Rex

CAROLYN ARNOLD

THE SECRET OF THE LOST PHARAOH

HIBBERT&STILES
PUBLISHING INC.

Hibbert & Stiles Publishing Inc.
www.hspubinc.com

This is a work of fiction. Names, characters, places, and incidents are the products of the author's imagination or are used fictitiously. Any resemblance to actual events, locales, or persons, living or dead, is entirely coincidental.

Publisher's Cataloging-In-Publication Data
(Prepared by The Donohue Group, Inc.)

Names: Arnold, Carolyn.
Title: The secret of the lost pharaoh / Carolyn Arnold.
Description: 2018 Hibbert & Stiles Publishing Inc. edition. |
    [London, Ontario] : Hibbert & Stiles Publishing Inc., [2018] |
    Series: Matthew Connor adventure series ; book 2
Identifiers: ISBN 9781988353685 (paperback, 4.25x7) | ISBN
    9781988353678 (ebook)
Subjects: LCSH: Archaeologists--Egypt--Fiction. | Pharaohs--
    Fiction. | Cuneiform tablets--Egypt--Fiction. | Good and evil-
    -Fiction. | LCGFT: Action and adventure fiction. | Thrillers
    (Fiction)
Classification: LCC PR9199.4.A76 S43 2018 (print) | LCC
    PR9199.4.A76 (ebook) | DDC 813/.6--dc23

Additional formats:
ISBN (5 x 8 paperback): 978-1-988353-69-2
ISBN (6.13 x 9.21 hardcover): 978-1-988353-70-8

THE SECRET
OF THE LOST
PHARAOH

PROLOGUE

THE SUN HAD BARELY BROKEN the horizon, but Alex was wide-awake and strapped into her safety harness. She had dreamed of this moment her entire life, and now that it was becoming reality, she could hardly believe it. Here she was at the age of forty and leading her first archaeological dig in Egypt's Western Desert. Even more incredible was the fact that she and her team were on the brink of a monumental discovery.

They had detected a manmade tunnel that ran thirty-five feet beneath the ground and over 3,600 feet to the east. Where the tunnel ended, there was in a large open space that the ground-penetrating radar couldn't identify.

Alex stood at the opening of the hole with her site foreman, Jeff Webb; a hieroglyphics expert named Jasper Blair; and two of four laborers, Seth and Timal. They would be responsible for lowering her down.

She took a deep breath, preparing her mind for the descent and the cramped space. Her team had only dug out a well of about four feet in diameter. The position she was in when she went down would be the way she'd stay, as there would be no room to flip over.

She wiped the back of her arm across her forehead to wick away the sweat that kept dripping down her face. She pinched her eyes shut, wishing she had her favorite blue sweatband from high school, when wearing one had been all the rage—back around the time when belonging to a Tape of the Month Club was *the* thing to do.

She let her long, blond hair down from the ponytail she'd had it in and redid it, tighter this time, pulling it into a messy bun. Back home in northern Michigan, she rarely put her hair up, reserving that for times when she was focused on her work or studies, but in this part of the world, she often wore it up. Even a warm breeze on the back of her neck was better than none at all.

"Good thing you skipped the second course last night," Jeff teased her.

Not that size was an issue for either of them. She was lean and athletic, and while Jeff had a solid build, he was trim with narrow shoulders.

"Same goes for you," she tossed back with a smile. She'd known him for years and worked on several digs with him. He'd been the one who had removed two of the stone bricks from the tunnel's ceiling to create the small opening through which they could descend. He'd been down there to set up a radio module and transmitting antenna that enabled communication between whoever was underground and whoever was on the surface.

Jeff moved behind her and tightened her harness. "Ah!" She sucked air in through gritted teeth. "Maybe just leave enough room for me to breathe."

He loosened the restraints slightly. "Good?"

She managed to slip her fingers between the straps and her rib cage. "It'll do."

He turned to face her again. "Here's your radio." Jeff handed her an earpiece that worked with the radio he'd put in place.

"Talk into it for me," he told her.

She tapped a button on the earpiece and said, "Hello, hello, hello." She smirked at her mock echo.

Jeff laughed. "I heard you loud and clear. In surround sound, actually. All right, one more thing." He popped a miner hat on her head, and she fastened the chin strap. "I think it's best if we lower you feetfirst so that you can be positioned upright in the tunnel." Jeff's demeanor became serious.

Alex nodded and looked down again. It was a good thing that she wasn't claustrophobic or afraid of being suspended by a rope and lowered helplessly into the ground. And while she might not battle with many fears, part of her was as terrified as she was excited about the prospect of setting foot where no one—besides Jeff briefly—had likely been in thousands of years. But this was just meant to be a brief look-see, and she'd be going solo. When she set out in earnest to explore the tunnel, she'd take members of her team with her.

She reached for the gold chain around her neck and pinched the tiny pendant that dangled from it. The Eye of Horus, also known as the Eye of Ra, was an ancient Egyptian symbol of protection. Out here in the desert, she needed all the help she could get. She kissed it and tucked it back beneath her shirt.

"Are you ready?" Jeff asked.

She met Jeff's eyes and flicked on the headlamp. "I'm ready."

Jeff pulled an LED flare from his back pocket, turned it on, and tossed it into the hole. Watching the light descend emphasized just how far down it was to the tunnel.

Once it hit the ground, Jeff rolled his hand toward Seth and Timal. "You heard her. Down she goes."

More sweat dripped from her brow, and she wiped her forehead again. And things were just heating up out here—if you could call already being a hundred degrees "just heating up." As it was, waves of heat were cutting through the air like ribbons on the horizon, and it was only eight o'clock in the morning.

She looked around at her crew, steadying her thoughts and locking on to her resolve to make history. Great men and women made a habit of stepping outside their comfort zones, living on the edge, and testing out unchartered waters. And she wanted to be among them, to make a difference in the world by unearthing what remained of long gone great empires. Sometimes that required delving into the unknown.

She shook her fanciful musings aside. After all, they may not have discovered anything more than an empty tunnel.

She sat on the ledge, dangling her legs inside the hole. She tugged on the rope secured to her harness, which was connected to a rigging system that Seth and Timal would use to lower her. She glanced at Seth and Timal, confident in their abilities to guide her safely down and back up again. And with one more look at Jeff, she pushed off, letting herself become suspended.

Her heart thumped against her rib cage as she was lowered. She reached out and touched the makeshift walls that her men had put in place to prevent a cave-in. Her fingertips brushed against some sand, and it was slightly cool to the touch, but the air around her was still hot. A few of the granules sprinkled down the shaft.

About six feet beneath the ground, she felt incredibly alone. Although, it was also quiet and peaceful.

As Jeff's form continued to become smaller above her and the space she was in became more shadowed, brief apprehension lanced through her. But the allure of what lie ahead silenced her anxiety.

"Looks like you're almost to the bottom," Jeff said to her over the radio.

She looked down. "There are probably only a few more feet to go."

"Press the button," Jeff shouted into the hole. "I can't hear you."

She rectified her oversight before repeating herself.

Seth and Timal slowed the speed of the rope they were giving her. Seconds later, she was extending her feet so the tips of her boots met with the stone blocks at the sides of the opening. Straddling it, she looked down again. "I'm about five feet from the bottom," she said into her radio.

Jeff's voice carried down the hole as an incoherent mumble. Into the radio, he said, "They're just going to lower you the rest of the way nice and easy. Extra slow."

Alex closed her eyes briefly and replayed the ritual with her necklace in her mind. She took a deep breath, stepped back into the air, and was lowered the rest of the way.

Her feet touched the floor of the tunnel. "I'm here." Her gaze followed the light from the flare until it met with darkness, about thirty feet or so into the tunnel. The radio module was there, and the transmitting antenna was looped and laid out on the floor.

She felt the hair rise on the back of her neck, and her sweat suddenly felt like ice pellets on her skin. She pulled out her necklace and squeezed the pendant between her fingers.

Alex drew her eyes back to the area immediately in front of her. Letting go of her pendant, she pressed her fingertips to the stone bricks that formed the walls. She pulled her hand back, looking at the sand on it before wiping it off on her pants. The walls were made of the same stone bricks as the ceiling, just as Jeff had reported. And the tunnel was about five feet high.

What was beyond the light? She crept forward without thinking, angling her head to the side so as not to hit the ceiling. Images of a pharaoh's tomb and great treasure filling her mind. She pictured the media coverage the discovery would attract, the flashing lights of cameras. Her name would go down in history books, and her career would really take off.

"Alex, are you all right?"

Jeff's voice plucked her from her daydream long enough to say, "Give me forty feet of slack." She had to find out where this tunnel led. Exploring was in her blood.

"Don't do anything careless." Jeff sounded like a father warning his child, but he was only eleven years older than she was. His personal roles as a husband and father to two daughters must have been creeping in.

"I know what I'm doing, Jeff," she replied curtly.

"This was only to be a brief evaluation of the tunnel," Jeff added. He was nothing if not stubborn.

"I'm aware of that." She didn't want to pull out the fact that she was his boss, but she would if she had to. She had no intention of returning to the surface right now.

Jeff didn't respond, but more rope fell to the floor of the tunnel.

"That's forty. Let me know if you need more," he said through the radio.

"Will do." She walked hunched over toward the edge of darkness, letting her hand trail along the wall, her fingertips gathering dust and sand as she went. She was about five feet from where the light from the flare's reach ended when she ran out of rope. Maybe it was a sign to turn around, but she'd never been good at heeding caution. "I need at least ten or fifteen more feet."

She felt the rope go slack and turned back to see more coming into the tunnel. Jeff hadn't even bothered to verbally acknowledge her request the second time, which meant he might be in a bit of a snit.

Still, she pressed on. In the light cast from her hat, she saw something on the wall about ten feet ahead of her. There was a texture to the area. Carvings, perhaps?

She picked up her speed. "I think I found something."

"What are you doing, Alex?"

She was panting. The limited oxygen underground didn't facilitate moving quickly. "I think I—" She reached the spot and stared. There was definitely something marked on the wall. She wiped the sand away, revealing hieroglyphics inside an oval frame. She started laughing.

"Alex?" Jeff pressed in her ear.

"I found a cartouche!" Her eyes trailed over the inscription, and even though her ability to read hieroglyphics was limited, she recognized part of this one from history books.

Khufu.

Her heart hammered in her chest. Khufu was an Egyptian pharaoh who had ruled during the Fourth Dynasty. But his tomb had already been found, and it was located hundreds of miles from her dig, beneath the Great Pyramid of Giza. So why would his name be in this tunnel?

The clue was probably in the lettering above and below his name, but that would require Jasper's expertise to decipher.

She walked farther down the tunnel as if something was magnetically drawing her forward. Tremors quaked through her as doubt flooded her. But then she spotted more hieroglyphics.

"I'm going to need Jasper down here right now," she said.

"What for?" Jeff's words were tight and clipped.

A wave of anger crashed over her at his questioning. "Just send him down."

Jeff's end of the radio went silent, and she imagined him pacing with formed fists and a clamped jaw. That was his typical reaction when she did something that he considered to be going off the rails.

"Jeff?" she prompted.

"We're getting him rigged up. Give us a few minutes."

She waited for what seemed much longer than mere minutes and then heard a scuffle in the tunnel behind her. She turned, putting her back to the darkness, and saw Jasper coming toward her.

"This way." She waved him on, hoping that he'd hustle. But given his six-foot frame and the constraints of the tunnel, she'd probably be out of luck with getting too much speed from him.

"This must be good if you couldn't wait." Jasper walked with his neck craned to the side and knees bent. He reached where she was standing next to the cartouche.

"This says *Khufu* from my knowledge, but what is this?" She pointed to the symbols she didn't recognize.

Jasper leaned in. "The top part says '*son of*.'"

She stared at him blankly. "'Son of Khufu?' But he had nine sons. Are you sure it doesn't give the name of which one?"

Jasper stared at her, not about to dignify her question with an answer. "Well, these lines at the top and bottom—"

"Indicate the name enclosed within them is royalty," she finished.

"Uh-huh." His tone was terse at her interruption.

She gave him a small apologetic smile but continued anyway. "So this son of Khufu ruled as pharaoh at one time." Her heart fluttered, followed by her stomach. "But only two of Khufu's sons were believed to have been successors to the throne, and the pyramids housing their tombs have been found…"

"I'm just telling you what it says."

"What does the bottom part say?"

"It indicates that his tomb is nearby."

She grinned and her eyes beaded with tears. "You're positive?"

Jasper's mouth turned downward, indicating he wasn't about to reconfirm.

"Wow." She stood there, basking in Jasper's interpretation. It seemed certain now that she was on the verge of finding a lost pharaoh's tomb. *Just wow.* "There's something else I need you to see." She hurried toward the second set of hieroglyphics, then turned around to gesture Jasper forward. But she came face-to-face with him. She stepped back. "You move pretty quickly, considering." She smiled awkwardly. Her entire body was shaking with excitement, and the only thing that would calm her down would be getting some answers.

Jasper looked away from her to the hieroglyphics, and he started reading.

Waiting on him was doing little to quell her nerves. "Even if you can't make out all of it, anything would help." She was all but tapping a foot.

Jasper drew his gaze from the wall. His mouth was set in a straight line at first but transformed into a genuine smile. "If I tell you what it says, you won't believe me anyway."

"Try me." Exhilaration rushed through her, stealing her breath.

"It mentions the Emerald Tablets and says that this tunnel is the path to great enlightenment."

"The Emerald—" She slapped a hand over her mouth, her eyes scanning his. She lowered her hand. "Are you kidding me? As in the tablets that are rumored to possess the ability to turn base metal into gold? To give man the ability to traverse Heaven and Earth?"

He raised an eyebrow. "I'm not sure if there are any other Emerald Tablets."

She swallowed, uneasy. She'd always clung to reason in the past, and it had served her well. "There's no way they can be real."

"Well, according to this—" Jasper pointed toward the hieroglyphics "—they are real and we're on our way to finding them."

"Whoa." Alex took a few steps and looped back. "But if they are real and we find them, and they fall into the wrong hands, it could mean the end of the world as we know it. And terrorists, world powers, they'd all be clamoring to get ahold of them. Their discovery could destroy the global economy." She paused, the enormity of this find sinking in with a sickening swirl in her gut. She locked eyes with Jasper. "If all this is true, then the fate of the world could be at stake."

"Not to make too dramatic a statement, but yes, it could be."

She stood there, her gaze going through him. This was certainly a case of "Be careful what you wish for because you just might get it"—and then some.

"You look like you're going to be sick," Jasper said.

"Probably because I *feel* like I'm going to be sick."

"You find the Tablets, and you will make history."

"I'll make history all right," she mumbled. "But will there be anyone around to learn about it?"

"As you said, if they fall into the wrong hands…"

The risks were great, but the reward—if managed properly—could be, too. Her thoughts went back to the cartouche and what else it could mean. "The open space that didn't read properly on the ground-penetrating radar could be a tomb, then."

"It could be."

Her breathing shallowed. It seemed the prospect of finding a lost tomb was paired with a legend that, if found, could destroy the world. But could she give herself over to accepting the implausible? That these tablets did exist and that they actually contained the knowledge of the universe? She'd always sided with the indisputable, the scientific, the logical. But the Emerald Tablets were attested to in the hieroglyphics mere feet away from her... Surely, that alone should be enough for her to consider the possibility of their existence. And legend *did* associate the Tablets with Khufu. In fact, it was believed by some that they lay hidden in a chamber beneath the Great Pyramid—the construction of which Khufu had allegedly commissioned. But hiding them out here, miles from his burial site, would be a far safer location to store something of such great value. Regardless of whether there was merit to the Tablets' existence or not, though, she couldn't just walk away from an unnamed pharaoh's tomb.

She looked thoughtfully at Jasper, her mind going over the possible repercussions if she were to find them. Worst case, there'd be global annihilation. Best case, she could save the world. After all, it was better that they wind up in her hands than someone else's. And she expected that the private party funding her dig would be ecstatic. Her pulse began to speed up again, the promise of what lay ahead stealing her breath.

And while it would be best to keep her team to a close few, she knew just the man who would love to join her. It had been at least five years since she'd worked with him, but they'd become fast friends, and he'd had a fascination with the Emerald Tablets even then. From what she understood, he now made it his business to uncover legends and myths. In fact, just less than a year ago, she'd read about him finding the Incas' lost City of Gold.

"How are you making out down there?" Jeff asked in her earpiece.

"We're just about to come up," Alex answered, not wanting to disclose everything over the radio, just in case an outside party picked up on their frequency. But once she got to the surface, she'd call Matthew Connor from a secured line and invite him to join her for the discovery of a lifetime.

CHAPTER
1

THE ROOT GLACIER, WRANGELL-ST. ELIAS NATIONAL PARK, ALASKA
TUESDAY, JUNE 22

MATTHEW SWUNG THE ICE AXE with his right hand until it found solid purchase in the face of the glacier. He repeated the process with the axe in his left hand, then carefully stepped up one leg at a time and pushed his feet against the ice. The crampons on his boots bit into the glacier and gave him solid footing—or the best footing one could hope for out here.

But the uncertainty, the danger, was all part of the fun, part of the rush, and it's what kept him coming back for more. Even today, the first day of summer, when his friends would be back home in Toronto seeking out a patio, he'd opted for glacier climbing in Alaska. There was just something invigorating about being bundled up with the cold air nipping at his nose.

But it wasn't just this particular extreme sport that lured him in. His friends had called him an adrenaline junkie on more than one occasion, and he definitely deserved the label. Whether it was skydiving, bungee jumping, white-water kayaking, or snowboarding, he was in. He'd even jumped off a cliff in a wingsuit like Lara Croft in *The Cradle of Life*. These activities were a great way to fill the time between expeditions, and they kept him physically fit and on his game. And while he welcomed the rush, adventure had to be tempered with caution so that he could live to do it again another day. He really didn't have a death wish.

He looked up and figured he'd be cresting the moulin within minutes. But instead of urging himself onward, he paused and glanced down—something any experienced guide would discourage. Easily forty feet beneath him, water rushed by, sweeping away everything in its path without prejudice. Yet, there was something peaceful about being here, essentially suspended in the air with no one around to request anything of him. He savored the quiet that came with this excursion almost as much as he did the adrenaline rush.

But now wasn't the time to sink into meditative thought. He had to focus on the task at hand. Sure, he wore a harness that was attached to a line secured at the top of the moulin and monitored by a guide, but screws didn't always hold, and people sometimes made mistakes. That's why axe placement and solid footing were crucial. One misstep or error in judgment would leave him dangling. If the screw gave way at the same time, well, then it would be sayonara.

He swung out again and took another step. As he did, the rope went slack and fell behind him.

Was this really happening? Blood rushed into his head, and he smiled.

Bring it on.

He focused on the glacier, on keeping his grip on the axes strong and his balance steady. All he'd have to do was hold his position until another rope was sent down for him.

"Hold on," his guide shouted.

Matthew rolled his eyes. Really, what else was he supposed to do?

Then he felt his right axe give. He looked up, his heart racing. The axe was, indeed, slipping in the ice. At least the left one was holding strong. The weight of the rope dangling from his harness and gravity were conspiring against him. He had to break free of it as soon as possible.

He let go of the right axe and unclipped the rope from his harness. He watched as it cut through the air, twirling like a ribbon until it met with the water below. Shifting his attention back to the abandoned axe, he slowly reached out for the handle. As he grabbed hold, the axe broke free of the ice.

He pushed his body against the glacier, clinging to it as if it would have mercy on him and save him. But he was down to one handhold and two footholds.

I've got this...

He took a few seconds to center himself and dug the freed axe into another section of ice. Thankfully, it bit in. Yet, he was still afraid to breathe in case it upset his precarious balance.

"Another rope's coming down. Just hook yourself to it," the guide called to him.

Matthew was starting to regret telling the guide to have a hands-off approach with him.

He looked up for the rope, and his gaze drifted to his left hand. It was cramping up, and his grip on the handle was slipping.

"Just grab the rope," the guide repeated.

Okay, Captain Obvious.

The promised rope snaked into his peripheral vision on his right. He'd have to shift his weight to his feet and rely on them and the axe in his left hand to keep him from falling to his death.

He squeezed his eyes shut, a dark part of him tempting him to just give up and surrender to the icy water.

Hell no!

He opened his eyes and looked over at the rope without moving his head. It was within a foot of where he was—a rather easy reach. But it would require trusting his holds.

"It's right beside you. Grab the rope."

If it's so easy, you get down here and take my place.

Matthew counted to three in his head and reached out. His gloved fingers touched the rope but failed to hold on to it. The momentum had him going off balance and swinging back to the left, making him feel like a human pendulum and giving him a brief sensation of weightlessness.

Now his right foot was breaking free of the ice. He struggled desperately to shift it but had to do so carefully or risk—

Both his footholds collapsed. Now the only thing anchoring him to the glacier was his left axe, and his grip on it was compromised. Searing pain shot through his shoulder and up his neck.

Shit! Shit! Shit!

He struggled to get some sort of hold reestablished with his feet and found shaky purchase.

"I'm coming down," his guide said.

I'll be dead before you get here...

Gravity was working like an anchor and pulling on him. He didn't have time to wait for the guide if he wanted to survive. But the rope that had been a foot away was now swaying from his earlier attempt to reach it, placing it easily three to three and a half feet away. He'd have to time his move for when the rope came closer.

One, two—

The remaining axe slipped some more.

He pushed on the glacier with his left foot to nudge himself to the right. His fingers played over the rope and—

In an instant, his life flashed before his eyes. Images of past expeditions layered on top of one another—the finds he'd made, the legends he'd proven real—and then his father's face, as clear as if he were standing in front of him. Matthew imagined the newspapers' headlines back home reading something like, MAYOR'S SON DEAD AFTER GLACIER CLIMBING ACCIDENT IN ALASKA. Then he saw the faces of his friends Cal, Cal's fiancée Sophie, and Robyn. Ah, beautiful Robyn, the love of Matthew's life. Only he'd die without her knowing just how much he loved her. He'd die without having left behind a—

He got a firm grasp on the rope just as his left axe dislodged from the ice. He released it and gripped the rope with both hands. His feet fell out of their holds, and he pinched the rope between his boots.

Now, I can breathe...

"You weren't kidding when you said you had this under control." The guide lowered down beside him and hooked the clasp at the end of the rope to Matthew's harness.

Moments later, Matthew was climbing on top of the moulin. His legs were shaky beneath him and threatened to give out. He bent over, set his elbows on his knees, and took a few deep breaths.

The guide slapped him on the back. "Way to go."

Matthew straightened up, ready to lay into the man about what a useless piece of—

The guide was grinning. "I'm sure that was a rush you'll never forget."

Matthew let out a whoop and raised his arms in the air. He'd faced death but had survived. God, that was worth celebrating!

"Uh, hey, man, you're ringing." The guide pointed toward Matthew's chest.

Matthew smiled at the guide. With the man's laid-back attitude, he would fit in quite well beachside in California, catching waves and chasing bikinis. Matthew took out the satellite phone he had tucked inside his coat. "Hello?"

"Is this Matthew Connor?" a female voice asked.

"It is."

"Well, you may not remember me, but this is Alexandria Leonard."

It took him only a few seconds to place her. Hot sun, sand, and mummies. "Alex? It's been awhile."

"That it has, and you're not the easiest person to get ahold of." She went silent briefly. "But I have an expedition I think you'll be quite interested in…"

CHAPTER
2

Matthew rushed back to Toronto on the first flight he could get out of Alaska. The plane had touched down at Pearson International Airport around three o'clock in the morning.

Now it was nine o'clock, and he was in his office, feet up on his desk with a book in his lap. He wasn't reading at the moment, though, but rather admiring how the stained-glass ornament on the window caught the morning sunlight and painted his floor with strokes of color.

His suite was situated in the south wing of his father's estate, a 26,000-square foot mansion in Toronto's affluent Bridle Path neighborhood. That was how William Connor did things—big.

Only two other people shared the mansion with him and his father: Lauren Hale, their housekeeper, and Daniel Iverson, the property manager whose duties varied widely.

Yes, Matthew lived at home, but the house was palatial, with plenty of space to stretch out in. His father lived his life and respected Matthew's privacy. And Matthew's two-story suite with loft had all the amenities most would want in a house. He had walk-in closets, a private bathroom, an office, a living room, and a king-size bed. To top it off, a wall of windows extended from the first floor to the second-floor ceiling on one side, and he had a balcony with a view of the tennis court in the backyard. All that and he was rarely even home. When he wasn't traveling for an expedition, he was away for recreational purposes.

He looked down at the tome he'd been reading. It was dedicated to the Emerald Tablets, and he was reacquainting himself with the legends that surrounded them—not that he'd ever actually forget such an intriguing "myth." But brushing up on them seemed like a good use of his time, especially given that he was too excited to sleep and needed to kill some time before approaching his friends.

When he'd mentioned Robyn and Cal to Alex, she seemed hesitant to bring in more people, but he, Robyn, and Cal were a package deal. She'd take all three of them or he'd decline her offer. The line had gone silent after his ultimatum, and just when he was starting to regret putting it to her that way, she'd said, "Tell me about them." So he had.

Robyn's work as a curator at the Royal Ontario Museum and her love for ancient culture, with her special enthusiasm for Egyptian history, made her ideal for the expedition. Cal was a renowned photographer, and his work appeared in many prestigious magazines, including *National Geographic*. He took a little more selling, though. Alex already had someone on her team who took *pictures*, but there was weakness in her word choice. Matthew had managed to capitalize on that slip and finally sold her on the importance of having a professional take *photographs*. Of course, if the Tablets were found, they'd be kept out of the media and away from Cal's lens. But if they found the pharaoh's tomb, that was fair game.

Matthew glanced at his desk and his closed laptop, wishing that he could look at the cartouche and hieroglyphics that Alex and her team had found. But she had been adamant about not sending them through cyberspace. She wouldn't even share the details of the expedition until he could get to a secure phone line. But, man, it had been nice to hear her voice.

When he'd worked with Alex on a different dig in Egypt five years ago, he'd just gotten his doctorate, and he was wide-eyed and curious, soaking in everything around him. He had spent his days yapping her ear off about the pharaohs and what life must have been like in ancient Egypt. But his fascination with the legend of the Emerald Tablets was never far from his mind since the day he'd first learned of it. And from there, he'd found himself obsessing about other myths.

At the time, Reda Ghannam, the Egyptian Minister of Antiquities—then and now—had told him to get his "head out of the sky." Matthew hadn't been able to gather the courage to correct the idiom. But the man's point had been clear, even if Matthew decided not to heed his advice.

And really, clinging to the intangible had come to define him. He was borderline obsessive about trying to prove the existence of what everyone else had given up on. It had become his life purpose, and it was the legacy he'd leave behind.

Legacy. That was what he was thinking about when he was losing his grip on the glacier. He didn't want to die without leaving behind a legacy.

Many people said that having children was the way to create a legacy, but legacies came in many forms, and they weren't always flesh and blood. Restoring artifacts and lost cities to the world had to be, in itself, a legacy. People would enjoy his discoveries long after he was gone. And if that wasn't a legacy, what was?

He turned his attention back to his book, realizing that he had steamed through it and only had a handful of pages left. First, he'd finish up, and then he'd go see Robyn at the museum.

There was a knock on the door.

He straightened up, removed his legs from his desk, earmarked the page in his book, closed it, and flipped it over in his lap with the cover facing down. "Come in."

Daniel entered holding a tray with coffee. "Good day, sir."

"How many times do I need to tell you not to call me 'sir'?"

"Call it an occupational hazard."

Daniel had worked for his father for as long as Matthew could remember. And in the past few years, he had also helped Matthew prepare for his expeditions by arranging local contacts, flights, passports, legalities, and things like that. Daniel often presented Matthew with a buffet of potential expeditions to tantalize him. But today that wouldn't be needed.

Daniel held the tray out in front of Matthew. "It's made just the way you like it."

"You have no idea how badly I need this today." Matthew picked up the cup and took a long draw. "Thank you."

"Of course." Daniel pointed at the book on Matthew's lap. "Is that the reason you need the coffee?"

Matthew tightened his grip on the book and covered more of it with his arms. "Yes and no. I hardly slept last night." He took another sip of the brew.

"Let me guess, sir—*Matthew*—you can sleep when you're dead?"

Matthew smiled at Daniel's dry attempt at humor. "Something like that."

Daniel set his tray on a corner of Matthew's desk and sat in a chair across from Matthew. His gray, Norwegian eyes fixed on Matthew. "The tomb of a missing pharaoh, eh? That's exciting."

"That's right." Matthew had told Daniel that much earlier this morning, and that's all he would share. The Tablets would remain with him, because the fewer people who knew, the better.

Daniel was still watching him, as if he expected an elaboration, and while Matthew owed him no explanation, he wanted to extend something.

"From the look of it, the tomb may belong to a son of Khufu." Matthew delivered this with mild excitement. But when compared to the Emerald Tablets, the Tablets would win every time. Even if the pharaoh's reign had previously been unknown.

"Then you have your mind set on this expedition?" Daniel came across leery and unconvinced, proving the man's strong detection skills once again.

"An opportunity like this? How can I refuse?" Matthew leaned back with his coffee, careful not to upset the book that was still on his lap.

Daniel remained silent for a few seconds. "We've always communicated openly." He paused, seeming hesitant.

Matthew gestured for him to continue.

"I just never expected the day to come when you'd go back to working on a regular archaeological dig." Daniel scanned Matthew's eyes.

Matthew held the man's gaze. "Because it's not in search of a legend?"

"That's right."

"Well, this is a unique opportunity for me." Matthew shifted in his chair. "And it's intriguing. Khufu was buried beneath his pyramid, so why would his son be buried nearly two hundred miles away from him? Something's not adding up."

Daniel nodded slowly, still unconvinced. "What do you need me to do for you?"

"I'll take care of this one." If Robyn and Cal were joining him, it would only be another awkward thing to explain. If Matthew were just taking part in a regular archeological dig, there'd be no reason for them to go.

Daniel's gaze drifted to the book in Matthew's lap again. "Very well." Daniel crossed his legs. "And when do you plan to leave?"

"Tomorrow morning."

Daniel uncrossed his legs and leaned forward. "Tomorrow? Why the rush?"

"The—" Matthew clamped his mouth shut. He'd almost said *the Emerald Tablets.* "If I want to be a part of this historic find, I have to move quickly. Alex and her team are already under way."

"Beg your pardon, but he's been buried this long—"

"And that's why he needs to be found." Matthew looked past Daniel toward the door, giving Daniel the nudge to leave.

Daniel settled back into his chair. "You said Alex. Do you mean Alexandria Leonard?"

"That's right." Matthew was impressed by Daniel's memory. "You remember her?"

"I do. She came to visit once."

"Wow. That was a long time ago. She only stayed a couple days."

"Yes, but she got you to play tourist with her—the CN Tower, Canada's Wonderland, the zoo. You even went to a Blue Jays game." Daniel inclined his head.

"I know," Matthew said with a laugh. "And I hate baseball."

Daniel watched him knowingly, and Matthew felt his old feelings for Alex coming to the surface. When he'd gone to Egypt that first time, it hadn't been long since he and Robyn had broken up. He'd been vulnerable, and the first chance he got, he'd invited Alex to Toronto. He'd whisked her around the city in a poor, pathetic attempt at stealing her heart away from her fiancé. Vying for her affections at the time was not one of his more noble moments.

"She was engaged, if I recall correctly," Daniel said. "So she'd be married now..."

"Unless she's already divorced." That came out too quickly for his comfort, and he struggled to backpedal. "Statistically, most marriages do end in divorce."

Daniel pulled his head back and tucked his chin downward. "Uh-huh."

"Anyway…" Matthew looked at the clock on the wall: *9:30*. Robyn should be at work now, and he wanted to speak with her before he broached the subject with Cal. "Well, I better get going." He stood up, hugging the book about the Emerald Tablets to his chest, and exited the room, no doubt leaving behind a confused and curious Daniel.

CHAPTER

3

ROBYN GARCIA STARED AT THE e-mail she'd just read with disbelief. The artifacts she'd requested for the African exhibit were being delayed for another three months. Unbelievable. After all the time that she'd put into securing them, and after she'd boasted to her boss about turning this around so quickly… Now she'd have to tell him it was on hold, but she wouldn't be giving him any sort of ETA, not even a ballpark one. Why risk making another promise she may not be able to keep?

She scanned her desk, observing her meticulous organization. Her in-tray was nearly empty, and she was well aware of everything that was still in there. And short of earth-shattering miracles, none of them would be resolved today. She had a holder for her pens, pencils, and highlighters, but it only contained a couple of each. No sense cluttering up the space by overstocking her office supplies. Her laptop sat next to a desk calendar, and she had a spiral-bound notebook with a blue pen resting on top of it. There was only one other item on her desk, and while it wasn't necessary given the lettering on her office door, she couldn't bring herself to get rid of it.

She picked up the nameplate and ran her fingers over the etching as she read it: *Robyn Garcia, Curator of Fine Antiquities.*

It never got old, thinking about what she'd accomplished in her career. She'd had a life plan from the beginning, and she'd had intention. Really, it was no surprise that she'd ended up as a curator. But she'd never imagined herself taking part in treasure-hunting expeditions.

Or rather, they were more like *legend*-hunting expeditions. Regardless, she'd never seen that one coming.

She set the nameplate down again and turned her attention back to the e-mail. Her mind searched for a diplomatic response but came up empty. The message required one. Normally she didn't have a problem stringing together a bunch of respectful words, but right now, she could only imagine one thing happening if she kept looking at the e-mail: she'd be tempted to fire back something impulsive, bordering on rude. Maybe it was a good time to step away and check on a few exhibits to make sure everything was fine and in order with them.

She went to get up when her door opened and Matthew Connor strolled in. His eyes were bluer than she remembered. She swept some of her dark hair behind an ear. "What are you doing here?"

"Well, it's been awhile since we've seen each other," he responded casually.

"You're the one who took off to Alaska, and before that to—" She stopped talking before it came across like she was keeping track of his schedule. "It's good to see you."

And it was. It always was. They'd been friends since college and lovers there for a while, too. But just when things started to get serious between them, she'd been offered this job. And with her life plan coming together and Matthew's selfless understanding, they'd ended things so she could focus on her career. She'd even gone so far as to avoid expeditions with him for a time, claiming they were too dangerous.

"You too." He flashed her a smile that could stop her heart if she allowed it to.

"If you had been around yesterday, you could have joined us at Gretzky's." By *us*, she meant, Cal, Sophie, and herself, but Matthew would know that.

He was still smiling as he sat down in the chair across from her. "I figured you'd end up on a patio for drinks."

"Uh-huh."

She regarded the light in his eyes but also picked up on shadows of secrecy. He got that look when he was thinking about an expedition. But she didn't have time to go away to wherever it was he had in mind. Maybe he had the luxury of dropping everything on a whim, but she didn't. She was tethered to a job she loved, and Lord knew she had enough that needed taking care of. The e-mail about the African exhibit was far from being the only thing on her to-do list.

"If you're here about an expedition, I can't go," she stated, certain she was getting in front of what he'd come here to ask.

"You don't even know when I'm going." Matthew leaned forward, one corner of his mouth lifting as if it had been raised by a hook. It was a carefree and devilish expression, and one that she found titillating, whether she wanted it to or not. And she didn't want it to. They were better off as friends. It was so much less complicated. He did his thing; she did hers. And when they did go on quests together, it was an experience they shared as friends.

"It doesn't matter." She was shaking her head. "I have too much to do here."

Matthew's gaze went to her tidy desk before meeting her eyes. "It doesn't look like it."

"You know that my desk isn't an indication of my workload. Do you want to see my in-box?" She gestured toward her monitor and then set her hand down on her desk.

Matthew reached forward and put his hand on top of hers. Her heart began to beat faster. She pulled her hand away and swallowed, hoping he hadn't sensed how uncomfortable his touch made her.

His gaze dropped to her desk but then tracked up to meet her eyes. "You seem a little jumpy. I think someone needs a vacation."

"Ha!" She mocked laughter. "You have no idea." Truth be told, she hadn't taken time off since the better part of a year ago, when they had gone in search of the City of Gold.

Matthew splayed out his hands. "No time like the present, then."

She narrowed her eyes at him. "An expedition"—she pointed a swirling finger at him—"isn't a vacation. It's work."

Matthew sat back in his chair and bobbed his head side to side. "Fun work. And in this case, it could affect the fate of the world."

"Excuse me while I roll my eyes. *The fate of the world?* Really?" She expected him to smile or laugh, but his eyes darkened and his mouth fell into a straight line. "You're serious?"

"I am dead serious."

"So what is this mission that could affect the fate of the world?" She'd started off armed with cynicism but found that her shield was starting to lower. What was wrong with her? Was he really baiting her with *the fate of the world*? Was she that desperate for time off that she was buying into his hyperbole?

"Before I continue," he said, "I just want to make sure you realize that what I'm about to tell you is highly confidential."

The skin pricked at the back of her neck, and tingles ran over her shoulders. "Why don't we move over there?" She got up and gestured toward a small seating area with a dark-green leather couch and chair. It wasn't to her taste, but she hadn't footed the bill for the furniture, either.

Matthew sat on the chair, and Robyn took the couch.

"Lock the door, please?" Matthew requested. "Just in case someone walks in."

"Ah, like you did." She smirked, got up again, and did as he'd asked.

"Hey—" he put his hands up in surrender "—Gloria wasn't at her desk."

That explained how Matthew had gotten past her assistant, who was responsible for announcing visitors.

She took a seat again and folded her hands in her lap. "All right. Talk to me. Tell me about this find that can affect the fate of the world."

"It's the Emerald Tablets." He put it out there with stark seriousness, but there was no way he could be.

She leaned back, sinking deeper into the couch. "You're kidding me, right? They're a myth. You really think they—"

"There's evidence indicating that they do exist," he cut in, perfectly anticipating what she was going to say.

He'd come to her before with wild stories about the Tablets and speculations on their whereabouts, but he'd always come back down to Earth. "What evidence? Do you have it with you?"

"Not exactly, but—"

Robyn smiled and shook her head.

"Do you remember how bizarre the lost City of Gold sounded to us at first?" He showed no sign that her indifference was affecting him. "But it existed, and we went in search of it on less information than I have now."

"We were sort of forced into it." The words came out harsher than she'd intended, and she softened her delivery. "I didn't mean that the way it sounded."

He dismissed it with a wave of his hand. "It's fine."

Silence fell between them, and Robyn wondered if he was also remembering what had truly spurred on the expedition: Sophie had been kidnapped, and the ransom had been finding the city. They'd pulled it off, but it was a taboo subject with Cal and Sophie, for obvious reasons.

"Are you considering asking Cal?" She broached the subject with the diplomacy she normally used in her position at work.

"I am." His voice held conviction but was also peppered with apprehension.

"Really, it doesn't matter what you have to say about the expedition. I can't take the time off."

"You brought this museum several artifacts from the Incas' lost City of Gold." Matthew paused, as if hoping to drive home his point, but she was opting to play hard to get. "*The* City of Gold. This museum owes you for the media attention you brought them."

"They gave me a large raise for that." For some reason, verbalizing that right now made her question if it truly had been enough.

"I'm just saying that I'm sure your boss would understand." And there he was, applying another twist on her arm to break down her defenses. She guessed he'd try anything to make her entertain the idea of going with him, to believe that it was even an option.

"The Tablets, Matt? Really?" Her heart cinched in her chest as she watched hurt sweep over his face at her obvious disbelief. "You said you had evidence? Hit me with it," she asked, surrendering to hearing him out. They were friends, after all.

"I received a call from Egypt and…"

Matthew continued to talk, but she was stuck on *Egypt*. Because the child in her, the one whose life plan was to work as a curator in a museum, also had grandiose dreams of visiting Egypt before she died. But it hadn't happened yet.

"…So we're all vouched for." He stopped talking, and his serious expression gave way to a smile that touched his eyes. "Were you listening to anything I said?"

"I heard 'Egypt,'" she confessed with a wince.

"And women say men don't listen," he teased. "Alex has found evidence that's led her to believe that she and her team are on the verge of finding the Tablets."

"And this *evidence*?" The pitch of her voice carried a plea. "You still haven't said what it is exactly."

"Well, I did, but apparently, you tuned me out completely." He tsked. "She found hieroglyphics that mentioned the Tablets." He paused, seeming to notice her confusion. "You didn't hear that, either?"

"Sorry." She winced again.

He smirked, not seeming to take the fact that she'd zoned out on him personally. "You've always wanted to go to Egypt. Now's your chance."

"Let me think about it." The words sank in her gut. Maybe this *was* her once-in-a-lifetime opportunity.

Matthew laughed. "You really didn't hear a thing I said, did you? If you had, you probably wouldn't have anything to think over. There's also an indication that a son of Khufu might be buried in the Western Desert, over one hundred and fifty miles from the Great Pyramid."

How in the world had she missed that?

"A son of Khufu?" She leaned forward, perching on the edge of the couch cushion. "History indicates that two of his nine sons served as pharaoh: Djedfera and Khafre. But their tombs have already been found. That leaves Kawab, Djedfhor, Baufra, Babaef, Khufukhaf, Minkhaf, and Horbear. Of these, Baufra has never been archaeologically attested to. He was only mentioned in a couple of unverified documents."

Matthew leaned back in his chair. "No one can say you don't know your Egyptian history. You'd be perfect to have on this trip."

She was too concentrated on Khufu's family line to fall victim to his flattery. "Two of Khufu's sons proceeded him on the throne but not his eldest. Kawab died before the end of Khufu's reign." She paused, meeting his eyes, and they were sparkling. She was certain they were mirroring her own excitement. "I don't understand why a son of Khufu would be buried so far away from the Great Pyramid…"

"Exactly. And there's only one way to find out for sure." Matthew's hook was baited again, and she was circling.

Damn him. She was intrigued by the mystery, and mysteries needed to be solved.

"Don't take too long to mull this over," he said.

"Why?"

"The plane leaves tomorrow morning at eight."

"Tomorrow?" Anxiety ratcheted up in her chest. "You can't be serious? What's the rush this time?" To save Sophie, they'd been given a deadline, but she couldn't imagine what was imposing a time crunch on this expedition.

"You don't remember much about the Tablets, do you?"

"Um." She licked her lips and turned away. But in her defense, one couldn't know everything...

"Let's just say that we need to get our hands on them before the wrong people do."

She nodded slowly. "And you know this Alex person well?"

"Well enough," Matthew said.

She took a deep, heaving breath. "How long do you think the expedition will take?"

"I'd say to count on a month."

She gasped. "Thirty days?"

"That's what a month is," he said it offhandedly, as if it were no big deal, and maybe in his world, it wasn't.

"I don't see how I can swing that." The e-mails that were stacking up, the diplomatic negotiations, the current exhibits she was responsible for taking care of...

"Bring your laptop. They do have the Internet over there."

She raised a brow. "In the middle of the desert?"

"Ah, so you *did* hear some of what I said."

"I'd just assumed—Egyptian pharaoh and all."

He laughed. "The desert? An Egyptian pharaoh? I'd say they have a connection."

"Matthew, be serious." She found herself smiling.

"Fine." He smirked and held up a hand. "In all seriousness, I'm sure they'll have access through a satellite network."

She didn't say anything for a few seconds. He'd made a convincing argument, and she was grappling with finding a way to refute his logic. The thought of bringing work with her didn't sound appealing, but he planned on leaving tomorrow. Still, she couldn't just cut and run that fast. "I'll have to get back to you."

"All right." Matthew patted the arms of the chair before he got up. "Let me know tonight?"

She nodded absentmindedly.

He stopped at the door, his hand on the knob. "And I'm going to call Cal. Wish me luck."

"Luck…" she said softly, already lost in her thoughts.

Matthew closed the door behind him. She'd wanted a distraction from that cursed e-mail, and boy, had she gotten one. This could be her chance to go to Egypt. And it would be so much more important than simply fulfilling a personal goal. She'd be on an actual expedition. She'd be making a contribution to the world—and saving it, if she surrendered herself to the legend of the Tablets.

She smiled to herself in her empty office, as she let her mind get carried away with thoughts of pyramids and mummies. But her musings were short-lived. Who was she kidding? The timing was lousy. Besides her job, she was pretty certain that tomorrow night she had a date. It was a blind date, no less, but one Sophie had arranged. And she'd promised Sophie she wouldn't back out of it. The fact that she hadn't been on a date in six months, maybe more, deepened the commitment. After all, she owed it to herself to get out and meet someone. But the more she tried to convince herself to stay, the more she wanted to go. As for the guy, she could get together with him when she got back. She just hoped Sophie would understand.

CHAPTER

4

MATTHEW HADN'T BEEN THIS UNSURE SINCE... Actually, he'd never been this unsure. The more he thought about asking Cal to come on the trip, the worse an idea it became. Sure, they'd scraped through brushes with death on past quests, but what had happened to Sophie last time had changed Cal. And Matthew got it—he really did. Sophie had been held hostage, her life had been threatened, and she'd almost been raped. That was a lot of emotional garbage to work through. Matthew had put going on expeditions on hold for himself because it wouldn't be the same without Cal, and he knew Cal wouldn't be joining him. They had drifted apart over the past months, too, with Cal sticking close to home and only partaking in "safe" recreation. But this opportunity was too big for Matthew to turn his back on.

He got into his Jeep Patriot, turned the ignition, and waited for the AC to kick in.

"Call Cal," he commanded the vehicle's hands-free system.

The line rang over the speakers.

"Matt?" Cal answered, sounding surprised by Matthew's calling.

"How are you, man?"

"Good." Cal drew out the word. "Is everything all right? Aren't you in Alaska?"

"I was, but I'm back now."

"Great. Let's get together tonight. You can come over and have dinner with me and Sophie. Say about seven?"

Matthew was hoping for sooner than tonight, but good things couldn't be rushed—or something to that effect. And maybe by the time seven o'clock came around, he'd have a way of making his offer irresistible. "That works."

"But hey," Cal said, "why did you actually call? I doubt it was to get invited over for dinner."

Matthew was searching for a way to say that he had something to talk about without coming right out and saying it, but he had nada.

"Matt?"

He'd obviously remained silent a little too long. Maybe he *should* just come out with it. "There's something I need to talk to you about."

Cal's end went quiet now.

"It's important," Matthew added.

"And it's about some expedition," Cal deadpanned.

"It's about saving the world." Maybe if he presented it this way, his friend would use the time from now until this evening to think things through.

"Yeah, so an expedition. Well, don't you dare say a word about it around Sophie." Cal's breathing came over the line.

"I don't want to upset either of you." Maybe he should have just let this be. Bring Robyn along but leave Cal out of this one. But he wanted his best friend with him, and Cal had been so melancholy the last few times Matthew had seen him. Cal used to have a fondness for risk-taking, too, and he'd loved going on expeditions. "I just know how much fun you used to have—"

"*Used to*, Matt. We barely got out of the last one alive. And what about Sophie? I can't put her through—" Cal stopped talking. "See you at seven?"

"Yeah."

Cal hung up, and Matthew's gut churned. It had been self-serving to call Cal. He should have left Cal out of this. Maybe he should just accept that going on expeditions with Cal was a thing of the past. But there was something in Cal's reaction that Matthew couldn't help but cling to: *Don't you dare say a word about it around Sophie.* It made Matthew think Cal was curious. And as closed off as Cal's last comment might have been, Matthew was having a hard time accepting that his friend's love for adventure was gone.

Someone honked a horn, yanking him from his thoughts. He looked in his rearview mirror to see a BMW sedan. The male driver was gesturing emphatically to prompt Matthew out of his parking spot.

For that, a part of him felt inclined to stay there with his engine running for just a while longer, but he had things to take care of and a trip to prepare for. He pulled out of the space, crawling along, while the BMW driver screamed and waved his fists. Did the guy have any idea how crazy he looked?

Matthew tossed out a smile and a wave once he'd cleared the spot, and the driver gave him the finger. Matthew laughed and shook his head.

And people think Canadians all are sweet and easygoing.

Matthew merged into traffic and headed home. He'd make the necessary phone calls from there and get started on packing. Nothing like moving out of one suitcase and into another, but this was the life he'd chosen. He didn't regret any of it for a moment.

Okay, maybe he regretted *one* thing: Robyn. But he had to believe someday, when the time was right, they'd find their way back to each other. She'd looked so beautiful when he'd shown up at her office— her tan Latina skin, her chocolate eyes, and long dark hair. The way she'd tucked a strand of hair behind an ear and held eye contact with him while she did so. It all drove him mad, but in a good, deliciously torturous way.

But for now, he had to accept that things between them had to remain platonic. And if he had a choice of friendship or nothing, the decision was an easy one. God, he hoped that she'd be able to maneuver her schedule and come to Egypt. But he also understood how important her work at the museum was to her. Still, the way she had lit up at the mention of Egypt... He'd noticed it right away but had carried on anyhow.

He pulled into the estate's driveway in what felt like no time. But his mind had been busy. He parked his vehicle, went inside the house, and headed straight for his room. While he walked, he pulled out his phone and selected the airline charter service from his contact list.

"Good morning. This is Blue Skies. Charlene speaking." Her professional tone carried a reserved friendliness.

"Charlene, this is Matthew Connor. I'll need a plane for tomorrow morning at eight o'clock please." While that surely seemed like a tight turnaround to most people, Blue Skies had always accommodated his last-minute flight needs.

"Sure, Mr. Connor. To what destination?"

"Cairo, Egypt."

"One minute, please, while I check plane availability." Charlene put him on hold, and soft music came over the line. It stopped a few seconds later when Charlene returned. "Thank you for holding. I can go ahead and book a plane for you now."

"That would be wonderful." They said that when things were meant to be, circumstances came together effortlessly. So far, it seemed to be true.

"How many passengers?" she asked.

Good question, was what he thought, but he was nothing if not optimistic. "Three." Besides, if Robyn and Cal weren't coming, it would be easy enough for them to change the passenger manifest.

"Very well. I will require the information for all the passengers."

He reached his bedroom and entered, walked over to the wall of windows, and looked out at the tennis court.

Charlene continued. "For each, that includes name, gender, date of birth, nationality, country of residence, travel documentation, i.e., passport and number."

He could provide everything for himself, Robyn, and Cal, except their passport numbers. Daniel surely had all this information stored away somewhere, but that didn't help him right now. And to go to Daniel would rouse his suspicions about why his friends would be accompanying him to Egypt to explore a pharaoh's tomb. He pinched the bridge of his nose.

"Mr. Connor?" Charlene prompted.

He might just have to wait until he had confirmation that Robyn and Cal were going and get their information directly from them. "How long would it take to adjust the manifest in the morning?"

"It shouldn't take the pilot long, but please keep in mind that a manifest has to be finalized one hour before takeoff."

He let out a deep breath. He'd have to get their answers tonight; otherwise, it could affect the flight schedule. But an hour gave him wiggle room if one or both of them were still on the fence about going.

"All right, that should be fine."

"What should be fine, Mr. Connor?"

"What I meant is just put me down as reserving the plane, and I'll provide the passenger list in the morning before seven."

"Please do so no later than six to give the pilot time," she started. "Will you be a passenger on this flight, Mr. Connor?"

"I will be."

"I will make a note of that," she said.

"Do you have all my information, then?"

"Yes, it's on file." There was a slight pause on her end of the line. "Your plane is booked for tomorrow morning at eight. Please arrive no later than six if you will be providing other passengers' information at that time."

"Actually, do you have Cal Myers's and Robyn Garcia's info on file, as well?" It stood to reason if they had his, since Cal and Robyn normally traveled with him, they might have theirs already, as well.

"Let me check for you." Only a few seconds passed. She had him confirm their dates of birth, and then she said, "I do have their information. Are they the other passengers?"

He hesitated. There was some saying about counting your chickens before they hatched. But, surely, he could convince them. A stab of conscience had him remaining silent.

"Mr. Connor?"

"Ah, I'm not sure yet."

"No problem. As I mentioned, if anyone else will be joining you, just have their information to us no later than six." She paused. "Is there anything else I can help you with, Mr. Connor?"

"No, that will be all."

"Thank you, and have a good day."

"You too." He hung up.

Time would tell if Robyn or Cal were coming. He sure hoped they would be, but regardless, booking the plane could be checked off his list. He also didn't need to worry about Egyptian work visas for the three of them. Alex had e-mailed him on his way to see Robyn, saying that she'd take care of the matter. When he'd called Alex back, he'd run with the assumption that they'd jump at this opportunity, but so far, it seemed he may have gotten carried away. Then again, it was too soon to say. For one, he'd sprung it on Robyn, and she said she'd think about it. For two, Cal hadn't fully shot him down. He seemed more concerned about Sophie hearing about it than finding out what Matthew had to say.

So for now, he'd hold positive thoughts that his friends would be joining him. And while he did that, he had better start packing. It was one thing to toss items together for a recreational trip and quite another to prepare for hitting the desert for an actual dig. He had to ensure that he had his backpack, a tent, flares, flashlights, a couple hats, his clothing, a canteen, and far more gear than his mind could inventory right now. Often he'd take a gun with him, too, but given that Egypt was experiencing a period of civil unrest, it might be best to leave that item at home. He just hoped he wouldn't need it.

CHAPTER

5

CAL HAD GOTTEN MATTHEW'S CALL at a Starbucks about an hour ago, and he was still sitting in the chair he'd dropped into after hanging up. And his plan had just been to grab a coffee and go. It was a good thing he didn't have anything he needed to do today. His thoughts were all over the place.

As for tonight, Sophie would accommodate the impromptu invitation he'd extended to Matthew, but she'd stress about what to cook for dinner and the fact she wouldn't have much wind-down time. She'd told him before leaving the house this morning that she had a full day of showings booked, too. But all he could think about when he'd heard his friend's voice was seeing him. It had been too long. Cal could always cook or pick something up.

That wasn't the real problem, though. The problem was that he couldn't stop speculating about what this expedition might be. Knowing his best friend, Cal was sure Matthew had something exciting and dangerous to entice him, but there was no point in wagering a guess. He'd have to wait until later that night when Matthew told him what was going on.

But it felt like it was days away instead of hours. He was quivering inside, not from nerves but rather eager anticipation. Still, why was he giving this any consideration? It was his globe-trotting with Matthew to dig up legends that had dug up so much trouble. The fact remained that his "adventures," as Sophie called them, had almost gotten her killed.

Really, it was a miracle she'd forgiven him. Her ability to bounce back just proved what an amazing and resilient woman she was—and how lucky he was to have her in his life. So how could he even flirt with saying yes to whatever it was Matthew was going to offer him? He had to let it go, to pass it up for Sophie, for their future. He loved her too much. And while nothing was guaranteed in life, if one tacked treasure hunting on to a standard existence, then the sentiment took on even greater meaning. There were always obstacles to overcome and risks that had to be taken. Whether it was the elements or people trying to beat you to the finish line. Even when you won, you could lose. After all, Sophie's kidnapping had been a direct result of his involvement in obtaining the Pandu artifact in India before another interested party could get to it.

How could Cal even think about saying yes without knowing what Matthew had to say? He had to be desperate for some excitement in life, and honestly, he had been playing it safe now for far too long. Well, ever since proposing to Sophie soon after discovering the City of Gold. All one had to do was look at his calendar to see just how safe. Just earlier this week, he'd returned from photographing the Grand Canyon for a travel piece. The most dangerous part—if you wanted to call it that—had been the helicopter ride he had taken to get the aerial shots.

He used to live for the chase and the adrenaline rush that came with working alongside Matthew. And this expedition was about saving the world? Now he remembered that's what Matthew had said. But was he exaggerating? Matthew had said something similar about the City of Gold, something along the lines that the discovery would change the world. Yes, he'd used the word *change*. At first impression, it was similar to the current situation, but really, the difference between the two words was enormous. And Matthew had made good on his other promise: finding the City of Gold *had* changed the world. It had certainly changed his and Sophie's world, anyway.

This venture, though, was pitched as *saving* the world, which was not something to be taken lightly. It was much more significant than simply a payday. And saving the world would include Sophie. He shook his head at his attempt to justify going. He didn't even know where he'd be going yet! Besides, how could a relic from the past really spell doom for the world if it *wasn't* found?

Maybe he should just count his blessings and be happy with what he had now and the memories of the adventures he'd been a part of. It's not like declining Matthew's offer would mean Cal would never travel the globe again. It just meant he wouldn't literally be putting his neck on the line or endangering Sophie. Despite popular opinion, lightning could strike the same place twice.

But he desperately needed to get away. He hadn't left North America since finding the City of Gold, with the exception of a trip to Bora-Bora where he and Sophie had celebrated their engagement.

Even if he didn't go on this expedition, he needed to start accepting photography jobs that took him to interesting and exotic locales. He'd fallen in love with the world by looking through the lens, and it was a passion rooted deep within him. But seeking out fresh landscapes and experiences were part of what made his profession invigorating and more of a calling than a job.

He ran a hand down his face and stared blankly across the coffee shop, seeing people but not really taking them in. The logical thing to do would be to let it go, get on with his day, and deal with whatever came his way tonight. Okay, that's what he was going to do. And the first thing to take care of was calling Sophie about the change of plans.

He pulled out his cell phone and pressed Sophie's name in his favorites. Her phone rang twice, and he was shuffled to voice mail. It told him that Sophie had refused his call, but that was all right. It was a system they'd worked out that just meant she was otherwise engaged.

As he listened to Sophie's greeting, he found himself somewhat relieved that he could leave the information about tonight in a message. She'd have time to think before reacting, which wasn't something Sophie was prone to doing naturally. No one could say she didn't know how to speak her mind, and even though he sometimes got the brunt of her knee-jerk reactions, it was one of the qualities he loved most about her.

The beep came, and he proceeded to lay out the evening's plan, leaving out any indication that Matthew wanted to talk to him about an expedition. Like he'd told Matthew, it was best he didn't bring it up around Sophie.

"Love you," Cal said, ending his call. His gaze had been unfocused as he'd concentrated on what he was saying to Sophie, but now his vision settled on a young couple entering the Starbucks arm in arm. The woman was leaning against the man's shoulder and periodically looking up at him with sultry eyes and a smile.

Guilt laced through him, along with a stab of pain. If he went away with Matthew, he could probably kiss Sophie's smile goodbye. But was he truly prepared to give up these adventures altogether? That wouldn't be a fulfilled existence, either. But then again, maybe he was blowing what he thought Sophie's reaction would be out of proportion. Maybe she'd be happy for him. Surely, she must have noticed how he'd been merely going through life on autopilot lately, without challenge, without bliss. A different kind of guilt slammed into him. Sophie did make him happy. Was he slime for wanting more out of life? For wanting to go on adventures with Matthew and Robyn?

Cal's insides twisted with indecision. He probably had a long night ahead of him. Yet it was better to be proactive than reactive. He'd stop by the florist and pick up three dozen red roses just in case he couldn't resist Matthew's offer. It would be easier to deliver the news if he went in armed.

CHAPTER

6

Matthew didn't want to open his eyes, but he had a feeling that it was time to get up, even though all his body wanted to do was stay put. He forced his eyes to open and focused on the clock on his nightstand. *6:15 PM.*

Holy crap!

He jumped out of bed. He was supposed to be at Cal's in forty-five minutes, and his place was a half hour drive without traffic. And in Toronto, especially at this hour, he'd have to contend with bumper-to-bumper congestion and pedestrian-clogged sidewalks.

He fumbled for his phone on his nightstand and keyed a text to Cal just to let him know he was running late. He tried to shake off his grogginess, but his head felt like it was stuffed with cobwebs.

He dashed around the room, took a quick shower, and slipped into a pair of light-gray, fitted cargo pants and a white T-shirt. The last item he put on before his shoes was a watch—ironic, given his current tardiness.

It wasn't until seven thirty that he pulled into Cal and Sophie's circular drive, regretting that he didn't have anything more to bring them than a bottle of wine he'd grabbed on the way over. But they were good friends, and he probably could have shown up empty-handed with a bowl on his head and wearing yesterday's shorts without offending them. Though, he might never live it down.

Cal answered the door partway through the bell's chime. He smiled at Matthew and reached for the wine. "Welcome home."

"Thanks." Matthew returned the smile and let go of the bottle. He was trying to read his friend's eyes, searching for any tell as to how he was feeling this evening. While Matthew had been packing that afternoon, he'd replayed the conversation he'd had with Cal several times. One benefit to being in such a hurry to get here was not having time to dwell on his regrets for piquing Cal's interest in an expedition.

"Well, are you going to come in or stay outside all night?" Cal razzed.

Matthew narrowed his eyes and played like he was going to sock Cal in the gut. Instead, they ended up in a brief hug.

Cal pulled out of the embrace first and gripped one of Matthew's shoulders. "Glad to see you made it out of Alaska alive."

"Yeah, me too." Shivers laced through him, Cal's words a reminder that Matthew almost hadn't been that lucky.

"So how was it?" Cal asked, gesturing Matthew inside and closing the door behind them.

"It was great. A real rush." Matthew didn't need to tell Cal about the little incident that had left him clinging for dear life on the side of a glacier.

Cal was leaning in toward him, obviously hungry for a good story—and possibly for an adventure himself. Maybe bringing up the expedition earlier in the day hadn't been a good idea. But it wasn't like he could really back out of it now. And if Matthew were in a relationship like Cal's, he sure wouldn't want to mess it up.

"Hey, Matthew." Sophie walked toward the front door and hugged him as he was slipping out of his shoes. She smelled of perfume and... roses? "Looking great as always," she added.

"Watch it, woman, or you're going to make me mad with jealousy," Cal teased.

Matthew laughed, and Sophie sank back against Cal. He wrapped his arms around her. His six-foot-five frame swallowed her small one of just over five feet.

"Hope you didn't have your heart set on anything fancy for dinner. We've just got a couple steaks for the grill and green salad. This guy"—she nudged Cal's chest with her shoulder—"kind of sprung tonight on me."

Cal harrumphed dramatically. "For someone who says they like surprises—"

Sophie spun and held a finger to Cal's lips. She giggled and raised up on her tiptoes to kiss him.

A twinge of jealousy laced through Matthew, and he hated himself for it. Of course, he was happy that his friend had found love. Matthew just wished he could have it for himself, too. But then again, he hadn't met Ms. Right yet. Well, he had, but it apparently wasn't meant to be.

The doorbell rang.

Cal cocked his head. "Are we expecting someone else?"

"Oh, that must be Robyn." Sophie wrestled out of Cal's grip to answer the door, her short dreads swaying with the effort.

"Robyn?" Matthew asked, surprise gripping him.

Sophie looked him straight in the eye. "I figured Cal invited you, so I'd invite Robyn."

Matthew and Cal stepped back and made eye contact. The smile that had been on Cal's face seemed to fade in increments, then disappeared completely.

Sophie opened the door, and Robyn stepped inside. She was wearing a black off-the-shoulder top paired with cream shorts. The women hugged, and Robyn handed Sophie a bottle of wine.

"They say great minds." Cal held up the bottle that Matthew had brought.

The four of them stood there grinning for a moment.

"Well, let's not waste time standing around here when there's drinking to be done." Sophie brushed between Matthew and Cal and headed in the direction of the kitchen.

Matthew looked at Robyn, and she trailed her gaze from him to Cal, the unspoken message easy to read. "Not yet," Matthew said when Sophie was well out of earshot.

"He's going to tell me what this latest—" Cal pressed his lips together, no doubt to take the place of *adventure, quest, expedition,* or another word along those lines "—is tonight."

Robyn's mouth formed an *O,* and she turned to Matthew. "Do you think that's a good idea?"

"Guess we'll find out," was all he said.

Robyn's mouth set in a straight line.

"What about you? Have you made up your mind?" Matthew asked her.

"She knows before I do?" Cal rushed out loudly. He slapped a hand over his mouth.

"I wasn't sure how you were going to take my asking." Matthew kept his volume low as he tried to do damage control. But based on Cal's scowl, Matthew wasn't doing a good job.

"So you two were talking about me behind my back?" Cal seemed to be getting worked up, a trait inherent to his volatile nature.

Robyn put a hand on Cal's arm. "It wasn't like that."

"But you were discussing me, right?"

Whatever Cal was so agitated about had to go beyond their immediate conversation, and given the storm in Cal's eyes, Matthew would peg his friend as feeling conflicted. And it was probably Matthew's fault.

"It's not like we were gossiping about you, Cal." Robyn rubbed his arm.

Cal's eyes went to her hand, and his shoulders relaxed. "I know things have been a little different lately, and it's been a long time since—"

"Are you guys going to join me or stay in the foyer all night?" Sophie called out, peeking her head around the corner to look at them. She held up an open wine bottle. "I have wine."

Matthew looked at Cal and Robyn, and watched as both his friends smiled in response to Sophie's invitation. Matthew followed suit.

"Pour me a big glass, Soph," Robyn told her friend as she padded off to the kitchen.

"You got it." Sophie's voice carried a light, wistful note as she ducked back out of view.

Matthew and Cal stayed in the entryway.

"Why don't you tell me now, before dinner," Cal said. "Then at least I can eat in peace."

"You've never been good with suspense," Matthew replied with some amusement.

"Do you know anyone who is?" Cal countered, a flicker of enthusiasm dancing across his eyes. It was the same flicker that presented itself often when on an expedition, the sort of flicker that testified to his friend feeling very much alive and excited about life.

"Fine. Why don't we grab a glass of wine and head to your office?"

Cal nodded. "Sounds good to me."

In the brief time it took for Matthew and Cal to decide their game plan and pour their drinks, the women had already curled up on a couch, wineglasses in hand. The living room was off the kitchen to the right and past the dining table, upon which sat a vase full of roses. They had to pass all this to reach Cal's office.

"Where are you guys going?" Sophie asked, stopping in the middle of something she had been saying to Robyn.

"I'm just going to show Matthew some of the pictures I took of the Grand Canyon," Cal responded.

"Okay, but don't take too long," Sophie said. "I'll want you to put the steaks on the grill soon."

"That's fine." Cal turned back to Matthew and continued to lead the way to his office, which was decorated in glass and metal with touches of teal. Cal closed the door behind them.

Matthew sat on a couch and Cal on the chair he'd dubbed "the King's Chair." It had cream-colored upholstery with a rounded back and nailhead accents.

"So what is it this time?" Cal asked.

It was probably best they get to the point right away in case the women walked in on them. He had faith that Robyn would do what she could to avoid that from happening, but when Sophie had her mind made up, it didn't always matter.

"The Emerald Tablets in Egypt," Matthew said.

Cal took a sip of his wine and looked away from Matthew. "Usually people go to Egypt to uncover pharaoh's tombs."

So, Cal remembered the Tablets and Matthew's obsession with them, but like Robyn, didn't buy into their existence. "That too," Matthew said.

Cal's eyes narrowed marginally, and he drank some more wine. "When are you planning to leave?"

"Tomorrow morning."

Cal spat out his wine, red mist shooting across his office. "Do you have something against planning ahead these days?"

Matthew pulled his gaze from the splotches of red on the floor to his friend, whose focus was solely on him. "You heard me when I said *the* Emerald Tablets?"

"Uh-huh."

"And you know that they're said to contain great power?"

"I remember a rumor to that effect."

"A rumor?" Matthew shook his head. "Well, they exist, and I believe their power is real."

Cal didn't say anything, just kept looking at Matthew. Matthew had to wonder if the skepticism was a ploy Cal was using to distance himself from this expedition.

"You want to come, don't you?" Matthew asked.

"I'd follow you to the ends of the Earth right now." Cal glanced away and rubbed his jaw. "But that's not an option."

Matthew leaned forward. "Of course, it is."

"No." Cal was shaking his head. "Not after what happened the last time. I can't do that to Sophie."

"Sophie has known for a long time that you love going on these expeditions."

"That doesn't necessarily mean anything."

"It should." Matthew let that marinate and came to realize that his wording may have been a little harsh. "I didn't mean that the way it came out. You and Sophie are engaged now. You've made a real commitment. And Sophie's great."

"That she is." Cal bobbed his head.

"She'll understand." Oh, what was he doing? Somewhere he'd stopped thinking about Cal's needs and switched his focus to the fact that he wanted Cal to come with him.

"I'm not so sure. After everything she went through, almost dying, almost being raped…" Cal raised his voice with the last statement. "I could never forgive myself if…"

Matthew swallowed the urge to make more assurances he wasn't qualified to make. "Only you know your relationship, Cal. But I know that Sophie loves you." He paused and flashed a lopsided grin. "After all, she did agree to marry you despite all that crap you put her through."

"Ha-ha." Cal raised his gaze to meet Matthew's. "You're right, though. If there was any time she should have hated me…"

Matthew held out his hands. "There you go."

"Guess it wouldn't hurt to talk to her about all this." Cal took another sip of his wine, but his features seemed to weigh heavy with hesitancy. "Tomorrow's rather quick, though."

"The Emerald Tablets are powerful. We can't afford them winding up in the wrong person's hands."

"I'm assuming you have a good lead to suspect they're in Egypt."

Matthew noticed his friend didn't even bother to ask for an elaboration on the Tablets' powers. "An old colleague has invited us to be a part of—"

"*Us?* So she knows about me?"

"You and Robyn."

Cal sank back into his chair. "How could you even be sure I'd agree?"

"I couldn't. I just mentioned that I normally go on expeditions with my close friends." Maybe he'd been a little presumptuous that Cal would agree to go along with him. There was one thing that was giving away his friend's true feelings, though. "Why all the roses, Cal?"

Cal clenched his jaw briefly and tapped a hand on the edge of the chair. "I thought it might be easier to tell her I'm going away for a while if— Oh, why am I explaining myself to you?" Cal met Matthew's eyes. "I'd love to go with you, Lord knows, but I just don't know how Sophie will take it."

"You won't know until you tell her."

Cal drained the rest of his glass. "You're right." He sounded sure of himself, the liquid suddenly arming him with confidence. "How long do you plan on being in Egypt?"

Matthew shrugged. "As long as it takes."

Cal shook his head and smirked. "Seriously? Can you be any more vague?"

"Don't you mean can't I be any *vaguer*?" Matthew smirked.

Cal shook his head. "And now he's correcting my grammar."

Matthew laughed.

"Just spit it out," Cal said. "How long?"

"Plan on a month."

A deep breath, then, "And we'd leave tomorrow?"

Matthew made note of *we'd* but thought it best not to celebrate just yet. "That's right. Takeoff is at eight in the morning. If you're coming, be there no later than six."

Cal's eyes glazed over, and Matthew wasn't sure if it was the wine, thoughts about breaking the news to Sophie, or simply feeling overwhelmed about preparing for the trip on such short notice.

"Just pack the essentials," Matthew said, skimming over the enormity of the task. "You've been there, done that before."

"Not in Egypt."

"You know what I mean. On expeditions. And everything's in place for us to dig once we're in Egypt. Basically, all you have to do is grab your passport and camera, and we're off."

Cal laughed. "I wish it were that easy. I've been dying for something like this to come along. Maybe I have a mental problem, but why do I need to face death to feel alive?"

"If you find the answer to that one, my friend, I hope you'll share the wisdom with me." Matthew lifted his glass in a toast but remembered Cal's drink was gone. Matthew knocked back the rest of his.

Cal's face became serious. "When do you need to know if I'm coming?"

"The sooner the better." Matthew paused. "The pilot needs to know for the manifest no later than six in the morning. Do you think you could—"

"Let you know by then?" Cal finished and nodded.

It was in the way Cal locked eyes with him that disclosed that Cal already knew what he wanted. It was just a matter of whether or not he was brave enough to follow through with his decision.

"All right. Sounds good."

Cal stood up and headed for the office door. "We better get back to the girls before—"

The door opened, and Sophie was standing in the doorway with Robyn behind her.

Robyn was wincing and mouthed, *Sorry*.

"Before what, Cal?" Sophie asked.

"Before…before," Cal stammered.

"Before you beautiful ladies go hungry," Matthew stepped in.

Sophie slid her gaze from Cal to Matthew and back to Cal, who hadn't moved. "Well?"

"Well," Cal repeated and pulled Sophie into his arms.

Matthew grabbed his friend's wineglass, and Cal dipped Sophie.

"Would you…cut it out?" Sophie was laughing and slapping Cal in the chest.

He set her upright but grabbed her sides. "I don't know…"

"Mr. Myers, I order you—"

"*Order* me?" Cal's demeanor became stony. He let go of her.

Sophie's eyes were darting about, her gaze shifting among the three of them. "I didn't mean *order* you, as in I'm your boss." Each of Sophie's words came out as if she was confused by the need to defend herself.

"That's good, because you're not," Cal snapped. He snatched the wineglass from Matthew and left the room, Sophie trailing behind him. "What's going on with you? We were just playing around..."

Matthew was left in the office face-to-face with Robyn. Her eyebrows hitched upward slightly, and she crossed her arms. "I don't think I even have to ask how everything went in here," she said.

Matthew raked a hand through his hair. Maybe he should have just left the matter alone and accept that his days of unearthing legends with Cal were over. That sounded so righteous in theory, but Cal wasn't happy that way. Matthew had known Cal long enough to read his friend's energy, and playing it safe by simply photographing landmarks wasn't something that sparked life in him the way treasure hunting did.

"He's not happy," Matthew said.

Robyn tilted her head upward. "It's not up to you to decide that."

He pointed toward the hallway. "I can tell."

"Did he give you an answer about going?"

Matthew was relieved that she was moving on from the topic of Cal's happiness. But it almost felt like an "out of the frying pan and into the fire" type of situation. Especially given the mild scowl on her face. "Not really, but I think he's going to come." He let his gaze trace over Robyn, taking in how her long, brown hair spilled over her tanned shoulders. "What about you?" he asked, attempting to detour himself from going down a rabbit hole that would only lead to a painful reality check. "Did you talk with your boss? Tell him how important this expedition was? Leaving out the Tablets, of course?"

"I did." She tightened her crossed arms, hoisting up her bosom with the action.

He was enough of a gentleman not to look...for long. But he was a man. He met her eyes. "And?"

"And I don't know, Matt." A glimmer danced across her eyes, betraying her.

"Your boss would be fine with you going," he stated.

She looked away. That was enough to stab home the loneliness he'd felt watching Cal and Sophie earlier, and while thinking about Robyn on that glacier.

"That's fine. I understand." Matthew moved to pass Robyn and leave the room, but she caught him by the crook of his elbow.

"It's just that I had plans."

"Had?"

Robyn pinched her eyes closed for a few seconds. When she opened them, her gaze met his. "As in, I canceled them."

A smile spread across his face. "So you're coming?"

She smiled. "Yes, I'm coming."

"Why give me such a hard time, then? I thought you were going to say you weren't."

"I like to keep you guessing," she said with a wink.

She had no idea just how often she did that.

CHAPTER

7

IT WAS ELEVEN O'CLOCK BY the time Matthew entered his father's study. William Connor was sitting next to the fireplace in a wingback chair reading a book. The man certainly fit the image of an affluent intellectual with his silver hair and gray eyes. Even at this time of night, his father was dressed in pressed slacks and a collared shirt. The only hints at his being casual were that the top two buttons of his shirt were undone and there was no sign of a tie.

His father turned the hardcover upside down on his lap, took off his reading glasses, and regarded his son. "Are you going away?"

Matthew nodded. No one could say that his father was slow, though Matthew's news must have been clear from the look on his face. He'd never been good at hiding his feelings, and his excitement and anxiousness must have been evident. The latter wasn't so much due to the trip or the expedition itself, but rather what he had potentially set in motion on Cal's home front.

"Where to this time?" his father asked.

"Egypt." Matthew took a seat in a chair facing his father, appreciating the relatively newfound openness they had between them. For years, Matthew hid what he really did for a living under the pseudonym of Gideon Barnes—all because he didn't think his father would understand. But when the truth came out after finding the City of Gold, his father had accepted what Matthew did in stride.

His father tapped his glasses on the arm of the chair. "I thought we promised to be honest with each other."

"I am being honest." Matthew felt the skin on the back of his neck tighten, even though he had prepared for the likelihood that his father would see right through him and know he was withholding something important.

"So you're going on an archaeological dig in Egypt?" There was only one reason his father would state the obvious as a question like that. He was mining for information. And under his father's watchful—and judgmental—eye, slivers of self-condemnation pricked at his conscience. But sharing more wasn't a matter of choice; it was a matter of protecting his father.

"That's right," Matthew said with a nod.

"What specifically has you going back there?" His father stopped tapping his glasses. "And tell me the truth."

This was the only thing about keeping his father in the loop: it made him feel like a child explaining his comings and goings.

"A pharaoh's tomb." Not fully forthcoming, but it was short, sweet, and honest.

"Uh-huh. I guess we're back to half-truths." His father looked toward the door as if encouraging Matthew to use it.

"I'm telling you the truth," Matthew started, earning his father's gaze again. "But yes, there is more to it."

"Well, I'd love to hear it."

Matthew pulled his shoulders back. "I can't tell you."

"Then why come in here at all?" he asked hotly, his frustration seeping through. "You're an adult. You don't have to explain yourself to me."

"I realize that, but I just thought you might notice if I wasn't around for the next month. I didn't want you to worry, but—" Matthew got to his feet.

"Sit down." His father's stern directive had Matthew sitting again despite not wanting to. It was no wonder the man was successful in business and politics. His father's posture relaxed, if only slightly. "Tell me what you can."

So much for not needing to explain myself...

"I've told you everything I can."

"Ah." His father studied him, and it was probably his skill at drawing out the truth that had been the real reason Matthew had avoided him in the past.

"Some of this expedition is confidential," Matthew said.

"But it's not dangerous." His father managed to phrase this as more of a stipulation than an inquiry.

How did his father expect him to answer? Surely, he knew that unearthing legends was a dangerous business. Though, it was even more so when it involved the Emerald Tablets...

"Keeping quiet on that point, I see." His father stuffed a bookmark into his book and put it on the side table. "That means it is. But you mentioned a pharaoh's tomb. That doesn't sound too risky." His father was nothing if not relentless.

"We're still talking about the desert here, and there are—"

"Risks involved with that alone," his father finished. "Are you being pressured into this?"

Sophie's kidnapping came to Matthew's mind. "Like with the City of Gold?"

His father nodded.

"No. I'm going completely of my own free will," Matthew promised.

"Very well. Whose tomb is it supposed to be?"

"We have reason to believe it belongs to a son of Khufu."

His father regarded him silently, the name going right over his head, and it had Matthew wondering why his father had asked whose tomb it was in the first place. The man's strength was in politics, not history.

"When do you head out?" he asked.

Matthew straightened his back, readying to defend himself. "Tomorrow morning."

His father's nostrils flared slightly. "*Tomorrow morning?* Isn't that a little soon? Or have you been preparing for a while and merely never said anything?"

His father always had a plan, while Matthew liked to go with the flow, regardless of where life took him. "It's an urgent matter."

"A long-dead pharaoh's tomb is *urgent*?" His father's eyes lit with revelation. "Ah, I see. It's what you're not telling me about that is so urgent." He paused for a few seconds. "Are Cal and Robyn going with you?"

His father's question propelled his mind back to earlier in the evening. Cal had come out and told Sophie that he was going to Egypt and that he didn't answer to her. Sophie had fired back that if Cal wanted that kind of freedom, then *maybe*... And she'd left that one word to dangle out there. Then the yelling had started. Matthew and Robyn had excused themselves not much past eight and picked up dinner at a fast-food joint.

"Robyn is," Matthew said. "I'm not sure about Cal yet."

"Boy, all you kids sure love leaving things until the last minute."

"We'll be fine," Matthew assured him, not even about to touch the "kids" comment.

His father pulled back and pursed his lips. "Seems you have everything figured out."

Matthew tapped a hand on the arm of his chair. *Everything* was a big word, and its scope made him gravely uncomfortable. There were always unforeseen situations that arose in his line of work, adjustments that needed to be made, quick judgments and reactions in the moment.

His father pointed toward him with his entire hand. "You *do* have everything figured out."

"I know what I'm getting myself into." He hoped he was coming across confident. "I've been there before and came back alive."

"Let's hope the record stays that way." His father offered him a genuine smile. "When you get back, you'll have to tell me all about it. Or what you can anyway."

"I will." Matthew got up to leave and considered whether or not to hug his father. The man had never been a hugger, but when Matthew was shipping off for an expedition, it seemed like it was the practical thing to do. Who knew if he'd be returning home?

"Good night, Son, and safe travels." His father's gaze drifted to the door as he put his glasses on again and grabbed his book.

"Good night." Matthew left the room, instantly wishing that he'd given the man a hug.

CHAPTER
8

THE NEXT MORNING, Matthew was pacing the VIP lounge at Pearson International Airport, thinking about last night and feeling completely responsible. What a disaster! If it hadn't been for him, Cal and Sophie wouldn't have had a big fight, and he wouldn't have been on the receiving end of Sophie's hard-ass glare. She may come in a small package, but she could hold her own.

He half expected Cal to change his mind, but on the other hand, Cal could be just as every bit hotheaded and stubborn as Sophie.

He dropped into a chair and let out a deep breath. Pacing wouldn't get his friends there any faster. Not that they needed to be there right that instant. Blue Skies already had their information for the flight manifest.

He caught sight of Cal and stood up. He waved, and Cal came over.

"How are you?" Matthew cursed himself instantly. What a stupid thing to ask. There was no way the guy could be good.

"I'm here, and I'm doing this." Resolve soaked Cal's tone, but it was sapped of enthusiasm.

"I'm sorry I even asked you to come along."

Cal shook his head. "Don't be. The topic was bound to come up at some point."

"And you and Sophie?" Matthew broached the subject directly, figuring he'd already ventured this far.

Cal dropped the bag he'd been holding to the floor. He was also wearing a backpack. "We'll be fine. Eventually."

Matthew felt his chest expand for a breath, but it wasn't a full one. *Eventually* didn't sound too promising.

"We made relative peace before I left, but I don't know..." Cal shook his head. "If she can't accept me for who I am..."

Matthew didn't know what to say. What advice could he possibly have to offer about relationships? Cal was looking at him like he expected him to say something. Maybe if he just approached it from a more detached standpoint, leaving out reassurances...

"Sophie's always accepted you," he said.

Cal's shoulders stiffened. "So you're on her side?"

Matthew held up his hands. "I'm not taking sides."

"Well, she's told me many times that as long as I'm happy, she's happy. But whenever an expedition comes up, I watch the light fade from her eyes. It's been that way since I started going on them." Cal clenched his jaw briefly and then let it relax. "I know it's not the safest thing for me to be doing, but that's why I love it. Does that make sense to you?"

"Ah—"

"Wait a minute, look who I'm asking." Cal laughed.

"Yeah, you should have known better." Matthew was smiling, and he looked past Cal to see Robyn coming toward them.

"Hey, losers," Robyn called out, grinning.

The greeting was uncharacteristic for Robyn, but the playful nature at the outset of an expedition was not—at least when they weren't being coerced.

Robyn's enthusiasm dimmed when she reached them, and she put a hand on Cal's shoulder. Cal and Robyn made eye contact, and Matthew picked up on their silent conversation. He figured it was something along the lines of her being sorry for how things went with Cal and Sophie.

Robyn pulled her hand back from Cal and adjusted a strap from her backpack. She'd also come armed with a wheeled hardside suitcase.

"You know what she told me?" Cal looked up at the ceiling and shook his head. "Sophie said that if I die over there, she'll just leave my body there because I made the choice to go. She's not even going to bury me. Yeah, she went so far as to add that. Can you believe it? This from the woman I'm going to marry."

A wave of nausea rolled over Matthew at the pain in Cal's eyes.

"Well, maybe the time away will do you both good, give you both perspective to realize how much you love each other." Robyn's voice was as delicate as a flower petal.

"I can only hope." Cal paused. "She gets so worked up sometimes that she shoots me these glares that remind me of Medusa. I fear turning to stone."

Matthew wasn't going to correct Cal's recounting of the Greek myth. It was technically just looking upon Medusa's face that did the trick.

"And here we are this morning, saying goodbye and pretending for the moment that everything between us is okay." Heartache spilled into Cal's voice, and he cleared his throat. "We're all about not going to bed mad at each other or going our separate ways without kissing goodbye. But this morning..." He deflected and pointed at Robyn. "She's mad at you, too, you know."

"Me? Why?" Robyn shot Matthew a look as if to imply that if Sophie should be mad at anyone else, it should be him.

Matthew narrowed his eyes at her. "Gee, thanks," he muttered.

Cal glanced at Matthew, then back to Robyn. "You broke your date with... Oh, I can't remember his name right now. But she set you up. You promised her you would follow through with it."

"Yes, and I told her I'd go out with him when I got back." Robyn avoided eye contact with Matthew despite his staring her down, which only amplified his curiosity.

"Who's this guy?" he asked.

"Someone Sophie works with," Cal answered. "She thinks that he and Robyn will hit it off."

Giving real thought to Robyn dating drilled an ache into Matthew's heart. But thinking Robyn would *hit it off* with someone other than him hurt even more.

Robyn was shaking her head. "Who likes blind dates anyway? It was nice of me to agree to go in the first place."

"It's not the date so much as the fact that you broke your word because of..." Cal didn't need to finish. It was because of the expedition.

Robyn's face fell, and she swept a hand through her hair. "I'll message her from the plane."

"Oh, I wouldn't do that," Cal cautioned. "I think putting space between you and her might not be a bad idea."

"Well, this isn't personal." Robyn tilted her chin upward. "And she knows what all of us do by this point. I am incredibly sorry for all she went through in the past due to our explorations, but we make a difference by doing it." She was putting up a tough front, but sadness crept into her eyes.

Matthew wanted to comfort her, but it wasn't his place. Not anymore. That was a job for whomever she was dating. And as much as it wounded him that Robyn was dating at all, he had to expect it. She was beautiful and intelligent. He was just grateful he had her in his life.

"Okay, let's get outta here," Matthew said enthusiastically, corralling his friends for what promised to be not only the adventure of a lifetime but a means of saving the world.

CHAPTER
9

Robyn had woken up in a hotel room in Cairo. The time difference had messed with her and disrupted her sleep, but she was infused with energy regardless. Or her mind was anyhow. One of her lifelong dreams had finally manifested. She was really in Egypt. At the moment, she was in the hotel restaurant with Cal and Matthew, their luggage beside their table. Matthew's contact, Alex Leonard, was going to pick them up in the lobby about seven o'clock. They had about half an hour until then.

Robyn sucked back her coffee, hoping that the caffeine would jolt her body into submission.

"Are you going to make it?" Cal quirked an eyebrow, looking at her over his mug.

I'm in Egypt.

"Of course, I will." She found herself smiling despite her exhaustion.

"Maybe we should have skipped the nightcap," Matthew teased and smiled back at her. She envied how rested he looked. He was drinking coffee, too, but didn't have a death grip on his mug like she and Cal did.

"No." She shook her head. "Being here deserved a toast...or two."

"I can't believe I didn't think of this until now, especially with everything going on with Sophie, but don't pharaohs' tombs have curses?" Cal asked out of nowhere. "I know there was one on King

Tut's tomb." His words relayed more concern than his expression, but maybe that was just because he wasn't awake enough to project it. He was prone to paranoia, though.

Maybe she could have some fun with this…

Robyn turned to Matthew. "Is now a good time to tell him that curses are standard for Egyptian tombs?"

Matthew frowned. "Probably not."

"What?" Cal leaned across the table and threw his arms up in the air. "Are you guys being serious?"

Now he was waking up. It took all of Robyn's self-control not to burst out laughing. What she had said was the truth, but reality had a way of invalidating the curses' sway.

Cal scowled, and his shoulders sank. "You think I'm being crazy."

Matthew pinched his fingers together, leaving a small space between them. "Just a little."

Robyn glanced at Matthew. His belief that some ancient tablets had the power to destroy the world was about as far-fetched as any pharaoh's curse. Not that she was going to voice her disbelief out loud at the risk of hurting him the way she had in her office.

"Sophie told me she won't bury me if I die out here," Cal said.

So that's what this was about. "I'm sure she didn't mean that," Robyn assured him. "Besides, we've got your back."

"You said there are curses. We could be in real danger, besides the scorpions, the snakes, sandstorms."

"Those are the *real* dangers," Matthew pointed out.

Cal straightened his posture, and he stretched out his neck. "A mosquito bite took out the man who found Tut's tomb. Who else in the history of the world has died from a mosquito bite?"

"Mosquitoes infect people with deadly viruses all the time," Robyn started. "Surely you've heard of malaria and West Nile virus."

"No." Cal was shaking his head. "What happened to that man was different. It was brought on by an ancient evil. I feel it."

Robyn burst out laughing and so did Matthew.

Cal narrowed his eyes. "You think I'm getting carried away?"

Robyn pinched her fingers to almost touching, just as Matthew had done.

"Well, don't come crying to me if we unearth an evil that hunts us down to kill us." Given his raised voice, he wasn't saying this simply to be amusing.

Robyn looked at Matthew, and they said, "We promise," at the same time.

"Very well. And you guys will bury me if I die out here?"

Again, Robyn and Matthew chimed in together. "We promise."

"All right, I'm hungry now." Cal got up from the table and hit the buffet line.

"Good ole Cal," she said. "From fear to food in seconds."

She watched Matthew's smile fade, and her mind turned to valid dangers they could face. In dire situations, it was best to have people around who could be trusted. While she trusted Matthew and Cal, she didn't know anyone else on this expedition. She'd asked about Alex before but was inclined to again. "So how well do you know this Alex person?"

"I worked with her when I came over here after getting my doctorate."

Robyn remembered that time well because they'd broken up not long before he'd left. It had been a hard time for—

Wait, her?

"Alex is a woman?" Robyn's throat felt as if it had been stitched shut. If he'd mentioned Alex's gender before, she must have missed it.

"Yeah. Alexandria."

"Very Egyptian-like." Robyn could have palm-slapped herself in the forehead for the awkward turn this conversation had taken. Really, why should it matter if Alex was a woman? Even if she had been a rebound fling for Matthew, that was years ago. Still, while Robyn had been wallowing in Canada, he'd been here…

"She's American. Though, she spends as much time as she can over here. That used to be the case anyway."

"You haven't stayed in touch?"

"No. I was actually surprised when I heard from her."

So they hadn't been in touch in years, but she calls Matthew out of the blue and invites him on her dig? It could just be a matter of Alex knowing Matthew would be interested in this particular expedition, but it made Robyn suspicious. Why didn't Alex keep the find to herself? It certainly wasn't an expedition that should be broadcasted. Maybe Robyn should have considered this before, but in her defense, the trip had been sprung on her and getting to this point had been a whirlwind.

Cal returned with a croissant, scrambled eggs, bacon, hash browns, and a six-inch-diameter pancake drenched with syrup.

"Eating for two?" Robyn jested. If she'd had a brother, she'd have wanted him to be like Cal. He was just too easy to harass.

"I figure if I'm going to die, I might as well do so with a full belly." Cal scooped up a forkful of eggs and stuffed it into his mouth.

Robyn wasn't sure if he was kidding or being serious. Sure, he had the tendency to exaggerate and jump to conclusions, but probably because he spent so much time around Sophie, who often got strong "feelings" about things. Thinking of Sophie, Robyn realized that her friend still hadn't responded to her text message. As a real estate agent, Sophie lived on her phone, so it was likely she'd seen it. She hoped that Sophie would find a way to forgive her. Even if Sophie couldn't get past the expedition, Egypt was a place most people never got to visit.

Robyn drained the rest of her coffee. As she had the cup to her lips, her gaze went across the room to the hostess stand. A strikingly beautiful blonde was talking to the hostess, her head turning as she searched the restaurant. Her face broke into a smile.

Robyn followed the woman's gaze, and the blonde was looking at Matthew. He was grinning back at her and waving.

Alex?

But it couldn't be seven o'clock already. They'd just sat down here not long ago. Robyn consulted her phone. *6:30.*

The blonde walked toward their table, all legs and sun-kissed skin. Matthew got to his feet and greeted her with a peck on her cheek.

"The years have been good to you," she purred.

Or at least it sounded like purring to Robyn. There had to have been something more to Matthew and Alex's relationship than he had let on.

"You look good yourself, Alex." Matthew doled out the compliment with natural debonair flair. "How's Shane?"

"Oh, Shane and I called off our engagement not long after I came back from playing tourist in Canada."

"Hope I didn't have anything to do with it."

Robyn's suspicions flared again, along with her curiosity.

"Leave it to a guy to want to take the credit for something like that." Alex held out her hand to Robyn. "I'm Alex Leonard."

She took her hand. "Robyn Garcia."

"That's Cal." Matthew pointed at him just as he was unloading another forkful of food into his mouth.

Alex laughed a sweet, innocent type of chortle. Very feminine.

"Matthew speaks highly of both of you. Pleasure to meet you." She carried off the pleasantry with sincerity. "Everything has been taken care of with the Egyptian government, as I told Matthew yesterday. All three of you have the green light to dig with my team."

"I'm glad to have that reconfirmed, seeing as we've come all this way." Matthew nudged his shoulder into Alex's, and it had Robyn's cheeks heating up from discomfort.

"Here, take a seat." Matthew pulled out a chair for Alex, and she sat down. "We're just finishing up breakfast."

Alex's gaze scanned the table, taking in the coffee cups and the still-wrapped cutlery in front of Robyn and Matthew. "Looks like you two haven't started."

Matthew took his seat again without saying anything.

If Matthew was feeling the way Robyn was, then his stomach wasn't awake yet. Back in Toronto, it was around one in the morning.

"Well, I suggest you eat something before we leave. It's going to be a busy day." Alex shuffled her chair closer to the table.

Matthew made no move to get up. "How did you know you'd find us in here?"

"Best guess. It's breakfast time."

Matthew jacked a thumb toward Alex. "She'd make a good detective."

His eyes met Robyn's, and she shook her head subtly. He was trying far too hard.

Matthew stood. "If you'll excuse me, I'm going to grab some food."

"You're excused." Alex jumped on that with a sultry smile. She watched Matthew as he walked toward the buffet.

"You and Matthew were close?" Robyn blurted out, instantly regretting doing so. There was something to be said for thinking before speaking. She attempted to recover by smiling, but Alex was eyeing Matthew like a tigress tracking her prey.

"We were good friends," Alex answered but didn't look at Robyn when she replied.

Good friends, as in merely platonic? Or was Alex glossing it over?

Robyn had been heartbroken when she and Matthew had ended things. But she'd buried herself in her work as a distraction. And while she had been doing that Matthew could have been burying himself in—

"You really should eat something." Alex withdrew her gaze from Matthew and looked at Robyn.

Robyn tilted her mug and eyed the bottom of it. She could indulge in a refill. "Suppose I should." She didn't like how agreeing made her feel like she was appeasing a parent. She got up anyway and joined Matthew. He was dishing some hash browns onto his plate.

"Looks like someone found his appetite," Robyn said.

Matthew handed her the serving spoon, and she shook her head. He put it down. "She's right. We need to eat."

She didn't know why his agreeing with Alex had her recoiling, but all the old feelings from when she and Matthew had broken up were resurfacing. The anger, the disappointment, and the heartbreak had been gone for so long, it was hard to know how to deal with them.

"You like her, don't you?" Robyn pulled off the question in a purely buddy-buddy manner, but she hated that she even thought of it as something she had to pull off.

"I don't really know her anymore," he said.

"I suppose that's true." She smirked at him, wishing her twinges of jealousy would go away. His lips curled upward, and she pointed to his mouth. "But that's something you'd like to change."

"Fine. I'll admit that I think she's beautiful, but that's not why I'm here. I mean, why *we're* here."

"I sure hope not, because you've made a couple big promises that made me come along in the first place."

"Who are you kidding? I had you at *Egypt.*" He winked and went back to the table.

He had no idea the effect he sometimes had on her. And they'd been friends for years—she should have adapted to parameters of the relationship by now. Curse this Alex for showing up and disrupting Robyn's mojo. Except *this Alex* was the reason Robyn was in Egypt at all. She sighed and looked at the spread of food. She ended up grabbing a muffin and a package of butter, but her stomach was a mess.

Alex pointed to Robyn's plate once she joined everyone at the table. "That's not much food."

"Well, maybe if Cal and Matthew left me some…" Robyn smiled at Alex and let the expression trail to Matthew.

"Well, we do have food out at base camp," Alex assured her. "And speaking of…"

"We should get going?" Matthew finished.

Alex nodded. "We probably should. It gets hot quickly around here, and we still have a two-and-a-half-hour drive to camp."

Matthew flagged down a nearby waitress. "Could we get the bill, please?"

The waitress nodded and walked off.

"So has any progress been made with the dig?" Robyn cut her muffin in half and smeared on some butter.

Alex had been looking at Matthew's profile and smiling. She turned from him and flashed a mischievous grin. "Yes, some very exciting discoveries, too. But I'll share those with you once we're at base camp."

"Now who sounds like a nasty tease?" Matthew asked.

Alex hit Matthew's shoulder. It was probably an inside joke that had lasted, despite the years and the distance between them, because Robyn certainly didn't get it. She looked away, uncomfortable with their display. She was in Egypt, it was true, but this was going to be a very long month.

CHAPTER
10

IT WAS TERRIFIC TO SEE Alex again, but it was odd admitting his attraction to Alex to Robyn. Wasn't there some kind of unspoken rule that they shouldn't discuss their romantic lives?

"Our rides are this way." Alex took off down the breezeway of the hotel to the front of the building. He followed alongside her to the drop-off area, which was a roundabout covered by an overhang. It provided shelter from the sun, but the air was intensely warm and dry.

Two open-roofed Jeeps were parked bumper-to-bumper, and two men wearing panama hats stood waiting next to them.

"Everyone, this is Jeff Webb." Alex gestured toward the man standing by the second Jeep, and she swept back a wisp of her hair. He looked like he was around fifty and wore a wedding band. "He's my site foreman."

"Hey—" Matthew held out a hand to Jeff "—Matthew Connor."

"*Doctor* Connor," Alex corrected him with a smile.

It had been a long time since he'd been introduced with his formal title, and it felt surprisingly good.

"Nice to meet you." Jeff had a firm grip, but his hands were sweaty and calloused.

"And this is Jasper Blair," Alex said, introducing the other man. "He's an expert at reading and deciphering hieroglyphics."

Matthew shook Jasper's hand, as well. He was easily in his fifties with leathery-looking skin and a face that hadn't seen a razor in a while.

Matthew stepped back and turned toward Robyn and Cal. "These are my friends and colleagues, Robyn Garcia and Cal Myers. Robyn is a curator at the Royal Ontario Museum in Toronto, and Cal is a world-renowned photographer."

Jasper settled a skeptical gaze on Cal.

Matthew had the urge to defend his presence. "When we find what we're after, and even for the journey, his work will document our expedition on film. With the exception of…you know."

"Well, not film exactly. Digital file." Cal lifted the camera that was dangling around his neck and snapped a photo of Jasper. The man grimaced. "I'd like to take a group photo." Cal waved for them to squeeze in next to one another. Once everyone did, Cal said, "Smile." He snapped the shot and lowered his camera.

Matthew put a hand on Cal's shoulder. "As you can see, he's got us covered." Jasper was still looking at Cal cynically.

"The three of them were responsible for finding the Incas' lost City of Gold." Alex sang their praises in a manner that bespoke of mediation. "And I look forward to working with every one of them. As I told both of you—" Alex glanced at Jeff, then Jasper "—Matthew and I worked together on a dig here in Egypt years ago."

"Have you been to Egypt before?" Jasper could have been asking the question of both Robyn and Cal, but his attention was on Cal.

"Nope. First time," Cal responded.

"Same for me," Robyn added.

Jasper didn't take his eyes off Cal. "It's a different world over here."

"It's a different country, anyhow." Cal's nonchalant demeanor gave no indication the man's disdain was getting to him.

Jasper remained quiet but kept his eye on Cal.

Matthew wished he knew what Jasper's problem was.

"Well, shall we get underway?" Alex's voice was full of enthusiasm. "We'll need to split up. Some of us will go with Jeff, and some with Jasper. I figured with your luggage, we'll need the space."

The two men got behind the wheels of their Jeeps.

Cal leaned in toward Matthew. "I'll go with Jeff."

Matthew looked at his friend. "I don't blame you." He chose to go with Jasper, though, and Alex tagged along while Robyn joined Cal and Jeff. They loaded their luggage into the two Jeeps, and then Matthew, Cal, and Robyn pulled out hats.

Matthew buckled up in the back seat behind Jasper so that he could easily talk with Alex, who was riding shotgun. In mere moments, the two Jeeps were pulling out single file, leaving the hotel in their rearview mirrors, along with the protection of the overhang.

The sun's heat was relentless, and the movement of the vehicle and the hat on his head did little to compensate. It was as if Matthew had gone from a sauna to a convection oven. He ran a hand under the brim of his hat, and it came out soaked with sweat.

"Believe it or not, it's better with the top off." Alex was looking over a shoulder and must have noticed what he'd just done.

"I forgot just how hot it gets over here. Wow." Sweat was running down his back in rivulets, and he almost questioned if wearing a hat was the wisest choice. Sure, it blocked out the sun, but it also kept the heat in.

Alex chuckled. "You'll get used to it soon enough."

"Or die trying," Matthew quipped.

He looked around, taking in the scenery and noting how much things had changed in the last five years. Cairo was more built-up and commercialized, and though that was disheartening, it was to be expected. Tourists held certain standards when traveling, and Egypt wasn't exempt from them.

Alex shifted toward the console, making it easier for them to carry on a conversation. "Reda's coming by the camp around noon and will be joining us for lunch and then going out to the site with us."

The Egyptian minister of antiquities had Egypt in his blood, and not just because he had been born in the country. He had been featured in most documentaries surrounding Egyptian pharaohs, tombs, and artifacts.

"He's never going to retire, is he?" It was a definite observation, a rhetorical question they knew the answer to.

"Not of his own volition," Alex answered anyhow. "But that's a good thing. He's an amazing man and brings a lot to this country." Alex's voice took on a note of pride when she mentioned *this country*. She obviously thought of Egypt as her own, despite being an American.

"Do you go back to the States often?" he asked.

Alex swept hair out of her face as Jasper made a right turn. "Not really. Technically, this is my second home, but I think of it as my first."

It could have been her love for Egypt that had eventually spelled doom for her relationship with Shane, but he wasn't going to bring that up. Instead, his mind wandered to one of his last interactions with Reda. It had him recoiling, and it didn't go unnoticed.

"What is it?" Puzzlement toyed with the edges of her mouth.

"I don't know if I should say anything."

"Oh, this must be good." She rubbed her hands together.

Images of the pottery vase slipping from his hands and hitting the ground were still so vivid after all these years. As was the scowl on Reda's face. If only the man hadn't made him so nervous. "It's just one of the last times I worked with him, I might have…"

"What did you do, Matt?" she said with a laugh.

He loved hearing the abbreviation of his name coming from her lips. It rolled off her tongue as if she was talking to a longtime friend, one she'd never lost touch with.

"I might have dropped something," he admitted.

"Oh no." Her eyes widened. "What was it? Did it break?"

Matthew shook his head. "No, thank goodness. That's probably the only reason I'm allowed back into the country."

Alex laughed again, and Matthew appreciated the lighthearted ring to it.

"It was just a fluke that it didn't break," Matthew went on. "Reda laid into me about being more careful, but it was his fault that I dropped it in the first place."

"Leave it to a guy to pass the blame." She tsked.

"You know the man." He wasn't about to become apologetic. "He could make coffee nervous."

She smiled. "He's not that bad."

"When it comes to cataloging, he's meticulous in how he oversees everything."

"And that's one reason why I love him."

"*Love* him?" The question slipped out and carried much more implication than he cared for.

Alex laughed. "Not *love* him, as in more than a friend. It's a figure of speech. Don't they have them up in Canada?"

"Yes, they do." He could try to dig himself out, but had a feeling that would make things worse and more awkward than it already was. At least for him.

"I just meant that's why I *respect* him," she clarified further.

"I was wondering there for a moment," he teased, attempting to wipe out the brief tinges of possessiveness he was feeling while, at the same time, trying to make sense of why they were even there at all.

Light danced across her eyes, and he wished he could read her mind. She turned away first.

Ahead of them were miles of road, but from here out, they'd see desert all around them. Just thinking that seemed to tick up the thermostat a few degrees.

Matthew took off his hat and ran a hand over his head. He was, again, instantly sorry that he had. But in the scope of things, a little sweat was a small sacrifice, given what lay ahead.

"So you made some progress with the dig?" He tried dancing around the matter, hoping that she'd make an exception and fill him in on their "exciting discoveries" now.

Alex gave him a sly, knowing look. "I'll tell everyone at base camp."

Matthew caught Jasper glancing at him in the rearview mirror. "You don't like outsiders, do you?"

"Alex speaks very highly of you," Jasper replied, skirting around Matthew's allegation, yet by doing so, he confirmed its truth.

"Jasper's a very private person," Alex explained. "And leery of new people."

"I think with a discovery of this magnitude, it should have been limited to a mere few of us." Jasper's voice was firm, and he looked over at Alex.

"As you've made clear many times." There was the burden of conflict burrowed into Alex's brow. Matthew would guess the two of them had had their share of heated arguments in the last couple of days.

"And we don't really need another photographer. We have Seth." Jasper was being relentless, and Alex was shaking her head.

"I know you like Seth, but he's not a professional," she countered.

"But he's one of us." Resentment coated every word, giving Matthew some insight into Jasper's strong reaction to Cal.

"And now Cal is, too." Alex clamped her jaw shut, and by doing so, she shut down the discussion.

They traveled for some time without anyone speaking a word, and Matthew wondered how Cal and Robyn were making out with Jeff in the other Jeep.

CHAPTER

11

THE SUN WAS ALMOST UNBEARABLE, but the journey was exciting nonetheless. Cal had read about how hot deserts could get, but reading about it and experiencing it were two different things. The temperature came close to that of the jungles of Mexico, but unlike Mexico's moist air, the dry heat of the Sahara seared down his throat and into his lungs whenever he breathed in too deeply.

Jeff had broken off from the road awhile back, and they were making their way across the desert. Cal was spending most of the ride looking through the lens of his camera, letting his mind wander the landscape. But even thousands of miles from home, his thoughts weren't far from Sophie. They'd said their goodbyes, but their argument had still been a pile of hot, glowing embers when he'd left.

Maybe he should have regretted his decision to come here, but he had needed to get away, to go someplace different, someplace that carried a real potential for danger to spike his adrenaline. And given the look of the vast, open space around him, he was certain he'd come to the right place.

The land itself could be life-threatening, if not respected. And that was the case *without* giving credibility to superstitions and the possibility of ancient curses. It was hard to shake Sophie's harsh reaction to his going and not let it dampen his excitement. Maybe it was because she'd made some valid points, the foremost of which being that his adventures had almost gotten them both killed. Not that he needed her to remind him of that.

He'd countered with the fact that they had money because of his adventures. But what he thought had been a strong defense backfired. She said that was all the more reason not to go. She failed to grasp that his primary motivation for going on expeditions was that they made him happy. And her not understanding that, even after all their years together, cut him the deepest. Her previous claim that she was happy as long as he was happy had sunk with the weight of hypocrisy.

He hated that all this was making him question the stability of their relationship. But how could he marry someone who didn't respect and appreciate his choices, his dreams? Maybe he was seeing things too black-and-white. She didn't need to agree with everything he said or did. And given their history, that had never been the case. Life would be rather boring if they never saw things from different perspectives. What ate at him the most was how his going on expeditions had become an increasingly sore subject. Heck, there were times he felt as though he had to hide how much he loved them, as if she'd take it as him loving her less.

But he did appreciate how his decisions affected Sophie, and if they ever had children, it would affect them, too. Yet, he'd always returned home safely in the past, and he had no intention of changing that this time around. Of course, people typically didn't intend to die.

"You're awfully quiet back there," Robyn said, cutting through his musings.

Cal had heard her and Jeff talking away, but most of their conversation had been a drone in the background.

"I'm just doing what I'm here for." He kept his camera in place, thankful for the portal of escape it provided. It allowed him to hide his emotions from the rest of the world and delve into his work.

"Guess we'll have a lot of shots of sand," Jeff said in an easygoing manner.

Sure, the terrain was sand, but it wasn't without its beauty. The sunlight refracted off the surface, making it look like a sea of diamonds. He also loved how the heat visibly coursed through the air like strands of ribbon on the horizon line. And while he preferred to take photos while standing still, his camera was one of the best money could buy and enabled him to take high-quality shots on the move. Adjusting the shutter speed was only one part of it.

Sweat trickled down the side of his face and had him lowering the camera to wipe it away. In the front seat, Robyn was fanning herself with her hand.

"You realize that will only make you hotter," Cal tossed out.

She stopped moving and looked back at him, narrowing her eyes.

Cal held up his free hand. "I'm just saying…"

She went back to fanning herself.

Cal returned to looking at their surroundings. There really wasn't much to see besides sand. "One could easily get lost out here."

"And you should know all about that." Robyn smiled at him over her shoulder.

"Really?" He felt himself stiffen. "You're going there?"

"When we were retrieving an artifact from India, this guy—" she jacked a thumb over a shoulder at him "—tells us to go a certain way and… Why don't you tell the rest, Cal?"

You make one mistake…

Cal rolled his eyes and took a steadying breath. He saw that Jeff was looking at him in the rearview mirror.

"You're leaving out something rather important to begin with, don't you think?" Cal raised his brows.

"Fill us in," Robyn prodded, seeming to enjoy having fun at his expense.

"Come on. Don't be shy," Jeff prompted.

"Guys were shooting at us." Cal was sick of telling this story, but he obliged anyhow. "So it wasn't exactly like we were calmly standing around taking in the scenery, when Robyn and Matthew asked me which way we should go."

"Oh, you remember things a little differently." Robyn turned and pointed at him. "I don't remember us asking. I just remember you telling us."

"Potato, potahto." He was tempted to just lift his camera again and ignore this conversation.

"Okay, so tell Jeff where you led us." Robyn was unyielding, and for fun or not, it was starting to tick him off.

"You could have suggested another route," Cal pointed out.

"But we trusted you."

"Humph." Cal waited a few beats, and given the silence, it was apparent both Robyn and Jeff expected him to continue. "I led us to a dead end."

Robyn was smiling and picked up the story. "So we're being fired at, as Cal said, and our only options are to surrender the artifact they're after and hope we'll be extended mercy or take a flying leap."

"A flying leap?" Jeff's voice became animated, his eyes wide in the rearview mirror.

"That's right," Robyn confirmed. "He led us to a steep ravine that dropped off to white water below."

Jeff gasped. "What happened?"

"We went with the flying-leap option." Robyn laughed.

"Hey, that was Matthew's choice." And Cal had experienced nightmares for months. He swore it had been a touch of PTSD.

"Potato, potahto," she volleyed back at Cal.

Jeff looked over at Robyn and back at Cal in the mirror again. "Seems it turned out all right, though. You're here to tell about it."

"Yep." Cal certainly wasn't bringing up the night terrors or the fact that it had taken him awhile to forgive Matthew.

"Do you guys normally attract danger? I read all about your expedition for the City of Gold. It was your girlfriend who was abducted, wasn't it?"

Cal was reluctant to confirm it, and he hated that Jeff knew it had been Sophie. They'd tried to keep her name out of the media, even utilized Mayor Connor's clout, but their efforts had failed. Sophie had told him how hard it was seeing her name immortalized in print attesting to her ordeal. Cal figured it had made her healing a longer process. Eventually, he nodded.

"You all got lucky," Jeff said.

Lucky... Luck was an uncontrollable variable but one he was thankful for nonetheless. He could have lost the love of his life. But he hadn't. And how did he show the universe—show Sophie—his gratitude? He ran straight back into danger. Not *straight* exactly, as time had lapsed, but maybe this should be his last expedition. The thought dropped like a rock in the pit of his stomach.

He lifted his camera back up to his face, and as he looked out the lens, he began breathing a little easier. There certainly was something peaceful and calming about viewing the world through a camera. For him, it was therapy, and for now, he'd take it.

CHAPTER

12

THE CAMPSITE CONSISTED OF A large main tent and seven smaller ones surrounding it. If it was one person per tent, this was a small team for such a monumental expedition.

Jeff pulled up beside where Jasper had parked and everyone got out, congregating at the rear of the Jeeps.

"How many of you are working the site?" Matthew asked.

"Seven," Alex answered. "Jeff and Jasper, you've met. Me, obviously. Then there are four laborers. Two of them are at the dig site right now, keeping watch. The other two should be around here somewhere."

Matthew glanced at Robyn, who was struggling to haul her backpack out of the vehicle. Cal helped her with it and received a mild glare and a reluctant thank-you for his trouble. It was just like Robyn to appreciate the help but prefer to take care of things herself.

Robyn pushed her sunglasses up her nose and looked around, searching the horizon. "And how far from here is the site?"

"About a ten-minute drive. Just past that." Alex pointed to a large sand dune in the distance.

Matthew kept his gaze on the dune and took a deep, slow breath. He didn't think he'd ever come back here, and yet, here he was. And it felt right. But it also felt like they were running against the clock somehow. Just the significance of what was at stake, he supposed. From the look of it, though, they didn't have other teams encroaching on their territory. But if word got out about the Tablets, that could change at any time.

"You struck it pretty lucky," he said. "Finding the tunnel this close to where you set up camp."

"Uh-huh, very lucky." Alex wet her lips. "Our early probing missions proved to be very informative."

"So what was it that brought you out here in the first place?" Robyn lifted her sunglasses to the top of her head but quickly put them back in place.

"The tunnel. Well, what we believed to be aqueducts running beneath the desert to divert water from—"

"Tombs," Robyn finished with a knowing smile.

"That's right," Alex said. "More specifically, hopefully a pharaoh's tomb."

"Many famous archaeologists believe aqueducts are false readings on ground-penetrating radar," Robyn continued.

"Guess we've proven them wrong. At least in this case. Although…" There was a slight curl to Alex's lips that hinted at a personal victory. "It's technically not an aqueduct. It's a tunnel. Which is even better. And we have found something else since we spoke." Alex glanced at Matthew. "A couple discoveries, actually."

His heartbeat hammered with anticipation. "What are they?"

Alex let out a small chuckle. "I appreciate that you're excited, but I suggest that you guys get your tents set up before it gets too hot out here. Then we'll meet in the main tent and go over everything."

Matthew's jaw dropped open slightly. "Now you're just being cruel."

"Come on, suspense is good for the heart."

"Not sure about that." It had been four days since Alex had called him, but it felt like much longer than that. He hadn't even seen the hieroglyphics that had spurred her to seek him out in the first place. But she was right about the sun. It was rising in the sky, and in about two hours, it would reach its peak. As if encouraged by his thoughts, a fresh stream of sweat trickled down his back. "But I guess we should get set up before it warms up any more."

"I'd say so." Cal hoisted his bags from the Jeep. He put his arms through his backpack straps and grabbed his other bag.

"Now, you can set up your tents wherever you wish around the main tent, but I suggest you stay as close as possible to the rest of us," Alex directed. "The toilet and shower are around the back side of the main tent. Unfortunately, we have to share with the men." Alex pressed her lips into a frown and passed a sympathetic look to Robyn.

Both women smiled then, leaving Matthew to take minor offense to the connotation until his mind veered into the gutter. "You heard her. You have to *share* the shower." He bobbed his eyebrows.

"Matt!" Robyn swatted his arm with the back of her hand.

Alex laughed and so did the guys.

"You have to watch him sometimes. He can take things very literally." Robyn squinted at Matthew. Sunglasses or not, he could still make out her eyes.

"Only when it suits me." He smiled, certain his grin was stretching ear to ear.

"Brat." Robyn shook her head as she donned her backpack and grabbed her suitcase. She headed off in the direction of the main tent and turned left. Cal wasn't far behind her.

"Well, I'm going to check on Andres and Danny at the dig site," Jeff said, hopping back into a Jeep.

"Andres and Danny are two of the laborers under Jeff's management," Alex explained.

Jasper walked off toward the main tent without a word, leaving Matthew alone with Alex.

She was smiling at him, but her eyes were prying, and Matthew sensed a bit of jealousy. But that had to be his imagination. She'd have no reason to be jealous. That was, unless...

"Do you need any help setting up your tent?" She was staring blankly at him now.

She'd make for good company, and he'd like to spend more time with her, but he had a method that got his tent erected in no time. He gulped at his own double entendre. This was all Robyn's fault—asking him if he liked Alex. That had messed with his mind.

"I'll be fine." He grabbed his backpack by one strap, put it on, and then took out his second bag.

"Suit yourself. I'll see you in the main tent." She stepped away, leaving him wanting more. And he wasn't just referring to the information she had yet to share about the dig.

CHAPTER
13

COULD SHE HAVE BEEN ANY more obvious about her attraction to the man? She'd been peering into his eyes like a lost puppy! It had to be because she'd been out in the desert far too long. Lord knew her love life was in a severe drought. But no excuses. There were far more important things that required her attention than her raging hormones. Besides, Matthew and Robyn seemed rather close. Alex wasn't sure if they were a couple, but there was a definite chemistry between them. It was probably best she stay out of their way.

Alex pulled back the door flap on the main tent and stepped inside. She expected Seth and Timal to be milling about, but only Jasper was inside.

She headed to the kitchen area and poured herself some water to take with her to the computer workstation that was set up at the other end of the tent. That's where Jasper was standing in front of a free-standing magnetic whiteboard that displayed enlarged photographs of the hieroglyphics they'd discovered.

Jasper's energy was quiet and brooding, as well as uninviting, but she stepped up next to him anyhow.

"I know you didn't want to bring others in on this," she said, unsure why she was initiating a conversation on the subject again. They'd been over it several times. "But I really do think they will be an asset."

Jasper turned his head slowly to look at her. "You're the boss."

"Don't be like that."

"It's your call." Jasper's tone struck her as detached, but she knew better.

"I trust Matthew, and the three of them have experience hunting down legends as a team. And the Emerald Tablets are, by far, one of the greatest."

Jasper's usual combativeness was replaced with surprising calm. "I appreciate that, but I feel like we could have taken care of this on our own. That's all."

Alex took a deep breath. "We've been down there. We haven't gotten anywhere yet."

"We haven't exactly explored the tunnel for hours," he countered. "Just tell me what you think Matthew brings to the table."

"I told you. He's a skilled treasure hunter and archaeologist, and he's passionate and knowledgeable about the Emerald Tablets specifically." Guilt snaked through her core because that wasn't the whole truth.

"You're skilled, I'm skilled, and we have this." Jasper directed her gaze to the photograph of another set of hieroglyphics she had yet to tell Matthew and his friends about.

In fact, it was this particular discovery that was killing her to withhold from them. But it was far too sensitive to disclose without the proper measures being taken. Sure, she probably could have told Matthew on the way out here, but that wouldn't have been fair to the rest of his team. It was also certain to distract him from setting up his tent, and that needed to be taken care of.

She traced her finger along the outside of the photograph. She took in the hieroglyphics, mostly understanding what they meant because Jasper had worked through them with her already. The symbols dissected and pulled apart were a different story. Her mind could only store the details of the interpretation, not identify the meaning of each image.

Jasper crossed his arms over his chest. "Why don't you just be honest with me as to why you called him here?"

"Why are you being like this?" she snapped, growing more exasperated by the second. He apparently knew exactly why and was trying to bait her into saying it out loud.

"I want you to be honest with me about this."

"Honesty? That's rich coming from you." While she'd known Jasper for years, she knew very little about the man's personal life, aside from the fact that he'd been orphaned when his parents died in a car accident while on holiday in Greece. And as far as orphans went, Jasper had gotten lucky. He had been taken in by a wealthy aunt and given the best education money could buy. This still left a lot of gaps in Jasper's life, though, and here he was, insisting on honesty *from her*.

"He brings something to the table you don't have," Jasper said.

Her chest was burning with fire, and her breathing was quickening. She clenched her jaw.

"Why don't you just say it, Alex? He'll bring you fame. He's high profile, and he'll bring attention to you, to this dig, to your discovery. He's here to make a name for you."

She raised a hand to slap him, but she stopped short. To do so would only confirm that what he was saying touched on the truth, and she didn't like how despicable that made her feel.

Jasper looked at her hand and raised his brows. "Yep, I'm right on the nose."

Her gaze fell to the table next to the whiteboard, where the two stone bricks that had been pulled from the tunnel were on display. The moment she did, she regretted her silence and aversion to eye contact. It would only cement his accusation. She was beyond damage control, but she could still defend any honor she had left. She raised her head and looked him in the eye. "He and his team bring unique abilities to this expedition."

Jasper shook his head, reeking of smugness. "Tell yourself what you want—"

He stopped short as Matthew and his friends walked into the tent. Robyn was holding a laptop under her arm.

"Hey." Alex set her water glass on the table and gave Jasper a heated glare, hoping the others wouldn't catch it. She plastered on a smile and went to meet them. "You get everything set up okay?"

"We did," Matthew answered. "We even took a quick look around and found the washroom and shower."

"The *bathroom*, you mean," Alex teased, remembering how fun it was to have a Canadian or two around.

Matthew rolled his eyes. "Don't you start."

She laughed. "Ah, so this is—" she gestured around the space "—our main hub. Not that I really need to point it out, but we have a small kitchen at this end and our workstations are at the other end. And we eat at these fancy tables." Not that the two picnic tables just inside the door needed explanation.

Robyn adjusted the laptop under her arm. "Do you have Internet access?"

"We do, but it's through satellite, so it's not the best."

Robyn narrowed her eyes at Matthew. He held up his hands. "Hey, I didn't promise it'd be top-of-the-line."

"I told my boss at the museum that I would be available if he needed to reach me." Robyn was staring Matthew down. "It was part of his agreeing to let me take off for so long and at the last minute."

"Well, as I said, we have it. It's just a little spotty." Alex's gaze traced over Matthew and Robyn. Her posture was rigid, and if looks could kill...

Matthew seemed oblivious.

"I guess I'll have to make it work." Robyn set her laptop on a picnic table, pulled an elastic off her wrist, and swept her hair into a ponytail. She had such a beautiful face, and her cheeks were flushed from heat.

"It's nothing like Canada here, is it?" Alex wasn't sure what propelled her to initiate banter, but it was too late now.

Robyn shrugged. "It gets hot there, too. It's just a different kind of heat."

"Yeah, despite the stereotypes, we don't all say *eh*, live in igloos, and play hockey," Matthew added.

"Some of us don't even like hockey," Cal chimed in. "Myself and my fiancée included."

"Yet, I'm still friends with them." Matthew smiled, but Alex sensed a restlessness coming from him. In fact, Alex sensed it coming from all of them. It probably had to do with the fact that they were eager for more information about the expedition.

"Well, if you want to help yourselves to a glass of water or something to eat, please feel free," Alex said.

"I'll speak for all of us when I say we just want to see what you've found. Do we need to wait for Reda?" Matthew asked.

Alex shook her head. "He was out here last night, and he's been filled in already."

"Thank God." Matthew's posture relaxed. "I'm not sure I can wait any longer."

Cal took off toward the cooler, though, and Robyn followed.

"Guess we're getting something to drink first." Matthew left to join his friends.

"I'll be down at the other end," Alex said.

A second later, Cal rushed out, "The water is warm."

Alex stopped and turned around to see Cal's face scrunched up in disgust. He maneuvered himself so he could see behind the cooler. "It's not even plugged in."

"Room temperature or warm water is better for you out here," Alex explained.

"I get that, but it was in a *cooler,* so I figured…" Cal puckered his lips.

"In this case, the cooler is just the dispensing method." She spun to continue heading to the workstation area.

"You should really warn people," Cal mumbled.

She reached the worktable and turned back to see Cal pulling on the fridge handle.

"Tell me the *fridge* is plugged in," Cal said.

"We do have a generator," Alex replied. "You might have heard it or seen it when you were around back setting up your tent."

Cal stuck his head inside the fridge. "Aw, now that's what I'm talking about." He straightened out and put his glass of water inside. "I'll just put this in here—cool it off a few degrees."

"As I said, warm water is better for you." There was no helping some people, but she had to try. "In the desert heat, even cool water will make you hotter."

Cal regarded her skeptically. "That's possible?"

Alex held up a hand. "I don't make the rules, but it's a fact."

Cal looked at Matthew as if seeking a second opinion.

"She's right," Matthew assured him.

"Oh man." Cal opened the fridge door, carrying on almost incoherently about things not being able to get any hotter out here. It was only when he pressed his glass to his lips that he went silent. Everyone's eyes were on him. He took a sip, albeit hesitantly. He lowered the glass, his cheeks puffed out from a mouth full of water, and he crossed his eyes.

Alex started laughing, and Matthew and Robyn joined in.

Cal gulped it down. "As long as you are all amused." He was flicking his tongue out like a cat with hair on its tongue after cleaning itself.

This friend of Matthew's was certainly good for entertainment, but it was time to get down to business. "If you guys would join me over here, I'll share our discoveries." Alex stood next to the whiteboard. Jasper, who had ended up sitting at a computer, came up next to her with a sideways glance that had guilt ripping through her again. But she had to get a grip. She had her reasons for bringing Matthew here— so what? She wasn't the first person to work another's prestige to her advantage, and she certainly wouldn't be the last. Surely Matthew would understand if she told him. At least, that's how she was pitching it to herself.

Matthew, Cal, and Robyn came over.

"I'll start from the beginning," Alex began. "I'm sure Matthew filled you in on the basics, and so you know that we discovered a tunnel. We also found a cartouche that mentioned the son of Khufu, leading us to believe his tomb is nearby." She let her gaze trace over the three friends. None of them looked lost so far. "And you also know that we found a grouping of hieroglyphics that testified to the Emerald Tablets, as well."

Matthew stepped toward her and the whiteboard. "And these are pictures of those hieroglyphics?"

Alex nodded. "They are."

Robyn and Cal huddled in on each side of Matthew.

Alex pointed to a few printouts that were also on the board. "These are readouts from ground-penetrating radar. Now, the tunnel is about eleven hundred meters long. About forty feet from where we entered the tunnel, we've found a staircase." Alex smiled. "That's one of the new discoveries I wanted to share with you."

"A staircase? Interesting," Matthew said. "It's certainly not an aqueduct."

"Now, the readout indicates a void," Alex said.

"That could be where the pharaoh's tomb is located," Robyn jumped in, her voice ticked up with excitement.

"It's possible. It's definitely large."

"How large?" Robyn asked.

"At least five thousand square meters."

"*At least?* So you don't really know how big it is yet." It was clear that Robyn was the most serious of the three friends.

"No," Alex confirmed.

"All right, so it's probably not *all* a tomb. What do you think it is, then?" Matthew raised his eyebrows.

"We know some of it's water because we've been to the edge of it. That's another recent finding," Alex started. "But there's more..." She looked at Jasper, who snatched a photograph of hieroglyphics from the whiteboard.

"What is that?" Matthew nudged in closer to Jasper.

"That is an ancient Egyptian treasure map," Alex said, a smile curving her lips. "And according to Jasper's interpretation, it should lead us straight to the pharaoh's tomb *and* the Emerald Tablets."

CHAPTER

14

MATTHEW COULD HARDLY BELIEVE WHAT he was hearing. "A map? This is terrific! Have you followed it yet?"

Alex shook her head. "We were waiting for you before we set out in earnest."

"But you said you reached the edge of the anomaly and came to water," Robyn tossed back.

"That's right, but we didn't go into the water. We decided to wait."

Alex said it as if she'd done them a favor. But he hadn't come all this way—and carted his friends along with him—to turn right back around and head home. "We appreciate that." Matthew turned to Jasper. "Explain the map to us?"

Jasper looked at Alex, and she gestured for him to go ahead. He pointed to the symbols on the photograph he was holding. "It starts off saying to follow the path, and it's actually quite similar to the first set of hieroglyphics, which basically said that the tunnel was the path to enlightenment."

Matthew's heart galloped. *Enlightenment.* That was a common word used in reference to the Emerald Tablets.

"From there," Jasper continued, "it mentions passage through water."

Matthew's breath caught. "The water you've already found."

Alex bobbed her head. "We think so."

"You said the anomaly is *at least* five thousand square meters?" Robyn's body visibly tensed.

"That's right," Alex confirmed.

"Why not just keep going until you reach the edge of it aboveground, then dig down there? It might put you right at the tomb." Cal suggested, then hitched his shoulders. "It seems like it would be easier."

"As I said, we have no idea where it ends, and it could take us a long time to find that out. If we even can find out." Alex paused. "Ground-penetrating radar can reach up to a depth of one hundred feet, except when moist clay or rock is involved. Then the signal can easily be blocked."

"So you think there could be rock underneath hindering the reading?" Robyn asked.

"Why not?" Alex said nonchalantly. "It could even be a limestone cave. There are many in Egypt, and"—she waved a hand over the table, drawing Matthew's eye to a couple of stone bricks—"these were pulled from the ceiling of the tunnel."

Matthew reached for the one closest to him, realizing a part of him must have been waiting for permission. It was about two feet long by one foot wide by five inches high, and it was smooth. To think that someone had sanded it down thousands of years ago, and he was touching it now… A rush of euphoria ran over him.

"How far down is the anomaly showing?" Robyn inquired, breaking his concentration.

"It's showing at thirty feet," Alex replied.

"So it's something interfering with the reading." It seemed obvious to Matthew, anyhow.

"Seems so." Alex gestured to Jasper.

He took the floor. "Now, the reason Alex mentioned limestone caves is because another marker on the map is a cave that comes after a hill. Whether that indicates a rise in elevation or the opposite, the hieroglyphics are not clear."

"Let's hope the entrance isn't under the water." Cal nudged Matthew's elbow. "Of all the times to have left home without my scuba gear…"

Matthew smiled at his friend. "You and me both."

"We don't think it's under water," Jasper said firmly.

Robyn stepped back from the table. "But you don't know for sure."

Jasper looked at Robyn. "Well, it would be unlikely."

"Why's that?" Matthew asked.

"Because of other indicators on the map, which we'll get to," Jasper replied.

"Going back to the radar…" Robyn drew Jasper's attention to her. "How far down is the tunnel you found? Did its limestone ceiling affect the radar?"

"The tunnel is thirty-five feet beneath the ground."

"Five feet deeper than the anomaly," Matthew stated.

"That's right," Alex picked up for Jasper. "Given that the radar could penetrate farther down on the outside of the tunnel, it was clear to distinguish its existence."

"But it could have just been a natural rock formation," Cal suggested.

"It could have been, that's true, but it wasn't." Alex reached for her water glass, took a sip, and set the glass back down.

Matthew mentally ran through the landmarks noted on the map thus far. There was, at minimum, one thing missing that would help immensely. "Were any measurements noted on this map?"

"None," Jasper answered.

"But just the fact that there's a map to something of this importance…" Alex's eyes lit up, and her voice softened as if she'd given herself over to rapture. "I'm sure you know that rarely do treasure maps even factor in, let alone lead you, right to your desired find."

Wasn't that the truth. He'd known it had been a leap when he'd asked about the measurements, but so far, all of this almost seemed too easy, too convenient. First, the mention of a tomb. Second, hieroglyphics that would notify anyone who read it that the Tablets were ahead. Third, an actual map. They had to be missing something. There had to be more to the puzzle that had yet to be uncovered and overcome.

"Going back to the water," Cal said, slicing through the brief silence that had fallen. "You said you didn't go farther than the water? So you never went in?"

Alex shook her head. "We know that it's fresh water, though, and the temperature is seventy-three degrees Fahrenheit."

Cal turned to Matthew. "I'm not too good at my conversions to Celsius."

Matthew smiled at his friend. "That's about twenty-three degrees Celsius. And our body temperature is around thirty-seven."

Cal mocked shivers but did a convincing job. "Brrr, that's cold."

"It's *cool*, yes," Matthew assured him. This conversation took Matthew back to the time he swam in the Ik Kil cenote in the Yucatán. He didn't have the heart to point out that twenty-three degrees felt even colder when the body was overheated. Matthew locked eyes with Alex, and she quickly turned her attention back to the hieroglyphic treasure map.

"So the water, the hill, the cave… Anything else?" Matthew asked Alex, but she slid her gaze to Jasper.

"Asps," Jasper replied.

"There are snakes?" Robyn rubbed the base of her throat.

"Seems that way," Jasper said flatly, clearly indifferent to Robyn's fear.

"And they're poisonous, aren't they?" Cal's eyes were darting among them.

Jasper blinked slowly, as if exasperated. "Very."

Cal paced a few steps and settled his gaze on Matthew. "Remember, I can't die out here. She won't bury me."

Matthew looked over at Robyn, not that he was sure what he expected her to do. But she did have a way of making things better with her positive attitude. But Robyn was flushed and staring into space.

Matthew was on his own this time.

"Who is *she*?" Alex inquired.

"Sophie. My fiancée," Cal said quickly. "It's a long story."

"No one's going to die if I can help it," Jasper retorted.

Cal's gaze went straight to Jasper, and it had Matthew doing the same.

"Do you know a lot about snakes?" Cal asked. "You sound pretty confident."

Alex put her hand on Jasper's shoulder. "We call him the Snake Whisperer around here."

Jasper tapped a snake hook that was attached to his waistband. At that, Cal sighed, and Robyn's shoulders relaxed.

"There's nothing much to wrangling them," Jasper said. "It's a lot about attitude and approach. But mostly about attitude."

"Well, we're lucky yours is so good, then." Alex's words may have been meant to instill confidence, but her compliment came across flat.

"The asp, also called the Egyptian cobra, was revered by the ancient Egyptians." Robyn's pallor was returning to normal as she spoke. "They were seen as a symbol of divine royalty."

"It's also believed that Cleopatra and two of her attendants committed suicide by letting themselves be bitten by an asp," Alex added.

The women smiled at each other, and it pleased Matthew they were getting along as well as he'd hoped they would. With both of them loving ancient Egypt, he wasn't sure how they could dislike each other. And while he loved a history lesson more than most, he was eager to get out to the dig site. He consulted his watch. *11:50*. Reda would be arriving any minute.

"You said there were a couple discoveries you made since you spoke to Matthew the other day," Cal said, directing his comment to Alex. "The map, I assume, was one of them. And the other?"

"That was the staircase I mentioned," Alex said. "We dug it out and have topside access to it now."

"Which is another indicator that this tunnel had a greater purpose than directing water away from a tomb," Matthew concluded.

Alex smiled at him. "Exactly."

The rumble of a vehicle's engine reached inside the tent.

"That must be Reda." Alex rushed toward the door when the flap was pulled back, and the minister of antiquities stepped inside.

Even though over five years had passed, Matthew would have recognized the man anywhere. He still had a mop of gray hair, although it had thinned out considerably on top. But it was his resting scowl and the way his brown eyes took in everyone with skepticism that was all too familiar.

Matthew gulped as Reda came toward him.

CHAPTER
15

BREATHING WAS BECOMING A STRUGGLE. With each step Reda took toward him, Matthew's chest tightened, anxiety clenching his lungs as if they were being squeezed by fists. He may as well have been catapulted into the past, standing there stricken as the pottery fell to the ground. But maybe he'd get lucky and Reda wouldn't remember him.

"Dr. Connor." Reda extended a hand toward Matthew.

So much for that...

"Good day, Minister," he responded, keeping things formal, as they shook hands.

"Now, I'd be lying if I said that I remembered your name, but I was given your information ahead of time—" Reda gestured to Alex "—along with those of your companions. But even without that, I never forget a face. Nice that we meet again."

If the man had forgotten Matthew's name, maybe the matter of the dropped artifact had been long erased from his memory, as well. Matthew could hope. "Likewise. These are my colleagues, Robyn Garcia and Cal Myers."

"Pleasure, I'm sure." Reda dipped his head to Robyn and Cal but didn't shake their hands.

This reminded Matthew of when he first met Reda. He had been guarded then, too. Obviously the fact that Robyn and Cal were here on Matthew's merit wasn't enough for Reda to simply open his arms and willingly accept them into the fold.

"Ms. Garcia works as a curator at the Royal Ontario Museum in Toronto," Matthew started, trying to warm the man up to them. "And Mr. Myers is a world-renowned travel photographer. His pictures have been sold to many prestigious magazines, including *National Geographic*."

Reda barely looked at the two of them. "I'm sure they'll both contribute greatly to this expedition." His sentiment came out lacking sincerity.

They may have been in the desert, but it was feeling awfully chilly. Apparently, it would take more to impress the man. Matthew went on. "They have accompanied me on many expeditions, including the quest for the Incas' lost City of Gold. And as you likely know, we found it."

"I did read that. Quite impressive." Reda regarded Robyn and Cal again, and his gaze lingered on Robyn. It was more like a leer, though, and Matthew's respect for the minister was fading, along with his nerves.

"Mr. Ghannam, what an honor to meet you." Robyn was either oblivious to how he was looking at her or she didn't care. She had a deer-in-headlights look on her face. "I read about your most recent discovery in an archaeological digest, but to have been there… Wow." Robyn was smiling and slowly shook her head. "It must have been amazing to have been a part of that."

"Yes, my dear—" Reda took one of Robyn's hands in both of his "—it was quite the discovery." He paused, assessing each of the team members briefly, possibly to see if everyone knew what the two of them were talking about. He waved a hand in dismissal, missing the dazed expression on Cal's face that had his brow pinching and mouth gaping open slightly. "Look who I'm surrounded by. I'm sure you all know that Ms. Garcia is referring to the centuries-old sarcophagus we recently discovered. Both it and the mummy inside were in pristine shape, as if they had just been buried earlier that day." He drew in a deep breath through his mouth, the air making a subtle whistle as it skimmed over his teeth. "It *was* remarkable."

Reda and Robyn held eye contact for a moment, and finally, the older man let go of her hand.

"Well—" Alex's voice pierced the otherwise silent room "—we were just talking about the map when you arrived."

"Wonderful." Reda took his eyes off Robyn to look at Matthew. "I'm sure you never got that lucky with tracking down the City of Gold."

"That thought occurred to me as we were discussing this one,"

Matthew admitted. "Jasper and Alex have filled us in on some of the markers to watch for, but I'm not sure that we made it all the way to the end."

"After the snakes, there's a door." Jasper held up the photograph of the hieroglyphics again and pointed to an image in the bottom right-hand corner.

"It looks like a drawing of two men in a boat." Cal leaned in closer. "And a bug?"

"It's a scarab beetle," Robyn corrected him. "And the two men would represent two forms of Osiris worshiping the scarab."

Jasper looked at Robyn. "That's right."

"Osiris? Who is he again?" Cal asked.

"He's the god of the underworld, or more specifically, the dead pharaoh who was believed to have become Osiris," Robyn answered.

"You really know a lot about ancient Egypt," Jasper complimented her.

Robyn seemed to just let Jasper's words roll off her.

"So why is Osiris bowing to a bug?" Cal arched his eyebrows.

"Scarabs were often used to represent Khepri, the god of the morning sun, who was a subordinate to Ra," Alex said. She pulled out a necklace from beneath her shirt and squeezed the silver pendant in her palm. She met Matthew's gaze and tucked it away again.

"Scarabs were chosen to depict Khepri because the scarab beetle rolls dung across the sand. As it does so, the dung forms a ball. The ancient Egyptians saw it as a symbol of the sun moving across the sky," Robyn explained.

"I'd say they had time on their hands." Cal laughed, but no one else did. "Hmm. Tough crowd."

Matthew smirked.

Cal pressed his lips together. "And the boat?"

"Egyptians believed crossing over into the afterlife required a journey by boat." Matthew figured he might as well get involved, maybe impress the minister at the same time. "In fact, in 1954, Khufu's boat was discovered in a pit next to the Great Pyramid of Giza. It was unassembled, but the wood was in pristine condition."

"A notable part about that discovery," Reda said, taking over, "was that there was no rigging for sails or an area for men to paddle. It wasn't designed to be used on water, but rather as a ritual vessel that would carry the resurrected king, along with Ra, through to the afterlife. You can see the vessel for yourself, if you'd like, while you're in Egypt. In fact, I highly recommend that you do. It's been assembled and is showcased inside the Solar Boat Museum. That's all that the museum offers, but it is worth it."

"So the map ends with what seems to be a depiction of starting the journey into the afterlife, but there's more to it." Jasper steered the conversation back to their dig. "There's another symbol here that represents a bolted door, and behind it, there's the depiction of Thoth, simply as an ibis." He pointed to the image of a man with the head of a bird.

Thoth was often depicted in different ways, and how he appeared was dependent on both the time period and the characteristic of the god that the artist wanted to portray. "Thoth was the god of knowledge, among other things, and he—" Matthew paused to breathe. It's like the more they discussed Thoth, the more it set in that he was actually here and about to embark on finding the Tablets. "Thoth was said to be one of the gods who created the Emerald Tablets and delivered them to Earth."

Alex caught his eye and smiled. God, he was happy she'd invited him along for this!

"Thoth is also associated with magic," Matthew added. "And I'd say knowledge of the secrets of the universe would qualify."

Jasper nodded. "Going back to the bolted door, it could mean there is a literal door that seals off a room containing the Tablets. But this other section indicates that the key to enlightenment lies with the pharaoh."

"And that's how the map ends?" Matthew asked.

"It is," Jasper assured him.

"All right." Alex clapped her hands. "Now that we're all caught up, let's get a bite to eat and head out to the dig site."

Matthew understood the need for food before heading out, even if they'd just be taking a quick look around, but he was dying inside. With all this talk about the map and the Tablets, and after seeing pictures of the hieroglyphics, he was ready to get started.

CHAPTER
16

ROBYN WAS HAVING A HARD time prying her eyes from the minister of antiquities. She hadn't felt this way since she had attended her first rock concert as a teenager and had fallen in love with the lead singer. Of course, that had been starry-eyed infatuation, but comparably, she was close to pinching herself. She was in the same room as Reda Ghannam, a man she was used to seeing on documentaries and reading about. People always warned against meeting one's heroes because it would shatter the illusion, but so far, Reda was holding his own against her perception of him. So what if he had been a little standoffish at first? Many people were. She just couldn't believe it had taken her so long to travel to Egypt and meet the man.

The group of them had eaten a quick lunch in the main tent, and if the others had been like her, they had swallowed mouthfuls of food without chewing much, if at all, in order to speed things along. But that was behind them now. Reda and Jasper went in Reda's Land Rover, and Robyn went with Alex, Cal, and Matthew in the Jeep. She hoped that the drive would help calm her down.

She sat in the back with Cal, and Matthew was riding shotgun while Alex drove. Matthew was looking all over the place, and even in profile, she could tell he was smiling like the Cheshire cat.

Cal's face was behind his camera, and he rarely lowered it. She envied him the ability to hide behind something and wondered if that was part of photography's appeal to Cal. If she had a camera, she'd lift it every time Alex made Matthew laugh. Then her eyes would be covered and he wouldn't be able to witness the lick of jealousy she assumed was visible there.

Matthew shifted his body to the far right and turned to look back at Cal. "What can you possibly be taking pictures of?"

"He was like that most of the way to base camp, too." Robyn chuckled.

Matthew let his smile carry to Robyn, and it warmed her insides. "Just don't use up all the space on your memory card on shots of the sand," he said to Cal. "There will be a lot of exciting things to photograph before this trip is over."

Cal lowered his camera and regarded them with an expression that bordered a scowl and a smirk. "I have plenty of data storage with me, don't you worry."

Matthew faced forward again, but Robyn could tell from his profile that he was still grinning.

Cal picked his camera up again and disappeared behind the lens.

"So we'll go down and look around a bit today," Alex said, holding her hat in place as she drove. They were clipping along at a good pace and crested the large dune they'd seen from base camp. "We'll set out in earnest tomorrow morning, though, and see how far we can get."

"Sounds great," Robyn said. And it did, but she wished they could get started "in earnest" today. Right now, in fact.

"We'll start at the staircase, and I'll show you where we found the cartouche," Alex went on, "and the first set of hieroglyphics that mentioned the Emerald Tablets."

"What about the map? I'd love to see that with my own eyes," Matthew said.

"It's farther down the tunnel, not far from the water's edge. I'd prefer we leave that for tomorrow." She looked over at Matthew. "Just to be safe."

He nodded.

"Today we'll just take a brief look, nothing with us but the basics and a radio, just as a precaution. There are some portable lights already in place, but not as far along as the first set of hieroglyphics." Alex paused a moment. "And you all brought your miner hats and water with you, so you'll bring that, too, of course. Not that you can go anywhere around here without water."

"Don't get me started on drinking hot water again." Cal kept his camera in place as he spoke.

Robyn laughed at Cal's exaggeration and woe-is-me humor. He was good at making her smile.

A few moments later, Alex added, "We've also got portable oxygen concentrators out at the dig site, which I'd like us to take along, as well. Again, just to be safe. There's a lot of dust, and it's been sealed up for a long time down there."

Reda's Land Rover was parked about twenty feet ahead of them, and beside it, there was a small open-sided tent set up with a table and a few chairs. The top of the tent gusted up and down with the wind as it blew across the desert.

She poked Cal's leg, and he lowered the camera rather begrudgingly and shot her a glare. She pointed toward the site, and his mouth relaxed. But it was only a second before the camera was back in his face.

Alex parked the Jeep, and the four of them grabbed items from the back, including the miner hats and water canteens. Cal had managed to set aside the camera while they did that.

As Robyn moved toward the men, her feet sank into the sand, the granules fine and plentiful. It took a surprising amount of labor to make headway, even more so than walking on a regular beach.

Two unfamiliar faces were watching the newcomers with marks of curiosity etching their features. But Robyn was doing the same as she noted the assault rifles strung over their chests.

"This is Andres and Danny," Alex introduced the armed men, gesturing to each of them as she did so. Both men smiled as she gave their names, but Robyn was too fixated on the weapons to care. "You'll have to excuse the guns." Alex made eye contact with Robyn, seemingly noting her concern. "But we have something highly valuable to protect."

Robyn dismissed it with a wave. She understood, of course, but that didn't mean she had to like it. Usually when weapons were around, they became *involved*. And she should know. She'd been shot before, back when they were searching for the City of Gold.

Robyn's gaze drifted to Jeff. His shirt was stained with sweat, and his brow was gritty from the blowing sand clinging to his flesh. He smiled at her, though, giving no indication that being out in the blazing sun affected him at all. Robyn, however, had already taken off her hat and was fanning herself with it.

She put the hat back on her head, and as she did so, she was more than ready to exchange it for her miner hat.

"Now, you said we'd be going down with radios," Matthew began, "so I'm assuming you're using something like through-the-earth signaling to communicate from underground to those on the surface?"

Robyn looked at him. Sometimes the breadth of his knowledge surprised her. It's not like they'd used that technology during previous expeditions. Not the ones she'd went on, anyhow.

"That's exactly what we're using. Also known as magnetic induction communication." Jeff pressed his lips together and nodded to Matthew, seemingly impressed. He glanced at Robyn and Cal, though, and must have noticed their confusion as he continued. "It's commonly used in mines and caves, and uses low-frequency waves that can penetrate rock. It works with a magnetic field and doesn't require line of sight." Jeff pointed toward a cable that was looped in a figure eight pattern across the sand and fed into a box near him. "The cable is a transmitting antenna, and it's plugged into a transmitter module. There's another set just like this already in the tunnel. Both are waterproof."

Robyn pointed to the radio clipped to Jeff's belt. "Otherwise it works like a normal radio?"

Jeff held up the radio for her to see and put it back on his hip. "Yes. We also have earpiece comms around here, too. This allows us to transmit data, in addition to two-way communication."

"And it provides a secure transmission between our two units," Alex added.

Matthew nodded. "Important, given the information that we'll be sharing."

"For sure," Jeff said. "As Alex touched on, these units are linked, but there's an alert button that can be pushed, which is detectable by any modules within range." He crouched and pointed to a panel on the module where a red light appeared. "This is the operational mode indicator and tells us how strong the signal is."

The markers on the panel looked like a gauge with longer dashes at the top and shorter and shorter dashes as it went down. The red light was next to the second dash from the top.

"So that means we have a strong signal right now?" Robyn asked.

"Uh-huh." Jeff straightened back up and looked at Alex. "We're good to go from this perspective."

Alex rubbed her hands together and smiled at each of them in turn.

Robyn bumped Cal's elbow to get him to lower his camera.

"Before we head out, Jeff will hand out the portable oxygen tanks." Alex put her hands on her hips and stretched out her back.

Jeff snapped his fingers at Andres and Danny. They hurried to retrieve strapped bags from the tent just beside them.

The men came back and handed bags to her, Matthew, Cal, Alex, Reda, and Jasper. Robyn unzipped the top flap to look inside: a standard-issue portable oxygen supply and mask. She closed it back up.

Alex pointed to her bag. "Now, given our needs, the bags are waterproof." She grabbed a small shovel from nearby. "Everyone ready?"

Matthew pointed to Jeff's empty hands. "Jeff's not coming down with us?"

Alex shook her head. "Not today, but he will tomorrow."

"Someone has to stay up here and keep an eye on these guys." Jeff smiled.

"All right. Let's get our hats on. The staircase is this way." Alex trudged toward an opening in the ground.

With each step Robyn took, her heart raced faster. She was really here. It was almost too much to fathom. She eyed the mouth of the staircase and stopped in front of it, purposely standing still simply to breathe in this moment. And God, what a moment.

To think this was just the beginning…

CHAPTER
17

ALEX GESTURED MATTHEW TOWARD THE STAIRCASE. "Would you like to go down first?"

He looked at the others and shook his head. He'd rather go last. Then he could move at his own speed without anyone rushing him. After all, he'd made it to the dig site. There was no need to hurry now. Rather, it was time to savor the start of what would undoubtedly be a remarkable journey.

It seemed Robyn was caught up in a similar rapture as he was, as she was just standing there looking at the opening, too.

"Robyn?" he prompted. She was standing closest to the staircase.

"Ah, sorry. What's up?" She glanced at him with a faraway look in her eyes.

"Are you going down?"

"You betcha." She turned on her headlamp and started for the opening, but Cal snuck in front of her.

He must have had a pang of conscience because he turned and pressed his palms together. "Can I go first?"

Robyn snickered. "Sure, go ahead."

"Thanks." Cal flicked on the light on his hat, as well, and was off, his back to them as he descended. Surprisingly, his camera was dangling from around his neck, bouncing against his chest. Figured that he'd have satisfied his shutterbug urges on the landscape, and now he actually had something of interest to take photographs of.

Matthew hung back until everyone had entered the staircase, then followed. The space was only about two feet wide, and he was grateful for his narrow shoulders. He turned his headlamp on and held his breath as he took each step slowly and methodically.

The staircase was hewn out of rock, likely limestone, and each step was about ten inches deep and about twelve inches high.

"I've reached the bottom," Cal cried out. "This is incredible."

"Isn't it?" Alex's voice pulsated with delight.

"I can't believe I'm here," Robyn said, awed.

Matthew smiled. He was so happy that she'd reworked her schedule to come along. And he couldn't say he was upset that her date had gotten canceled in the process. He felt like a chump for even thinking that, but apparently, jealousy had no bounds for it to strike here, of all places—in the middle of the desert on an ancient staircase built by slaves or servants of an Egyptian pharaoh.

He touched the walls as he descended, appreciating the cool stone against his hot fingertips. It didn't stop the sweat from running down his back, but it provided a whisper of relief.

He wasn't counting the steps as he went, but he turned to look back once he reached the bottom. Fourteen steps and taking his estimate of twelve inches high that would mean they were only fourteen feet down.

"Alex," he called out and faced forward again. His breath caught in his throat. This time he really took in what was ahead of him. The tunnel was all stone brick—the floor, the walls, and the ceiling—and it was milled and smooth. The portable lights that Alex had mentioned brightened the space, illuminating details that would otherwise be left in shadow. The lights from everyone's hats were pretty much unnecessary so far. He craned his neck to look around, and he figured the tunnel was only about five feet high and maybe that wide.

"Matthew?" Alex's head peeked out from behind Robyn. "You called me?"

"I did."

She made her way back to him and stopped a few feet away. "Incredible, isn't it?"

"Sure is. But how deep underground did you say the tunnel was?"

"Thirty-five feet." She paused, and before he could say anything, she added, "But remember that's how much sand we needed to clear to reach the tunnel. The staircase was also buried."

"Okay, that explains it. I was just looking at the staircase and doing some quick math."

"Ugh. Math. Not my favorite subject." She smiled. "I'm partial to Egyptology."

He laughed. "I never would have guessed."

"Follow me. I'll take you to the cartouche." She spun and took a few steps. "Actually, it looks like the others are almost there already."

Matthew maneuvered to look past her and saw the other four up ahead, standing next to one another and all facing the same wall. He stepped under an aperture that served as a skylight and cast illumination on the snaking loops of another transmitting antenna that was on the ground. The transmitter module wasn't much farther ahead.

He stopped walking and looked up the hole to the blue sky beyond it. Alex stopped next to him. "That's how I came in. To think I was only about forty feet from the stairs."

He could only imagine the thrill of the descent, though, and what it must have been like being the first to set foot in the tunnel.

They reached the others, and Reda was at the end closest to them.

"Seeing these—" Reda pointed at the cartouche "—never gets old. It's too bad I am, because otherwise, I would do this type of thing forever."

The minister's comment took Matthew back to the conversation he'd had with Alex about the man. But he also understood how Reda felt. For Matthew, it was more about unearthing legends than studying ancient civilizations, but close enough. Some might have disagreed and said the comparison between Egyptology and myths was like scientific fact versus the existence of aliens and the supernatural. But when scaled back, all those areas of study boiled down to a lot of mystery.

"As I shared with the others—" Jasper stepped back to get a line of sight to Matthew "—this is the cartouche in which the son of Khufu is mentioned."

Matthew moved toward Reda, who shuffled down, along with the others, to allow Matthew to stand right in front of it. He reached out and let his fingers skim over the cartouche, imagining the person who had etched it into the stone. What kind of person had they been? Had they been single or married? A willing servant or begrudging slave? Had they had any idea that it would take thousands of years for another living person to stumble across their creation?

He heard the shuffling of feet and looked ahead to realize that Jasper, Robyn, and Cal were continuing down the tunnel. Alex was still on his left and Reda on his right.

"Too incredible to leave, isn't it?" the minister asked.

The man's eyes glistened in the light, and Matthew was inspired by the minister's devotion after all these years. He'd certainly found what he was passionate about in life and was holding on tight.

Matthew smiled. "And from what I understand, there's even more excitement ahead of us."

"Well, you go on ahead. I'm going to stand here a moment longer." Reda made no movement to leave.

Matthew maneuvered past him and so did Alex. The others had wandered off far enough that they were but shadows in the distance. The reach of the portable lights didn't stretch quite as far as they were.

He was about thirty feet from Jasper, Cal, and Robyn when there was a deafening crack and the ground shook. Dust sprinkled down from the ceiling, and his stomach roiled as he turned around to see the tunnel caving in behind him.

The minister!

"Reda!" Matthew screamed, pushing past Alex and running toward him. Alex pulled back on Matthew's shoulder.

"We have to move, Matt!" she yelled, ratcheting the urgency of the situation.

"But the—" Matthew watched Reda watching him as a cloud of stone and sand dropped into the tunnel between them, cutting through the ceiling as if it were made of tissue.

His eyes went to the transmitter module on the ground and the antenna cable that fed into it. His mind was whirling.

Waterproof...

He snatched the box, closed the lid, and tugged on the cable. But it was stuck on something. Part of it must have been under rock.

"Matthew!" Robyn's piercing cry hit his ears and prompted him into action.

He pulled harder, and thankfully, the cable broke free. He gathered it to him as he spun and ran toward the others, Alex in front of him. He coughed deeply. Ahead, he could hear the rest of them hacking, as well.

"We don't have a choice," Alex said and barreled past Cal and Robyn. The next sound to hit Matthew's ears was splashing water.

Matthew looked beyond his two close friends and saw the ledge where the tunnel ended and the water began. It was only about a foot's jump to the water's surface. Alex and Jasper were already treading water. As he stood there, it seemed as if time had come to a standstill and everything around him was moving in slow motion.

Turning to look back, the tunnel was crumbling piece by piece, like a row of tumbling dominoes coming straight for them.

Matthew looked at the water, then back at the tunnel. There was nowhere else to go.

"Go!" he yelled to Cal and Robyn. Splashes of water hit his face and arms as they jumped in, and then he was right behind them.

The water hit his body like a thousand frozen spikes. He went beneath the water and resurfaced. When he looked up, the air was a cloud of dust and the tunnel was gone.

CHAPTER
18

SOMETHING WAS WRAPPED AROUND CAL'S feet as he struggled to reach the surface of the water. It felt like a vine was constricting his movements. He managed to pop his face up out of the water, and he gasped for air through his mouth before he was quickly tugged back under. He had to reach his ankles to free himself from whatever it was. But the oxygen bag was getting in the way of him bringing his legs up so he could reach—

Someone pulled him up by one shoulder, but whatever was around his legs fought against their efforts. He opened his eyes underwater, but the light from the miner hat was useless down there. He couldn't make anything out.

He briefly broke the surface again. "There's something on my—"

And under he went again.

Would this be how it all ended for him? He wasn't prepared to die. Despite Sophie's pleas and repeated admonitions about how dangerous his adventures could be, he still didn't believe he would die on one. He was too young. He had too much to live for. Too much to still do. More love to give Sophie.

But as her face flashed in his mind, he started to lose the fight. She'd said she would leave his body in the desert. She was mad at him, and they had a huge difference of opinion about his expeditions. What if him coming here had been enough to push her away for good? Then he'd have no reason to survive. She was his best friend, his favorite person in the world.

Through his depressing thoughts, he felt hands working around his legs.

He wanted to yell for help, but if he did, his lungs would fill with water. Instead, he screamed in his head.

Finally, his legs were free, and he kicked hard in a fight for his life. He also felt hands pulling him upward.

When his head was finally above water, he gulped in the air, but as soon as it reached his lungs, he started coughing violently. He had yet to open his eyes, but as he did so now, the air was a hazy blur. He could make out, though, that Matthew was right in front of him and his hands were under Cal's arms, as if he would go back under without the help.

"I'm—" Another cough erupted from deep in his lungs. He was chilled to the bone, and he felt something move against his side. His heartbeat ticked up, and he flinched. "There's—"

Matthew pulled his hand out from under the water, and he was holding the antenna cable. "This was wrapped around your legs. I was holding it and the transmitter module when we jumped into the water."

At least it hadn't been a man-eating anaconda like the one they'd found while searching for the City of Gold.

"Is everyone okay?" Matthew called out, then coughed himself.

"I'm fine," Alex said, handing the module to Matthew. He must have passed it off to her to hold while he had worked to free Cal's legs.

"I'm here, too," Jasper confirmed.

Then silence.

Where was Robyn? Cal looked around, not that he could see too much, but he could see the shadows of the others through the beams of light from their miner hats. The air was heavy with dust, and the grit went into his lungs, making each inhale and exhale painful. He counted heads and came to a total of three.

"Robyn?" Cal yelled, but it didn't come out nearly as loud as he'd intended. Still, his voice echoed back to him.

Matthew let go of him and treaded in a circle.

"I'm...okay."

The sound of Robyn's voice let Cal breathe easier, if only for a mere second. Both his friends were alive.

But now what? Everyone was hacking. They literally had to wait for the dust to settle because any exertion would suffocate them. And even then, where would they go?

The oxygen…

Cal reached to his side and felt the bag, wishing for nothing more than a hit of fresh, clean oxygen. But there would be no way to utilize the tank while in the water. The bag was waterproof, not the machine. Thankfully, he'd managed to think fast enough to stick his camera inside when the tunnel started caving in. And luck was on his side when there was room in the bag for it. He'd lost one camera to water on a previous expedition, and he wasn't willing to lose another. As the thought sank in, he started to laugh.

"Cal? What's going on?" Matthew asked.

Cal heaved, trying to keep his laughter shallow but to no avail. It was cough, laugh, cough, laugh…

"Has he lost it?" Robyn asked.

Cal couldn't talk between laughing and coughing. Poor timing, but what could he do? His musings about his camera struck him as funny. How ridiculous it was to be concerned about such a thing when his life and others' lives were at stake. He considered how to stop this hysterical bout, this teetering on the brink of insanity, and looked back to where the tunnel had been. A sickening weight balled in his stomach.

The dust had cleared enough to see that the tunnel was gone. Sand and rock had blocked it off. There was no way they could go back the way they came. What were they going to do? Were they going to just bob in the water until someone dug them out? That could take days.

"What are we going to do?" The weak timbre of his voice struck his own ears as if it belonged to a stranger.

"What about Reda?" Robyn was splashing water as she spun around. "Did he—" She didn't finish her question, but it was clear she was wondering if he'd survived.

"He could have gotten out," Matthew offered, but his sentiment sounded like it lacked faith.

"The world lost a treasure if he didn't," Robyn lamented.

Things fell silent among them again, and everyone's coughing calmed. But the quiet became its own noise. Screaming doubts and uncertainties cried out, begging to be pacified. But there would be no appeasement coming because there were no answers, no guarantees. And he wasn't even going to give too much thought to what might be in the water with them or exactly how long it would be before they took their last breaths.

"There's no way they can get to us in time, is there?" Asking the question stamped in their desperate predicament.

"I don't see how," Alex said softly.

"By the time they'd dig out the tunnel and get to us"—Jasper, who had a flashlight, swept its beam around the space—"and that's assuming they could, we'd be dead."

A somber dose of reality pierced through Cal. Again, this could be it. Maybe he only loved the thrill that came with risk-taking because he was under the delusion that he was in control.

"We might be able to let them know we're alive," Alex began. "That's if it will work, of course."

"Jeff said it was waterproof," Matthew reasoned.

"Yes, but it might be out of range," Alex countered. "Can you hold it steady above the water?"

"I can."

Alex worked to open the lid on the module and frowned. "There's no signal strength."

"What about the alert feature Jeff told us about?" Robyn asked and swam closer. Jasper, who had been near her, followed. "Does that need a signal?"

"I would think so." But Alex didn't sound too sure.

"Put it on for a minute or two—" The tension in Robyn's voice gave away her terror "—even if there's only a small chance someone will detect it."

Alex nodded. "But we don't want to drain the battery."

She was worried about a battery? "We have far bigger problems," Cal pointed out.

"Okay." Alex pushed something on the module, and a series of red lights began flashing.

"Let's say your guys get the signal, what are they going to do? Even if they know we're alive, as Jasper said, they might not make it to us in time." Cal's chest tightened with fear. "We can't just give up, though."

Matthew faced him, his headlamp shining in Cal's eyes. "No one said anything about giving up."

"Great, then what's next?" Cal looked hopefully at Matthew. His friend was good at getting them out of jams.

There was a pregnant pause. "We get what we came to Egypt for." Matthew sounded as if he had everything under control. If he or anyone else said anything about making lemonade out of lemons, Cal might have to hold their head under the water.

"We're...we're not fully prepared," Alex stammered.

"Things happen. I know it's not ideal, but we really don't have any other choice." Matthew was holding strong.

"Well, we can't go back the way we came." Jasper shone a flashlight on what used to be the tunnel.

"I guess we're doing this, then." Alex took a breath deep enough that Cal could hear it.

"We have water, then a hill, a cave, and snakes, right?" Matthew rhymed off, obviously having committed the map to memory.

"Correct," Jasper confirmed. "And after the snakes, there should be a door to the tomb."

"Then I say, let's get a move on." Matthew held the module out toward Alex. She turned off the alarm and closed the lid.

"How long will the battery last?" Robyn asked.

"Up to twenty-four hours on standby, or eight hours of active use," Alex said.

Similar claims were often made about a lot of things, from phone batteries to camera batteries, but that's usually all they were—*claims*. "Let's hope the manufacturer's telling the truth," Cal groaned.

"Let's," Alex agreed. "No one will want to hear this, but it's probably down about eight hours. We were going to charge it up tonight so it would be ready for tomorrow."

"All right, guys, is everyone okay and ready to swim?" Matthew asked, ignoring Alex's comment and pressing them all into action instead.

"As ready as I'll ever be," Cal conceded. If they were moving forward, there was hope. Staying put would be waiting to die.

CHAPTER
19

MATTHEW COULDN'T SHAKE THE FEELING that the tunnel caving in was a bad sign of things to come. Not that he believed in omens, or that it made a difference. But still, dread was pinching the skin at the back of his neck. He brought up the rear once again so he could watch over the others. Alex had insisted that she stay with him. He hadn't argued, because it gave him immediate company and someone to ensure his safety, too.

As he swam, he looked up periodically. The ceiling was a good twenty feet above them, and the surface was natural rock. It hadn't been worked by man's hands, as the stones of the tunnel had been. Maybe that was in their favor, and it would continue to hold as it had for who knew how many years already.

The air became clearer the farther they swam, and he could finally detect the smell of the water, which was fresh and carried the hint of fish. Assuming there was aquatic life down here, they were leaving him and the others alone. So he could rule out those of the carnivorous variety. Then again, it was possible those creatures just weren't aware they had company. But he'd learned a long time ago not to dwell on the unknown too much or it could drive him mad. In this case, it could literally weigh him down. And with the oxygen bag, the module, and the cable, he was already toting more than he would have liked to be. He had to believe that this special radio would somehow serve as a literal lifeline, even if it was off to a bad start.

"I feel like we're going in circles," Robyn said, her strokes stopping and making everything that much quieter.

"We can't be. Please don't tell me we're—" Cal didn't finish.

Matthew looked around, seeking out any sort of landmark that would differentiate this location from where they had first entered the water. It was just more rock above them and more water around them. He couldn't see where the water ended in any direction. He couldn't even see the ledge where the tunnel had been.

He turned onto his back, floating there and fixing his eyes a particular section of rock that was jutting out from the ceiling. One of his hands was still clenched around the handle on the module and the antenna cable was spooled around his upper arm. He rested the oxygen bag on his abdomen. He stayed as motionless as possible, relaxing his body. He wanted to see if the water was flowing in any direction, though he wasn't sure that information would even be useful.

But none of that mattered. A few seconds passed, and he hadn't moved. He straightened back up.

"Were you checking the current?" Jasper asked.

"Yeah, but there isn't one."

Jasper's face hardened. "The map showed the water coming after the tunnel, and there was an indication that the water was to the east of the tunnel."

"Which is the way we came out of the tunnel," Matthew said.

"Uh-huh. But seeing you on your back, I was thinking there may be more to the water being to the east of the tunnel. It could be that the water flows that way toward the next marker on the map."

Maybe Jasper was having a hard time hearing or he just wasn't comprehending. Either way, tension was snaking into Matthew's chest. "As I said, the water's not moving."

Jasper didn't say anything.

"What do we do?" Robyn asked, looking to Matthew for direction.

Their only option was to keep moving and hope they found land. It was a crappy plan, but this was a crappy situation. "We need to keep swimming and hope we get lucky."

"Hope we get lucky?" Cal exclaimed. "I'd say we're running on the wrong side of luck right now."

Sometimes it was best to keep quiet, and Matthew was fresh out of assurances. What he did have was the will to survive and a determination to get everyone else out alive, as well. Still, the thought of being trapped down here scared him, and he wasn't scared of much.

He took some strokes, cutting between Jasper and Robyn, to lead the way. Splashes from behind him confirmed the others were following. Not that he knew where he was going. He just knew that if he didn't stay positive, the near pitch-black of the underground cavern would close in on him and suffocate the fight right out of him. As it was, all they had were the lights on their hats and a flashlight Jasper had.

A sense of foreboding tingled over his body, taunting him to give in. But as a Connor, he didn't know or accept failure. His father had drilled that into him from a young age.

Sometime later, Matthew let himself rest, and he bobbed there with as little effort as possible. His arms and legs were aching from exertion, his throat dry from thirst.

The others reached him and treaded water.

"I just need a little break," he told them. "And some water."

"You don't have enough?" Cal asked.

Matthew took the question as dense sarcasm, but when he looked at Cal, his friend crossed his eyes.

People said humor helped during times of tragedy, but it was difficult for Matthew to find comfort in that right now. "Here. Hold this for a bit."

He handed Cal the module and snaked the cable through his arm. Then he worked his hands beneath the water to free his canteen from his waist where it was clipped to his pants. His arms were fatigued, and all he wanted to do was crawl onto land, drink water, and breathe for a while. He treaded water with his legs only and brought the canteen to his lips, gulping back the water. He started choking. The particles of dirt and dust were like tiny stones going down his throat. He coughed, his eyes filling with tears and his stomach threatening to bring up lunch.

Robyn swam over to him. "Matt?"

He held up a hand and worked through the worst of it. After a few deep breaths, he took another go at the canteen, drinking more slowly this time.

The beam of Jasper's flashlight bounced along the ceiling, then ahead of him and behind him. There was nothing but water around them and stone above. Nothing new.

"All right, is it just me or is the cavern ceiling getting lower as we go?" Jasper turned the light back the way they had come.

Matthew scrutinized the ceiling. It was hard to tell for sure, but here it was about fifteen feet from the surface of the water.

Jasper shifted and shone his flashlight in the direction they'd been heading. "Look at how close it's getting to the surface of the water ahead of us."

Matthew saw what Jasper meant, and his insides felt like they'd turned to stone. "Let's hope it's not a dead end."

"Oh, please don't even say that," Robyn moaned.

"We probably should go back," Cal said.

He turned to his friend. "Go back to where? There's no way for us to get out back there."

Cal was fiercely shaking his head. "I shouldn't have come."

Pain shot through Matthew. Whatever happened to his friends down here was on him. Cal might never see the love of his life again, and Robyn had finally made it to Egypt, her dream come true, and it was turning into a nightmare. He had to rally them. "We'll get out of here."

On a wing and a prayer...

"I appreciate you saying that, but you don't know that," Cal said.

"We'll get out of this, Cal. Matthew is right," Alex chimed in. Matthew looked at her, appreciating her backing him up.

"I have no plans of dying down here." That was probably the closest Jasper came to offering reassurances. He spoke with his gaze glued to the ceiling ahead of them. Again, assuming that was *ahead*. With no reliable way of gauging what direction they were going, they could be swimming in circles.

"Me neither," Robyn agreed.

A few beats of silence passed.

"That has to mean something..." Cal squinted when everyone's lights hit him. "The ceiling getting lower," he clarified.

Matthew wasn't going to bring up the possibility of it being a dead end again.

Jasper's flashlight cut out, and he resumed swimming.

"Where are you going?" Alex called out to him.

A few strokes later, Jasper replied, "I'm not going to just stay still and hope to be rescued."

Alex turned to Matthew, and fear burrowed into every crease on her face. "I'm going to follow him."

"We all should. We need to stay together." Matthew hurried to clip his canteen back onto his pants. He and the others swam quickly, trying to catch up to Jasper, who had a solid head start. Matthew's heart was thumping against his rib cage in no time.

"Do you see anything?" Alex sounded desperate.

Jasper stopped swimming. "The ceiling is definitely getting lower. I'd say it's about ten feet from the surface of the water here."

Did that even mean anything? Matthew longed to say something inspiring and motivational to light them with hope. But that would be a tall order, as he was struggling to stay positive himself. After all, it would only be a matter of time before they'd tire out and drown if there wasn't divine intervention or some miraculous twist of fate.

They finally reached Jasper and gathered around him. He had his flashlight out again and was shining it ahead of them.

Matthew strained to see past the light into the shadows and beyond that into the darkness. He was trying to force himself to see something that didn't exist. Still, he thought he could see shapes. He was probably succumbing to his exhaustion in much the same way a traveler in the desert does to a mirage. It was likely sheer determination that was inserting hope into an otherwise hopeless situation.

"I think there might be…" Alex snatched Jasper's flashlight and began swimming with one arm while the other directed the flashlight.

"Might be, what?" Matthew followed her, and as he got closer, he was certain formations were emerging from the shadows.

"Is that…?" Alex's words trailed off.

Jasper and Robyn caught up with them. Cal was still a bit behind, holding the module and antenna. Matthew grabbed the flashlight from Alex and set off, cutting through the water.

He slowed down when he was able to confirm his eyes weren't playing tricks on him. Here, the ceiling was only about eight feet above the water. And better yet, about two hundred feet ahead, there was land.

CHAPTER

20

ROBYN'S BODY COULDN'T TAKE MUCH more swimming, but catching a glimpse of land instilled her with newfound strength. Her muscle aches and pains started to fade away. She became determined to reach land. She even steeled her mind against the snakes they might find there. She'd never been a fan of the scaly reptiles, and these wouldn't be harmless, run-of-the-mill garter snakes. The map had said asps, and they were extremely dangerous, not to mention poisonous. Venom from one bite could down an elephant. And snakes didn't exist alone. They always had friends, and they made many babies…

Not that she was a snake expert, but if she remembered correctly from her trips to the zoo, cobras laid forty or so eggs at one time. She shuddered. Something in their favor, though, was that the snakes couldn't survive solely underground, so that could indicate a possible way out.

Her stomach sank as logic told her that snakes would be able to burrow through the sand. Something she and her companions obviously didn't have the option of doing. But given that two items could be checked off as landmarks thus far—the water and the promise of land—she was going to have faith there would be a door and a pharaoh's tomb. Maybe they'd get out through there somehow.

But tombs were sealed with slabs of stone…

Oh man. Thinking probably wasn't the best thing for her to do right now. She had to keep her eyes fixed ahead. And she wouldn't look around, either, or she'd risk sending her imagination into a tailspin. Not that such a thing was difficult right now. While Matthew was doing his best to sound positive, she'd known him for long enough to hear the uncertainty in his voice.

Had she really come all the way to Egypt to die? To think that Egypt had been on her bucket list, too. The irony wasn't lost on her. But she was only thirty. She had a lot of life left to live and more sights to see.

She kept swimming, though both her arms and her legs were still trying to rebel. They had to have been in the water for hours by this point—and the better part of that, they had been moving. She thought about reaching for her phone to check the time but quickly realized the stupidity in doing so. It would be destroy—

Something brushed up against her right leg, and she squirmed.

Oh, there it was again! This time near her left ankle.

"Gah!" she cried out, torquing her body. "Something's— Ah!" She was outright shrieking now, and the sound of it rang back in her own ears.

"Robyn!" Matthew spun to face her.

She couldn't breathe. Her heart was racing. "God, there it is again!" she screamed as she felt it against her skin. The perspiration on her brow nearly chilled into a sheet of ice. She had a bad feeling about this, but if she let her body go still to inspect what was going on, her panic would cause her to sink. Instead, she kept swimming, slicing through the water past Matthew. Maybe if she ignored what she was feeling, that meant it wasn't happening. But it was. And did again.

The light on her hat caught the water, and dark strands of something were wriggling close beneath the surface. It was the very thing she had been wishing it wasn't. "Snakes!" Robyn yelled, her voice echoing in the cavern.

"Oh, something just touched me," Alex said with a start.

"Me too," Cal added.

"Let's focus on getting to land," Matthew directed. He swam up to Robyn and touched her shoulder.

She flinched. Even with him next to her, she wished she were somewhere else, pretty much *anywhere* else. As her light skipped over the surface, her worst nightmare came to life with the realization that the water was getting thicker with snakes. And they were squirming against her.

The land… She had to focus as Matthew had said. But it was still about twenty feet away.

"You've got this, Robyn," Matthew assured her. "I'm right here."

She couldn't look over at him, but she soaked up what she could of his confidence. And she needed all the help she could get because adrenaline seemed to be letting her down.

Oh! More writhing snakes brushed against her, pushing her to the brink of hysteria. It was a tangible feeling that welled up in the back of her throat.

Ten feet left to go. Why was she making such slow progress?

Move, damn it!

With each stroke, she found herself sinking deeper into the water, and it was becoming laborious to swim. She tried to coax herself to keep moving, but her mind was a cluttered frenzy. She couldn't do it. She couldn't pull herself together. Her arms became heavy and stopped moving, and her legs were going down. "Matthew!"

"I'm right here," he repeated and reached for her. Before he touched her, her legs went straight beneath her. She held her breath as she prepared to go under. But then her feet hit a flat surface. "I'm touching the bottom!"

Alex started laughing. "Me too."

"It seems we've reached our third landmark," Jasper said casually. He was certainly a man who took things in stride. You'd think he had a map *and* a way out of here.

"Wasn't there supposed to be a hill and a cave before the snakes?" Cal asked.

Robyn looked over a shoulder at him, willing her focus to stay on her friend and not the snakes still slithering around her and breaking the surface of the water.

Okay, they aren't snakes. They are black streamers cutting through the water. Just streamers.

Shivers ran through her, and goose bumps rose on her arms.

"It's a matter of interpretation," Jasper said. "The three things could appear all at once. We're touching the bottom and walking toward the land now, so maybe the hill is underwater and leading us upward."

He was so collected and matter-of-fact. Robyn envied his composure.

But he *was* the Snake Whisperer. That's what Alex had said back at the main tent. She looked at Alex, and while her face was contorted in her own discomfort from the snakes, terror wasn't etched on her features.

Robyn took a steadying breath as she walked through the water. Facing forward again, her light revealed a similar nightmare to the one she had been living in the water.

The landmass was about twenty feet wide at the water, but a good portion of it was covered with writhing snakes.

Robyn froze for a moment and then pointed ahead. "How are we supposed to—" Oh, she felt so queasy and weak. Maybe they should turn back and pray for a timely rescue. Another few hours of swimming couldn't be that bad…

"I'll take care of them." Jasper trudged past her and Matthew. Jasper was either a man with a death wish or just hungrier to move forward than the rest of them. Possibly a combination of both.

He stopped once the water came to his knees and unclipped the snake hook from his belt. Thank God, he still had that with him.

"Everyone be quiet," he cautioned without turning around. "And stay back."

Cal and Alex came up behind her and Matthew, and the four of them did as directed.

Jasper held out one of his hands, his index finger pointed in the air, and moved it back and forth slowly. As he did so, he took cautious, methodical steps. The snakes were hissing, their tongues flicking out, no doubt smelling and sizing up their prey. They were definitely from the cobra family, and they weren't too impressed with their visitors. Some were showing off their hooded heads, staring at Jasper and poised to strike.

She was cringing inside. One bite… That's all it would take.

Jasper didn't seem affected at all, though. He kept moving, only slowing periodically.

One lunged toward him, and Robyn flinched.

Jasper responded swiftly, hooking the snake and catching it midflight.

Her heart was hammering in her chest, her breathing erratic.

The snake Jasper had caught writhed in the air, and she wanted to look away but couldn't bring herself to do it. Sort of like the way a car accident made most people gawk.

Jasper used the hook like an expert and got the snake under control, then thrust out the hook, tossing the snake feet away from him. Robyn followed the snake's airborne trajectory and watched as it hit the water and swam away. She couldn't help but wonder what would happen if it came back. No doubt it would be even more pissed off than it had been before its efforts were squashed.

Looking back at Jasper, he was wrangling another cobra and cleared it away, as well. The rest of the snakes were starting to spread out from where they had been concentrated. Some went to the left, others to the right, most sticking to land but some slithering into the water.

Tremors shot through her, and Matthew reached out to comfort her but stopped shy of physical contact. It was a good thing, too, because if anything—or anyone—else touched her right now, she'd scream.

"You guys can come ashore now," Jasper said. "Just take your time."

But all she heard was they could go on to the land, and she trudged ahead quickly. Out of the water, the snakes—if she was lucky—would move away from her. At least they wouldn't be rubbing up against her.

"Slowly," Jasper said again, firmly and with authority. And given what he'd just done, she obeyed.

She held up her hands in surrender as she took her last step out of the water. The snakes had wriggled away, apparently not interested in human company or being hurled into the water like their friends. She didn't know where they had gone, but it didn't matter. They were gone and she was relieved. Now, she could breathe.

She bent over and braced her hands on her knees. Her legs were unsteady beneath her, rubbery and wobbly, both from her phobia and the workout. She essentially had to get her land legs back, as it were. But God, it was so nice to have solid earth beneath her feet. Would a snake-free expedition from here on out be too much to ask?

CHAPTER
21

MATTHEW HAULED HIMSELF UP ONTO the ground next to Robyn, with Alex and Cal following. The ceiling here was about eight feet above his head, and the landmass was composed of rock and sand. His legs felt like jelly, and from the looks of everyone else, they were catching their breath. Well, all except for Jasper, who may as well have just gone on a leisurely stroll, rather than an hours-long swim. Matthew looked at his watch. It had been an expensive accessory, but its manufacturer claimed it was indestructible.

What do you know? The damn thing is still ticking.

He smiled at his investment, which told him they had been swimming for close to four hours. He looked at the others. Alex had her canteen to her lips, Cal was setting the module and the antenna on the ground, Jasper had his back to Matthew, and Robyn was standing with her eyes shut, panting.

No one seemed to notice that he'd looked at his watch, so why bring it up unprompted? If anything, it might discourage them more.

Robyn opened her eyes and met Matthew's gaze. "I've never seen so many snakes in my life."

It seemed they'd gone off, doing whatever it was snakes did. "I think they're gone now. We're safe."

Robyn stepped back. "Safe? No." She shook her head. "We're far from *safe*, but..."

He'd never seen her quite like this before. Showing her fears was something new for him to witness, as she typically liked to suck them up and make out like nothing was getting to her. And *she* was normally the group's cheerleader.

"They are asps," Jasper interjected. "One bite can kill you. Even if you get help quickly."

Robyn swigged water from her canteen, her eyes pinched shut. Matthew sensed she was trying to distance herself from the situation.

"Sounds like a good reason not to let them bite you," Cal said drily.

"I'd say so," Matthew agreed.

Jasper carried on, either obtuse or insensitive to Robyn's fear. "They'll only attack if they feel threatened or if you have the wrong energy."

Robyn used the back of her arm to wipe her mouth. She grimaced and dropped her arm, probably because she realized her skin was wetter—and dirtier—than her lips. "The wrong energy?"

"Remember how I said part of being a snake whisperer is attitude? You have to mask your fear. If you don't, like most things in nature, they'll smell your weakness and exploit it. Heck, you could say that about some humans, too."

"The less evolved of the species, anyhow." Alex stepped up next to Matthew. "We should probably get moving, figure out where this goes."

"Oh, we know where this goes," Jasper said, squaring his shoulders and alluding to absolute confidence as if he'd been there before.

"Let's hope the rest of the map is right." Alex's gaze dropped to the ground.

"This is not a good time to be entertaining doubts. Hello?" Cal waved his hand to get Alex's attention. "I'm just sayin'…"

Matthew put a hand on her shoulder. "He's right, Alex."

She shifted her gaze to him. "I know. It's just…" She paused. "I can't help but think about Reda. He's probably dead. And all because of me." Her words hinted at a breakdown, but otherwise, her demeanor struck Matthew as composed. "All I wanted was to discover something important, and it's going to get us killed."

"You couldn't have known the tunnel was going to cave in," he offered as delicately as possible.

Alex eventually nodded. "You're right."

He smirked. "Of course I am."

She laughed. "We might have to work on your modesty."

Matthew loved the sound of the word *we* coming from her lips. For that matter, he loved the sound of her laugh. And he loved the way her wet hair cascaded over her shoulders, already drying into soft curls. But Alex seemed unaware of his admiration and walked away.

He picked up the module and antenna from where Cal had set them down and went to follow, but he sensed eyes on him. He looked around and found that Robyn was watching him. She rubbed her cheek against a shoulder and pressed her lips together. For a brief second, he'd almost peg her as jealous of Alex, but that was ridiculous. He and Alex were friends, just as he and Robyn were. But he had wished for a romance with Alex in the past, and it had been poor timing. And Robyn, well, the romance between them was long in the past, buried like some of the relics they uncovered. She was dating other men, and he dated other women.

Robyn smiled at him and tucked a strand of hair behind an ear. He smiled back and tilted his head in the direction the others were walking, encouraging her to follow. Then he turned and started after them.

More snakes were curled up on the sand and stone, their tongues flicking the air, smelling their visitors and assessing if they were a threat. But the snakes made no move to attack.

There was a wall on the right, and as they rounded a curve in the landmass, a wall appeared on the left.

"The cave," Matthew said.

"I'd say this qualifies." There was a lightness to Alex's voice, and he detected she was smiling, though she didn't look back at him.

As they moved along, the terrain didn't change, and it made Matthew think of pictures he'd seen of the moon—barren with nothing but rocks and dips and valleys. Here, the latter would be closer to knolls and traps for twisting your ankle. The fine layer of sand that coated the stone made it slippery, too.

They carried on walking for an hour or so before stopping to take a rest. They gathered in a circle, and Matthew took everyone in. When he met Alex's eyes, he realized she was doing the same thing, and they smiled at each other.

"I don't know about anyone else, but I'm hungry," Cal said.

"I think we all are," Matthew conceded. "But I don't think any of us has food on our person."

Alex shook her head, and her chin quivered ever so slightly.

Matthew gripped her elbow. "None of this is your fault. Please know that."

She sniffled and ran a hand under her nose. She nodded. "I know. I just feel like I should have known better."

"You couldn't have known, Alex. Jeez." Jasper shook his head, impatience oozing from the man. "Reda's dead. There's nothing any of us can do about it now, and there's nothing any of us could have done to prevent it."

Matthew glared at Jasper. It wasn't exactly the best pep talk he'd ever heard.

"I know you're right, but..." Alex sighed.

"Listen, it's not doing you or me, or any of us—" Jasper swept his arms over everyone "—any good to bemoan what happened. We just have to keep moving forward. In fact, that's our only option."

Something thudding against the ground drew Matthew's attention away from Jasper. He walked in the direction the noise had come from. And there it was again. He treaded lightly and slowly, despite his urge to rush to investigate.

"What is it?" Robyn asked him.

"Does anyone else hear—" And more thudding.

He stepped around a stone formation that made him think of a stalagmite and found the source of the thudding noise. He looked back at the others. "Snakes are dropping from somewhere. But they can't be coming through the rock... Maybe the sand?"

Jasper rushed in front of Matthew. "The door..." He took out his snake hook again, but the snakes were slithering away from him. Still seeming unafraid, Jasper went up to the wall as if a snake wouldn't be popping its head out at any second and wiped it down. "I think it's the door."

Matthew didn't need another invitation to join him. As he ran his hand along the wall, his fingers dipped into a crevice. He looked at Jasper. "You're right!"

"The snakes are coming through a gap on this side between the stone door and the frame," Jasper concluded.

The flow of snakes coming out of the wall seemed to have stopped, and it was a blessed miracle.

Matthew and Jasper worked to clear the sand from around the doorframe. For the most part, only a fine crack outlined the door. Where the snakes had come in, the crack was about three inches wide.

"How are we supposed to move the door?" Cal asked, coming up behind Matthew and Jasper. "It's not like there's a handle and hinges."

"Look." Jasper was standing to the right of the door now, running his hand over the wall there. "Stone blocks like the ones in the tunnel."

"We can pry those out and find a way in." Alex sounded confident, and when Matthew turned to look at her, she was holding a compact shovel.

"Where did you get that?" He hadn't seen it on her person, and it seemed to have manifested out of nowhere.

"I grabbed it before we headed down into the tunnel. I keep it here." She tapped her lower back. "It clips onto my belt. You probably just didn't notice it." She went over to Jasper, who stepped back to give her access to the bricks. She wedged the point of the shovel into the wall and worked to pry the crack wider. She took a few stabs at it and seemed to get a good hold on her fifth attempt. She spread the blocks apart about half an inch and pushed the shovel in farther. "Can you get a grip on one of the blocks?"

Matthew wasn't sure if she was talking to him or Jasper, or if it mattered who responded. Matthew got there first and grabbed on to the stone, working his fingers into the smaller crack on the left of the block.

Eventually, by her shimming the shovel in the crevice between the blocks, they shifted the blocks enough that he could really get his hands firmly on the one. It was jutting out about half an inch at the top. He put his hands around it and pulled. Very little movement. Maybe they were thicker than the five-inch ones used in the tunnel.

"Here." Jasper took the shovel from Alex and came to where Matthew was working. Matthew stepped back, and Jasper put the shovel into the left side of the block and shimmied it looser still.

Alex grabbed her end, and Matthew moved in to help her. Their hands touched, and their eyes met. For a fraction of a second, it seemed as if time had stopped.

Matthew cleared his throat and did his best not to get caught up in the floral overtures of her perfume, which somehow still clung to her after all that time in the water. He looked back at the block and pulled again. It shifted outward, then fell at their feet.

"It's always that first one that's the bitch." Jasper passed the shovel back to Alex and grabbed hold of another block. Matthew watched it come out easily. He followed Jasper's lead and took out another block, as did Alex.

Matthew looked over his shoulder at Cal and Robyn. They were watching intently, smiling and eager.

"You guys aren't ready to get out of here yet, are you?" Matthew laughed.

"Oh yes, we are," Robyn fired back. "I just hope there are no more snakes on that side."

"I wouldn't count on it," Jasper replied.

By the time Matthew looked back at the wall, six blocks had been removed—three horizontally, two vertically. They'd have to get down on their knees, but it was passable.

The five of them moved to the opening, scrunched in next to one another, and bent down. Their headlamps cast light into the hole.

A large cobra was staring back at them. It lifted its head.

"Oh no!" Robyn shrieked and backed up, prancing in place and fluttering her hands rapidly.

"Stop moving," Jasper growled barely above a whisper. "And keep quiet." He unclipped his snake hook again. "The rest of you step back nice and slow."

He didn't have to tell any of them twice.

Matthew sensed dueling energies within Jasper—one dominant and one submissive. The snake's attention went to Jasper. Watching Jasper work with the snake made him think it really was mind over matter, and maybe that was exactly what he was witnessing. Still, he wouldn't want to be the one trying it.

Jasper held out his free hand, his index finger pointed again as he engaged in a silent battle of wills with a deadly reptile.

The snake shot its head forward, but it seemed to be intended as a warning rather than an attack. But it had moved closer to the opening, regardless. The snake sprang ahead again, and Jasper got it on the hook this time. He maneuvered his body away from them, and the snake's tail flicked through the air. But its attempts to break free of Jasper were futile. He stepped away from the group and tossed the snake away from him, as he had with the others.

Matthew was the first to brave it back to the opening, and this time, he got a better look at what was on the other side. He didn't see any more snakes, but he made another observation. "There's another tunnel."

"Let's hope it shows us a way out," Cal said.

"Oh, I'm hoping for a lot more than that." Alex grinned and then slipped through the opening.

"Me too." Matthew followed right after her, eager to uncover what they'd come to Egypt to find in the first place. And for a brief moment, his mortality and their dire predicament faded from his mind.

CHAPTER
22

Once inside the tunnel, Alex rose to her full height. She took the flashlight and shone the beam ahead of her, to the left, then to the right. It was about the same width as the previous tunnel but tall enough that she could stand up straight. It was probably closer to seven feet tall than the previous one's five. So far there were no hieroglyphics on the walls. Still, she got the feeling that they were closing in on the pharaoh's tomb and the Tablets. She didn't know which discovery she would celebrate more, but the thoughts of sipping champagne and making toasts at galas around the world popped with stark reality.

Reda was most likely dead. And while she had heard the logic in Matthew's and Jasper's reassurances that she wasn't to blame, she had a hard time accepting it. After all, they could still all die down here—just because she'd invited them. And what if this tunnel was nothing more than an endless underground labyrinth that led nowhere? How could she ever forgive herself if they remained trapped down here?

She pulled strength from within, taking deep breaths. If she was ever going to find the level of success she craved, she'd have to get a grip on her emotions, become hardened. All she had to do was look at any number of successful people to see the sacrifices they'd made and heartaches they'd overcome to get to where they were. Hopefully, all this would just become a brief blip in her life journey.

"I'm happy to see there are no more snakes," Robyn said, and it made Alex smile.

Other than Robyn's obvious dislike—phobia?—of snakes, she had been so composed and professional. She certainly knew her history, and she had an easygoing nature that made people relax around her. And she was beautiful. It kept coming back to that. Well, that and the status of her relationship with Matthew.

The way he went to her in the water to help her cope with the snakes and the way he'd smile at her sometimes, as if they shared a secret, made it seem like they were lovers. But then there was the spark that had fired between Alex and Matthew when they touched hands…

"What came after the door on the map again?" Cal asked, his voice cutting through the quiet.

"The pharaoh's tomb," Jasper replied.

Actually, it had been the journey to the afterlife, but Alex refrained from correcting him.

As Alex listened to their footsteps shuffling along the tunnel, she put her fingers to the stone. They were coated in sand and cool to the touch. She wished she had some way of seeing what was behind the walls. Did the tomb lay beyond them? Her imagination certainly was running wild, and in more ways than one. She'd lose herself in moments that struck her as surreal and had her high on euphoria. But that rush would cave in, much like the tunnel had, and the floods of grief would pour in and nearly drown her.

Ahead of them, there was nothing but unexplored darkness. How long was the tunnel, and where did it end? How nice it would be if the map had provided measurements? Swim X number of cubits—the Egyptians' main form of measuring length—then go Y number of cubits in the cave to the door, and go another however many cubits to reach the tomb itself. But that probably would have been too easy.

"You're awfully quiet," Matthew said, coming up on her left.

She turned to face him. "I'm just doing a lot of thinking."

"I hear you there." His face was a solemn mask of hardened lines. "We've got to get everyone out of this."

"I plan on it." She attempted a smile, but it was a futile endeavor. There was an energy to the air down here—bittersweet and tangible.

"Me too," Matthew assured her.

She looked straight ahead again and still saw nothing but darkness and the shadows created by their headlamps. Surely, there had to be some light at the end of the tunnel. She chuckled at the thought.

"What is it?" Matthew sounded concerned.

"I was just think—" Her laughter was making it hard to talk. "Ahem. I was just thinking that there has to be some light at the end of the tunnel."

Silence. Then after a few seconds, everyone was laughing.

"Oh!" Matthew bounded ahead of her and pointed to the right side of the tunnel. "There's an opening up here!"

She glanced back at the others, then hustled toward Matthew. As she stood in front of the opening, tingles ran up her arms and around her neck. They seemed to grip her throat and squeeze. She rested her hand there, trying to will away the creepy feeling that was overwhelming her. It felt otherworldly and made her fearful. But then again, maybe it was nothing more than her nerves getting to her and her imagination playing tricks.

"I think we might have just found the entrance to the tomb." Matthew's grin was contagious, and if he was experiencing anything close to what she was, there was no physical tell.

"Yes!" Robyn cried out in glee, followed by Cal.

Jasper remained quiet, but it was in his character to be cautious and skeptical.

"You first, madam." Matthew playfully extended his arm toward the opening. One would think they were safely on land somewhere, not tens of feet beneath the ground without a way out.

But feeding on his enthusiasm, she let her inner child win and shook aside her reservations, fears, and regrets. She had dreamed about this day for as long as she could remember. She pulled out her pendant, squeezed it, and then kissed it for extra luck.

Her heart was hammering in her chest as she led the way inside, and the sensation sweeping over her body only intensified with each step she took. The space here was much narrower and dictated that they walk in strict single file. She had a feeling this was a corridor, and corridors led to tombs.

When she reached the end, she let out a gasp and covered her mouth. She was in a small room encased in smooth stone bricks to her left and right. On the wall ahead of her, though, she could make out distinct imagery under a dusting of sand.

Then something on the ground moved. Alex dropped her hand. "Jasp—"

A large cobra slithered toward her.

"Everyone get inside the room and move aside," Jasper said. "I'm going to get it and fling it down the corridor we just came up."

Alex bumped into Cal in her haste to get out of the way. "Sorry."

Cal waved his hand as if to indicate *no worries*, and Robyn tucked herself behind Matthew.

Jasper did his Snake Whisperer thing and cleared it from the room. He clipped his snake hook back on his belt. "Now I can get to work." He rubbed his hands together and headed to the hieroglyphics on the back wall.

Jasper pulled out a small brush from one of his pockets. He fanned the bristles and wiped them on his pants to dry them. He then worked to remove the veil of dust that time had put in place.

Sand-covered artifacts were stacked around the perimeter of the room, but where the mural was, the piles were only a couple feet high, as opposed to five feet high in other areas. That made it easier for Jasper to reach.

She watched him for a short while as he revealed colorful snippets of a painting but then left him to do what he was good at. She took in the room. Matthew and Robyn seemed to be making themselves at home as they were walking around, and Cal was taking pictures.

"Your camera?" Alex started. "It's okay?"

"I was able to get it into the oxygen bag on the run. You said they were waterproof," Cal answered without lowering his camera.

So he might not have been a history major, but he sure was a quick thinker.

She meandered, scanning the items on the floor. Even beneath a thick coating of sand and dust, many had distinguishable outlines: pottery vessels, jars, wine amphorae, dishes—

"Okay, what are those?"

She turned to see Cal pointing to the far-right corner of the room. She followed the direction of his finger.

"Cat mummies," Matthew and Alex said at the same time.

"What?" Cal blurted out.

"Cat mummies," Alex repeated. "Cats were considered sacred, and it was common for them to be sacrificed as an offering and then mummified."

"It was actually a profitable business in ancient Egypt," Robyn interjected. "Even people who were not royalty would pay to have cats mummified." She glanced at Alex and smiled when their eyes met.

Alex nodded. "And the more money a person had, the more elaborate the wrappings and ritual."

"There's much I need to learn," Cal admitted and lifted his camera back to his face.

Alex returned her focus to the items in front of her. Cal's camera flash was going off like a paparazzo's in Hollywood, but it didn't bother her one bit.

"This is amazing." Alex smiled. She wouldn't be surprised if the expression became permanent. She'd done it. She'd led a dig that had uncovered what appeared to be a pharaoh's tomb. And now, as self-criticism and doubt danced around the edges of her consciousness, she refused to acknowledge them. Even if she died down here, no one could take her claim to this discovery.

Robyn and Cal spread out, although the space wasn't very large—maybe eleven feet deep by fifteen feet wide. Matthew stuck by Alex's side, but she drifted off in her own thoughts as she took an inventory of what she could see without touching anything.

She counted fifty cat mummies, but in addition to her initial observations, there were also footstools, crates of wine, oils, baskets, and games. This wouldn't be the treasury room, though, not if the layout followed a similar pattern to King Tut's tomb. In his case, the corridor fed into the antechamber, which served as the main hub and access point to the other rooms. Seven hundred items had been catalogued in Tut's antechamber alone.

And while it could make sense that this was their pharaoh's antechamber, she had a feeling it wasn't going to be the only one. Sure, it was possible this tomb was much smaller than Tut's. Just call it a hunch.

"I can't believe I'm really here," Robyn said.

Alex grinned and couldn't hold back her excitement any longer. "We're in a tomb!" She wrapped her arms around Matthew's neck and knocked his hat off in the process. He fumbled to catch it, but he'd reacted too slowly and it fell to the ground.

"I'm sorry." Alex winced, and they both went to pick it up and bumped heads. Then they both straightened up, and she put her hands in the air and stepped back.

He smirked at her, retrieved his hat, and put it back on his head.

Alex locked eyes with Robyn. "Oh, I probably shouldn't have..." Alex looked from Matthew to Robyn.

"Shouldn't have what?" Robyn asked.

Alex felt like she was a bug and Robyn had her under a microscope in the sun.

"The hug." Alex put a few more feet between herself and Matthew. "I didn't mean anything by it."

"By the hug?" Robyn had a dazed look on her face. "Why are you looking at me?"

"I mean...you are..." Alex looked at Matthew and back to Robyn. "You're together, aren't you?"

"No," Matthew rushed out, but a flicker of pain danced across his eyes.

Alex looked back at Robyn, and she clenched her jaw. "Oh," Alex said, "I just thought—"

"You thought wrong," Robyn cut in.

"All right. Then I guess I had nothing to apologize for."

"Smile," Cal said to Robyn. He held up his camera and snapped a photo.

"Oh." Robyn winced and squinted from the flash. "Be careful where you point that thing."

"Sorry." Cal turned around and aimed his camera at Alex and Matthew.

Alex put up a hand preemptively to stave off the flash, but none came. She dropped her hand to see that Cal had also lowered his camera.

He pointed directly across the room from where he was standing. "There's another doorway."

She turned and faced the stacks of items she'd been looking at before.

"Right there," Cal said, still pointing.

Alex and Matthew went about six feet down the wall, and sure enough, there was a doorway obscured by the stacks of artifacts.

"This *is* a secondary antechamber," Alex said.

"Do you think it will lead us out of here?" Cal let go of his camera, leaving it to dangle from the strap around his neck. He hustled past Matthew and through the doorway.

He obviously wasn't waiting for an answer, but she replied anyhow. "Let's go find out."

Robyn went in after Cal, and Matthew touched Alex's elbow. "Go ahead."

"Thanks." She smiled, a little skip to her step as she entered ahead of him.

"Uh, everyone?" Jasper's two words had all of them stopping and retracing their steps into the secondary antechamber. "Look familiar?" The bristles of Jasper's brush rested next to a painting of a boat with a scarab and the two representations of Osiris.

"From the map." Alex's response carried on an exhale, and she turned to Matthew again, about to hug him, but shifted her attention back to Jasper. "What else does it say? Is the pharaoh named?"

"Excuse me for a second." Cal stepped in and took a picture of the painting. When he finished, he told Jasper, "You can go on."

"How nice of you." Jasper's tone was bitter, and Alex flashed him a silent reprimand. He might have had an issue with them being here, but they were certainly all in this together now.

"So?" Alex pressed.

"No name that I've seen yet, but I did find this." Jasper stepped to the side and drew everyone's eye to what looked like three green rectangles of similar size with yellow rays coming out from them. They'd been painted within a yellow triangle. And to the right of that triangle were two more, but they were solid yellow. Above that, there were hieroglyphics.

Alex guessed at the images' interpretation, and her stomach sank. "The Emerald Tablets are in the Great Pyramid?"

"They are at least connected with it somehow."

She was going to be sick. She'd go down in history books as a failure. The one who fell for an ancient treasure map, set out to find the goods, only to get herself and those who came along with her killed. That was if she was even deemed worthy of making the pages of a history book.

Matthew stepped up to the wall. "What do the lines coming out of the rectangles represent, and the hieroglyphics?" He didn't seem at all fazed by the possibility that the Tablets weren't in this tomb. Still, there had to be a clue here, something that would lead them to precisely where the Tablets were.

Please give me that much.

Jasper's brow tweaked upward, and he looked at Matthew. "You've heard the myths? The ones that say aliens helped the Egyptians build the pyramids?"

"Of course," Matthew said matter-of-factly. "That's what this is saying?" Skepticism drenched his question.

Jasper turned back to the wall. "Not exactly, but it's saying that they were assisted by heavenly beings."

"Well, the Emerald Tablets are said to contain universal wisdom." Matthew lolled his head to the side.

"As much as I'm enjoying all this—aliens, heavenly beings, and whatnot," Cal began, "can we come back to this after we've found a way out of here?"

Matthew nodded. "He's got a point."

Jasper turned to Cal. "Why did you come?"

Cal's gaze slid to Matthew, then back to Jasper. "Excuse me?"

"You heard me. Unless you're hard of hearing..."

"Jasper, that's enough," Alex intervened.

Cal's nostrils flared, and he lunged toward Jasper. "I don't know what your problem is with me, but I've done nothing to you."

Alex put herself between them, facing Jasper. "Please, let's just work together and find a way out of here."

Jasper looked her in the eye. "You're on his side? I should have known."

His verbal slap stung and catapulted her back to their conversation from that morning. His dislike for Matthew and his friends being here was all too clear, and he wouldn't let her forget it. In fact, she should have enjoyed the reprieve she'd had from his judgment since the tunnel caved in on them.

"We can fight later," Robyn said firmly. "We've already been down here for hours. Who knows how many more we have ahead of us."

Alex regarded Robyn. She had no idea what she was getting in the middle of, but Alex appreciated her involvement. And she liked the woman. It would be so much easier if she didn't. In fact, all of this would be easier if she didn't give a damn about other people. But the implication behind Jasper's words still cut her to the core. She didn't use people.

CHAPTER
23

ROBYN KNEW THE WISE THING to do was search for a way out, but she could have stayed in the secondary antechamber, as Alex had coined it, for hours on end. Looking at the artifacts instilled a sense of calm in her somehow, as if their lives weren't in danger.

As she moved through the second corridor, her legs felt heavy and unwilling to move. She was in good physical shape and worked out five times a week—if she could at all help it—so it wasn't all the exercise. It had to be fear. Logically, they still might not make it out of here alive.

But she had to be positive and envision herself and the others finding a way out. From there, she'd picture how they'd return and start cataloging the find. Not that she, Matthew, and Cal could stay long enough to see it all through. Tut's tomb had taken years to catalog. And who knew how much more there was to find here? Her mind went to Julian, her boss from the museum. There was no way she could stay past the month. As it was, he was probably trying to reach her. She obviously had a good reason for being unreachable, but she just hoped he'd understand. He was a good man overall, but he detested excuses, no matter the packaging.

Cal would be hopping on a plane to get back to Sophie after a month, for sure. Matthew might stay longer. In fact, Matthew had a reason to stay besides the discovery: Alex.

Their attraction was blatantly obvious. And what was all that about a bit ago? The hug, the apology, and Matthew's quick correction when

Alex had asked if they were together… Robyn had pushed down her emotional response at the time, but his rush to clear the air had been hurtful. He'd acted as if she was the last person he'd be seeing, as if he was superior to her, as if the idea of dating her again was unimaginable.

Still, she wondered if Matthew had picked up on the fact that something was going on behind the scenes with Alex and Jasper. He'd have to be blind not to. The tension had risen up so quickly between them. The source of their conflict had to rest closely beneath the surface. Did it have something to do with Jasper's seeming dislike of Cal? Was there a hidden agenda to this expedition? Would it hurt Matthew? Then again, Robyn could be getting carried away, building on her earlier reservations about why Alex had called on Matthew. She'd already had a team in place and a grandiose prospect. Sure, Matthew was an experienced adventurer, but was that the only thing that had gotten him the invite to join the expedition?

Maybe Robyn had just grown skeptical and suspicious. After all, this line of work came with its share of double crosses. But she'd set aside all this mental banter for now, though, because they needed to work as a team. And the only way she could do that would be by giving them the benefit of the doubt.

As she trudged on, she was happy that she hadn't seen any snakes for a while.

No one was saying a word. They must have been doing a lot of thinking, too.

She took in the walls, noticing the smooth stone bricks that bore no hieroglyphics. No other rooms had yet come off the corridor, nor had it fed into one. But given the burning in her thighs, she'd say the corridor ran uphill.

Flashes lit up the space, assaulting her vision like bolts of lightning, even though the source came from behind her. Cal was snapping pictures again.

At least there was someone she could count on in this world. Cal was like the brother she'd never had, one of the good guys. He loved Sophie fiercely and loyally, and coming on this trip, leaving things how they were at home, must have been tearing him up inside. She could sense it coming off him at times, but he was doing a good job masking his emotions behind his camera.

"Did you find anything else in the hieroglyphics back there, Jasper?" Alex asked without turning around.

"Well, I didn't finish uncovering all of it, but there was a curse called down on any who disturbed the tomb."

"But no name," Alex mumbled.

"A curse?" Cal's voice cracked. "See, I told you! I swear that shit is real."

"Just like leprechauns at the end of the rainbow," Jasper said drily. It was obvious he had no concern for Cal's feelings.

"I've got your back, Cal," Robyn said, finding herself coming to his defense, despite having teased him about his belief in curses just that morning. "The underworld will have to come through me."

"Why doesn't that make me feel better?" Cal paused. "Oh, maybe because you have no experience with such things."

"How would you know?" She was being silly, the madness of being down here getting to her.

Camera flashes bounced off the walls.

"What could you possibly be taking pictures of?" Jasper asked.

"None of your—"

"There's another room," Alex cried out with excitement.

Robyn watched as the light from Alex's headlamp expanded ahead. She turned to look over her shoulder and was met with a blinding explosion of light.

"Cal!" She couldn't see anything but dark circles.

"Everything all right back there?" Alex asked.

"We're fine," Robyn mumbled.

Blind maybe, but fine.

"I flashed her." Cal snickered, and Robyn stopped walking so that he ran right into her back.

"My, a party's going on and I'm missing it." Alex laughed and stepped out of view.

"I just meant—" Cal's words died on his lips when Robyn glowered at him over her shoulder. He cleared his throat. "Nothing."

Robyn resumed walking, although she could only make out light and shadows. She stepped out of the corridor, joining Alex in a room that was much larger than the secondary antechamber. And it contained a lot more treasure. She was certain her mouth was gaping open. As her vision cleared, she took in the sights before her. More artifacts were stacked around the room, and they went as high as the ceiling in some places. She guessed it was eight feet tall.

Cal came in after Robyn, followed by Matthew and Jasper. Their combined headlamps made everything easier to discern: couches, statues, beds, chests, models of ships, golden trinkets, swaths of fabric, arrows, and the list went on. She walked around the room, so tempted to put her hands on everything, but she wouldn't want the oils from her skin to ruin or soil the artifacts. Still, she couldn't fully resist and swiped away a thick coating of sand from the arm of a chair.

"It's gold," she exclaimed and noticed Matthew smiling. "Well, technically, it's gilded wood, but—"

"You touched it," Alex said. It wasn't as much a statement as it was an accusation.

Robyn felt the back of her neck stiffen. "I do have experience working with precious antiquities."

"I don't mean to insult you, but—"

Robyn stood her ground. "I understand and respect how valuable these artifacts are."

"Fine, but please, don't touch anything else."

Robyn caught Matthew's eye, but he gave no indication that he was about to come to her defense. She felt her cheeks heat.

Sure, take her side…

Robyn jutted out her chin, took a deep breath, and turned away from him.

Cal was back to snapping pictures, and even though there was so much here to photograph, part of her couldn't help but think he was getting more shots of sand right now. She could only imagine how breathtaking everything would be once they got the rest of Alex's crew down here and started cataloging everything.

Robyn walked clockwise around the room. She took in all the jewels, fine garments, and gilded statues. Being here was like living in the photographs she'd seen of King Tut's tomb. Remarkable and equally unbelievable.

She came to a doorway, the light from her miner hat delivering some good news. "I found another corridor."

"Please tell me it will lead us out of here," Cal said.

Alex came hustling over. She took the first step inside when Matthew called out from the other side of the treasure room, "I think I found the burial chamber."

Robyn's breath hitched, and Alex's movements halted. It was clear she was as conflicted as Robyn was. She'd love to have the assurance of a way out, but at the same time, Matthew was talking about a burial chamber.

Robyn turned to look at Matthew, but she couldn't see him past the piles of artifacts in the room.

"Where are you?" she asked while moving to the opposite end of the room in the general direction of where his voice had come from.

"I'm behind the statue with the cow's head." He stepped out into a bit of a clearing and waved his arms as if he were flagging down a cab or trying to draw attention to himself in a crowd. Between that and the boyish grin on his face, Robyn found herself smiling.

"What makes you think—" Alex stopped talking, and Robyn understood why.

Both of them had rounded a statue of the cow-headed Hathor at the same time and had come face-to-face with two other statues, which were representations of a pharaoh, likely the one whose tomb they were in. They stood floor-to-ceiling on either side of a doorway—*guarding* said doorway.

Robyn started laughing, and Alex joined her. Jasper and Cal stood next to Matthew, and the three men were looking at them with amusement.

"We did it." Alex turned to Robyn. "And that means that this here—" she pointed to the floor "—is likely the main antechamber. The first one we entered was either the secondary one, as I suspected, or an annex if we're basing it on the layout of—"

"Tut's tomb," Robyn finished.

Alex nodded with a smile. "That's right."

"So now that we've found the tomb, will we live to tell about it?" Cal lowered his camera, a grim foreboding gripping his features.

Robyn went over to her friend and nodded. "We have to stay positive."

"Easier said than done, don't you think?" Cal served back, the strength of his emotions telling her he was thinking about Sophie.

"We'll all walk away from this," she assured him, but as they met each other's gaze, she found herself withdrawing. She was in no position to make any such claim, but she had to stay positive for him, for Matthew, for Alex, even for Jasper. "We still have another corridor to explore. Let's see if it leads to a way out of here."

"If it does, it's probably buried beneath tens of feet of sand," Cal mumbled.

And blocked by a stone seal like in most tombs, she thought, but she wasn't going to say that out loud.

CHAPTER

24

KING TUT'S TOMB HAD COME UP, but Matthew noted one glaring difference between this tomb and Tut's. "Khufu served during the Fourth Dynasty, and Tut reigned in the Eighteenth. That puts nearly twelve hundred years between them, with Tut coming after Khufu. And since this tomb resembles Tut's, it stands to reason that Tut's tomb was designed with this tomb in mind, not the other way around."

"It's possible," Alex conceded.

"And look at this." Robyn walked up next to what looked like a large chest that sat on a flat of wood.

"The canopic shrine." Alex's voice was breathy.

Matthew always thought history was sexy, but these two women took it to another level. He smiled and looked at the shrine more closely. There were inscriptions on the side, and there were heads of raised cobras with disks representing the sun at the top. Statues of female divinities were on the two sides that were visible, but he'd wager there would be four in total—one for each side. That was, if it was indeed the canopic shrine.

Alex brushed against him as she moved in next to him. She pointed to the goddess on the side who had what looked like a rectangle above her head with hieroglyphics on it. "That's Isis, goddess of magic and life, and this one—" Alex pointed to the second visible one "—is Sereket, the scorpion goddess. See the scorpion on her head."

"The scorpion goddess?" Cal asked incredulously. "They had gods for everything."

"Well, she is identified by the scorpion on her head. She was believed to heal the bites from venomous reptiles," Robyn elaborated. "The protective goddesses on Tut's shrine were Isis, Sereket, Nephthys, and Neith. Each of them had their arms stretched out to their sides and were put in place to protect a package of viscera."

Cal cocked an eyebrow. "Viscera?"

"Basically, the main organs of the abdominal cavities." Alex answered, then added, "The lungs, stomach, intestines, and liver."

"Okay, that I understand. Plain English does wonders sometimes." Cal snickered.

Jasper didn't say anything but looked sideways at Cal. It was hard to tell what the man was feeling beyond irritation.

"In the case of King Tut, inside the shrine they found a canopic chest made of alabaster. Inside that were jars that contained mini gold-inlaid coffins. The Egyptians liked to nest things, as if it would provide more protection," Robyn added.

She was certainly in her element here. But, then again, what had he sentenced her to? They were essentially trapped down here. They still had a corridor to investigate, but his optimism was waning.

Matthew could feel Jasper's breath on the back of his neck and stepped to the side to give him a direct line of sight to the shrine. He leaned forward and cleaned some of the dust off with his brush.

"What are you doing?" Alex touched Jasper's arm, and he stopped moving.

"I'm trying to read the hieroglyphics. It's what I'm here for." The latter part came across a little snide.

Alex looked from Jasper to Robyn and back to Jasper. "Just be careful."

Matthew looked at Robyn, and her jaw was clenched. There were double standards in play. He probably should have defended Robyn when she'd touched the gilded chair.

Cal came up on his left, snapping more photographs. Matthew looked away and took in more items that his eye must have skipped over the last time he scanned the room. He paced slowly. There were lamps, musical instruments, walking sticks of ebony and ivory, golden fans, small jars that likely contained oils and perfumes, more jars of wine, and clothing made of the finest linen. Really, it was a mishmash of anything and everything to make the pharaoh comfortable in the afterlife. And to the Egyptians, the afterlife was just as real as the physical one. Hence all the planning and care taken to make their deceased comfortable.

Matthew was itching to touch the objects, but he dared not or he'd risk bringing Alex's wrath down on his head. He looked back to see Alex and found that she, Robyn, and Jasper were still back at the shrine. Jasper was muttering something under his breath, seemingly engrossed by the writing on the shrine.

"What are these?" Cal lowered his camera and was pointing to several small statues, on the floor near the shrine. They were grouped together as a troop and each was about ten inches tall.

"They are most commonly known as shabti or ushabti," Matthew said.

"You remember what I said about English being a good language?" Cal smirked.

Alex came over to them, Robyn trailing her. "Ushabti *is* the English term," Alex said. "Just like *viscera* was."

Cal looked at Matthew and crossed his eyes. Matthew laughed.

"And what are they exactly?" Cal asked.

"Figurines that represent those who were to serve the pharaoh in his afterlife. They are often found in rooms containing treasure, as they are meant to protect it."

"Okay, I'm still stuck on how these could service a dead guy," Cal said.

"In many ways," Alex began. "On each ushabti, there will be a spell, for example."

"Also known as a shabti formula," Robyn interjected. "It would detail what that individual ushabti's responsibilities are. Each will have different tools with them—hoes, baskets, chisels, other tools for manual labor. But the list could go on."

Alex nodded. "Surely you've heard about *The Book of the Dead*?" She directed her question to Cal.

"I've heard of it, but I've never read it. It's not something I can pick up at the bookstore, though, is it?" Cal passed Matthew a smart-alecky grin.

Matthew shook his head and smiled. *Leave it to Cal to make light of an ancient book of spells.*

"Well," Alex started with only vague amusement tracing her features, "there are many spells found in the book, which covers a number of topics, including invoking protection. But one spell is specifically for calling out to the ushabti to awaken and perform their duties."

"Ooh." Cal wriggled as if a shiver had run down his spine.

"It was so their master, in this case, a pharaoh, could live a relaxing afterlife," Alex added. "They found three hundred sixty-five ushabti in Tut's tomb."

"One for every day of the year?" Cal guessed.

"That's right, but he was also given forty-eight overseers," Matthew added, pulling from his university days for this tidbit.

"Four hundred thirteen little statues," Cal summarized.

Alex's mouth dropped, and Matthew sensed it was from Cal's seeming downplay of their importance.

"They are much more than that," Alex said, her tone hot.

Cal held up his hands. "I didn't mean to offend you."

"Ushabti took the place of retainer sacrifices," Alex went on, paying Cal no attention.

Cal looked at Matthew, and his confusion was obvious.

"During the First Dynasty," Matthew explained, "servants of the pharaoh were killed and buried with him."

"Oof. Would've sucked to be a commoner, then." Cal gave a little smile, but no one else seemed amused. "I'm hungry, so I'm a little off my game and distracted," he said defensively.

"I think we're all hungry," Jasper snapped, the sting in his voice driving home the fact that starving to death was a real possibility down here. But Matthew had enough of this man treating Cal like a piece of garbage.

"What is your problem?" Matthew asked.

Jasper looked at him. "I'm hungry. *Apparently.*"

Alex put a hand on Jasper's shoulder, but he shrugged her off, holding eye contact with Matthew the entire time.

"I think you have more problems than that." Matthew could feel the hair rising on the back of his neck, usually a precursor to him punching someone.

"Matthew." Robyn's voice cooled his heating temper. "We have to remember none of us are at our best right now, and we should be more patient with one another."

Matthew was still seething, but her mild and logical request was working its way in. He let out a deep breath. "Fine. We're all tired and cranky at this point, and we don't know how long we'll be down here together."

Robyn tilted her head down and eyeballed Matthew.

He held up a hand. "I say we check out the other corridor and see if we can find a way out of here before we do anything else."

Jasper's eyebrows shot up. "And leave the burial chamber?"

"It's not going anywhere." Matthew stepped away from the group in the direction of the corridor Robyn had found.

"What time is it anyhow?" Cal asked. "Not like anyone would—"

"About eight at night." Matthew held up his wristwatch. "Seven fifty-five precisely."

"You've had that all this time?" Alex stared at him. "We must have been swimming for—"

"Four hours."

"No wonder I'm exhausted," Robyn said.

Cal's brow furrowed. "Wait, you said seven fifty-five?"

"Yeah. Why?"

"Well, you know Sophie's into numerology, and if I remember right, fives indicate a change is coming."

"Tell me it's a good one. A way out perhaps?" Matthew smiled, not sure he really bought into the idea that numbers contained messages.

"It means *change*, but that doesn't always mean it's going to be good change," Cal clarified.

"Let's hope this time it does." With each step Matthew took, he hoped they'd find a way out, but he wasn't getting too carried away with that notion yet.

CHAPTER
25

AFTER ABOUT THIRTY FEET, Matthew reached the end of the third corridor and came to a set of stairs. He turned, holding his hand out behind him toward Jasper. "Flashlight." Jasper put it in his palm. Matthew hated being so ill-equipped, but it's not like getting stuck down here had been the plan. He directed the light up the staircase and could see the top. What he saw wasn't a surprise, but it curdled his stomach.

"What do you see?" Robyn prompted.

Alex was pretty much pressed against his back trying to get a look.

"It's an entrance or exit, depending on how you look at it, but there's a slab of stone sealing it off."

Cal let out a moan of defeat, and it only cemented how Matthew was feeling in this moment. Surely, they had to catch a break that would get them out of here. But it was getting harder to believe they would.

"There's no way we can move it," Alex said. "I thought this might happen."

"Even if we could move the stone, sand would come pouring in," Robyn pointed out.

"So you're saying that we can't get out of here? We have a door, but we can't use it?" Cal's voice ratcheted up in volume with each word. He maneuvered his way past the others and pushed on the stone. "None of you happen to have any dynamite handy, do you?" There was nothing jovial about his tone when he asked.

"Trust me, you wouldn't want it anyway. It would cause a cave-in, not to mention destroy a historical find." Alex glowered at Cal.

Matthew looked at Alex. Her priorities were a little off-kilter.

Cal turned to face them all, the light from his miner hat dancing as he shook his head. "How are we going to get out of here?"

"Good question." Normally, Matthew could pull out an ounce of optimism to use in a pinch, but he was all out.

Alex nudged Matthew in the back. "We need to set up the module and the antenna and give it a try. Just in case."

"In case what?" Cal spat.

"In case my crew is in range."

"They don't even know we're alive," Cal countered, seeming to have resigned himself to the fact that their fate was sealed, just as their way out was.

Alex took the module and transmitting antenna from Matthew, who hadn't set them down since they'd entered the tomb. "We have to believe they do."

"There are a lot of things we'd need to believe in before then," Cal said. "One, that they know we're still alive so they are actually looking for us. Two, that the transmitter has battery left, and three, your crew is in this vicinity." Cal's discouragement was tangible and infectious. Matthew could feel it bringing his spirits down further, but Alex continued, looping the cable and laying it out in the corridor.

She plugged the antenna into the module. "Very weak signal strength, but I'm giving it a go anyhow." She punched some keys on the module and held the radio that had been inside the case to her mouth. She pushed a button on the side. "Jeff Webber, do you read me? Over."

The silence in response was deafening.

"Jeff Webber, do you read me? Over," she repeated.

Seconds ticked off, and nothing came through.

Alex lowered the radio and bit her bottom lip. "One more time," she said to them. Then, "Jeff Webber, do you read me? Over."

More silence.

"It's not working. We're going to die down here." Cal sat down on a step.

"I'll turn on the emergency signal for a bit," Alex said, ignoring him.

"What about the battery, though?" Robyn asked, stepping up close to Matthew's back. "It can't stay on for too long."

Alex looked at Robyn, and Matthew could read the resolve on Alex's face. "We need to wait it out for a few minutes."

And each second of each minute felt like an hour. Matthew imagined hearing Jeff's voice coming over the radio and telling them they had a fix on their position. But nothing came.

Alex pressed a button on the module. "I'll turn it off for now and save the battery."

No one said anything.

"My crew won't just give up on us," Alex assured them. "They might not know for sure we're alive, but they won't stop searching for us until that's been proven."

"That's a scary thought," Cal said. "They could be back at the original tunnel still, and we have to be miles from there now."

Alex looked at Matthew as if to say, *Is this guy for real?*

Matthew hitched his shoulders. "He calls things how he sees them. He always has." He stepped up the stairs, observing that this section was composed of more stone bricks. Maybe they weren't entirely out of options. "We could free these bricks, maybe get out that way?"

"You're forgetting about all the sand that's above our heads. If we remove any bricks, sand will come pouring in. Sorry to be bleak, but…" Alex pressed her lips together. "If anyone has any other ideas, now's the time to share them." She stared directly at Matthew, as if expecting him to present another one. But his mind was blank.

Not taking action would get them killed. But taking action would also get them killed.

Alex broke her eye contact. "Maybe we should just get comfortable and—"

"Are you kidding me?" Cal's eyes were wide. "We can't just give up."

"I'm not saying that we give up, but we might need to wait on some outside help," Alex said. "And if you pray, pray. Rest probably wouldn't hurt, either. Get our brains functioning at capacity again."

Cal turned to him. "Matthew?"

Surely there had to be something he was missing. Besides, he wasn't the wait-and-see type of person, and he definitely wasn't someone who relied on luck. He'd never been religious, either. But he'd been known to call on a greater being from time to time. It was far better to be proactive than roll over in defeat. In his mind, he walked through the parts of the tomb they'd seen on their journey up until to this point. "The snakes," he blurted out.

"Matthew?" Robyn prompted, her tone laced with fear.

He met her eyes. "The way out of here has to lie with them."

"Can't they burrow through sand?" Cal asked.

"I want to believe they found an easier way in." Matthew was still thinking as he spoke, not even sure where he was headed.

"What are you thinking?" Alex asked.

"Specifically about the snake that came into what we're calling the secondary antechamber." His eyes widened. "I'd like to see what's on the other side of that wall."

Alex perked up. "It's not uncommon for tombs to have hidden rooms."

"You're thinking there's one that might lead to the surface?" Robyn asked, her voice carrying hope, but then she shook her head. "There'd still be sand, and likely another sealed door."

"Only one way to find out." Matthew started back down the corridor.

"That wall has a priceless mural on it," Alex ground out, keeping up with him. "We can't just destroy it."

He bit back any response, giving her a momentary pass on drawing attention to her skewed priorities. But when they reached the secondary antechamber, Alex stood back from the wall, hands on her hips. "It just breaks my heart that we have to damage this painting."

Matthew couldn't hold back any longer. "It could be the painting or our lives. You do realize that, don't you?"

Alex blushed. "I didn't mean it in the way you seem to have taken it. Of course, our lives are more important."

"Then help us move some of these artifacts out of the way," he said to her as he and the others started to clear the area beneath the painting.

Alex got down next to Matthew and reached for the first object with hesitancy. He made eye contact with her but spoke to everyone else. "Just be careful not to break anything."

The corners of Alex's mouth curved up slightly, and she deliberately blinked as if thanking him.

They set aside the priceless objects one at a time, doing so with thoughtful execution.

"Oh!" Robyn gasped and stepped back across the room. A cobra was slithering out from behind a basket, and its focus was on her.

"Don't move." Jasper quickly jumped into action. He wielded the snake hook and got in close to Robyn. He finessed the snake's attention away from her and on to him. "Everyone back out of the room *slowly*."

Matthew waited until Robyn was free from danger, and the four of them crammed into the corridor that lead to the main antechamber and watched from the doorway.

Jasper got a hold of the snake, its head swaying through the air, its tongue flicking, and its body wriggling. He carried it like this and turned to the opening of the corridor that led back to the tunnel and thrust the snake inside it.

Robyn was the first back into the room with Jasper. "The Snake Whisperer to the rescue. Thank you, Jasper."

"Yeah, don't mention it." He wiped his forehead and pointed to a small hole between two stone bricks. "Guess we know how the snakes are getting in."

"But is there a room and way out behind this wall?" Cal cocked an eyebrow. "Or just a bunch of sand?"

Matthew stepped up next to the wall and reached out a hand to Alex. "Shovel?" She passed it to him. Then Matthew got down on the floor next to the hole and turned to Cal. "Help me out here."

Cal joined him on the floor. Matthew stuck the shovel between the two bricks.

"Wait a minute," Alex burst out.

Matthew looked up at her.

"Let's clear off the picture first and have Cal take a picture of it, just in case it gets destroyed."

Matthew glanced at Cal, then back to Alex. "Let me just remove a couple of the bricks from the floor level, nowhere near the painting, and see what I see first."

"No. I'm sorry, but no. We can't take the chance that the wall won't crumble."

"And why doesn't that make me feel all warm and gooey inside?" Cal lamented.

Matthew shot him a glare. They had just started to latch on to the idea of hope, and he didn't need Cal's sarcasm sucking them back into a defeatist attitude. Although, Alex's comment had opened the door.

"Very well."

Alex flicked a finger toward the painting. "Jasper, please clean it off."

Matthew and Cal got to their feet. Jasper brushed off the painting as everyone watched him.

"Tell us if you see a name," Alex said.

Jasper shook his head.

"I'm sorry if you guys don't understand where I'm coming from," Alex added, pressing her fists into her hips. "But I'm very passionate about what I do."

"And we're passionate about living," Cal shot back.

Alex narrowed her eyes. "So am I." She paused, her mouth opening and shutting a few times as if she were a fish gasping for air. "I'm just a very optimistic person." She shrugged. "There's no reason to believe we're getting out of here alive, but I can only accept that we are. And because of that, I don't want to be responsible for ruining this tomb, its artifacts, and its artwork."

Her sincerity was obvious. Maybe Matthew had been a little rash to think the find meant more to her than their lives.

"All right, there we go." Jasper stepped back from the painting and its vibrant colors. "And before you ask again, Alex, there was no name, but I didn't read everything as I worked, by any means."

Alex nodded, and contentment rested on her features, as Cal took a series of pictures.

Matthew moved toward the wall, and Cal followed suit. "We'll be careful and move slowly," he assured Alex.

"Thank you."

Matthew put his hand back on the shovel that was still lodged between the two bricks. He moved it and pried a larger space between them. He grasped on to the brick on one end, and Cal grabbed the other. They jostled it until it broke loose. Sand didn't filter into the room, so that was a good indicator that there might be a room on the other side.

He and Cal continued working. The second, third, and fourth bricks came out more easily.

He passed the shovel to Cal, who handed it off to Alex, and crouched even lower so he could look inside. His headlamp revealed a good-sized room and, thankfully, no snakes.

"What do you see?" Alex asked.

"Well, it's definitely a room," he said.

"Do you see a way out?" Cal lowered himself again, pushing Matthew aside.

"Do you mind?" Matthew shot him a glare.

Cal eased back, giving Matthew space to look again. "Excuse me."

"I can't see that much from here. I'd have to go in." He already had his head inside when someone tugged on his shirt. There wasn't enough space for him to look over his shoulder, so he wriggled back out.

Jasper was standing over him. "Let me go in. Just in case there are more snakes."

"I don't see any."

"That doesn't mean more won't come."

"Please, Matthew," Robyn said. He looked at her, and her eyes were full of concern.

He moved aside, though he didn't really want to. He just wanted to find an exit. While he was still determined to find the Tablets, he was a bit of a realist, unlike Alex, and time wasn't slowing down. They had limited water and oxygen down here, and no food. They had the portable oxygen tanks for when they needed a hit, but it wouldn't tide them over for long. His gaze went to the hole and Jasper's larger frame.

"Can you fit through there?" Matthew asked.

"I'll manage." Jasper was up to his shoulders in no time. Not long later, his hips disappeared, then his legs and feet. "I'm in," he said, as if they needed verbal confirmation.

Matthew was watching him through the opening. Cal got up, and Alex joined Matthew on the floor.

Jasper's flashlight was making it easier to see the actual size of the room. Although Matthew pegged it at seven feet high and ten to twelve feet wide, he couldn't see to the back wall. But from what he could see, he'd guess it was at least twenty feet long. He also made out something else, just as Japer made an announcement.

"There are more snakes," Jasper told everyone.

Matthew watched as Jasper did his thing with the hook. But instead of thrusting them aside, he used the tool to help maneuver past them.

Awhile later, Jasper provided an update. "I've cleared the snakes, and there's a staircase."

"Be careful, Jasper," Alex cautioned.

"It's just like the other one." His voice was becoming distant. "It's made of stone bricks and there is a door, but it's sealed."

Soon Jasper was walking back toward the opening in the secondary antechamber. The snakes didn't seem to be paying him much mind on the return trip, though.

Matthew and Alex backed up and got to their feet so Jasper could come into the room.

"I see where the snakes are coming in," he said. "There is another hole between two bricks up there and a spill of sand on the stairs."

At that, an idea struck Matthew. But it was probably just as lethal as sitting down here, doing nothing, and waiting for a rescue. They could pry those bricks loose and run from the room. Maybe the additional space would accommodate the sand that would likely come pouring in. He'd call it his hourglass strategy.

The sand would fill up the room they'd just discovered, come through the opening they'd just made in the secondary antechamber, and hopefully stop there. But then again, it's not like he had any way of knowing how much it would fill up. And it would significantly deplete their oxygen. Then, they'd have to dig through the sand to the surface when all they had was one tiny shovel.

"You look deep in thought," Alex said, watching him.

"It's nothing."

She scanned his eyes, and he hoped she wasn't a mind reader. Because it wasn't nothing; it was potentially the thing they might have to try if they ever wanted to see their loved ones again. But he wasn't going to mention it until they had no other choice—not that they really had any options now. But before they could even think of trying to pull off what he had in mind, they needed rest. "Why don't we check out the burial chamber now and then get some sleep," he suggested.

"You're not giving up on me, I hope," Alex said, a subtle smile on her lips.

"Not at all."

CHAPTER
26

ALEX HAD SEEN HER SHARE of sarcophagi, but they were always housed behind plate glass in museums. Now here she was, mere feet from a sarcophagus that allegedly belonged to a son of Khufu—a firsthand discovery. It was beyond incredible and certainly spiritual.

Ushabti lined the perimeter of the coffin, and the walls were covered with murals. They likely depicted the pharaoh's life, his death, and his journey into the afterlife. If she and the others were lucky, they'd find a name here somewhere, too.

She felt some sort of a connection to this room, but it was one she was unable to put into words. Tingles spread over her shoulders and down her back. This time the sensation didn't scare her, and instead, she embraced the experience. After all, it's not like a dead king really held any sway over her fate. No matter how convinced Cal seemed to be that pharaohs' curses had merit, she couldn't allow herself to give in to such foolishness. She could assign no logic to it. They were stuck down here because of unforeseen circumstances and a bad turn of events. It had nothing to do with some ancient hex.

In fact, Alex had the overwhelming urge to pry off the lid to the sarcophagus right now and look inside. Was there a mummy inside? Were the Tablets in there with him? But she had to fight this moment of weakness. Her values and her respect for the sarcophagus and the dead pharaoh inside it dictated that she make sure everything was done properly and followed protocol. Anything else would be a violation.

And that wasn't even touching on the likelihood that the group of them might not be strong enough. It had taken eight men to remove the lid to Tut's sarcophagus.

Robyn was pacing the room, seeming to be doing her best to stick close to the walls and avoid knocking over any ushabti. "This is incredible."

"Is it just me, or is anyone else dying to see inside?" Matthew was standing there, staring at the sarcophagus, his energy eager and curious.

"Someone died to get inside already," Cal said, lowering his camera and smiling.

"Hardy har har." Matthew smiled at his friend.

Alex had to remain in control of her impulses and not buckle under the pressure. "We need to leave the sarcophagus the way we found it to protect—"

Something clattered across the floor and stopped her cold.

Cal's mouth dropped open, and his eyes widened. He was looking at everyone but her.

"I...I...didn't mean to," he stammered.

She looked at his feet, and a few ushabti had been knocked over. Thankfully that's all it had been, but even so, anger coursed through her and she clenched her jaw to keep from snapping at him. She wasn't normally so quickly roused to lashing out, and she didn't like the feeling. It had to be because she was hungry and tired.

Everyone but Jasper was silently watching her. He was swiping some dust off a mural.

"It was an accident," she said to the rest of them, doing her best to slough it off, but she was trembling with aggravation.

"Forget an accident..." Cal's face fell as panic swept over his features. "I've probably really pissed him off now."

Alex narrowed her eyes. "Who?"

"The pharaoh. Who else?" Cal's words held conviction. He really bought in to all that curse nonsense. "He'll probably call on his usha—whatever they are—and have them kill me."

Jasper turned from working on the mural and rolled his eyes.

Alex fought a smirk. "I'm sure you'll be fine."

"No." Cal was shaking his head. "We're going to die down here."

"Why are you being so dramatic, Cal?" Robyn asked.

"Dramatic?" Cal screeched. "We've just upset the burial chamber of a pharaoh, Robyn. We've got to get the hell out of here."

"The pharaoh is dead. He's in a coffin," Jasper said slowly and matter-of factly, his eyes back on the mural. "He can't harm you."

"Are you sure about that? The Egyptians had a strong belief in the afterlife." Cal was shaking, and sweat was beading on his forehead.

"Come here, Cal." Alex guided him to join her in the main antechamber. Matthew and Robyn came along, as well. They truly were like the Three Musketeers. *All for one. One for all.*

"Do you believe in an afterlife?" Alex asked. She'd been raised to be respectful of others' beliefs, and as much of a stretch as a curse was for *her*, Cal was convinced of their validity. Maybe if she could reason with him, he'd calm down.

Cal looked from her to his friends and back to her. "What does it matter what I believe?"

"Well, if you believe in it, then sure, maybe you have a right to be a little nervous. But if you don't, what do you have to be afraid of?" It sounded reasonable to her own ears, but Cal's brow pinched in thought. He apparently had to consider it. She continued. "If you ask me, supposing there is an afterlife, I'm sure the dead have more important things to do than hang around worrying about who is visiting their tomb. Again, that's assuming a belief in the existence of an afterlife."

Cal's gaze darted back toward the burial chamber.

"Do you think he's here?" Alex pressed.

He met her eyes. "I feel something down here," he admitted. "I don't know what, but I don't like it."

"Fear, I'm sure. We're all facing that." Even given her earlier speech, she felt far less certain than she let on.

"You said that you were optimistic we'd get out of here." Cal lifted his chin and studied her. "I'd love to hear how that's going to happen."

God, she wished she had a response. Instead, doubts rushed in on her, weighing her down. They all could very possibly die down here. She thought she was hungry now, but wait until tomorrow and the day after. If they didn't get out of here, their futures included agonizing death.

Cal inclined his head. "Nothing, eh?"

She smiled at him.

"Why are you—"

"Canadian, *eh*?" Deflection and humor. Sometimes that's all one could hope for.

"Hey, watch it. You're outnumbered down here," Matthew warned with a smile.

Alex held up her hands in surrender. She was laughing when Jasper stuck his head out of the burial chamber and then joined them in the main antechamber.

"While it's not good for those who believe in hocus-pocus"—Jasper slid his gaze to Cal, then back to Alex—"the wall says our pharaoh was assassinated and his name was stripped from him. It goes on to say that his spirit would be at unrest for eternity."

Cal rubbed his arms and stared into space.

"Does it say why his name was stripped?" Matthew asked.

"To protect his remains, his treasure, and the world. Now how he died, I can make out: it was his brother who killed him. But I don't think it was just for the throne. There's mention of the pharaoh practicing dark magic."

"Wait a minute. To protect the world? Dark magic?" Matthew assumed a confident stance, all hard lines and rigid body language. "It has to be related to the Emerald Tablets."

"It might not all be about the Tablets, though," Alex said. "It's possible that this pharaoh was buried this far away from the Great Pyramid because he was being shamed. But all the offerings he was given for the afterlife allude to him being revered by the people he'd ruled. So they didn't entirely turn their backs on him."

Cal tapped his foot against the floor. "People do a lot out of fear."

Alex bobbed her head from side to side. "I was thinking more along the lines of people doing a lot for their religion. It was very important in ancient Egypt. And while our pharaoh may have practiced dark magic, he also seemed to have a respect for common Egyptian deities."

"Alex has a point," Robyn said. "They wouldn't fill his chamber with depictions of their gods if he didn't worship them at all."

Alex nodded. "Completely agree."

Jasper motioned for them to follow him back into the burial chamber. Once they were inside, he pointed to the image of a man with the head of a baboon. "There's another depiction of Thoth."

The fact that it was Thoth, a god associated with the Tablets, wasn't lost on her. "He was depicted as an ibis on the map, but this depiction here—" Alex gestured toward the wall "—shows him as A'an, the god of equilibrium. In other words, in a state of physical and emotional calm and balance."

"He had quite the identity crisis going," Cal jested. If jokes helped him deal with his fear, so be it.

"Is there any other mention of the Tablets?" Matthew asked, obviously disregarding his friend's attempt at humor.

"Not that I've come across yet." Jasper paused. "I think it's only a matter of time, though."

"And time is something we're running out of," Cal said in a no-nonsense tone.

"We don't need you to keep reminding us." Alex tried to keep the irritation from dripping into her voice, but she was pretty certain she'd failed. "We're all in the same boat."

"Yeah, and we're going to be in the boat with the scarab," Cal shot back.

Matthew gripped Cal's shoulder. "You'll feel better once you've gotten some rest."

"And something to eat," Cal countered.

"Well, I can't do anything about that."

"We were going to have steak back at the camp tonight," Jasper put out there. "*Barbecued* steak."

Alex sliced a hand across her neck for him to stop there, and Jasper laughed.

"Hey, a man can fantasize," he said, defending himself.

"Oh, yes, he can." Cal licked his lips, and Alex laughed.

She scanned the group of them and settled her gaze on Matthew, whose smile didn't quite touch his eyes.

"I don't know about the rest of you," he began, "but I say we sleep and dream up an exit strategy."

"Sleep? Down here?" Cal's brows shot upward.

Alex was stuck on the *dream up an exit strategy* part. There seemed to be a small spark of hope in his words, and she had a feeling he had something in mind. But given his somber energy, it wasn't promising.

"Sleep might not be a—" Robyn yawned. She shook her head. "Sorry.

I was going to say sleep might not be a bad idea."

"I agree," Alex said.

"If we all go to sleep and one of those cobras attacks, we won't have to worry about waking up," Jasper stated plainly.

"Oh, yes, the snakes," Robyn said, as if she'd forgotten about them.

"We can't just stay up all night," Matthew replied.

Jasper shrugged. "We take turns keeping watch."

Matthew looked at Alex.

"That could work," she said.

"I suggest the Snake Whisperer takes the first shift," Cal said.

"Even though you won't be able to sleep?" Jasper was unrelenting, and Cal looked down at the floor. "Don't worry about it. I was going to volunteer."

"All right, then. It sounds like we have a plan." Alex faced Matthew again, and he still had that grim look on his face. What was he thinking and when would he share it?

Cal spun around. "Where are we going to sleep?"

Robyn walked into the main antechamber and got down on the floor. She lay on her side and curled up her legs. "Right here works." She yawned again.

Matthew sat next to her, and Alex on his other side.

Cal was still standing and pointed to the burial chamber. "Right here? In the room next to the dead guy?"

Alex smiled at him. "You could sleep in the room *with* the dead guy."

"We've been through this, Cal." Robyn patted the floor and flicked off her headlamp. "Sit down."

Alex closed her eyes, her body facing the burial chamber. Had they really come all this way and overcome all they had, to die down here and not be able to share this amazing discovery with the world?

CHAPTER
27

THE OTHERS ALL THOUGHT HE was crazy and overreacting, but Cal felt quite justified in assigning some merit to a pharaoh's curse. After all, right from the beginning of this expedition things had been going wrong. They had gone down into the tunnel to briefly investigate and it collapsed, forcing them to run and then swim for hours. Then had come the snakes. And if all that wasn't bad enough, there was no apparent way out of here.

He sat down, looking at the burial chamber. He could see the sarcophagus from this vantage point. Maybe if they'd just opened the coffin and he'd seen the mummy, he'd be able to get a grip. He would confirm that the pharaoh was nothing but a harmless rotting corpse. As it was, his imagination ran wild, and scenes from the Mummy movies came to his mind's eye all too clearly. Jasper had said the pharaoh's spirit would be at unrest for eternity. Cal got cranky when he didn't get a full eight hours, so he could only imagine how pissed off the dead pharaoh would be.

Matthew turned off his light, and so did Alex, leaving only Cal's and Jasper's, who was still in the burial chamber. There were shadows everywhere. Strange shapes and outlines. The objects towered over him, closing in on him. Shivers ran through him, and he hugged himself.

Dear God!

His heartbeat pounded in his ears, and the hair on the back of his neck was standing up. Was the curse at work or was it his active imagination? Either way, it was giving him a physical and emotional reaction—and he didn't like it one bit.

Through it all, his stomach continued to rumble, seemingly unaffected by his fear. Jasper had said they had been planning to serve steak for dinner back at the camp. He'd focus on that. Grilled to perfection, juicy and pink...his teeth sinking into the meat. As he let his mind slip into the fantasy, his thoughts shifted to the rest of Alex's team. Surely they were working hard to find them and hadn't given up hope that they'd survived the tunnel collapse. He hoped they hadn't anyway. He prayed they'd decided to scout out the area in search of their radio signal.

The radio! That's what he could do. It's not like he could fend off cobras like the Snake Whisperer, but he could push the button on the module intermittently. That wouldn't suck all the juice from the battery, and it could improve their odds of reaching someone on the surface.

"You're going to have to put your light out, Cal," Robyn said. "It's kind of hard to fall asleep with it on."

"It stays on," he replied.

"Why? Do you really think it will protect you from the ghost of the pharaoh or a curse?" Robyn grumbled.

Cal clenched his jaw. "Now you're mocking me."

Robyn laughed and so did Alex and Matthew.

"It's not funny, guys." It really wasn't. He was seriously frightened.

"It is, actually," Alex chimed in. "Trust me when I say he can't do anything to you."

"I'll believe what I want, and you believe what you want." Cal was drawing deep breaths through clenched teeth. "All right?"

"Sure," Alex said. "Whatever makes you happy."

Whatever makes me happy would be to get the hell out of here. But that doesn't seem to be an option...

His gaze went back to the burial chamber, his mind never far from the dead man inside it. A pharaoh who was into black magic. Dread shot up his back. If they thought he was going to actually rest next to the corpse—in the dark—they were all crazy.

He jumped to his feet.

"Where are you going?" Matthew asked.

"I'm going to see if I can reach someone on the surface. I'll turn on the module periodically, say in two-minute increments every ten or fifteen minutes."

Alex sat up. "That's a terrific idea."

"I mean, I can't sleep anyway, so…" And doing something might also fend off the shivers lacing down his spine.

"Do you know how to use it?" Alex asked.

He shrugged. "I just assumed it would be easy to figure out."

Alex told him what buttons to push. "You can switch between calling out over the radio and putting the alert signal on. Just be careful not to drain the battery altogether."

"I've got it." Not that he was sure why she was so concerned about the battery's life. It did them absolutely no good unless they used it to get rescued. Cal took a few steps in the direction of the corridor where the module and antenna were.

"Here." Matthew slipped off his wristwatch. "Take this with you to use for timing."

Cal took Matthew's watch and left the antechamber. He'd been so set on getting away from the dead guy, it wasn't until he reached the base of the staircase that he was clued in to the fact that he was on his own.

He made the sign of a cross, drawing from his Catholic upbringing, but his hands froze partway through. There were many religious symbols in this tomb. What if he insulted the spirits with his display and made them angry?

He took the stairs two at a time, as if by reaching the radio and the seal, he'd have put enough space between him and the spirits. *Ridiculous. They can traverse time and space.*

He gulped, sweat dripping down his back.

He found the module and antenna where they'd left them and breathed a sigh of relief. He didn't know where he'd expected for them to have gone, but he wouldn't put anything past angry gods and spirits at this point.

Sitting down next to the module, he flicked it on, picked up the radio, pressed the transmit button, and said what Alex had earlier. "Jeff Webber, do you read? Over."

Silence.

He repeated the process three times, and each time there was no response.

He set the radio down and pressed the buttons to turn on the alert signal, and he let it run for two minutes. His eyelids were getting heavy as he looked at Matthew's watch, and his eyes were feeling gritty from exhaustion. Something about being in this compact space with his back against a wall had him feeling less afraid of the dead pharaoh. His eyes fell shut.

A little while later, his eyes shot open.

He consulted Matthew's watch. It was one in the morning, and he'd been out for twelve minutes.

"Crap," he muttered and turned off the module.

If he dozed off again, he'd risk draining the battery. He looked back at the watch, taking in the high-tech gadget. It must have cost Matthew a small fortune. Surely, there was some way to set up an alarm on the thing. He fiddled with it until he found a countdown timer. He set it for thirty minutes, and as the numbers ticked down, they served to hypnotize him.

All he could hear was the sound of his breath, and it was getting extremely deep. He closed his eyes and saw Sophie's face. In some ways, he wished that he'd never left her. But even so, for a dying man, he hadn't felt this alive in a long time, either. He was pretty sure he fell asleep with a smile on his face.

CAL STARTLED AWAKE. He looked at Matthew's watch. It was eight in the morning. He'd been out for about seven hours. What happened to the timer? Surely he would have heard it if it had gone off.

Stupid technology.

His eyes landed on the module, and he bit back his criticism. Technology could be the only difference between them living or dying.

He shook his head, hoping the cobwebs would clear, and picked up the radio. "Jeff Webber, do you read? Copy... I mean, over." Copy? Over? Did it really matter?

Seconds passed and nothing.

Cal tried again and waited for a reply, *willing* a reply, but none came.

Don't they say the third time is the charm? He tried again.

"Jeff Webber, do you read? Over."

More silence. Cal's stomach knotted. They were going to die down here. Sophie's promise not to bury him didn't even matter anymore because the expedition would take care of that much.

Then there was a crackle of static.

Cal straightened up. He pressed the transmit button on the hand radio. "Jeff Webber, do you read? Over."

A second later, a jumbled mess of words came back to him.

"Yes!" Cal jumped up. "I have Jeff!" He ran down the corridor with the hand radio, hoping to God it would continue to transmit for a distance from the module. "Jeff, this is Cal. Over."

"Cal, is everyone all right? Over," Jeff came across, clearly this time.

"We're— Everyone wake up!" Cal shouted as he ran into the main antechamber.

Robyn, Matthew, and Alex stirred awake. Jasper was nowhere to be seen.

"What is it?" Robyn sounded groggy and was squinting. "My God, your light—"

"Cal? Alex? Are you there? Copy," Jeff said.

Alex shot to her feet, and Cal passed her the radio, his heart swelling with hope.

"Jeff," she said, "I'm here. Over."

Two beats.

"It's great to hear your voice. Over."

"Yours too. Over."

"Is everyone okay? Over."

"Reda didn't make it. Over." The sadness in Alex's tone was raw.

"Reda's fine. Over."

Tears fell down Alex's cheeks, and she palmed them. "He's fine? Copy?"

"Yes. Now we have to get you out of there. Over."

"Yes!" Robyn cheered. She got to her feet and so did Matthew. Cal felt like someone who was merely observing. He wanted to latch on to hope of a rescue but was afraid to quite yet.

"We'd love that. Over."

"We've triangulated your location and will start digging right away. Over."

Alex hugged the radio to her chest, grinning. She sniffled. "How far are we from base camp? Over."

"We've been on the move all night, hoping to find your signal—"

Alex smiled at Cal, and he remembered her assertion that Jeff wouldn't give up on them.

"You're only about a fifteen-minute drive from where you went down," Jeff continued, "but that's a distance of twelve miles. Over."

Everyone in the tomb went silent for a few moments.

"We found him, Jeff," Alex said. "We are in a pharaoh's tomb. Over."

"Any sign of the Emerald Tablets? Over."

Cal hoped it was a secure line.

"Not exactly. But there is treasure. Over."

"Wonderful. Now just hang tight, and we'll there as fast as we can. Over."

"How far down are we? Over."

"Fifteen feet. It will take hours of intense labor. Over."

"See you soon. Over." Alex shot her fists into the air.

The haze in Cal's mind began to clear, and his stomach rumbled. "I can taste that steak."

Robyn laughed.

Matthew gripped his shoulders. "Me too."

One by one, the three of them turned on their headlamps, lighting up the antechamber.

Jasper came into the room from the corridor that led to the secondary antechamber. "What's going on?"

"Jeff's coming," Alex exclaimed.

"I knew we all just had to calm down, keep our heads," Jasper said teasingly, and Alex hit his arm.

Alex turned to Cal. "We're going to be rescued thanks to you." She hugged him and kissed his cheek.

She backed away, and Cal put a hand to his cheek, smiling.

Robyn nudged his elbow and narrowed her eyes at him.

"I'm just a man," he said playfully, not that he'd ever had any impulse to cheat on Sophie. It just felt good to have done something that had helped. "But it's not all me. Matthew thought to grab the machine when the tunnel was collapsing."

"True, he did." Alex smiled at Matthew.

"So not only did you survive a night in a pharaoh's tomb, but now we're getting rescued," Robyn said to him. She raised an eyebrow. "Still believe in curses?"

He wouldn't dismiss his reservations until they were all safely on the surface. He hesitated just long enough to give Robyn his answer without needing to say a word.

Robyn shook her head with a smile. "He still does."

Cal held up a hand. "Hey, I'm reserving judgment until we get out of here."

"We're being rescued!" Alex did a little dance, holding the radio in the air as if she were toasting with it. Matthew came in close to her, put a hand on her hips, and moved with her.

Cal noticed Robyn watching them. The smile that had been on her face a moment before was gone. It seemed Robyn was still crazy about Matthew. Too bad he seemed too blind to see it for himself.

CHAPTER
28

HOURS HAD PASSED, and Alex was still grinning and practically jumping around Matthew. The professional archaeologist had been replaced by a college cheerleader, and it was a sad display. But Matthew seemed to be lapping it up. Then again, why wouldn't he? Alex was a beautiful and intelligent woman.

"When we get to the surface, what are you going to do first?" Alex asked Matthew.

"I'm going to bow down to the sun," he said.

"What about you, Robyn?" Alex looked straight at her.

"Me?" Robyn glanced at Matthew, who was smiling. "I'm going to celebrate. Yep, that's what I'm going to do." She wished the celebration could involve Matthew on a more personal level. Man, she had to pull herself together. They'd been there, done that.

"Well, we're all going to celebrate," Alex said. "Anything in particular?"

"Eat steak," Robyn offered pithily. Alex's face hardened. "I mean, steak's good," Robyn tossed out, hoping to somehow gloss over her *eat steak* comment. Responsibly, the first thing she should do was find a way to reach her boss and explain to him why she'd been incommunicado.

"And let's not forget champagne." Alex pranced in a circle around Matthew. His eyes were glued to her the entire time.

Gah! Watching them flirt was sickening.

The instant the thought laced through her, the guilt slammed into her. She should be happy for him. After all, they were friends. They traveled the world and uncovered legends together—that was a solid basis for a forever relationship, not romance. Besides, dating and going on quests together would affect their objectivity. There were times when tough decisions needed to be made, and if they were involved romantically, the right choice could be even more difficult to make. No, it was just best that she kept her feelings about Matthew to herself and let him go. That would be the show of real love for him.

But there was a niggling feeling in Robyn's gut. She wasn't sure if she questioned Alex's character or if it was just the fact that she wasn't ready to give herself over to reveling in a rescue just yet. "I have a question about the radio transmitter," she said.

"Shoot," Alex said.

"Does it give off our exact location? Or is it more of an approximate range?" Verbalizing her doubts and concerns turned her stomach. She wanted out of here just as much as the rest of them, but there was a part of her that was a realist. She'd fully give herself over to elation once she saw the light of day.

"It's supposed to provide an exact location."

Supposed to...

That assurance didn't settle well. Enough had happened to them already, and while Robyn prided herself on staying positive, she was struggling right now.

"I can tell you're worried," Alex began, "but Jeff's going to get us out of here."

"You have a lot of confidence," Jasper interjected. Robyn turned to look at him. He had been relatively quiet since Jeff's voice had come over the radio.

Alex arched her brows and crossed her arms. "Is there a reason I shouldn't be?"

"I never said that, but—"

"You don't think we'll be rescued?" Alex served back.

"Any number of things could go wrong." Jasper looked at Cal. "We're supposedly cursed, so..."

Alex rolled her eyes and shook her head as if she were exasperated with Jasper. Robyn, on the other hand, was livid.

"Making fun of someone's feelings is childish," Robyn said as she came to Cal's defense. "If Cal wants to believe in pharaoh's curses, that's his right. And I think all of us have to admit that we haven't had the best of luck since we stepped into that tunnel."

Everyone around her remained quiet. Cal was watching her with a subtle smile on his lips.

"Being a little hypocritical, don't you think?" Matthew asked, calling her out.

She steeled herself. "I was teasing him before, not actually making fun of him." Maybe it was a fine line between the two things, but she'd never said anything to hurt him. But Jasper had come across demeaning, and she wasn't about to stand for it.

"We're only five feet away now. Over," Jeff said.

Alex lifted the radio to her mouth. "Keep us posted. Over."

"Will do. Over."

With that, Jeff clicked off again, and they were back to the silence of the burial chambers. Robyn met Jasper's gaze. He looked exhausted. "You didn't trade off watch with anyone."

"I was fine staying up." Jasper was cut-and-dried. "Besides, you younger people need more sleep than us older dogs."

His metaphor rang false, but she wasn't going to touch it. "So how did you make out?"

"In regard to...?" Jasper asked.

"The snakes? Interpreting more of the hieroglyphics?"

Jasper moved his body, looking down at his legs and the length of his arms. "No bites."

"Well, that's a good thing," Robyn replied.

"Any come close to the antechamber?" Matthew asked, getting involved in the conversation.

Jasper turned to him. "Nope. It was all good."

"Even down in the secondary antechamber?" Cal asked.

Robyn regarded her friend with some confusion, then recalled that's where Jasper had come from.

"There were some there," Jasper said.

"You left us here unattended?" Alex asked sharply.

Jasper put up his hands. "The last place we saw snakes was in the secondary antechamber. I was just making sure none got into the corridor to come up here."

"Humph." Cal concentrated his gaze on Jasper.

"Don't look at me like I've done something wrong." Jasper's brow tensed, and a vertical line formed between his eyes.

"Did you find out any more about the Emerald Tablets' whereabouts?" All of Alex's earlier frivolity was long gone. Her gaze was serious, dark and judgmental.

So did Alex not trust Jasper? Was that at the base of the tension between them? But that wouldn't explain why Alex would bring him on board for her dig.

"I did find more hieroglyphics," Jasper admitted.

Matthew stepped closer to him. "Where?"

"In the hidden room we found. The one with the other staircase."

"You went in there with all those snakes? What if you were bitten?" Alex's pitch hit a higher octave than before.

"Then I would have been screwed." Jasper spoke like a man whose life wouldn't have been on the line, as if he had everything under control. "But I am the Snake Whisperer, remember?" He flashed an arrogant smirk.

Alex shook her head. "Unbelievable."

"What's unbelievable, Alex, is that you think I wouldn't explore down there," Jasper said. "We're in the tomb of a lost pharaoh."

"But we work as a team and move as a team," Alex corrected him.

"No harm was done."

Alex and Jasper locked eyes.

The radio crackled to life again. "A couple more feet. Over," Jeff said.

"Thanks, Jeff. Over," Alex replied, not taking her gaze off Jasper.

Robyn looked at Jasper, too. There was one thing about his story that was nagging at her. She crossed her arms. "I thought you were watching the corridor to make sure snakes didn't come up. So how could you do that from the hidden room?"

Jasper held up his hands. "Everyone's just fine."

Small wrinkles formed in Matthew's brow, a physical tell that he was agitated. "What did the hieroglyphics say?"

"More or less what I've already translated in here."

"Which is it, Jasper? More or less?" Matthew's icy glare lasered in on Jasper.

"Depends on how you look at it. No more on our dead pharaoh here or his love of dark magic." He glanced at Cal.

"What about the Tablets?" Matthew pressed.

"Just that the secret of the Tablets lies with the pharaoh." Jasper gestured haphazardly in the direction of the burial chamber.

"Not much different from the earlier hieroglyphics that said the key to enlightenment lies with the pharaoh," Matthew pointed out.

Jasper nodded. "That's why I said *more or less*."

"We're outside the tomb's entrance. Copy?" It was Jeff coming in over the radio, and they all hurried toward the corridor that led to the stairs and the stone seal.

Alex held the radio to her mouth and hit the button on the side. "Copy."

As she raced down the corridor with the others, Robyn could hear the grinding of stone moving against stone. They were going to survive this, after all.

"Keep back from the entrance," Jeff cautioned. "Copy?"

"Copy," Alex replied, stopping at the base of the stairs, the rest of them piling in behind her.

"The stone is moving. Get back if you're not already. Over."

"We're at a safe distance. Over," Alex assured him.

Light filtered down the stairs, and Robyn's heart felt like it was going to burst. She let out a squeal and had her arms around Alex before she had a chance to think it through. She backed out of the embrace, smiling awkwardly for a moment, but she had been rescued. *They* had been rescued. Now the world could enjoy their discovery. Their brush with death was behind them, and they'd be toasting with champagne and enjoying a feast in no time.

"Oh, I can feel my teeth sinking into that steak," Cal said, as if reading Robyn's mind.

Matthew was grinning. "I'm not gonna lie, it's going to taste amazing!"

Robyn laughed with her two closest friends in the world, not even wanting to imagine life without them. She *did* want to imagine food going into— Her stomach rumbled.

"Oh, someone's hungry," Cal teased.

She narrowed her eyes at him playfully and smacked him in the abdomen. Then she hugged him. Filled with gratitude, she held on to her friend. She let go of him and moved on to Matthew. She sank against him for a few seconds and squeezed him. She pulled back a moment later, a smile on her face as she looked up at him.

"What an adventure this has been," she said.

"You can say that again. And there's more ahead of us," Matthew countered.

Not that he needed to remind her. She figured he was referring to the search for the Tablets, but for her, just the thought of coming back down here and bathing the tomb in light was enough to excite her. She was eager to put her hands on the artifacts as she cleaned and cataloged them. But *after* she had some food and breathed in some fresh air.

CHAPTER
29

THERE WEREN'T WORDS IN THE English dictionary that could completely capture the way Matthew felt as daylight streamed down the staircase. Relieved, ecstatic, exuberant—all of them fell short. But while he was feeling all those things and more, his mind was on the sarcophagus and what they'd find inside.

He'd had a series of odd dreams while he'd slept, and they all had focused on the contents of the coffin. They'd find the pharaoh's remains, he was certain, given the canopic shrine they'd found, but if Matthew were to hide something of great value, putting it in with a dead body would be a pretty safe place. And while Jasper had mentioned that the hieroglyphics in the other room spoke of the Tablets, there hadn't exactly been an earth-shattering reveal as to their whereabouts.

"I heard that people were in need of a rescue," Jeff called down from the entrance to the tomb. With the sunlight at his back, he was a shadow coming down the stairs. A couple of men were close behind him.

"We're here," Alex cried out and hurried toward her site foreman, while the rest of them stayed at the base of the stairs.

"So you did it!" Jeff said to Alex.

"Treasure beyond imagining, Jeff," she started. "Think the scale of King Tut's tomb."

Alex turned around and came back down the stairs, Jeff right behind her.

"That much treasure?" he asked.

Alex was smirking. "Yes, pretty much."

"Sweet mother!" Jeff cried out. He waited a few beats, then added, "Can we see it now? I know you guys just probably want out of here…" Jeff looked around at them, his gaze landing first on Matthew, sweeping across the others, and then ending back on him, as well.

Seeing Jeff's excitement mirror his own reset the impulse to get aboveground as quickly as possible. Maybe it had something to do with the fact that they could leave anytime they wanted to now.

"We can show you," Alex offered. "But if anyone wants to go to the surface, you're free to do so."

Matthew turned to look at Cal, expecting he'd hop on that opportunity, but he shook his head.

"All right." Alex raised her shoulders in delight and wiggled her fingers for Jeff and the other two men to follow. Matthew recognized the men as two of Jeff's workers but couldn't remember their names. In his defense, though, he'd just met them briefly before all hell broke loose.

They stepped out of the corridor into the main antechamber.

Jeff gasped. "Oh my word! This is incredible."

"Isn't it?" Alex smiled.

"And there's a secondary antechamber with more artifacts," Matthew interjected.

"And a treasury?" Jeff asked.

Alex shook her head. "No room that comes off the burial chamber. There was, however, a hidden room behind the secondary antechamber."

"Maybe it was the treasury at one time? It could have been robbed," Jeff suggested.

"I don't think so." Jasper was quick to comment and sounded sure of himself.

Matthew snapped to face Jasper. Tingles raced through him, along with a suspicion that Jasper may have held something back. "Why's that?"

"Just a feeling based more on layout. There were also hieroglyphics in the hidden room we found, and nothing identified the room as a treasury."

Alex stepped next to Jeff. "They did mention the Tablets, though."

Matthew was watching Jasper, not quite sure what to think. He didn't much care for the fact that the man had left them unattended while he took a little side tour.

"But still no sign of them?" Jeff asked.

Alex's face fell. "No."

"Hmm. That's disappointing." Jeff rubbed his jaw. "Did you look inside the sarcophagus?"

"Of course not," Alex fired back, and her shoulders tensed.

"Because you think the lid will be heavy? There are more of us here now. We could all work to lift it off, I'm sure," Jeff said, seemingly oblivious to Alex's offense that they open it at all. "The Tablets could be in there," Jeff added when no one said anything.

To hear someone else conclude the same thing Matthew had thought spurred him to move. "This way."

"Matthew? What are you—" Alex rushed after him and tugged back on his arm.

He stopped moving and turned to look at her.

She scanned his eyes. "What are you doing?"

"I'm with Jeff," he said. "We should open the coffin."

"But it needs to be done the proper way. In a controlled environment at the hands of exp—" Alex's eyes diverted to Jeff, and her words ran dry.

"We are experts," Jeff said. "And the proper way will involve a lot more eyeballs. And that's the last thing we want if the Tablets are in there."

The room lapsed into silence.

"Fine," Alex conceded after some time had passed. "We can try to lift the lid."

"I say it's worth a try," Jeff countered.

Alex's cheeks flushed, and she held up a hand. "We have to carefully move the ushabti out of the way so they don't get damaged, though."

"There are ushabti?" Jeff asked. He didn't seem to be coming from a place of surprise but rather delight.

Alex smiled. "There are some in the main antechamber, but there are a lot of them on the floor around the sarcophagus."

They walked to the burial chamber, and Jeff stopped at the doorway. His gaze went to Cal. "Do we have pictures of this?"

"We do."

"Then let's work on clearing enough ushabti so that we can get into the sarcophagus." Jeff looked at Alex. It should have been her giving directions, but right now she seemed to be okay taking the back seat. Jeff snapped his fingers at his men. "Bring down some lights."

Matthew took the first ushabti and carefully passed it to Alex, who placed it in a corner of the antechamber next to a pile of other artifacts. As he worked farther inside the room, Robyn, Jeff, and Jasper joined him. They passed off the ushabti to Cal and Alex to put aside.

Jeff's laborers returned with some portable lights and aimed them inside the burial chamber.

With the room cleared enough to make room, Matthew, Robyn, Jeff, Jasper, and the two workers positioned themselves around the sarcophagus.

"Cal, get in here, too," Matthew directed his friend. If this lid was anywhere near as heavy as Tut's, they could use all the help they could get.

"Oh, I—"

"Now, Cal."

Cal came into the room and stood next to Robyn.

"We must be very careful with it," Alex said.

Matthew smiled at her and started the countdown. "One…two…three." He lifted his section of the lid and the others did the same. It was certainly heavy, but the group of them were effective. The seal broke, and the lid came free. "Let's set it down *carefully*," he said, intentionally using Alex's word.

What felt like a painstakingly long time later, they had the lid on the floor and he could finally get his first look inside.

Matthew took a deep breath, preparing himself to see another coffin or more than one nested inside, but when he peered down, he was looking right at the mummy. A burial mask covered its face, and its arms were crossed and hands clenched—a mark of royalty.

Matthew stared at the remains of a man who had once undoubtedly been a powerful ruler—one whose name still remained a mystery to them.

"Do we know his identity?" Jeff asked.

Jasper shook his head. "His name was taken from him."

Matthew took a closer look, trailing his gaze over the mummy. His heart sank. "There's no sign of the Emerald Tablets."

Alex straightened up. "There's nothing written inside the lid, either."

Oftentimes coffins were riddled with hieroglyphics and typically contained a cartouche giving the deceased pharaoh's name. But since this one had been stripped of his, Alex's discovery wasn't a surprise.

"Now that we've confirmed the Tablets aren't inside, let's put the lid back on." Alex's tone left no room for dispute.

The group of them did as she instructed.

"Now, we need to get some food and water, and some rest," Alex said, "And we'll come back fresh in the morning to get started."

Matthew wanted to challenge her, but he was exhausted. The uncertainty that they'd lived with over the past day had taken a lot out of him. Plus, he knew she was right.

Alex patted Jeff on the shoulder, and they led the way out of the burial chamber, through the antechamber, up the corridor, and to the staircase.

When Matthew's boots hit the sand, he could have fallen to his knees to worship the sun god. It was hot, and it had to be—he looked at his wrist to find that his watch was missing. Cal must still have it. "Hey, Cal, what time is it?"

"I don't— Oh." Cal came toward him with the watch dangling from his fingers and handed it to Matthew. "It's just after four in the afternoon."

He'd known it had been awhile, but there was something about doing the math. "Wow. We were down there for over twenty-four hours."

He looked around the area. There were two Jeeps, various lighting apparatuses, shovels, rope, and tools set up in the area, but there was also a shelter, a small table, and a couple of chairs. Jeff's other two workers, who hadn't come down to see the tomb, were seated there. So base camp was, for the moment, unattended. The workers stood and came over to them, handing out water bottles and protein bars. Matthew immediately unwrapped his and took a large bite.

Alex came up next to him with a mouthful herself. There was disappointment in her eyes. "I'm sorry we didn't find the Tablets."

"Yet." He smiled at her. Despite the odds, he was determined to remain positive. After all, there were a lot of artifacts down there that they hadn't yet inspected. And with the piles being so high, especially in the main antechamber, it was possible the Tablets were hidden there somewhere. "It doesn't mean they're not down there."

Alex smiled at him. "I like to think they are, too."

And while her voice sounded light and positive, Matthew realized another danger was coming to the forefront. There was a lot in the tomb alluding to the Tablets, and if that got out… They really were racing against the clock. Logically, he knew they needed rest, though. Still, while his physical hunger was starting to abate with the protein bar, another hunger needed satisfying. He couldn't wait to put his hands on the Emerald Tablets.

CHAPTER
30

ROBYN'S STOMACH WAS A BALL of knots, but she kept pushing the food into her mouth anyway, as if by eating faster, tomorrow would get there sooner. She was also trying to offset the champagne that had gone straight to her head. And she'd only had one small glass before changing over to water.

"Damn, this is good!" Cal shoveled another forkful of steak into his mouth.

"You might want to take it easy," Alex cautioned. "You could upset your stomach."

"The only thing my stomach is upset about is that it went hungry for so long," Cal said with cheeks full of food.

Alex laughed, and so did Robyn and Matthew. Jasper remained stone-faced. Jeff and the four laborers had stayed to guard the dig site while the rest of them were at base camp stuffing their faces and celebrating. Before the champagne and food, they'd all washed up and taken showers. Robyn had also checked her e-mail, and her boss had sent seven messages. She had called with the sat phone and explained why she hadn't replied to any of them. He had been surprisingly empathic about the entire ordeal she'd been through. Apparently, it only took a life-threatening situation to get that out of him.

Jasper put down his fork, his gaze straight on Alex. "I'm going to head back after dinner."

"I'd like for all of us to get a night's sleep before—"

"I'm fine, Alex," he assured her. "I just want to go back and get the tomb rigged with lighting so it's ready for morning. I can spend the night there, too, watch over it with the others."

Alex's jaw tightened. "Jeff and his men have it under—"

"I'm fine, and I'm going," he ground out.

Alex's cheeks flushed with anger. "You'll leave us without a Jeep."

"I'll send Andres and Danny back for the night. Worst case, someone will come back and pick you up in the morning."

"Fine."

Robyn was curious why, as the one in charge of the dig, Alex was letting Jasper call the shots. Maybe it had something to do with the conflict between the two of them and Alex didn't want to get into it in front of everyone. But if Robyn went along with Jasper, she could buddy up to him and maybe find out what had Alex and Jasper pitted against each other. She wouldn't be getting that out of Alex, who was too busy sticking to Matthew's hip.

"I wouldn't mind going with him," Robyn said.

Her declaration warranted a stern look from Matthew. "You should rest, too," he said.

"I appreciate your concern, but like Jasper, I'll be fine." Matthew's face didn't soften, but she trudged on. "You know being involved with an expedition like this has been a dream of mine for a long time." As she spoke, she started to feel miffed. Why was she defending herself to him? This was her life, not his. "I'm going with you, Jasper."

Jasper nodded and got up. "We'll leave in a bit, then? Say half an hour?"

"Sounds good." She stuffed another bite of food in her mouth, then set her fork down. She really needed to stop eating for the sake of eating.

Jasper left the tent.

"Guess it will just be the three of us," Alex said, nudging Matthew's shoulder with her own and smiling.

The laborers who'd be coming back weren't entering into Alex's equation, and it was apparent she wished it were just the *two* of them.

"Guess so." Matthew wasn't smiling, though, and his gaze was on Robyn.

She pushed her plate away and tried desperately to rein in her temper. "What?"

"Are you sure you don't want to spend the night here, and get up and at it well rested?"

"I'm an adult, Matt." She lowered her eyebrows, silently petitioning him to back off.

He eventually nodded.

Alex was studying her, and Robyn could only imagine what was going through her mind. Maybe she was silently celebrating that Robyn would be a twenty-five-minute drive away. Not that her presence was stopping Alex from flirting with Matthew.

"I just can't wait to get down there and light up that place," Robyn said, hating herself for smoothing over her earlier attitude. It only made sense she'd be eager to get to work on the tomb.

"I can't wait to see it that way, either," Alex said.

"I look forward to finding the Tablets," Matthew added.

Cal bulged his cheeks and patted his belly. "Whew, I think I'm done."

Robyn chuckled. Leave it to Cal to lighten a tense mood. "I hope it stays down for you."

"It will." Cal grinned like a cat who had just eaten a mouse, or in this case, the man who had just eaten a chunk of cow.

"Well, I should probably grab some things to take with me." Robyn got up just as Jasper slipped back inside the tent.

He grabbed some water bottles and then went over to a locked cabinet. He took out an assault rifle, which she guessed was an AK-something. And while Robyn didn't know a lot about guns, she knew it hurt like a son of a bitch to get shot.

"To protect the site, the men need to be armed," Alex explained, even though it wasn't necessary. They'd been through this before—back when they had first arrived at the dig site.

"I understand that," Robyn said. And she did, but that didn't stop her stomach from becoming a mess of fluttering butterflies. She was familiar with how to fire a gun, of course. Matthew often had them cart along a handgun on expeditions. It didn't mean she liked them or ever adjusted to being around them.

"Just be careful out there." Alex was being serious, and it shifted Robyn's mind from guns to cobras.

But she'd be fine. She took a deep breath. She'd have the Snake Whisperer with her. "I will be." She patted the table and passed one more look to Matthew, but he was leaning in toward Alex and laughing about something. Robyn shook her head and left the main tent, happy to be putting a little space between herself and them.

She grabbed a change of clothes, her pillow, and her sleeping bag from her tent and put them into her backpack. Jasper was waiting for her next to the Jeep by the time she got there.

"Sorry to hold you up."

Jasper didn't say anything, just got behind the wheel and turned on the vehicle. She tossed her bag onto the back seat and hopped into the passenger seat.

She looked over at him. "I thought I was the only one crazy enough to be in a hurry to go back."

Jasper slid her a sideways glance. "We're not crazy. We're smart." He looked forward again, and his scowl indicated he didn't feel much like talking.

So Jasper was the strong, silent type. He wasn't the first she'd run across, and he wouldn't be the last. She wasn't going to let him intimidate her.

"Do you think that Alex is crazy for holding off until tomorrow?"

Jasper's scowl deepened.

"You don't agree with her?" Robyn pressed harder, keeping her tone conversational.

"She's the boss around here." Jasper was staring intently ahead.

Robyn wasn't going to point out that he'd come across as the one in charge at dinner.

The Jeep rocked as Jasper drove over the dunes at a fast speed. It had her reaching for the roll bar.

"A find like this and she wants to sit around? We're talking about the Emerald Tablets," Jasper said. "Once word gets out about them, we won't have enough manpower—or firepower—to hold off the outsiders."

Robyn noted how he'd said *once* word gets out. "You think other people are going to find out we're looking for them?"

"I think too many people know already." He punched the gas, and the tires spun, searching for traction.

"You're talking about us."

"No offense, but yeah." The first part hinted at peace, but the latter part demolished it. He had a huge problem with them being here. Yet most of his derision had seemed projected at Cal until now.

"Are you worried we'll share the find with someone?"

Jasper looked over at her. "Your friend is snapping pictures all the time. He does that for a living. You expect me to believe he's not sharing his work online?"

"Not something like this," she spat. Now it was her turn to be angry.

Jasper pulled back. "I didn't mean to offend you."

It was the second time he'd made that claim in less than two minutes. "But you did. We're professionals. We know what's at stake when it comes to the Emerald Tablets and how their discovery—if they wind up in the hands of the wrong people—could destroy the world. Trust me when I say that's not something I—or any of us, including Cal—take lightly."

Jasper remained stoic, but he made a couple of rough adjustments with the wheel that jostled her like a ragdoll and had her wishing that she hadn't eaten so much.

Robyn put a hand on her stomach. "Is this why you're mad at Alex?"

He glanced over at her. "Who said I'm mad at Alex?"

He was a terrible actor. He wouldn't even get cast in a B-movie.

She raised an eyebrow. Jasper wasn't going to budge. "Fine, you're not going to talk? It's obvious you're upset with each other."

"We're not upset with each other."

She rolled her eyes. "He said through gritted teeth…"

Jasper looked at her again. "Do you really think it was a coincidence that Alex called up Matthew after all these years?"

"I'm not sure what you mean by that."

Jasper snapped his jaw shut. "I've probably said too much."

"Please, tell me what you mean," she pleaded.

"Your pal has quite the reputation in the archaeological community. Actually, he has a reach beyond that. He's known in certain circles as 'the Legend Hunter.'" He made air quotes with one hand.

Robyn turned her body toward him. "This is my first time hearing that."

Jasper hitched his shoulders. "Well."

"Well, what?" Surely, he couldn't just leave her hanging like that. But that's what he did.

In fact, the rest of the trip passed in deafening silence. Of course, she had no idea what this man was thinking, but he was definitely hiding something. She continued to mull over the conversation they'd just had. She ripped it apart, including the words *We're not upset with each other*. Did that mean only one of them was the pissed-off party? And how did that factor in to Matthew's reputation as "the Legend Hunter"?

Jasper parked beside the other Jeep, and Jeff walked toward them, brows arched in curiosity.

"What are you guys doing here?" Jeff asked. But his gaze trailed over Jasper to Robyn, so more specifically, it seemed he didn't understand why *she* was there.

"I'm just here to help," she said.

"You're eager to go back down?" Jeff shook his head. "You're too pretty to be nuts." It was said in a playful manner, but it grated nonetheless.

"This is too important a discovery to put off until tomorrow."

"I'd have to agree," Jeff conceded. "Well, make yourself comfortable. But there are only a couple tents for sleeping. You'll have to bunk with someone. Unless you want to sleep with the mummy again." He chuckled.

And the snakes…

"Ah, I'll pass on that one," she said.

"Good, then you'll share with someone."

"That's fine." As soon as she said the words, she realized that everyone here was male. It had her wishing for Cal's camera to hide behind.

Jasper pulled a tent from the back of the Jeep. "She can sleep in this one."

Jeff gestured to him. "Ah, good thinking."

"What about you, though?" Robyn turned to Jasper. "You stayed up all last night."

"I'll sleep when I'm dead," Jasper said drily but sprinkled in a brief smile. "And this is for you." He extended a handgun toward her. "You know how to fire one, don't you?"

"I do, but—"

"It's for your protection. I can't be around to save you from every snake."

She took the gun from Jasper.

Then he addressed Jeff. "Alex needs you to send a couple of guys back to base camp so they have a Jeep for the morning. I said Andres and Danny would probably go back."

"Sure, that's fine," Jeff said. "I'll let them know."

Jasper headed off in the direction of the two sleeping tents. He stopped once he got there and set down the tent he'd brought.

"It's not just snakes you have to watch out for," Jeff cautioned. "There's lot that can kill you out here at night. Anyhow, make yourself comfortable."

There's a lot that can kill you and *make yourself comfortable* weren't exactly two things she'd pair together…

"We've already rigged up most of the lighting," Jeff went on. "The find is incredible."

So she'd been able to talk with Jasper and get away from Alex and Matthew. And now she didn't need to work tonight. Talk about win-win-win.

She looked toward the entrance. "I can only imagine it's breathtaking down there."

"Well, no need to imagine. Go down and take a look around. Just don't touch anything." With that, Jeff walked off toward the open-sided tent.

"Oh, Jeff?" she called out. He stopped walking and turned around. "How's Reda? I know you told Alex that he made it out of the tunnel…"

"He got out just as the entrance collapsed. He's a lucky man." Jeff turned back around and spoke over a shoulder. "He's going to be here tomorrow to look at the find."

Of all the men to survive unscathed, and without the drama the rest of them went through… That right there debunked the validity of mummies' curses. If anyone would have one on their head, it would be Reda, who had unearthed several tombs in his lifetime.

She headed toward the staircase when one of the laborers stepped in front of her. He was tall and gangly, but all muscle. He had black eyes and tanned skin, and an assault rifle harnessed across his chest. She couldn't remember his name.

"Hi, ma'am," he said.

"Hi. Andres, right?"

"That's right, ma'am," he said with a smile.

One *ma'am* she could get past, but two in a row? Ouch.

"Ah, mine is—"

"Oh, I remember your name, pretty woman. It's Robyn." He wasn't leering at her, but a mild discomfort made her cringe inside anyway.

She pointed toward Jasper, thinking maybe she'd go with a change in plans. She didn't really want to go down into the tomb with Andres, so maybe she could help Jasper with the tent. But when she looked at him, he was finished with that already.

Her gaze went back to Andres—more specifically to his weapon. He lifted it from his chest to show her. "It's just in the case of grave robbers. We've got to protect what's ours."

A term any Egyptologist was well familiar with, but one she'd never heard used firsthand.

She looked over the makeshift camp, at the six men she was here with. Essentially, they were all strangers—and armed ones, at that—but on the upside she was away from Matthew and Alex. And she was here with a pharaoh's tomb at her disposal. Not very many people could say that.

"Well, I'm gonna—" She jacked a thumb toward the tomb's entrance and left Andres.

With each step she took into the earth, a creeping weight pressed down on her shoulders. It wasn't from thinking about snakes but rather the weaponry that was involved with securing the find. Speaking of, she looked down at the gun in her own hands and hoped she'd never have to use it—on a reptile, animal, or otherwise. But with her mind on life and death, her conversation with Jasper came back to her, including his mention of Matthew being "the Legend Hunter" and his allegation that Alex had invited Matthew here due to that reputation. Finally, it sank in. Jasper hadn't come right out and said it, but Alex was using Matthew.

CHAPTER

31

ROBYN WAS PROBABLY OUT AT the site by now, and Cal went back to packing food away. Matthew wondered where his friend was putting it.

"I thought you said you were done," Matthew said, then half-laughed and looked at Alex.

Cal narrowed his eyes at him and crammed another forkful into his mouth. "I *thought* I was done." He hitched his shoulders. "I wasn't."

Alex quirked an eyebrow at Matthew. "Do Canadians have a habit of speaking with their mouths full, or is this specific to Cal?"

"Oh, that's classic Cal."

Cal swallowed, and it looked like something the size of a rodent slid down his throat.

Matthew laughed, but Cal didn't give any indication of being amused. It turned Matthew's thoughts somber. They'd survived by pure luck, as far as he was concerned. So many delicate variables had aligned to make their rescue possible. If anything had been different, they wouldn't be here now. He lifted his champagne glass. "To surviving."

Cal lifted his glass without relinquishing his fork. Alex clinked her glass to Matthew's, then Cal's. "To finding the Emerald Tablets," Alex said.

Boy, could he drink to that. He tipped back his glass and emptied it.

Thinking about how close they were to the Tablets was almost painful. His ever-increasing anticipation had yet to be satisfied, leaving an ache in his chest. The hidden room they'd discovered taunted him. It had been empty, save the snakes, and led to a secondary staircase. What was its purpose? Did it have something to do with the Tablets? Where did the stairs go? What if Jasper knew something he wasn't telling others? He'd been the only one to actually enter the hidden room, and he had been in an awful hurry to get back out to the site. And he took Robyn along with him.

Matthew got to his feet and rubbed his jaw.

"What is it?" Alex sat back, drawing up one of her legs and resting her foot on the bench.

"I'm just thinking about the empty room we found and wondering why it was there." He wasn't going to say everything on his mind just yet.

"It was another exit," she said.

He shook his head. "Nah, I think there was more to it."

Alex put her leg down, and her brow wrinkled in confusion. "What are you saying? You think it has something to do with the Tablets?"

"Well, that and..." He paced a few steps. "What if they're hidden in there somewhere?"

"It was just an empty room. We both saw that." She was watching him as if he'd lost his mind.

"I remember what I saw, but it's hard to get a good look at something when it's mostly dark and you're at a distance."

"Jasper already told us what he found in that room." The set of Alex's jaw told Matthew she was confident that he had disclosed everything. It turned out keeping quiet about Jasper was probably the right call—at least until he determined where Jasper's loyalties lay.

Cal belched loudly. Normally, that wouldn't impress the ladies. But Alex was laughing, and Matthew found himself smiling. He loved the way her nose crinkled up and her eyes sparkled when she was amused.

"What? It's a natural bodily function," Cal said, defensive.

"Yeah, for a caveman." Matthew winked at Alex.

"Ahem." Cal cleared his throat. "Can I talk to you for a minute?"

Matthew nodded. "Fire away."

"In private."

"Ah, sure." He turned to Alex. "I'll be right back."

Cal led the way out of the tent. He let out another belch and rubbed his stomach. Surely his friend hadn't called him out here to ask for antacids. "What is it?"

Cal's eyes were ablaze. "I'm tempted to hit you upside the head."

Heat gripped Matthew's chest as aggravation sparked within him. "What? Why?"

Cal shook his head.

Matthew splayed his hands out in front of him. "What did I do?"

"Robyn's out in the desert…at night…with strangers. *Male* strangers, may I add."

"They're not strangers," Matthew fired back, and guilt snaked through him, especially given his earlier doubts about Jasper.

A pulse ticked in Cal's jaw. "I should have gone with Robyn. We don't really know anything about them other than their names."

"But Alex does."

"Ah, Alex." Cal threw his hands in the air.

Matthew shifted his weight. "I'm not a mind reader, Cal. What's this about?"

Cal stared at him pointedly. "Do you know why Robyn volunteered to spend the night out there?"

"This is a find of a lifetime and something she's dreamed about—"

"Don't play stupid."

That turned Matthew's temper up to a low boil. "Enlighten me."

"She didn't want to watch you carrying on with Alex."

"Come on. *Carrying on* with her? We're old friends." He squared his shoulders, insulted.

"Old friends who never got to be more than that."

The hairs rose on the back of Matthew's neck, along with his temperature. "Are you being serious right now? You're telling me that Robyn has a problem with Alex and me, and that's why she went back to the site?"

Cal stared at him but said nothing. He didn't have to; it was written all over his face.

"There's no reason my attraction to Alex should affect Robyn at all," Matthew said. "We're *friends*."

"She loves you." Cal's tone carried an inferred *duh!*

"As a friend. Just like I—"

"That's not what I'm saying, and you know it."

Matthew raked a hand through his hair. "Wow, just speak your mind."

"Well, it's the truth," Cal said, voice raised.

"She's dating; I'm dating. If you remember, we tried the whole romantic relationship thing and failed miserably."

"And you say I'm the dramatic one? 'Failed miserably'? Come on." Cal pursed his lips. "It was just the timing."

"Yeah, well, timing is everything." Just like how they got lucky being rescued. Cal had just happened to have the radio on at the right time.

"Ah, I see." Cal smirked and bobbed his head. "And now that Alex's fiancé is out of the way—"

"The timing with her is better." Matthew gritted his teeth.

"So the timing is better with Alex, but what about with Robyn? Maybe it's time to be with Robyn now."

Matthew's breath hitched. It would be a dream if that were the case. But he knew better. They worked better as friends. After all, wouldn't it complicate the hell out of everything if they ever were to become more again?

"Nothing to say to that, eh?" Cal pressed his lips. "I just wish you and Robyn would stop fooling yourselves. I hate seeing two of my best friends torn up because they're both too damn stubborn to admit their feelings for each other."

"Oh, we've admitted to them...*in the past.*" And it had happened all because Matthew had slipped and called her *baby* when she'd been shot.

His mind went back to the runway in Toronto when they'd returned home after finding the City of Gold.

"You know how I feel about you, Robyn."

She angles her head back to gaze into his eyes. "And you know how I feel."

He detects the softness in her tone, the fact that she feels the exact same way, but there is also sadness and regret there, too.

"I know it's not our time right now," he says.

Robyn shakes her head, and with it, she spears his heart.

"We're in the past," he blurted out, coming back to the present. "Robyn and I are friends, and that's all." Forget a simmer, his temper had escalated to a hard, vigorous boil. "And if you'll excuse—"

"She went out in the desert, Matthew, with snakes, scorpions, and

God knows what else just to get away from you and Alex. Think about that." Cal stormed off in the direction of his tent, leaving Matthew to do exactly that.

While he could have stood there, contemplating all the ways he'd messed up with Robyn, he'd end up coming back to the same conclusion he had so many times before: their friendship was everything to him, and he didn't want to risk screwing it up. What if they tried again and things didn't work out? Then where would they be? Would they be able to salvage any sort of relationship at that point? He'd rather have her as a friend than risk not having her at all.

"Matt?"

He turned to see that Alex had come outside. "Is everything all right?" she asked.

He pressed on a smile. "Yeah, everything's good. Do you want another glass of champagne?"

Alex smiled at him. "Sounds good to me." She spun to go inside the tent again, and he grabbed her arm, and she turned to face him.

He had to forget about Robyn, about the way her flesh had felt under his fingertips, about the light in her eyes when she'd spoken of loving him. And even though all this had been a while ago, he could conjure up the memories as if they'd happened mere moments ago. It hurt too much to dwell on, and it really was best for Robyn—and for him—if they just buried that part of their lives.

He looked at Alex and let his eyes fall to her lips, then moved toward her. His mouth met hers, and she melted against his body.

CHAPTER
32

THERE WAS SOMETHING TO BE said for riding through the desert in a Jeep with the top off and the breeze sweeping across your face. Matthew breathed in deeply, appreciating both his surroundings and his company. He looked over at Alex, who was driving. Cal was in the back seat and would frown on the physical contact, but Matthew reached for Alex's hand anyhow. At that moment, the vehicle dipped, drastically listing left, then right, then left again. It was like being on a ship in a storm. He ended up gripping the roll bar behind Alex's head to brace himself.

He looked back at Cal, and his arms were wrapped around his stomach.

"Not feeling so well?" Matthew asked.

Cal moaned. "I think I ate too much last night."

"We tried to tell you," Alex said.

Matthew turned back around, though he was tempted to give his friend an I-told-you-so smirk. Not that he'd been the one to caution him directly, but Cal had been advised to take it easy.

Matthew's hand was still on the bar behind Alex, and she glanced over at him and smiled. Her expression carried the hint of a secret between them. They hadn't slept together last night, but they had kissed—and more than once. After another small glass of champagne, they'd called it a night and headed their separate ways. It had been due to her willpower more than his own.

But he'd slept soundly and woken up feeling great and ready to go. It was a good thing, too, because they had a long day ahead of them. The plan was to stay at the site the entire day. They'd even packed protein bars to tide them over until dinner. And worst case, someone could always run back to the main tent for more food.

He was eager to return to the tomb and explore that hidden room more closely. That was, as long as the snakes were gone. But he knew the others would appreciate his help cleaning and cataloging artifacts, so he'd help out there, too.

Even if they came out of this not finding the Emerald Tablets, or even uncovering a substantive clue as to their whereabouts, they had found an unnamed pharaoh's tomb. That alone was something that would make history. But he had to admit that he'd be greatly disappointed if, in the end, the Emerald Tablets were never recovered. He'd been fascinated with them for years, ever since that spark of interest had been ignited while he had been getting his undergraduate degree. His archaeology professor had worked hard to drill the Tablets out of his head, telling him not to get so caught up in myth. He'd encouraged him, instead, to focus on "real history," as he'd put it. And he'd gone on to do that for a while, but finding them would provide him with some sort of justification for hanging on to the legend for all these years—even if his professor never found out about the find.

Alex slowed the vehicle, and Matthew looked ahead. Robyn, Seth, and Timal were huddled around the back of the other Jeep. Their movements were frantic. Robyn was hugging herself and shaking her head. Jasper stepped out of the tomb, holding a hand to his forehead and shielding himself from the sun. There was no sign of Jeff, but he could have been in one of the chambers.

"Hurry, Alex, hurry," Seth yelled.

Matthew looked over at her. "What's going on?"

"Good question." She parked next to the other Jeep and got out. Matthew followed.

"What is—" Alex stopped speaking.

The workers had stepped back, revealing Jeff in the back of the Jeep. Sweat was beaded on his face and forehead, and his eyes were rolled back in his head. His mouth gaped open and shut as if he wanted to say something but didn't have the strength.

"He was bitten by a cobra," Timal said.

Alex took Jeff's hand, worry in her eyes, though she was clearly trying not to panic. "Was he given the antivenom?" she asked.

Neither of the workers answered.

"He...he was, I think," Robyn said.

Matthew glanced at Robyn. She was barely holding herself together. She was trembling and biting down on her bottom lip. He put an arm around her for support.

"We've got to get him to a hospital. Now." Alex paused. Everyone was still. "What are you waiting for? Go!"

Seth dipped his head and got into the driver's seat, and Timal got in the passenger seat.

Alex was still holding Jeff's hand. Her chin was quivering. "Hang in there, buddy. You can pull through this. If anyone can—"

The engine started, but Alex hadn't let go of Jeff's hand yet. Cal stepped in and gently pulled her back.

Matthew watched on helplessly, knowing that Jeff's chances of survival were slim. He might have been given antivenom, but the nearest hospital was easily two and half hours from here.

Robyn was quaking beneath his arm, and he turned her toward him and enveloped her in a hug. They were so close that his lips brushed her forehead. He pinched his eyes shut. "It will be all right."

She backed out of the embrace and shook her head. She was looking past him, and Matthew followed the direction of her gaze to Jasper.

Matthew left Robyn and went over to him. "How did this happen?"

Jasper took a deep, heaving breath. His eyes glazed over. "I looked away for one second and..."

Alex stepped up next to Jasper. "You were with him when it happened?"

"No."

"This isn't your fault," Matthew assured him.

"Weren't you sticking together down there?" Alex's brow knotted, and her face was all hard lines and shadows, making it clear that she figured someone was to blame. "How many times do I have to—"

"He's the foreman," Jasper spat. "He knows the rules."

"Now you're blaming *him* for getting bit?" Alex gritted her teeth.

Matthew put his arms around Alex, hoping to calm her. But her shoulders were heaving and there was fire in her eyes. The sound of retching had him looking around. Cal was bent over next to the remaining Jeep.

Just perfect!

"I don't think he even knew I was holding his hand." Alex's gaze was on the horizon where the Jeep carrying Jeff was getting farther and farther away. Her eyes filled with tears, and she licked her lips.

Matthew didn't say anything but pulled her closer to his side. Sometimes silence was better than talking. And it was definitely better than saying the wrong thing at a time like this.

"I should have gone with them to the hospital." She shook her head. "I can't believe this happened."

Again, there was nothing he could really say. Any assurances would fall flat.

Alex looked directly at Jasper. "Where was he bit?"

"Seth told me he was in the hidden room we found," Jasper replied.

"So you don't know for sure?" she countered.

"I can't be everywhere," Jasper ground out.

Alex's face became bright red. "How can you be so blasé about this?"

Matthew gripped her tighter, and the glare she gave him was blistering. But she seemed close to hauling off and hitting Jasper. Matthew held eye contact with her, and eventually, she turned and fell against him.

She balled up a fistful of Matthew's shirt. He held her tightly, wishing to suck the poison of this tragedy from her system. He cupped the back of her head with one hand as she leaned her head against his chest.

Matthew looked over at Robyn. She was kicking at the sand, and her eyes were full of tears. Everyone knew Jeff's fate had been decided the moment he had been bitten. And even though Matthew hadn't known Jeff for long, he still had a knot in his chest. The incident had cast a dark cloud over the expedition, and really, it could have been any one of them. Heck, the five of them should technically still be buried. Living was about beating the odds. So maybe…

He rubbed Alex's back and pulled out of the embrace. "Keep being your optimistic self."

"Why would she?" Jasper scrunched up his face and gestured wildly toward the entrance of the tomb. "He was bitten by one of the most poisonous snakes in the world."

"He was given antivenom," Matthew served back. "Shouldn't that be worth something?"

Jasper clenched his jaw, shook his head, and walked off.

Alex threw her hands up in the air. "I can't believe him right now."

Matthew watched after Jasper, trying to figure out what was going through the man's mind. But Matthew knew that if he had been out here, he would have felt responsible, especially if he prided himself on being the Snake Whisperer.

Matthew closed the distance between him and Robyn. "How are you holding up?" It was such a stupid question, really. It was obvious just looking at her that she wasn't doing well.

She lifted her head. "I was in the antechamber looking at some artifacts and all I heard was Seth yelling, 'He's been bit.'"

"So Seth was with him when it happened?" Matthew asked.

"I think so? But I'm not sure."

Matthew wondered why Seth hadn't mentioned that to Alex when they'd first arrived, but maybe in the rush of everything that was happening, it hadn't occurred to him.

Cal started retching again.

"I think we should go back to base camp," Matthew said, feeling he needed to be the voice of reason. "Cal's not feeling well, and with Jeff..." He stopped talking. To think he had been in such a hurry to get back inside the tomb. Now he was ready to walk away.

"I'm going to the hospital." Alex's face was a mask of grief. "I should have gone with him."

Matthew understood. She was probably feeling she had somehow sealed his fate by not going along. "You want company?"

"I'd love it." Alex's gaze slid to Robyn. "You must be scared. I know you hate snakes to begin with."

"I'm fine," Robyn said gruffly and walked off toward Cal.

Matthew wasn't sure what that had been all about. Was it what Cal had tried to point out to him last night but he'd been too stubborn to accept? Was Robyn jealous of the connection between him and Alex? Then again, given what had happened, his ego must be involved for him to even think Robyn's coolness had anything to do with him.

"Jasper can stay here to watch the site," Alex said. "Your friends can, as well, if they want, or we could drop them off at base camp."

"I'll let you know." Matthew approached Cal and Robyn. Cal was holding his stomach, and Robyn was looking away from Matthew. "Are you going to be all right?" Matthew asked Cal.

Cal waved a dismissive hand. "I'll be fine. I think it's just that the champagne didn't agree with me. All that bubbly has made me—" Cal started gagging and covered his mouth.

Matthew turned away, feeling his own nausea coming on.

"It's okay, I was able to hold that one…back." Cal's voice sounded thick with saliva.

Ick.

"Well, we're headed to the hospital. You can come with us, get dropped off at base camp—"

"I'll stay here," Robyn interrupted. "I'm assuming that Jasper will be here to watch over the site?"

"Uh-huh," Alex replied, coming in behind Matthew.

He stared at Robyn, hoping to draw her eyes to him, but it was as if she was looking everywhere else but at him.

"What about you, Cal?" Matthew asked. "I'm assuming you want to go to base camp?"

Cal swiped a hand over his mouth. "No thanks. I'll stay here with Robyn."

Matthew wished he could say something to change their minds. He wasn't too keen on Jasper, but Cal and Robyn both seemed firm in their decisions. "You're sure you'll be fine?"

"Yep." Cal burped. "I'm feeling better already."

The smell of puke wafted to Matthew's nose and had him looking down. He cringed. Cal should be feeling better since his stomach contents were on the desert floor—and only about ten inches to the right of Matthew. He stepped back a bit.

"What exactly happened anyway? I only caught bits and pieces in the midst of…" Cal gestured to the ground, but there was no way Matthew was looking at the vomit again.

"Jeff was bitten by a cobra, and he's probably not going to make it," Robyn said, withholding all tact.

Matthew regarded her, not sure who she was at the moment. "We don't know that."

"We don't?" Robyn shot back. "It seems quite likely to me."

No one said anything. Alex's face was blank.

Matthew put a hand on Alex's back. "Okay, let's go." They shuffled a few feet, and Matthew felt compelled to confirm yet again that his friends were good to stay. "The hospital is quite a distance away. You're still good to—"

"I'm fine," Robyn said and walked off. She was surprisingly believable as an ice princess.

Matthew looked at Cal. "And you?"

He lifted his camera. "I'm going to take some pictures."

Robyn turned around and walked a few feet backward. Her gaze was on Matthew, and her eyes were a storm. "Be safe." Her sentiment came out curt, but Matthew took it as sincere. She flicked a glance at Alex, then resumed walking forward, headed toward the tomb's entrance. Cal trudged after her.

"You too." Matthew wasn't sure if they heard him, but he was lost as to what Robyn's attitude toward Alex was about. It had to be more than his attraction to her. "All right, it looks like it's just the two of us."

Alex nodded. "Looks like."

Matthew walked around to the passenger side of the Jeep and looked over a shoulder as he got in. Robyn and Cal were nowhere to be seen, so they must have already gone underground. He had a sick feeling in the bottom of his gut, and he wasn't sure if it was because a man's life was in the balance or if his friendship with Robyn might be, too.

CHAPTER
33

It was taking all Alex's resolve not to just break down altogether. Jeff most certainly had one foot in the grave. His wife and daughters would be left without a husband and father. Her own grief mingled with sympathy for them. A heavy weight sank in her stomach and an ache settled in her chest. And as much as she prided herself on being optimistic, she had a wrenching feeling in her gut that told her this time all the wishful thinking in the world wouldn't do an ounce of good.

Matthew was holding her hand, and she felt like such a traitor. Given Robyn's bitterness toward her, Jasper must have opened his mouth and told her why she'd brought them here. There was clear judgment in her eyes, anyhow. And yet, as she sat here, the man who'd she'd brought in to bring her expedition fame—and by extension, bolster her own reputation—was the only one truly supporting her. She didn't deserve him.

She slipped her hand out of his. "It's hot," she offered as an explanation and tossed out a brief smile.

"Say that again." Matthew wiped his brow.

She tried to concentrate on driving, but her mind was a jumbled mess. Maybe this was what she deserved for withholding her true intentions. Maybe if she'd just come out and told Matthew she wanted to use his fame in some archaeological circles, he'd have been agreeable. Then, at least, there wouldn't be any secrets between them now, no hidden agenda.

She glanced over at him. He was watching the landscape, and given the set of his mouth, he was deep in thought. It was probably about Robyn.

Alex shook her head, willing herself to let go of this competitive inclination she had toward Robyn, as if Matthew was a trophy to be won. Besides, none of it mattered now. Jeff was fighting for his life, and all her energy needed to be focused on him, not on satisfying her lust.

They were about five minutes from base camp when her satellite phone began ringing. She went to grab it from the center console, but Matthew got there first.

"You're driving," he said, as if they were on a road and subject to traffic laws. "Hello?" he answered.

Silence fell, and a tangible darkness along with it. She stopped the Jeep and looked over at Matthew. He met her eyes and shook his head solemnly.

In that second, all the strength she'd mustered to hold herself together crumbled. Her heart began to fracture, and her breathing became ragged. She heaved choppy breaths between sobs.

Matthew reached out to her, and when his hand touched her shoulder, she found herself pulling away. She didn't deserve his affection, his friendship, his empathy.

"Thanks for letting us know. Call Jasper." Matthew lowered the phone and stayed quiet for a few beats. "Jeff didn't make it."

She smacked the steering wheel.

Matthew didn't say a soothing word when she needed it the most. Why couldn't he just tell her that none of this was her fault, that Jeff's wife and children would be okay, that she'd be okay? The first dig she'd headed up and one of her men had died—a friend, at that. This was all her fault. She was the one in charge. If she had been there... If she'd insisted... Waves of self-chastisement kept crashing over her.

Matthew leaned toward her. "I'm sorry, Alex."

She couldn't bring herself to look at him right now, as if by doing so he'd see what an epic failure she was. She feared that her guard had fallen enough for him to witness the empty shell she'd become since they had first met. Of course, she still loved Egyptology, but the focus of her passion had changed over the years. She used to take part in expeditions for the sheer thrill of discovery, of touching artifacts that had long ago been buried. In recent years, though, she'd entered into a contest with herself, striving to do more, be more, attain more.

She sniffled. "Where are they taking him?"

"Still to the hospital to have him officially pronounced," he said tenderly.

Tears were streaming down her cheeks. She should follow after them, but there would be no point. Jeff was gone. Hearing the news directly from a doctor wouldn't change that.

She pressed on the gas pedal and headed for base camp.

Once there, she exited the vehicle without a word to Matthew. She heard him walking behind her, and he followed her into the main tent. She went straight to the fridge and grabbed an open champagne bottle.

"Do you think drinking is the smartest thing you could do right now?"

She pulled out the stopper and took a swig.

When she lowered it, his eyes were on her, and she didn't like the judgment she saw in them.

"Jeff and I go way back," she practically hissed. She paused and collected herself. "He has a wife and two daughters, and now I have to tell them—" she took another swig "—that he's dead because I talked him into coming out here in the first place." She ran a hand under her nose and sniffled. "What am I supposed to tell his family?"

A few seconds passed.

"Jeff knew the risks of coming out here, but he still wanted to be a part of this adventure." The way his eyes glazed over, she wondered if his statement had a broader implication. Was he talking about himself? Robyn? Cal? All of them?

"He still didn't know that it would be his last." Tears slid down her cheeks, and she wiped them with her free hand.

"But he *wanted* to come," Matthew emphasized. "He was an adult, and he made a choice."

Her gaze met his, and the starkness of the statement chilled her. Logically, he was right. Was life just one big cosmic game they were all rigged to lose at some point?

"I just feel so... I hurt." With that out there, she felt so raw and vulnerable. "And that could have been any of us out there," she added quickly to somehow salvage the exposure.

"When did you meet?" Matthew asked, sidestepping her last statement.

She bit her bottom lip, thankful he was there. He wasn't like other guys who got weird the moment emotions came into play, and his empathy for her grief seemed genuine. "We met on a dig here in Egypt," she said. "It was my first one, and he taught me a lot." Sorrow welled up in her throat, and she swallowed roughly, wishing that was all it took to purge the heartache.

Matthew nodded and reached for the bottle. She let him take it.

She wandered over to a table and sat down. "Reda's going to be here in a couple of hours, and I'm going to have to tell him what happened." She blew the air out of her lungs.

Matthew sat across from her as the tent flap opened. Andres entered. He and Danny had stayed behind to watch over base camp.

"Hel—" His greeting fell short. "Is everything all right?"

The flap opened again, and Danny walked in.

"Something's happened," Andres said to Danny.

Danny looked right at her. "What?"

The guilt burrowed in. She was more than the leader of this dig; she was responsible for each of her team members' lives, and she'd failed. She let one down. "Jeff…"

"There was an accident at the site," Matthew cut in, but she was thankful for it. He set the bottle on the table. "Jeff was bitten by a cobra, and he didn't survive."

Andres's and Danny's eyes narrowed, and Danny's gaze went to the bottle.

"Are you toasting to his death?" Danny accused.

The champagne's dryness became bitter on her tongue. "Absolutely not."

"It looks like you were." Danny's eyes were steely.

"Well, things aren't always what they look like," Matthew said with heat.

"I'm heartbroken by this," Alex said.

"As you should be," Andres snapped.

He may as well have shot her in the chest.

"There's no need to be like that," Matthew said sharply. "This wasn't

Alex's fault."

Danny arched his brows. "She's in charge of this dig, is she not?"

"And she put faith in Jasper's ability to keep the snakes away from the crew," Matthew said.

Alex pinched her eyes shut briefly. This could get uglier than it already was. She figured he'd probably said that in her defense, but it came across as Matthew throwing Jasper under the bus. And even though she'd initially charged at Jasper, she didn't care for the insinuation.

"It's not Jasper's fault, either." Alex held up her hands to stave off the laborers before their next verbal assault. "It's not anyone's fault." Saying that made her feel slightly better for a nanosecond. That was, until contempt hardened both men's facial features to stone.

"Sometimes things happen, and there's nothing that can be done to stop them," Matthew added.

Her men continued to look at her.

"You're going to call his wife?" Andres asked.

"Yes," she said. "Soon."

Andres nodded and hit Danny's arm. It broke the stare he had fixed on Alex, and she breathed easier because of it.

"Ah, we were coming in to grab something to eat." Andres gestured toward the fridge as if he thought they might be in the way.

"Of course. Go ahead," she told them.

The two men headed over to the kitchen area. She leaned forward, cupping her forehead, and her ponytail fell around the sides of her head to frame her face. Maybe if she just tucked herself away and pretended to be invisible, she'd somehow be relieved of this nightmare.

"I'm with you," Matthew said, "about telling Reda about Jeff."

His words struck her from out of nowhere, but then she remembered mentioning Reda just before Andres and Danny came in.

She lifted her head. "We have to. He has the right to know."

"You can't tell Reda." Danny was back at the table. He obviously had ears like a bat.

Alex's cheeks heated. "He has the right to know."

"He could shut us down, assign this expedition to someone else. Even kick us out of the country."

Just the mention of the prospect soured her gut. All the years, all her hard work... "Well, it's not like we can hide this from him. He knows

Jeff. He'll wonder where he is."

"So lie," Danny said without preamble. He apparently had no issue with deception.

Alex looked to Matthew for help.

"I believe it would dishonor Jeff's memory not to be upfront with the minister," he said.

Alex pressed her lips together and blinked slowly in an unspoken thank-you.

"Why would you think that?" Danny was relentless in his efforts to unnerve her.

"Danny, as you said, I'm in charge of this dig. That means I make the decisions. And I'm telling Reda what happened."

Danny threw up his hands and walked back to the kitchen area.

Alex leaned in closer to Matthew. "Am I missing something here? I don't understand why we're even discussing whether or not we should tell Reda. In fact, if we don't, it will look like we're trying to cover something up. He knows what's at stake. He could think we found the Tablets and killed Jeff ourselves for some reason."

Matthew's lips settled in a slight downward curve, the way they had in the car. He was deep in thought again. Was it her comment about them covering something up? Because she had to admit, slivers of doubt crawled through her. But that had to be all they were: doubts. She was probably merely looking for an explanation as to why Jeff's death had to happen. But the question of *why* was rarely satisfied when it came to losing someone. She knew well that grief had a way of taking the most rational person and turning them into a lunatic.

She pulled out on her pendant, squeezing it between her fingers. "Jeff was bitten by a snake. It was a tragic accident."

Matthew squinted. Words weren't needed. His assessment was plain to see in his eyes. She sounded as if she was chanting a mantra and trying to convince herself that's all it was while suspecting more. But did she?

She looked away from him. What kind of leader doubts their own team? People that she entrusted with responsibility in the first place? Admitting to questioning Seth's, Timal's, and Jasper's innocence would be equivalent to her questioning her own judgment. She shoved the wild notion aside. It had to be originating from a grieving, delusional mind.

"It was just an accident." Matthew pointed to her pendant. "I saw you doing that before. A ritual of yours?"

She looked down, then lifted her head. "I usually hold it when I'm stressed or about to do something dangerous."

"The pendant means a lot to you?"

Her gaze met his. His perceptiveness was impressive. "It does." She stopped there, debating how much she wanted to share. "It was a gift from my mother when I went off to college." She'd give him that much.

"You obviously always loved Egyptology," Matthew concluded. "Of course, I know that much from working with you before." He smiled, the expression reaching his eyes.

"I have. And I had this pendant when we worked together years ago, but I couldn't bring myself to wear it." From here, the story became more intimate and painful. "My mother died right before I came to Egypt for my first dig."

"I'm sorry," Matthew offered.

She nodded. "It was a long time ago now. But I just couldn't wear it back then. Maybe that sounds crazy. Some people would probably think wearing it would have been like bringing my mother with me, but I feared losing it out here. I kept it in my tent but never wore it."

"I can understand that."

"I started wearing it after Shane and I broke up," she went on. "People come into our lives, and they leave. Some stay longer than others, but the truth remains that, at some point, most leave our lives." She held up a hand, as it looked like Matthew was about to say something. She had a feeling she knew what it was going to be. "I'm not upset that Shane and I went our separate ways. Really, it was a long time coming. He was more about settling down and having a family while my heart belongs out here." The admission sliced her open. What if Danny had a point, and she was sent back to the States because of what had happened to Jeff? Even if it didn't come to that, she would probably never head up a dig again. She tucked her pendant back beneath her shirt and stood.

"I have some work to do before Reda gets here…" She fell quiet, thinking about the unpleasant task she had ahead of her. "You'll be fine to entertain yourself? Or did you want to go back to the site?"

"I'll stick around here and head out with Reda once he arrives."

"I should be finished with what I need to do before then and be able to join you."

Matthew reached for her hand just as she was stepping over the bench. "I'm here if you need to talk."

"Thank you."

She walked to the workstation area, despite the burning desire to just hunker down in her tent and get away from everyone. Everyone, that was, except for Matthew. His touch brought her comfort as much as it sent splinters of guilt piercing through her.

She sat in front of her computer, hungry for some distraction from what had transpired but knowing it wouldn't come. She'd update the journal she was keeping on the progress of the expedition before calling Jeff's wife. And to think that what she'd recorded that morning had been so upbeat. She risen early to document everything that had happened from the time Matthew and his friends showed up to them all being rescued from the tomb. To anyone else reading it, it would seem more like a diary, as she made sure to include her feelings as she went along. It humanized the expedition. After all, it was the desire to dig deeper into the understanding of human history, thought processes, and ways of life that had her and the rest of the team out here in the first place.

She started by dating the day's entry and logging the time, then typed, *Today, we lost Jeff.*

She stopped, her eyes on the blinking cursor, on the weight of those few words, and she let the tears fall.

CHAPTER
34

MATTHEW SPENT THE LAST COUPLE of hours pacing around base camp, refusing to go into the main tent, and wound up hanging out in his own. Alex needed some space to let Jeff's death sink in and to call his family. And she'd certainly need a lot more time.

Matthew knew all too well the sting death invoked, how it rendered loved ones left behind breathless, wrenched, and broken. He'd lost his mother at fifteen, and even now, at the age of twenty-eight, he could still conjure up the heartache with such vivid intensity that her death could have just occurred. When Alex had shared the story about the pendant and her own mother's death, he'd actually had a hard time keeping his emotions in check. They say the natural order of things is for parents to go before their children, but the children left behind would often gladly make the sacrifice in their place.

He was lying on his sleeping bag, staring at the ceiling of his tent, when he heard a vehicle approach. He got up quickly and was assaulted with mild vertigo, but he brushed it off on the move, riding it out like a night spent sipping whiskey.

Reda was getting out of his Land Rover. He saw Matthew and waved. Matthew waved back. Relief washed over him as he realized the last time he'd seen the man had been through a haze of sand and a collapsing tunnel. He'd thought it was going to be *the* last time he saw him.

Matthew reached Reda and held out a hand, but Reda pulled him in for a hug.

"Thank you for trying to save me—" Reda patted Matthew's back and then released him "—but I'm too stubborn to die." He tacked on a smile.

"I'm glad to hear it. I must admit I didn't think you had survived. None of us did." Matthew's voice turned a little a hoarse with the last sentence.

"Well, no sense getting worked up about what could have been. As you can see, I'm fine."

Matthew took in the older man, and he was right on point. There was no visible sign that he'd even had a brush with death—not so much as a scratch on his face. Matthew forced a smile and held back the flap on the main tent.

"Why, thank you," Reda said, walking inside. "I hope I'm not too early," he added when Alex walked over to them.

"No, not at all. Please take a seat." Alex waited for the minister to do just that before continuing. "We have something we need to tell you."

"You make this sound serious." Reda took off his hat and set it on the table in front of him.

Alex sat across from him, while Matthew opted to remain standing.

"It is," she replied. She pressed her left thumb into the palm of her right hand, kneading it. "There's no other way to say this than to come out with it… There's been an accident."

Reda leaned forward, worry lines etched into his brow. "Did something get damaged?"

Alex's chin quivered slightly, and she took a deep breath. "Jeff Webb was bitten by a cobra."

"He…" Reda gripped his chest. "Is he all right?"

Alex bit down on her bottom lip and shook her head.

"Oh."

"It was an accident," Alex rushed out. "No one's fault. I mean, it's not like you can control a cobra."

Matthew clenched his jaw as his suspicions about Jasper filtered in again. It was completely possible that Jasper hadn't been around at the time Jeff was bitten, but what if he had been? What if Jeff's death could have been prevented? Matthew tried to shake off the thought. It was probably just his mind playing with him in an effort to make sense of what had happened. Besides, what was he really thinking? That Jasper somehow provoked the snake and made it attack Jeff?

Reda scratched his hairline. "Did you call his wife?"

"I did," Alex replied.

The tent fell quiet, and Reda shook his head.

Alex continued after a few beats. "She's going to arrange for his body to be transported back to the States."

"Where is he? I mean, his body?"

Alex provided Reda with the name and location of the hospital where Seth and Timal had taken Jeff. Her voice cracked partway through, and she cleared her throat.

Reda reached forward to pat her forearm. "This is very sad. Very unfortunate. I'm so very sorry for your loss. For Egypt's loss. I've known him for years."

"Thank you, Mr. Ghannam." Tears beaded in the corners of Alex's eyes, and her voice strained to project volume. "His death is really a loss for the world. He made such an impact in the archaeological community."

"That he did." Reda had been quick to agree, but now he paused, seeming to give thought to his next words. "I will make sure to send his family my condolences."

"I'm sure they'd appreciate that." Alex sniffled and looked at Matthew. He wished he could heal her pain, but only time could do that. "Don't mistake our sorrow as a lack of enthusiasm about our find."

Reda sat back, and his brows pressed together. "Of course not."

"Well, Jeff wouldn't want us just sitting around." Alex got to her feet. "Let us share what we found with you."

"Sounds good." Reda placed his hat back on his head and stood. He addressed Matthew. "Where are your friends?"

"Both of them are out at the site," Matthew replied.

Reda dipped his head and didn't say anything, as if giving an impromptu moment of silence for Jeff. But it ended abruptly when Reda rubbed his hands together and said, "Let's get out there, then."

Matthew regarded him, picking up on the man's sudden shift from sorrow to elation. But really, who was he to judge someone else's grief? Everyone responded differently to tragedy. Some people liked to bury themselves in their work, and that's probably all it was with Reda. That, and Matthew's skepticism at play. But treasure hunting was riddled with danger, and trusting the wrong people could get one killed.

CHAPTER

35

CLOSE TO TWENTY-FIVE MINUTES LATER, Matthew spotted the site's tents on the horizon line. While his heart was still weighted down by Jeff's death, Matthew was ready to go back into the tomb. His primary interest was still in the hidden room—its existence for one, its purpose for another.

Alex was driving while Matthew sat in the back seat, having given Reda the front. Andres and Danny stayed behind at base camp to keep watch over things there.

As they approached the site, Matthew saw that Robyn, Cal, and Jasper were sitting under the shelter at the table.

Alex parked, and they joined the others. The three of them stood up and took turns welcoming Reda.

"I'm happy to see you're okay." Robyn extended her hand for a handshake.

Reda smiled at her and pulled her in for a hug. The older man seemed to hold on for an uncomfortable while. Or maybe it was just uncomfortable for Matthew.

Matthew cleared his throat. "We told him about Jeff."

Reda let go of Robyn. "Horrible tragedy," he said.

"That's why it's so important that we don't go down alone," Jasper said curtly.

Robyn turned her head quickly and looked at Jasper.

Reda quirked his brow. "He went off on his own?"

Matthew glanced at Alex, sensing the anger coming from her in waves. And he understood why. Nothing like blaming the dead guy for his own death. "Jeff's death was no one's fault, and it's best that we believe that." He felt like a hypocrite, given his musings about Jasper.

"Best for whom?" Jasper asked, angling his head and looking at Alex.

Matthew had picked up on the underlying tension between the two of them at different points since he and his friends had arrived, but it was running hotter than the desert sun at the moment. "Alex wasn't even here. You were, however. And you're the one who whispers to snakes." The hair rose on the back of his neck, despite his sweating.

Jasper held up both his hands and stepped back.

"Well." Reda offered the buffer word in an obvious attempt to move past the tension in the air.

Robyn picked up on it and added, "The tomb is unbelievable. It's in excellent condition."

Matthew concentrated on the sound of Robyn's voice, letting his temper fade away. His jaw slowly went slack. "It must look amazing bathed in light."

Robyn looked at him. "It's incredible."

Reda set his hands on his hips and pivoted toward Jasper. "I know Alex mentioned over the phone that the pharaoh's name had been taken from him. By chance, have you found any indication of his name since?"

Jasper tucked his hands in his pockets. "Nope. All we know is that he was a son of Khufu."

"That's better than nothing, I suppose," Reda said lightly. "What about the Tablets?"

"Mentioned in hieroglyphics, as you know, but we haven't found them," Jasper replied.

"From Jasper's interpretation, the key to the Tablets—or the key to enlightenment—lies with the pharaoh," Alex said, the look of anger gone from her mouth, though a trace of it still remained in her eyes.

Robyn looked around at the group of them. "Why don't we go down?"

"I was hoping someone would say that." Reda bent his arm and held it out for Robyn to slip hers through.

He was one crafty old man, Matthew gave him that. Using his position and his age as a means to innocently wear down a woman's defenses.

Alex turned to Matthew and waited to speak until Reda and Robyn were out of earshot. "He's a wily old man."

Matthew smirked and chuckled.

"What?"

"You know the expression 'great minds think alike'? Well, I was just thinking something similar."

She smiled at him. "Well, there you go."

"Excuse me—" Cal thrust an arm between Matthew and Alex "—coming through."

"Seems someone's feeling better," Matthew said to him.

Cal kept walking and facing forward. "Told you I was before you left."

Matthew watched after him and saw his friend lifting his camera to his face. He turned left and right. Taking, what? More pictures of the desert?

Hopefully his friend wasn't exaggerating when he'd said he brought a lot of data storage with him.

Alex turned to Matthew. "You ready?"

"I was born ready." He smiled at her, but his expression faded as he caught Jasper's eye. "You go on ahead. I'll be down."

"Oh—" Alex looked from him to Jasper and let out a hesitant, "Okay."

Matthew let Alex put distance between them before he spoke to Jasper. "Why are you giving her a hard time?"

"Why am I?" Jasper growled.

"You're upset with her for some reason. It's obvious."

"I don't want to get into it." Jasper's indifference was palpable, but maybe he was battling with grief himself.

"Did you and Jeff know each other well?" Matthew studied Jasper, but his body language was closed. That only served to stir up feelings of suspicion again.

"I've known him for a while." Jasper's tone was sharp, defensive.

"I'm sorry for your loss," Matthew offered sincerely.

Jasper bobbed his head.

It was probably best for Matthew to walk away now and leave behind the ridiculous suspicions that had wormed into his head. Jeff had died of a snake bite. It was completely plausible that it happened without intentional provocation. In fact, it was more logical than thinking that the snake was roused to strike. And, really, what was he getting at? That someone on this dig had murdered Jeff?

"So, Jeff was in the hidden room we found, and he was in there alone?" A question and answer that had been spoken before, but Matthew wanted confirmation again.

"Honestly, I don't know," Jasper admitted.

Rumbles of adrenaline fueled Matthew's system. "You as much as confirmed he was when everyone else was here a moment ago."

"I just know that he came out of the tomb looking peaked. He collapsed once he reached the surface."

Matthew recalled how Jasper had been coming out of the tomb after they'd arrived earlier that day. Had he gone back down for some reason?

"Where were Seth and Timal?" Matthew asked.

"As far as I know, both of them were in the tomb."

"But not with Jeff?"

"Not from my understanding."

Matthew nodded, not sure if he was buying Jasper's story, but at the same time, criticizing himself for not buying it.

"Is that it for the inquisition?" Jasper's hardened aura softened and gave way to a subtle smile.

Matthew's shoulders relaxed. "Yeah, that's it."

"Well, it was snake-free in the secondary antechamber and in the hidden room last I looked a few moments ago." Jasper walked away, leaving Matthew standing there to mull over thoughts spurred on by his crazy imagination. What reason would any of them have to kill Jeff anyhow? He hated that his mind had regurgitated a suspicion he had earlier: that they'd found something out about the Tablets—or the Tablets themselves—and Jeff wasn't part of the plan.

Jasper stopped and turned around. "You coming?"

"I am." Matthew hurried to catch up with Jasper, but as he neared the top of the staircase, his legs seemed to fuse to the desert floor. He was finding it a bit harder to breathe with each step he took. He was painfully aware that it was just yesterday that he thought he and his friends would die in the tomb. Sadly, that stirred up thoughts of Jeff, who hadn't been as fortunate as they had been on this expedition.

Matthew worked through his musings, though, and started breathing easier again. He lived for a challenge, after all. And he prided himself on not being afraid to look death in the face.

"This is incredible." Reda's voice carried through the air.

Moments later, Matthew joined Reda, Jasper, Cal, and the women in the main antechamber. He sucked in a breath through his mouth. The room was flooded in light, and gold peeked out from some artifacts despite the layers of dust—and there was *a lot* of gold in this room. Some of the pieces were quite intricate, and many objects were sculpted in the forms of various Egyptian gods.

"This is absolutely incredible." Reda's mouth gaped open in awe. "All of you should be extremely proud of yourselves."

"Thank you, Minister," Alex replied.

"No, my dear, thank you." Reda looked around at everyone. "Thanks to all of you. This is—" He covered his mouth briefly with a hand, and when he lowered it, he was smiling and shaking his head. "Absolutely incredible," he said again. Reda reached out toward some bottles but didn't touch them. "It must have stolen your breath to see all this. Wow. Just wow."

"We didn't see it in this much light, of course, but, yeah, I think I can speak for everyone when I say that it made us forget we were trapped down here," Alex said.

"Oh, I bet."

"But what a find, what a find." Reda whistled.

Everyone fell silent as they took in the room. Reda was the first to speak again, but a full minute or more had passed.

He smiled. "Now, you said that you found a pharaoh?"

"This way." Alex gestured for Reda to follow her, but everyone did.

Matthew might have had his mind set on getting into the hidden room, but he wasn't going to pass on seeing the sarcophagus and burial chamber again.

Alex stepped to the side of the burial chamber doorway to let the others in first.

Matthew's breath hitched as he entered the room. The makeshift lighting Jeff had his men put in place yesterday didn't even do the space justice. It was so bright in here now, and while the sarcophagus and murals hadn't been completely cleared of dust and sand, it was literally breathtaking.

"Incredible." The sentiment flowed from him.

Reda looked at him. "I have been thinking the same thing since I've come down here, Doctor."

"Matthew is fine, thank you."

"You've earned your title and have proven yourself repeatedly." Reda winked at him as if he were a loving father showing approval for his son, and it had Matthew gushing with pride.

He nodded.

"When we found it, ushabti were positioned all around the tomb," Alex explained. "We moved most out of the way."

"How many are down here?" Reda asked.

"We haven't counted them yet." Alex sounded like she was embarrassed to admit that, but it's not like they'd exactly had the opportunity.

"There will be plenty of time for that. You have had other things on your minds." Reda scanned the room. "Like survival, for one. And you were found all because of a radio..." Reda shook his head. "That's incredible, too. You have to love modern technology."

"When it's working, anyhow," Alex said offhandedly.

"True enough." Reda smiled at her. "Did you open the lid to the sarcophagus?"

"We figured, given the delicate nature of this situation, that it was best to look without a bunch of eyes on us."

"I can appreciate that." Reda became pensive. "Obviously you didn't find anything in there?"

"Besides the dead guy? No." Cal hitched his shoulders when everyone looked at him.

Leave it to Cal...

Matthew smiled, but the minister didn't look impressed.

"Yes, well..." Reda turned to Alex. "Shall we?" His inference being that they open the sarcophagus for him.

"Sure, I don't see what harm could come of it," Alex said.

The six of them stepped up and lifted the lid. Then they set it on the floor to the side of the coffin, as they'd done before.

Reda slipped on a pair of half-moon glasses he took from his shirt pocket and studied the mummy. "He looks like he was buried yesterday." He looked at Jasper. "We just know he was a son of Khufu?"

"That's right." Jasper didn't seem annoyed with the minister's repetitive questioning on this subject.

The minister's brow furrowed, disclosing his skepticism. "That's very interesting. Now, I am somewhat of a hieroglyphics expert myself, and no offense to you—" Reda gestured to Jasper "—but I will be looking over everything myself."

Jasper shrugged, unoffended. "I wouldn't expect anything less."

"I'll also be having the mummy taken to the Egyptian Museum in Cairo. He'll be examined forensically there. They have an entire lab in the basement that can accommodate this sort of thing. Hopefully they will be able to give us some answers as to his identity and confirm he was from Khufu's lineage. They were the ones who—" A flash from Cal's camera had Reda turning on him with a scowl.

Cal, who had been bent over the sarcophagus, was oblivious, though, and straightened up. "They can identify mummies?"

"Yes," Reda said rather impatiently. "They were the ones who conducted DNA analysis on Tut's remains and were able to confirm his identity. They even extracted DNA from two small fetuses found in his chamber and confirmed that they were his children. There was no written record of Tut having children." Reda looked at Alex. "See? There's that lovely technology again." His last sentence was dry, and he had his eye back on Cal.

"Cal's the photographer for this expedition," Alex said, clearly feeling the need to interject, even though Reda should have already known this from their first meeting. "He's taken pictures of the tomb and some of the different artifacts as we found them."

"And now that there's more light down here, I'll be taking more." Cal's edginess bespoke of agitation. "During the cleaning and cataloging, I'll take more again."

"Speaking of cataloging, a find like this is going to take some time," Reda said.

"We're prepared for that, and we'll see everything through, Minister," Alex replied.

Reda slipped his gaze to Cal. "And you?"

"If you're asking if I'm staying until the end…" Cal looked at Matthew.

"A venture like this could take years," Matthew said. "My friends and I came here prepared to stay for a month. With that said, if need be, I could stay a little longer if my work visa gets extended. Cal and Robyn need to get back, though."

Reda lifted his chin slightly and looked at Alex.

"We'll get another photographer," she assured him. "Or have Seth go back to taking pictures."

"Very well." Reda went quiet for a few seconds and gazed down at the mummy.

Matthew looked again, too, taking in how he'd been laid out—from the burial mask to body positioning.

Reda pointed at the mummy's crossed arms. "That indicates royalty."

"Well, he was a pharaoh," Cal said.

Reda didn't acknowledge Cal directly but he did clench his jaw. Matthew bugged out his eyes at his friend in reprimand and shook his head. Was Cal trying to get on the minister's bad side? Although, the minister was being rather touchy.

Reda walked over to the mural on the wall opposite the entry to the burial chamber. After a few minutes, he said, "From what I see, this man's name was taken away and he was into some very controversial beliefs. That's also what you interpreted, Jasper?"

"Yes," Jasper confirmed.

"With a slight variation," Matthew inserted. "Jasper said the pharaoh practiced dark magic."

Reda glanced at him, nodding. "Yes, I can appreciate that interpretation."

"We figured dark magic might allude to the Tablets," Matthew went on.

"It could," Reda agreed.

"Yet, despite being a pharaoh who didn't follow the mainstream religion, he was obviously well loved, given all the treasure he was buried with," Robyn stated, reminding Matthew that Alex had said something similar on another occasion.

"From what I see, he had a sect that followed him and believed as he did." Reda circled a finger around a series of images that showed what looked like people bowing with a line through them. "This doesn't mean that he lost these followers, but rather the reverse, that these followers cut themselves off from the rest of Egyptian society to serve under our nameless pharaoh here."

Matthew looked at Jasper, wondering why he'd withheld this and if it mattered that he had. It didn't help with feelings of goodwill toward him, though.

Reda continued. "He had two sons from what I see here. At least one died before him." He looked over the wall and pointed at the face of a female. "She was his wife for a time, but she never accepted his new beliefs, and he had her killed for her disloyalty." The minister took pause, licking his lips, then leaned over the coffin again. "Such a shame that there's no sign of the Tablets." He stood straight and put his glasses away. "Okay, then, let's put the lid back on."

They all cooperated to do as he'd asked. Once the lid was in place, Reda said, "I should have brought this up before coming down here, but I hope all the snakes are gone?" His voice rose as he spoke, injecting a question into what could otherwise be a statement.

"Jasper's assured me they are," Matthew answered.

Jasper cast an open hand toward Matthew. "As he said."

"All right, run me through the place," the minister said. "Take me to where Jeff was bitten."

"This way." Jasper led Reda and the rest of them out of the room and down the corridor to the secondary antechamber.

Reda stood in front of the mural there and spun around, pointing to the corridor that led to the tunnel they'd come up. "That is where you entered?"

"That's right," Alex confirmed.

"I can't imagine what was going through your minds at the time, but wow, just wow," Reda said.

"Well, that and fear of never being rescued." A smile played at the corners of Alex's mouth, but the expression didn't form. No doubt the recollections of actually facing her mortality—not to mention Jeff's death—zapped any attempt at joviality.

"I have no doubt." Reda gestured toward the hole in the wall under the mural. "Please tell me that you have pictures of how it was when you found it, before you removed some of the bricks."

Alex gestured toward Cal.

"She insisted," he replied.

"And we were careful not to ruin the wall more than we had to, but we were eager to find a way out of here," Matthew added. He noted that Reda's eyes were full of understanding. "If you want to go in, you'll have to get down on your hands and knees."

"This old man stopped crawling around years ago, but if there was any time to make an exception…" Reda was down in seconds, peering through the hole. "It's just a room?"

"There's a staircase at the end. Jeff and I spoke on the sat phones last night, and he and his men had mapped out the structure from aboveground using the ground-penetrating radar machine. They also took measurements, and Jeff drafted the layout by hand. Of course, that's before he..." Alex cleared her throat and took a few seconds to compose herself. "The plan was to dig out the second staircase."

"Hmm." Reda was mentally chewing on something. "But other than some snakes and a staircase, there was nothing else here?"

"Not exactly," Jasper said. "There are hieroglyphics on the wall that speak about the Tablets some more. It says that they are linked to the Great Pyramid."

"Nothing more specific than that?" Matthew blurted out the question, hating being so reliant on one person's interpretation and integrity.

Jasper shook his head.

Robyn held up a finger, as if she were waiting to be called upon, but she simply proceeded. "Just the fact that this is supposed to be the tomb of a son of Khufu could be that link. It doesn't mean that the Tablets aren't inside this tomb somewhere."

"I would think inside his coffin would have been a good spot to hide them," Reda said, verbalizing the same logic Matthew had thought. "But they weren't in there. It's certainly disappointing that we haven't found them yet."

No one said anything. No doubt everyone was in complete agreement with the minister.

"All right. I'm going in." Reda wormed through the opening into the hidden room they'd found. Matthew was right behind him.

"I found the hieroglyphics on the left, about halfway down," Jasper called out.

Matthew stood up to his full height, took a deep breath, and followed Jasper's directions. He saw no slithering reptiles around, so that was good. The bright lighting had probably scared them off. It also made the markings on the wall easy to find. Not that Matthew could read them, but maybe if he could just look at them... He didn't know what he expected, though. What he wished for were clear directions on where to find the Tablets, and such a thing was unrealistic.

"Ah yes." Reda had his spectacles perched on his nose again and stood in front of the hieroglyphics. "It is most definitely saying the Tablets are linked to the Great Pyramid." He arched back so he could see around Matthew.

Matthew followed the direction of Reda's gaze, and Jasper was coming toward them. He also saw that Robyn, Cal, and Alex were making their way into the room.

Jasper passed a glance to Cal. "It also calls down a curse on those who pursue them."

Cal's face paled, and Matthew imagined his friend was thinking about how a man *had* died.

"I don't recall seeing a treasury." Reda looked at Alex. "Was there one?"

"Not that we've found," she replied.

"Hmm."

Then it hit Matthew like a freight train. He gripped Alex's forearm. "You said that Jeff and his men had drafted a layout of the tomb?"

"Yes," Alex drew out the word slowly.

"And it's obviously to scale?"

"Absolutely." She looked down at her arm where he still had a hold on her. He let her go.

"May I look at it?"

"What are you thinking?" Alex raised her eyebrows.

Matthew turned to Reda. "You asked about a treasury. Well, King Tut had one connected to his burial chamber, and it only seems conceivable this pharaoh would have one, too. And this would be about where this pharaoh's burial chamber would be positioned." No one moved. No one said a word. Matthew continued. "What I'm thinking is that the Tablets might be behind—" Matthew pressed his hands to the wall "—here."

"Another hidden room?" Robyn's volume ratcheted with a peal of excitement.

"A hidden treasury. Somewhere between the burial chamber and this room."

Alex was immediately on the move toward the exit. Matthew was right behind her, and he couldn't move fast enough. The Emerald Tablets could be closer than they'd thought, after all.

CHAPTER
36

Sweat was dripping down Matthew's back, but he didn't care. He was with Alex, Robyn, and Reda under the open-sided tent. Cal and Jasper remained in the tomb—Cal to photograph and Jasper to watch for snakes.

Alex had already consulted the readouts from the ground-penetrating radar machine. Now she smoothed out the large piece of drafting paper Jeff had used to draw the layout of the tomb on the table. The wind licked at the edges. Matthew went around to the other side of the table and held down the top corners while Alex held down the bottom ones.

"There does seem to be an empty space that runs along here." Alex pointed to a blacked-out area between the burial chamber and the hidden room. "Oh." The bottom corner she'd lifted her hand from flew up, and Alex returned her hand to the paper.

"It could definitely be a room," Robyn said.

"Let's find out." Alex let go of the drafting paper, looking as if she was about to walk off.

Reda touched her arm. "You're going to break through the wall?"

"I was going to start with the ground-penetrating radar machine. I can use it to look through the wall." She went inside the first tent, came out, and went into the second one. Moments later, she returned with the machine in hand. It looked like an upright cart with wheels. The reader was at the bottom, and there was a spot for the readout module between the handles.

"How is it going to work for this application exactly?" Robyn asked.

"You'll see." Alex grabbed the readout module out of a cabinet. "Robyn, would you mind?" Alex tilted her head toward the table, silently requesting that Robyn put the layout away.

Robyn's posture stiffened, and she looked away as if she didn't understand Alex's unspoken request. But Robyn was great at reading people, so Matthew knew better.

He rolled the layout and snapped the rubber band around it. By the time he put it away, Robyn was following Alex and Reda toward the entrance to the tomb. Matthew grabbed a shovel that was propped up against one of the tent poles and caught up with them.

His steps were so light, he felt as if he were floating above the ground even as he was going beneath it. But he'd been disappointed when it came to the Tablets already, and logically, he needed to prepare himself to be again. But he had a feeling in his core that they were close to narrowing in on the Tablets' location. With the numerous mentions inside the tomb and the one on the map, it stood to reason that since the other landmarks had led them to the tomb, the Tablets were here somewhere.

The group of them, less Jasper and Cal who were off somewhere else, assembled in the burial chamber.

Alex connected the readout module to the ground-penetrating radar, but didn't secure it into place. "Now, I'm going to hold this, and you're"—Alex looked at Matthew—"going to take the machine and set it on its side, with the bottom against the wall."

He put down the shovel and picked up the machine.

"You think this is actually going to work?" Robyn asked. "What about the stone interfering with its readings?"

"It will work, yes," Alex said definitively. Then she addressed Matthew. "Now just move along the wall slowly." Only a few seconds had passed when she said, "Oh yeah, something's definitely back there."

"You're absolutely certain?" Reda asked. "Sometimes it can be hard to tell."

"We'll only know for sure if we get in there." Alex pressed her lips together and maintained eye contact with the minister.

"True enough." He let out a sigh. "We've come this far... Let's go through from the other side, though. There's less to potentially destroy there."

"Absolutely." Alex took back the machine, and Matthew grabbed the shovel.

"And your man should have pictures." Reda turned to Matthew.

He nodded, picking up on the man's paranoia. He'd brought up Cal's photography a few times now, and seemed quite concerned that Cal had taken pictures of everything the way it had been found.

They left the burial chamber, heading for the first hidden room they'd found. They ran into Jasper and Cal in the secondary antechamber.

"We think we've found another hidden room," Alex told them.

Matthew went straight to the hole in the wall and got to his knees. He slid the shovel through the opening and crawled in after it. Robyn came in next. He held out a hand to help her to her feet.

"I'm fine," she said, declining his offer. She wiped her hands on the front of her pants.

Next through the opening was the radar machine, and Matthew collected it. He extended his hand to Alex, and she took it with a smile and a thank-you.

Matthew looked over his shoulder at Robyn. She was standing in front of the hieroglyphics and paying neither him nor Alex any attention. Maybe Cal was right about Robyn being upset over Matthew's attraction to Alex. But then, his ego could be doing his thinking for him again. A man had lost his life and she was in the room where he'd gotten bit.

Jasper came through then, followed by Reda and Cal.

Flashes from Cal's camera flickered in the room.

Jasper spun to face Cal. "Can you give it a rest for a few seconds?"

Cal took a couple more photos, likely just out of spite, then lowered his camera. "Okay, I'll cut it out. *For now.*"

Matthew walked over to the wall where the hieroglyphics were and ran his hand along it. Somewhere behind here was a room. Did it contain the Tablets? He just wanted to have at this wall, but he had to show some restraint. What if he took out the wrong bricks or too many and jeopardized the structural integrity of the ceiling? The last thing they needed was another cave-in.

"Matthew?"

He turned to see Alex look at him, then at the machine and back at him.

"I'm on it." He picked up the machine and did as he had in the burial chamber.

About seven feet down the wall and three feet from the start of the hieroglyphics, Alex cried out, "Stop! Right there."

Matthew set down the machine and exchanged it for the shovel again. "Before we start taking out bricks, I think some of us should return to the surface. Just in case there's a collapse."

Robyn put her hands on her hips. "I'm not going anywhere."

"Me either. I'm the photographer." Cal lifted his camera just to emphasize his point.

"Don't look at me," Reda said. "An old man gets to live his dream. If I die down here, I die happy."

Matthew wondered if that resolve would remain if the minister were actually faced with death. He really wished that Cal and Robyn would go above ground where they'd be safe, but the fact that they wanted to stay didn't surprise him.

"Matthew's got a point." Alex looked at Jasper.

"Fine, I'll go." Jasper left, but based on the energy coming from him, he would have preferred to stay.

"We'll give it a few minutes to make sure Jasper gets out," Alex said.

Matthew nodded and consulted his watch. Every second was painful.

"Okay. It's the moment of truth." Matthew pressed the shovel into a crack between two bricks, and they gave way easily—much more so than he'd expected. "This might look like a brick wall, but I'm pretty sure these aren't bricks."

Reda's brow pinched. "What do you mean?"

"Just that... I think it might be a door." Matthew followed his gut instincts and got down on his knees, then put his fingers in the crack. He had planned to pull on it somehow, but nothing happened. Then he pushed against it and was met with the same result. He pushed to the right. And the wall slid.

"What do ya know?" He pulled a flashlight from a clip on his pants and shone it into the opening. He was grinning when he turned around. "Well, it's definitely a room."

Alex let out a brief holler, and Robyn and Reda smiled at each other. Cal had moved in front of Matthew and was blocking the doorway.

Matthew put a hand on his friend's shoulder. "I appreciate your enthusiasm, but—"

"But what, Matt?" A few flashes. "I'm taking pictures. That's why I'm here." A few more flashes, then he got out of Matthew's way.

"You sure I can go in now?" Matthew teased.

Cal tossed him a sardonic smile. "Sure, I'm good with it now."

"Why, thanks ever so much." Matthew laughed and turned his attention to the floor. He was looking for any sign that the room had been entered or disturbed recently. There was some sand on the floor but not much, and there were no scuff marks or anything to indicate someone had been inside.

He took a deep breath, dizzy with anticipation, and entered the room. It was about seven feet long by five feet wide and at least six feet tall. But he noticed something else. He turned and found himself pressed against Alex. He shuffled back just a bit, as did she.

"It's empty." He may as well have been punched in the stomach. All this day was bringing was misery, loss, and disappointment.

"I can't believe this." Alex sounded as if she'd taken a blow to the gut, too.

"Tomb robbers must have gotten to it," Reda said.

Matthew was shaking his head, but Reda's suggestion was entirely possible. The rest of the tomb was blocked off from this room. They could have found whatever was in here and thought they had everything. Matthew sure as hell hoped that didn't include the Tablets.

CHAPTER
37

THEY ENDED UP CALLING IT a day early. Jeff's death had drained them both physically and emotionally. It was around six o'clock when they reached base camp. Jasper had stayed at the site, and Andres and Danny would be joining him later. Matthew was happy that Robyn and Cal had returned with him, Alex, and Reda.

The minister got out of the Jeep and started in the direction of his Land Rover. "Well, I'm headed back to the city."

"You are more than welcome to spend the night," Alex offered.

Reda waved a dismissive hand. "I'll be back first thing in the morning, and we'll get started on cataloging." He got into his vehicle and turned the ignition. "Tomorrow's going to be a big day, and I love my own bed."

"I get that," Alex said.

With that, Reda drove off in the direction of civilization.

"I'm just going to catch a shower." Robyn unloaded her bag from the back of the Jeep. "I'll meet everyone in the main tent in a bit."

"I'm going to download today's pictures to my computer," Cal said, and headed toward the main tent.

That left Matthew with Alex. She was at the back of the Jeep and had just slung a bag over her shoulder.

"How are you doing?" he asked.

"It's been quite the day, hasn't it?" Her voice was monotone. She wasn't meeting his eyes, either.

He touched her upper arm. "That's not what I asked."

"I'm—" Alex looked down at his hand, and then her gray eyes flicked up and locked with his.

He wished he could kiss her and take away all her pain. But only time helped to lick that wound, and even then, it would fester and bleed, only to scab over and over again.

And if he kissed her, and she didn't appreciate his timing…

But she was still looking at him, and she tilted up her chin.

To hell with it!

He put his mouth on hers. Her lips parted and his tongue swept into her mouth, taking what he wanted and giving in equal measure. People said that heartbreak couldn't be healed in bed, but he believed it could be temporarily alleviated. But even if they weren't going to sleep together, he wanted her to know that she wasn't alone, that he was here for her.

She moaned, arousing him further. He cupped the back of her head, drawing her closer to him, and knocked off her hat. He dug his fingers through her locks of blond hair.

"We…should…" Her words came out on clipped breaths, and her bag fell to the ground at their feet.

He felt consumed by her. He wanted to rip her clothes off, to take her. He wanted all of her. He gripped the hem of her shirt, praying for the willpower to be strong. But his hands went under the fabric, grazing the skin at her waist. She wrapped her arms around his hips, and she pulled him against her. She seemed to want him just as badly as he wanted her.

It took all his resolve to put some distance between them, but this wasn't the place to be doing this. He caressed her cheek, his jaw clenched with hunger. His focus was fixed on her—on her lips, on the feel of her skin, on the sweet, hot spot between her legs.

"Do you want to—" He swallowed roughly.

She nodded, keeping her gaze locked on his. Her eyes were at half-mast, and her cheeks flushed.

He picked up the bag she had dropped and slipped the strap over a shoulder. They each wrapped an arm around the other, and with her free hand, she held on to his, which was draped over her shoulder, against her chest. She interlaced her fingers with his and rubbed his palm with the pad of her thumb.

They were rounding the main tent toward his tent when they ran into Cal.

His gaze went straight to Matthew. His eyes were full of judgment, and Matthew felt his temperature rising. "I thought you were backing up—"

Cal held up his hand, in which he held a data drive, and butted his head in the direction of the Jeep. "Looks like you forgot your hat."

Matthew and Alex turned around.

"Oh." Alex glanced at Matthew and smiled. "I should probably go get that."

Under different circumstances, Matthew would have volunteered to get it for her, but he had a pressing matter to deal with. The second Matthew figured she was out of earshot, he lowered his voice and growled, "Can you just mind your own...business?" It took restraint not to say *fucking business*.

"This *is* me minding my business." Cal smacked a hand over his heart. "You and Robyn are my closest friends besides Sophie. And if you screw things up with Alex, we'll be on the first plane home to Canada."

"She's not going to—"

"All we've been through will have been for nothing. Almost dying... would have been for no reason," Cal cut in, as if he hadn't heard a word Matthew had said.

Matthew didn't know how to respond, so he shook his head and gritted his teeth.

"You look like a raging bull when you do that. You do realize that?"

"Not the time, Cal."

"You're just mad because you know I'm right," Cal delivered pointedly. "And if you sleep with Alex, can you imagine how that will affect Robyn? Do you even care?"

"Robyn doesn't have any right to be upset." Matthew would stick with that justification because it held merit. They were friends.

"Whether you think she does or not, she is upset." Cal paused. "You saw her today."

"A man *died* today," he countered.

Cal cocked his head. "Is that what you're telling yourself? That she's only acting this way because of Jeff?"

Matthew knew there had to be more to Robyn's attitude than Jeff's death, as it seemed to get worse around Alex. "Listen, Robyn and I are both adults."

"If you say so." Cal shrugged.

Matthew glared at his friend for the insinuation that he wasn't one. "We're *both* adults," he repeated. "We are not dating, and I am free to see other people, as is she."

"Oh, you're obtuse."

"She told me that it wasn't our time."

"She told you that?" Everything from his friend's tone of voice and the high pitch of his question to his body language told Matthew that Cal was skeptical.

"Uh-huh." So it was a slight variation of the truth, but she had agreed when he'd said it.

"When did she say that?"

"You're relentless." Matthew looked over his shoulder. A breeze had carried off Alex's hat, and she was chasing after it.

"When?" Cal pressed.

Matthew faced Cal again. "When we got back from Bolivia."

"Ha! So almost a year ago."

"Nothing's changed."

"You really believe that?"

Matthew's insides turned cold. "I do."

"Fine," Cal punched out. "But you do realize that people rarely say what they mean." Cal studied Matthew. "Who said it wasn't the right time first?"

"What does it matter?" Matthew's chest tightened. Was Cal implying that Robyn had only agreed to save face?

"It *matters* because if you said it first, she could have just said it for your benefit or to avoid embarrassment."

Before Matthew could say anything, Alex walked up to them, all smiles.

"Sorry that took so long," she said.

Matthew turned to her. "Now who's apologizing like a Canadian?"

She tugged on his arm. "I guess you're rubbing off on me." Her smile faded, and she looked from Matthew to Cal and back again. "Is everything okay?"

Matthew held eye contact with Cal, silently daring him to speak. He didn't. Matthew turned to Alex. "Yeah."

"Hey, I thought I heard people out here." The man's voice came from behind him and Alex. He turned. Timal was walking up to them.

"Seth and I brought back a deep-dish pizza with all the toppings," Timal continued. "It's been sitting around a bit, but help yourselves. It's in the fridge."

Frustration and pent-up sexual energy coiled around Matthew's heart, restricting his airflow. He was breathing through his mouth but could still feel his nostrils flaring. He was living up to Cal's earlier observation of Matthew resembling a raging bull. He couldn't take Alex to his tent now. Not yet. Anger toward Cal was still pulsing beneath the surface, and he didn't want to rush things with Alex. She deserved better than that.

"Pizza sounds good." Matthew tried to come across as easygoing, but he wasn't sure he pulled it off. Still, he moved to the main tent, ignoring the fact that Alex was staring at his profile. She tagged along, and Matthew held the flap for her. He let it drop in front of Cal. Cal let himself inside and glared at Matthew.

He took two pizza boxes from the fridge and walked to the table. One of them felt especially light, and he opened it first. Empty. "Not sure why this got put away," he said.

Alex shook her head and smirked from across the room. "Go figure. And when there's leftovers, they're left to sit out and spoil."

He opened the second box, and there was an entire pizza inside. He tore off a slice, took a bite, and grabbed a seat. The food was good, but his mind was stuck on kissing Alex and how their bodies seemed to fit together perfectly. He wanted her naked flesh pressed against his, to feel her warm breath across his skin, to taste her, to savor her. Frustrated, he took another bite of pizza, and was clued into the fact that *all the toppings* would mean pepperoni, and he didn't care for the stuff. He started plucking it off and built a little pile on the table in front of him.

Cal grabbed a piece of pizza, too, and sat down across from Matthew. "What time are we heading out in the morning?" His voice was laced with seemingly genuine interest. The conversation he'd initiated outside appeared to have been forgotten. And he clearly wasn't feeling any remorse over sabotaging—or in delaying—Matthew's plans for the evening. Cal was carrying off an Academy Award–winning performance.

Matthew met his friend's eyes. "I have no idea. You'd have to ask Alex."

"What's that?" Alex, who had been in the kitchen area getting some water, walked up behind Matthew. She set her glass on the table and put her hands on his shoulders. The searing heat from her fingertips shot straight to his pants.

Cal eyeballed Matthew, and Alex's hands on him. "Never mind." Cal tapped the table and left.

Thank God for small miracles...

"What's wrong with Cal?" Alex sat down beside Matthew.

"Who knows," Matthew replied. It was a lie, but he wasn't getting into Cal's reasoning with Alex.

The flap of the tent opened, and Robyn came in.

"There's pizza," Alex said to her.

Robyn headed to the watercooler. "I can see that."

Guilt snaked through his gut, but that was ludicrous. It's not as if he was cheating on Robyn.

He gripped Alex's knee. "Do you want to get out of here?"

"I wish we never came in here." She laughed, tilting her head back just enough to expose her long, slender neck.

They left, practically running toward his tent. But they didn't make it there before their mouths crashed together. Hands searching, fumbling, grabbing. He struggled with the zipper of his tent with one hand, because his other one was busy under Alex's shirt. At this rate, they'd never get inside.

He pulled back. "Just a second."

"I hope you take longer than that." She narrowed her eyes at him, toying with him.

"Trust me. I'm going to take my time with you."

"Now, you're just teasing me." She traced a fingertip down his chest.

"No, sweetheart, I'm *promising* you." The tent finally cooperated, and he yanked her inside.

CHAPTER
38

The next morning, Robyn was working alongside Alex cataloging the ushabti. The plan was to clear the way for the sarcophagus to be removed and taken to the Egyptian Museum sooner rather than later. Cal was hovering and taking photographs as they cleaned the artifacts. And while Robyn should have been solely focused on what she was doing and the significance of this find, her mind kept wandering to Matthew, to Alex, to her own pathetic love life.

The blind date she'd canceled would have been her first date in six months. She tried to justify her avoidance of the dating world by saying she was too busy. And her job most certainly kept her that. But if finding Mr. Right had been a priority, she would have made the time. Still, from the dating sampler she'd partaken of—or her friends had—it was hard to get excited about what was on the market these days. Her last date had been more interested in his car and his hair than in her, and her friends had told her stories that would make any intelligent women either avoid dating altogether or in the least rule out men. There was one guy who had turned out to be a gigolo who pleasured married women. And another who had taken out a kitchen knife when her friend had decided to end things, and he had said, "Take it. Stab me in the heart. You have already anyway."

No one had time for that kind of drama.

Not that Robyn had always been so skeptical. She used to believe that knights in shining armor did exist, but life had popped that bubble.

Happily-ever-afters were restricted to fairytales.

She brushed off the ushabti she held in her hand and lifted it up to the light. It wasn't because she was inspecting her work. She'd done that numerous times already. But the more she immersed herself in the present moment, she could forget about her romantic feelings for Matthew. Especially when it was obvious he was feeling that way about Alex.

The way Matthew and Alex had been eyeing each other in the main tent the night before, and how quickly they had left together, had made Robyn suspicious. But it was the stricken look on Matthew's face this morning and the awkward exchange she'd had with him that cinched it. He had slept with Alex.

She considered warning Matthew that Alex was using him for his reputation. But what good could come of that? Would he even believe her?

"How are you making out over there?" Alex asked, cutting through Robyn's thoughts.

Robyn lowered the ushabti. "Fine."

"Hmm." Alex sounded skeptical.

Robyn looked at Alex, not sure whether to comment or ignore it altogether. She opted to go with the latter, even if it gave her heartburn. "What about you?"

"Going good." Alex smiled. "Great, actually. I keep thinking, *Wow, I'm really doing this.*" Alex held up her cleaned ushabti, and Cal took a picture. Then she wrapped it and carefully placed it in a crate.

"It does feel like a dream." Or a nightmare, depending on one's focus and perspective. Robyn held her piece up so Cal could photograph it, too, and then she packed it away. As she grabbed another ushabti, she noticed Alex watching her. Her mouth was opening and closing as if she was considering saying something.

Alex looked at Cal. "Could you give us a few minutes?"

"Sure." Cal stepped out of the room.

"I hope you're all right with..." Alex rolled her hand, surely using the gesture to allude to what had happened the night before.

"You and Matthew?" Robyn asked to confirm.

"Yeah."

Robyn gritted her teeth. Heat surged through her.

"Robyn?" Alex prompted.

She should just be the bigger person, let things between the two of them run its course, but her mouth seemed to have a mind of its own. "I'm not," she blurted.

Alex squinted, and her brow pinched. "You're—"

"Not fine with it," Robyn finished. It was too late to turn back now.

"I'm sorry. I didn't want to get in the middle of anything." Alex's words may have technically been an apology, but her energy was anything but apologetic.

"You're not. Trust me." Robyn wasn't sure if she was trying to convince Alex or herself. She was also debating whether or not she should confront Alex about using Matthew.

"Why do I not believe you?"

"Well, that's your prerogative." Robyn worked the brush over the ushabti in her hands.

"You love him," Alex said softly.

Robyn huffed out a derisive laugh. "No." She'd deny her feelings for Matthew with a gun to her head.

"What is it, then? You're obviously pissed off."

Robyn looked around to make sure no one was within earshot. She looked Alex in the eye. "I know you're using Matt."

Alex's face fell, and she wiped her cheek with the back of her hand. Unless an itch happened to strike right then, it was a nervous reaction to busy her hands. The accusation had come as a surprise. But Alex composed herself quickly and regarded Robyn with heat. "Who told you that?"

"What does that matter?" Robyn was fuming, her hands shaking.

Cal came up behind them. "You guys ready for me now?"

Robyn clenched her jaw as she and Alex stared each other down.

"Okay." Cal dragged out the word. "I'm leaving again." He was barely gone when Alex spoke.

"I'm not—" Alex swallowed roughly "—using him."

"You're really denying it?"

Alex's shoulders sagged. "I just wanted this find to make history."

"The pharaoh's tomb or the Tablets?" Robyn jutted out her chin. "Because the Tablets are not exactly something you can advertise."

Alex looked away. "Matthew's had a passion for them since—"

"So you're trying to spin this as doing him a favor?" Rage and adrenaline were crashing together and making her jittery.

"It's not like that," Alex began. "It's just—"

"He would bring your expedition a lot of media coverage." Robyn put down the ushabti she'd been working on and got to her feet. "I'm going to take a break."

When she reached the surface, Matthew was walking toward her.

"Hey," he said.

"Hey," she parroted. "Just taking a break. My neck is killing me." Not entirely a lie.

"Robyn?" Her name dangled out there, as if he wanted to say something else but was hesitant.

"Yeah?"

"Is everything all right with you?" His voice was tender and caring.

"Yeah. Of course. Everything's fine."

"I thought…I don't know, that you'd be happier." He attempted a smile and failed miserably. "Coming to Egypt and working on a dig has been a dream of yours for a long time."

She didn't need him to tell her what her dreams were. She took a deep breath, ready to lay into him. But the way he was regarding her with such rawness in his eyes, she didn't have the heart to do it. Besides, it wasn't really him she was mad at. It was Alex. But if Robyn told him about Alex using him, Matthew would likely write it off as her being jealous. Maybe there was no point in bringing it up to Matthew. Not right now. Possibly never. They'd be heading home within the month, and Alex would probably wind up being nothing more than a blip in Matthew's past.

His gaze was latched on to her, and Robyn felt compelled to fill the silence, to say *something*. "You and Alex seem to have hit it off."

"Yeah, she's pretty great," he admitted.

"She makes you happy?"

"She does." He smiled, stamping home what she had suspected. But to hear his confession made her feel like a horrible person. She should be happy for him, not jealous.

"There you are."

Robyn turned to see Alex approaching Matthew.

Robyn shook her head and resumed walking toward the tent, wishing that she were getting a bottle of Jack instead of a bottle of water.

She took a few deep breaths. It was going to be a long few weeks.

CHAPTER
39

It was depressing being back at Cairo International Airport. They'd spent the last three and a half weeks cataloging and hadn't found any more clues as to the location of the Emerald Tablets. There was a lot more to process, though. Still, Matthew hated that he was starting to give up hope that the Tablets were out there at all. That's probably why he was opting to return to Canada. He couldn't take any more disappointment.

But it's not like they were leaving without having had any success. Robyn was already negotiating with the Egyptian government to arrange for an exhibit of the tomb's contents at the Royal Ontario Museum. Matthew had no doubt she'd come out on the winning end with some of the artifacts. Egypt was stringent about what mummies and sarcophagi they lent out.

Alex pulled Matthew to the side. Robyn glanced over a shoulder and kept walking with Cal toward the terminal check-in for their airline.

"I'm going to miss you." Alex grabbed his shirt and pulled him down to kiss her.

"Well." He drew back, licking his lips, loving that he'd gotten to spend nearly a month with Alex getting reacquainted, getting *better* acquainted.

"*Well?* That's all you have to say? I must not have done that right."

She leaned toward him again, but this time, he assumed the role of aggressor and took her mouth with a hunger that needed satisfying.

A few seconds later, he ended the kiss.

"Well," she said and gave way to giggling. She fanned herself as if she were playing up the kiss, but she truly was flushed. "I'm gonna miss that," she added with a wink. "And this." She pinched his butt.

"Hey." He squirmed out of her reach. "Control yourself, woman, we're in a public place."

Her expression fell serious, casting shadows over her face.

"What is it?" He wished to God that she wasn't about to cry.

She bit down on her bottom lip. "I know it's more complicated than either of you are letting on." She pointed behind him, and Matthew turned to see Robyn laughing at something Cal must have said. Matthew caught her eye, then looked back at Alex.

She straightened the lay of his T-shirt. "But at least I had you for a brief time."

Matthew conjured his best goofy face, widening his eyes and letting his mouth go slack and fall open. He'd never tried it in front of a mirror, but it usually got women to laugh or roll their eyes.

She punched him lightly in the shoulder. She was trying to slough off his diversion, but was failing miserably. Sadness paraded across her features.

He took her hands. "Hey, this doesn't have to be the end. You could come visit me in Canada. I could come visit you."

Alex shook her head. "Long-distance relationships never work." Now, she was wielding reason like a knife, and he wasn't sure he cared for it.

"We could give it a try. Besides, you never know when I'll be in the States."

"I'm in Egypt ten months out of the year."

Matthew hitched his shoulders. "I have money for travel."

"Uh-huh. Well, I'm not just going to wait around for you. I do have a life to get on with."

"Ouch. From hot to cold in a flash." Matthew snapped his fingers with dramatic flair but was smiling. "Nasty," he teased.

Alex laughed and squeezed his hands. Her touch confirmed that this was the end of their relationship, or their tryst, or whatever it had been.

He'd just have to accept that what they'd had was over and go back to his life.

"I should probably check my bags." He let go of one of her hands to grab the bags at his feet.

"Stop there!" a man called out.

Matthew looked over his shoulder. A cop was heading straight for them, and he'd come with backup: five other officers and Reda Ghannam.

"What's going on, Minister?" Alex asked.

Three officers continued past them and headed toward Robyn and Cal. The cops were stripping them of their bags and handcuffing them.

An overeager officer started patting Matthew down. Another was apprehending Alex.

Adrenaline rushed through him, mingling with anger and confusion and raising his blood pressure. "What's going on here?"

"Minister?" Alex's voice was tense and high-pitched.

Reda stepped forward to within a few inches of Matthew's face. "As if you don't know."

"If I did, I wouldn't be asking," Matthew stamped out, wondering who this man was in front of him. Matthew had spent hours working with Reda at the site. In the last few weeks, they'd shared dinners and drank wine. But this wasn't the same man.

"I am so disappointed in you. And you!" Reda slid his gaze to Alex. "I have known you for many, many years." He spat on the floor by Alex's feet.

"Red— *Minister*, please. Tell us what's going on." Her plea was loaded with desperation.

"What's going on is that you are all thieves," Reda answered. "You disgrace Egypt with your lies and betrayal!"

"Thieves?" Matthew's head was spinning. Everything was coming at him so fast.

The officer who had been patting Matthew down pulled his arms behind his back and snapped cuffs on his wrists. The metal bit into Matthew's skin and had him seeing red.

"We're Canadians. Take us to an embassy," he ground out.

Other passengers were milling about the airport, gawking at them.

"Please, Mr. Connor, you are making a scene," Reda said in a calm but disgusted manner.

"*I'm* making a scene?" Matthew served back loudly. "It seems to me you're the one doing that." As he held eye contact with the minister, the way Reda had addressed Matthew as "mister" instead of "doctor" sank in. "Take us to an embassy," Matthew repeated, doing his best to get a grip on his nerves.

Reda glared at him. "Your crime has been committed against Egypt."

"You said that," Matthew protested, "but what is it we're alleged to have done?"

"Get him out of my sight." Reda made a sweeping motion with his hand, and the cop yanked on Matthew's cuffs, leading him toward the front doors of the airport.

"You better be taking me and my friends to the Canadian embassy," Matthew said, feeling sick. Reda wasn't listening to a word he was saying.

As the cop shuffled him off, he looked over his shoulder to find Alex wasn't far behind. And Robyn and Cal were being hauled along, too. The accompanying officers were getting their luggage.

The cop who had Matthew led him to one of four police cars parked bumper-to-bumper. He was put in the back with Alex. Robyn and Cal were placed in another cruiser. Their luggage was loaded into the trunks of the third and fourth police cars. The last of which, Reda got into. But not in the back like a criminal. He was riding shotgun.

Matthew's breath was coming in short, choppy gasps. What the hell had just happened? What the hell *was* happening? Reda had accused them of betraying Egypt. This had to involve the expedition, but how?

"Why are we being arrested?" Maybe if he asked instead of demanded, he'd have better luck.

The officer who was driving looked at him in the rearview mirror. "You have stolen from Egypt."

"We never stole anything," Matthew said, feeling utterly frantic but volatile at the same time. "Do you have any idea who my father is?" He hated playing that card, but William Connor knew people in influential positions all around the world. His father had clout, and when he found out about this travesty against Matthew and his friends, there'd be hell to pay.

"You were the ones in charge of the dig, and now an artifact is missing," the officer said, indifferent. He was following orders, but he certainly didn't come across as having any empathy for their situation, either.

"We…" Matthew's mind went blank, and the words he was going to say were gone. He looked at Alex, who was shaking her head.

Who the hell had stolen an artifact? It wasn't him or his friends. Sure, he'd had his suspicions about Jasper a few weeks back, but they had fallen away seeing as the man had stuck around to help with cataloging everything. In fact, Alex's entire crew had worked tirelessly over the past three and a half weeks. This was obviously a setup, but the challenge would be getting anyone to believe them.

CHAPTER
40

Robyn had never been so terrified in her life, not even when she had been trapped in the tomb, unsure if she'd survive. There, her future was certain to hold starvation and dehydration. In this scenario, she had no idea what was coming. The cops weren't listening to a thing they said. She'd heard Matthew requesting they be taken to the Canadian embassy, and she had followed his lead. But it had done no good. The cops who had cuffed her and Cal had ignored them. The little they did say was clipped and to the point: *Turn around. You're coming with us. Move it.* Then she and Cal had been stuffed into the back seat of a cruiser.

While some youths got in trouble with the cops, she'd never been one of them. The cuffs were heavy on her wrists, and her palms were wet. Sweat dripped down her spine, and her insides were fluttering as if she had a hundred hummingbirds in there.

The cop behind the wheel was talking to his partner with animated gestures, but he wasn't speaking English. She'd guess the language was Arabic, and it was one Robyn couldn't begin to understand. And right now, she was kicking herself for that limitation. Why couldn't they be speaking French or Spanish? She knew those languages well enough to carry on a conversation. But maybe now wasn't the best time for self-flagellation. She had enough problems.

She did her best to shove aside the nightmarish news stories about international incidents and innocent people being locked up for life in foreign countries. How some were beaten and starved. She thought back to how the cop who had patted her down had taken more liberties with his hands than he should have. How the women were assaulted and— She swallowed what felt like a rugged-edge stone, and her mouth gaped open.

Cal looked over at her. "What did we do?"

"*Alsamt!*" the cop from the passenger seat called back.

Robyn shook her head subtly at Cal, guessing that *alsamt* was Arabic for *shut up*, given the man's scowl. She racked her brain as to why they were being treated like this and kept coming back to the same answer: whatever they had allegedly done had something to do with the dig. That had to be the case. But it's not like they had broken any laws—or any that she knew of. They had been working in the country legally, but what if Alex had failed to file their work visas properly? Robyn dismissed that possibility. They'd been working with Reda, who would have surely checked on their backgrounds and documents. If there had been a problem with their paperwork, they'd have known long before now. Besides, such a transgression shouldn't warrant rough handling by local cops.

As for the site, they'd left it in good condition. While they had been there, they'd cataloged with the skill of the professionals they were. And then they'd left amicably. Reda had even hugged her goodbye and said, *Take care, my dear.*

So what was it exactly that he thought they'd done? And what was it that had them all under suspicion—even Alex?

Robyn's body jerked to the right as the driver took a left turn at a fast speed. She hissed in a breath as a searing pain shot up her spine to her neck. The damn cops hadn't even bothered with the seat belts. A moment later, they were slowing down and pulling into the lot of a huge, military-type building.

If this was the embassy, there was nothing to indicate it. In fact, there were no signs at all, and if there were, she probably wouldn't be able to read them anyhow.

"Is this the embassy?" Robyn asked, silently praying it was while panic swelled in her chest.

"*Alsamt!*" the cop in the passenger seat shouted again.

Fear shuddered through her. It felt as if her throat was constricting.

It was tough to swallow. She blinked tears from her eyes.

The car was parked, and both officers got out and retrieved her and Cal. She found herself longing for the back seat as they were shoved forward. There she had been relatively safe. Who knew what horrors awaited them inside this building?

It was intimidating enough to be hauled out of the airport, but with the yellow, brick building towering over her, she felt tiny and defenseless, and her legs didn't want to move.

The officer yanked on her and barked something at her. Again, the interpretation was left to her imagination and based more on body language than actual words. She'd wager he was telling her to move. Part of her wanted to resist him. The officers had shown no interest in obliging their requests to go to the embassy. But if she did pick up her speed, she'd find out what alleged crime they'd committed sooner rather than later and wouldn't be considered uncooperative. That might work in her favor.

He hurried her into the building and through some hallways. Cal was ushered in behind her.

She could barely catch a solid breath. It was as though she was being marched to death row without a trial and conviction.

The officer stopped next to a closed door. He opened it and said, "Get in."

That she understood, and she complied. The officers removed her cuffs and Cal's, then slammed the door.

Robyn rubbed her wrists, busying her hands to try to calm her mind. But her chin was quivering and chills buffeted her.

"Hey." Cal touched her arm. "Matt will get us out of here. We'll be fine."

She looked at him, her breathing slowing down. She nodded, and a tear trailed down her cheek.

"And no one wanted to believe me when I said that pharaoh's curses were real." He smirked.

She shook her head and found herself smiling despite his inappropriate timing. But really, it was that or buckle in defeat. "Only you would attribute all this to a curse."

Cal shrugged. "If you have a better explanation, I'd love to hear it."

"They think we did something. Something we didn't do, of course."

She finally managed a full, deep, satisfying breath. She stretched out a kink in her neck.

"It's gotta be bad." Cal paused. "And the curse at work." He was smiling, trying to make light of what he'd said, but she knew he believed it. And she must admit—to herself, anyway—that maybe, just *maybe*, a curse had some merit. Otherwise, how did they find themselves in this ludicrous predicament?

The door opened, and Matthew and Alex were escorted inside and their cuffs removed.

Robyn went over to Matthew. "What's going on?"

"They think we stole an artifact," Matthew said.

"That's insane," Robyn exclaimed. "Why would we do that?" She paced, stopped in front of Alex, and turned to look at Matthew. "We did our jobs. We cleaned, cataloged, and packaged everything that went past us. Have they investigated the people who were responsible for transporting the artifacts to the museum?"

"I don't know." Matthew sounded about as frustrated as she felt. "It's not like they've opened up to me."

Robyn's attention snapped to Alex. "This has something to do with you."

"Excuse me?" Alex barked and thrusted her chin upward.

"Robyn." Matthew's voice contained a warning for her to back off. He took it further and stepped up beside Alex and slid an arm around her waist.

"We hardly know her, Matt. You knew her years ago, but there are things you don't know." Robyn stared at Alex as she spoke.

Alex tightened her jaw. Her eyes were begging Robyn to stop there. But she didn't. "You don't want to tell him? Then I will."

"Tell me what? What are you talking about?" he asked, partially annoyed and obviously curious. His body was rigid, as if bracing for bad news.

"She's using you, Matt." Robyn expected to feel good about telling him, but anger flashed in his eyes.

"Using me for what?" He was making it sound as though *she* was the crazy one.

Robyn crossed her arms. "She didn't call you here because you're in love with the mystery of the Tablets. She called you because she wanted to make a name for herself by using your reputation. Apparently, you've been dubbed 'the Legend Hunter' in certain circles."

Matthew's shoulders sagged, and he removed his arm from Alex's waist. "Is this true?"

There was a blend of anger and betrayal in his tone, and Robyn hated herself for doing this to him. But really, all this was Alex's fault.

"Is it?" Matthew punched out, and Alex flinched. "Were you using me?"

Alex turned her back to Matthew and remained silent.

"Maybe the reason we're here is because *she* stole the artifact and is pinning it on us. That would make quite a story." Robyn was finding it hard to stop, her pent-up aggravation erupting like a geyser over which she had no control.

Matthew shook his head and pointed a finger at Robyn. "Now that's crazy. She's here just like the rest of us."

"What better way to look innocent?" Robyn sighed. "Fine, I don't know about us being her patsies, but I do know she was using you."

Matthew's Adam's apple heaved. Robyn looked at Cal, who pressed his lips together. Alex was still facing away from them, but Robyn could hear her sniffling.

Alex turned around, her face flushed. "She's telling you the truth." Her eyes were wet, but no tears were falling.

Matthew closed the distance between them. "You used me? All this time? And this—" he waved his arm between them "—was this a lie, too?"

"It wasn't, I swear to you." Alex reached for his arm, but he drew back.

Alex slid a flaming gaze to Robyn, but Robyn let it roll off her. Her loyalties lay with Matthew and Cal, and Matthew had a right to know.

"Please, let me explain," Alex petitioned.

"Let you explain why you used me?" Matthew turned away from her and shook his head. "I don't think there's anything to say." He clenched his jaw, a pulse tapping in his cheek.

"But there is. I remembered you were in love with the legend of the Tablets, and that's why I first thought of you," Alex said, her voice straining. "But yes, I admit that I was aware of your reputation."

Robyn watched Matthew's eyes harden to steel and had to look away.

She hated seeing him going through this pain.

"It was just business, Matthew." Alex was gentle but unapologetic.

"Huh, nice to know that's what I am to you."

"That's not what I mean," Alex said. "Not us. But digs cost money, and my dig was funded by an independent benefactor."

"You make it sound like you don't know their name," Robyn interjected and closed her mouth when Matthew glared at her.

"I don't. The money was sent directly to an account."

"And so, what? I was a big flashy name to throw out there?" Matthew ground out.

"I didn't—" Alex licked her lips "—I didn't mean to hurt you."

Silence fell over the room for only a brief second before the door swung open.

An officer pointed a finger at Matthew. "You. Come now."

Robyn stepped up to pull Matthew back, but Alex beat her to it.

"Why do you need him?" Alex demanded.

The officer said nothing but removed Alex's hand from Matthew's arm. He shuffled Matthew out of the room and slammed the door.

Alex turned around and glared at Robyn. "You told me you were just friends."

"Uh-huh. And friends warn each other if someone is out to screw them." Her insides were quaking with rage.

"But you haven't said a thing for the last few weeks. So why now?"

"I figured Matthew would go home and forget about you." Robyn paused as she watched the agony wash over Alex's face. Surprisingly, she felt some remorse for being so harsh. "I didn't see a point, I guess," she added in a lower voice, attempting to soften her earlier blow.

Alex bit her bottom lip, and tears filled her eyes.

It wasn't fair that Robyn was now feeling like crap. This was certainly backfiring. "Listen, maybe he'll come to under—"

Alex held up a hand. "Don't even start. You saw him before he left here. He's pissed. He's not going to forgive me."

"Then you don't know Matthew very well." Robyn crossed her arms and turned away from Alex.

"Did you stir all this up because you still have feelings for him? Is that why you—"

"I told you why." Robyn peacocked her stance. If this woman thought she was going to admit to having romantic feelings for Matthew, she was sorely mistaken. Besides, the second Robyn set foot back in Canada, she was going to find herself a great boyfriend. Call it an order already placed with the universe. After all, Sophie was a strong believer in the law of attraction—believe something strongly enough and it was yours. Maybe it was time to put that theory to the test.

Cal stepped between them. "Come on, ladies, let's—"

Alex looked around Cal to Robyn.

Robyn's body stiffened. "The truth is, we hardly know you."

"You know everything you need to." Alex clenched her jaw and stared at Robyn. "Do you need my star sign?"

"Not necessary." Robyn didn't want to hear excuses or explanations. She didn't want their relationship to become personal. Besides, she knew all she needed to. But then again, Matthew saw something in Alex. And the wounded look on his face had been genuine. He really cared about her. Robyn knew loving someone meant wanting them to be happy, and that sometimes meant setting aside one's personal feelings.

"I've dedicated my adult life to Egyptology," Alex went on. "I'd never, ever risk losing my status here in Egypt. And if you think I would, you're pretty stupid."

The stark reality of it was there in Alex's gaze, and her defense was credible. Robyn turned away from Alex to face Cal. "I don't think she's in on this."

"Gee, thanks," Alex said.

Robyn slowly faced Alex again. "You're welcome." She wanted to tell her not to drag Matthew into their conversations again, but if she repeated this point, she'd only prove she hadn't let go of Matthew yet. And that was to remain her secret for now.

CHAPTER

41

MATTHEW PRIDED HIMSELF ON FEARING very little, but being hauled into a foreign police station as if he were a criminal topped all previous death-defying moments. Even when he was hanging by one arm off the side of a glacier, he had felt more in control. Matthew had been escorted into an interrogation room and told to take a seat, and he hadn't been there long before the door opened again.

A broad-shouldered officer entered. His eyes told the story of a hard life, and the wrinkles and gray hair bespoke of a man in his fifties. Given the chevrons on the uniform the man wore, Matthew guessed he was a lieutenant or sergeant. Reda came in after him holding a file folder. He closed the door behind them and stood next to it.

"I demand to be taken to the embassy and given a phone call." Matthew ground his teeth and squared his shoulders, doing his best not to portray any signs of fear.

"I'm Sergeant Youssef." He took a seat across from Matthew, all calm and cool.

Matthew's chest tightened. "Did you hear a word I said?"

"Yes, I heard you." The sergeant was studying him.

Matthew's temper flared. "Then *listen*. My friends and I are Canadian. I request that you take us to the embassy." He only felt a little bad for leaving Alex out of his protest.

Youssef sank back into his chair and gave a smug smile. "I don't have to do any such thing."

Matthew balled his hands into fists under the table. "You said there's a missing artifact?" Maybe if he played along, he'd get somewhere.

The sergeant and the minister remained silent.

Matthew continued. "My friends, Alex, and myself have nothing to do with this. Do you have any proof that we are?" Maybe an appeal to logic would help shake something from this stone-faced bastard. Matthew looked at Reda. "You know that none of us would have done what you're accusing us of."

Reda's gaze swept over Matthew, analyzing, judging. "The four of you had unsupervised access to the site."

"You mean when you weren't around?"

"Yes, and the artifact under discussion went missing before cataloging began," Reda clarified.

Four of you... Before cataloging began...

But there were more than four of them who'd had access to the site before cataloging. There'd been Jasper, Seth, Timal, Andres, and Danny. Jeff, as well, but it's not like they could go after him.

"You said four," Matthew began, "but your math is off. Technically, ten people had unsupervised access to the site. Nine are still with us." Matthew glared at Reda defiantly. "Have you brought the others in for questioning?"

"Who we question is not your concern," Youssef stepped in.

Matthew clenched his jaw. "When you are violating my rights and my friends' rights, it is my concern." His earlier trepidation was long gone, morphed into indignant anger. "My friends and I are innocent."

Youssef opened his palms toward Matthew. "Prove your innocence, then."

"Funny," Matthew said drily, "but in North America, it's the job of law enforcement to prove guilt, not the other way around."

"Ah, but you are not in North America. Do you need a GPS? A map?" The sergeant smirked and glanced at Reda, who was still over by the door. "For an archaeologist, you need to study your geography."

"What is this artifact you think we stole?" Maybe if Matthew knew what it was, he'd be able to offer something, though he couldn't imagine what.

Reda walked up next to where Youssef was sitting. He pulled a sheet of paper from the folder he was holding and tossed it across the table.

It was a photograph of the main antechamber.

"This picture was taken the night you and your friends first discovered it," Reda said.

Matthew glanced at the sergeant, who seemed relaxed, settled into his chair as if he were at home on his couch watching TV.

Reda tossed out another photograph. "This was taken after the portable lights had been brought in but before cataloging began. Do you see a difference between the two?"

Matthew picked up the pictures, holding one in each hand. He searched both and came up empty. He shook his head.

Reda gestured to the pictures. "Keep looking."

Matthew studied them. "Listen, I've never been good at the *Where's Waldo?* thing." He set down the photographs.

Reda's face creased with confusion.

"They're puzzles where you try to spot a cartoon guy named Waldo in a crowd," Matthew clarified.

"Humph." Reda took another sheet from his folder, and this time he handed it directly to Matthew. "How about now?"

Matthew snatched the page, albeit reluctantly. It showed a comparison of three photos. All were of the same section of the main antechamber. At the top half of the page, the two images he'd already looked at were side by side. The one to the left was marked *Before* and the one on the right was labeled *After*. The bottom half of the page showed an enlarged version of the *Before* shot, with the focus on a section with a circle drawn around an artifact. It still had a coating of dust on it, but the shape was unique.

It mostly resembled a rectangular chest but turned vertically, and the top was the shape of a triangle. At its peak was what looked like a small disc. In the four corners, there were higher points that stood on their own and came to oval tips. Based on the artifacts around it and Matthew's memory of scale, he'd say it was about fifteen inches wide, twenty inches high, and roughly fifteen inches deep. He didn't recall seeing this specific artifact in person.

Matthew admitted to that and added, "It's possible that it's still in the tomb to be cataloged. Things were moved around."

Reda shook his head. "No. It's gone. Someone stole it, and I believe it was you, your friends, or Alex. Or all of you."

Matthew obviously wasn't getting anywhere claiming their innocence, so it was time to try another tactic. "Tell me why you think one of us stole it. What about Jasper, Seth, Timal, Dan—"

Reda held up a hand to silence him.

"No, this is crazy," Matthew rushed out. "You've known Alex forever. You've worked with me in the past. Give me one good reason why we'd take it."

"This particular artifact is priceless," Reda ground out, maintaining eye contact with him.

Tingles shot up the back of Matthew's neck and cascaded down and over his shoulders. A blanket of clammy chills clung to him. This artifact must be connected in some way with the Emerald Tablets for Reda to be fixated on him and his friends. Reda knew how important finding them was to Matthew, how important it was to Alex. Matthew looked at the sergeant, unsure whether or not to mention them in front of the man. He was also worried that by bringing up the Tablets in reference to the artifact at all, it would somehow suggest guilt.

There was a knock on the door, and Youssef answered it. He stepped into the hall for a moment.

Reda continued to hold eye contact with Matthew during this time but said nothing.

The sergeant came back into the room but didn't take a seat again. He addressed Reda. "Their bags checked out. No sign of the missing artifact."

"I told you," Matthew spat.

Reda spoke to Youssef, still keeping his eyes on Matthew. "It still doesn't mean they're innocent. They could have hidden it or sold it."

"We've already started tracing their electronic footprints and have the records coming in from their phones."

"Another violation of our rights," Matthew growled.

The sergeant slid him a cool glance.

"Right, I'm not in North America." Matthew crossed his arms and slouched back into his chair.

Youssef continued, not paying Matthew any attention. "How do you wish for us to proceed, Minister?"

Reda regarded Matthew for a few seconds. "Why don't you leave us alone for a while? Maybe get the doctor a glass of water. Just knock before you reenter."

So he was *Doctor* again? Maybe his protests of innocence were finally getting through to the minister.

"As you wish," Youssef said and left the room.

Reda waited for a bit after the door had been shut. He looked over at the large mirror on the wall. No doubt it was one of those two-way mirror dealies like the ones Matthew had seen on cop shows. He wondered who was on the other side. Did they know about the Emerald Tablets? He still wanted to inquire if the artifact had something to do with the Tablets, but reason held him back.

"We need to talk." Reda's mouth set in a straight line, and he sat across from Matthew.

"I *have* been talking, but the problem is that you and the sergeant don't listen to a word I say."

Reda pressed a fingertip to the table. "This is a very sensitive matter, as I'm sure you can appreciate."

The hairs rose on the back of Matthew's neck. "Now you're trying to present yourself as my ally? Trying to make me feel like we can relate? You should have thought of that before accus—"

"I need your help," the minister interrupted.

"You need—" Matthew ground his teeth. "Do you listen to yourself when you speak? Why should I help you?"

"I know what I've put you through may seem unnecessary from your standpoint."

"You think?" Matthew snapped. "What makes you think I'd want to help you now?"

"Because if you don't, you'll spend your lives in an Egyptian prison."

"For what?" Matthew shook his head. The darkness in Reda's eyes told him that the man would concoct a charge if he had to. "You're threatening me, and I don't respond—"

"I'm *promising* you." Reda's gaze was relentless. "Someone stole that artifact, and you're going to help me get it back."

Matthew didn't even know the man in front of him anymore. The Egyptian Minister of Antiquities had been a man he'd revered. "Do threats normally work for you?"

Reda didn't respond, and Matthew straightened up in his seat.

"Listen, I know nothing about this artifact, but I'm sensing—"

Matthew paused, considering if he should come out and ask if the artifact was connected to the Tablets "—there's more importance to the artifact than it simply being a piece of ancient Egyptian history."

Reda regarded him with a well-groomed arrogance. "Isn't that enough?"

"Why don't you try being straightforward with me, and see where that gets you…" Matthew inclined his head.

There was a long silence.

"I believe it's connected to the Emerald Tablets," Reda eventually said.

To hear Matthew's suspicions confirmed didn't surprise him any. "Connected how?"

"From what can be made out, there are inscriptions on the sides. We believe the entire thing may provide directions to the Tablets."

Matthew looked down at the pictures on the table. "You can tell that through layers of dust?"

"I'm not without my resources," Reda began. "An enlargement was done of the artifact, and a graphic specialist was able to decipher the side that shows by utilizing light and shadows. They found definitive impressions."

"Hieroglyphics?" Matthew asked, and Reda nodded. "Were you able to read them?"

Reda regarded him with serious eyes. His posture was rigid, and he slid his jaw left, then right, and right, then left. "Are you going to help me get it back?"

"A moment ago, you didn't present it as if I had an option."

"I know that you are the most qualified to secure the artifact, and you're hungry to find the Tablets."

"You're also aware that my friends and I have other obligations and need to get back home." As it was, Robyn was dancing a fine line with her boss, given the spotty Internet connection. Cal needed to get home to Sophie. Matthew had to… "Our work visas were only valid for the month."

"Consider that taken care of."

"And the others? Are you going to question Jasper, Seth, Timal, Andres, and Danny?" If the minister was seeking his cooperation, Matthew wanted some in return.

"Andres and Danny have been cleared. Jasper, Seth, and Timal are currently in the wind."

"Huh, that's a sign right there that you should probably take a closer look at them."

"And, we are. But until we find them, I need your help."

"As you said." The minister's audacity was unbelievable.

"The artifact hinted at not only the Emerald Tablets but the hidden Library of Thoth."

Matthew straightened in his seat. According to myth, the Library would contain numerous scrolls and writings.

"I see this excites you," Reda said.

Matthew loosened his posture, hating that his body language had betrayed him. He wasn't going to add a verbal confirmation.

Reda must have sensed Matthew wasn't going to say anything, and he continued. "The directions that we can see in the photograph are incomplete."

"So get the artifact back from who stole it and follow the map you believe exists on it." Matthew shoved back with indifference.

"I thought that you prided yourself on hunting down legends, Dr. Connor. Your reputation says you're damn good at it, too."

Matthew let a few seconds pass in silence. That's exactly what he did, and he enjoyed the hell out of doing it. And maybe debunking cities and/or items people had relegated to fantasy had something to do with his rebellious streak and the need to prove people wrong. Still, there were times he found himself sliding straight to skepticism first. This was one of those times. While Matthew had tried to remain positive throughout the cataloging process in the last few weeks, he had to admit to having doubts about the Tablets' existence. But the source of his skepticism now wasn't so much in regard to the existence of the Library or the Tablets, but rather the faith Reda was placing in this artifact.

"What makes you think that this map leads right to them?" Matthew would cling to realism for the moment. "And even if you had directions, what's to say they'd be reliable anyway? There were other indications that they would have been with the pharaoh. We saw how that worked out."

"Some things you need to take on faith," Reda started. "But further examination of the hieroglyphics and drawings on the walls inside the tomb have provided us with other clues."

Matthew sat up straighter. "Why am I just hearing about this now?"

Reda regarded him for a few seconds, holding out in silence. "It's just recently come to light."

Matthew had this sinking suspicion that might not be the case.

Reda tapped a finger on the enlarged image of the artifact. "See the profile? There are tips sticking up in all four corners, and the top of the artifact comes to a point in the center and ends in a disc."

"Yes, I noticed."

Reda pulled out another photograph. "This was taken from the painting in the secondary antechamber. Look familiar?"

Matthew picked it up. "It looks like the artifact…"

"Uh-huh," Reda said. "And it gets better because the more I studied the hieroglyphics, I found snippets of what didn't seem to belong."

"I'm not following."

"Insertions, as it were. Random depictions in the midst of another story. Needless to say, they stood out to me."

Matthew's mind went straight to Jasper. He'd never mentioned anything striking him as being out of context when he'd interpreted the hieroglyphics. It seemed that may have been intentional.

"I think the murals also contain a partial map," Reda continued.

"Because the image of the artifact is next to the 'insertions'?" Matthew was grasping to understand.

"That and the hieroglyphics on the one side of the artifact was a duplicate of one we found in a mural."

"So there is a map on the artifact and enclosed in the murals?" Matthew just wanted to make sure he was hearing all this correctly.

"I believe so."

"Then why do you need the artifact?"

"As I mentioned, the murals only provide us with a partial map," Reda said.

Silence fell between them for a few seconds.

Reda studied him. "You thought that keeping the Tablets from falling into the wrong hands was important before? Well, now it is even more so. I believe whoever has this artifact may hold the key to finding both the Library and the Tablets. You wouldn't want that, would you?"

Now Reda was questioning his values? Who did this man think he was? But Matthew wasn't sure he had it in him to refuse this offering. And what if Reda made good on his threat of imprisonment? Matthew's back was against the wall. It wasn't much better than when the City of Gold had been the ransom for Sophie's freedom.

Setting aside his personal feelings, he assumed the weight of his moral obligation. "Guess we don't have much choice."

"I was hoping you'd see it that way." Reda got up, a smile resting on his face.

Oh how Matthew would have loved to wipe that grin right off.

CHAPTER

42

IT HAD BEEN HOURS SINCE Robyn had hurled out her accusation and exposed Alex to Matthew. But she still couldn't bring herself to look at Robyn. The assurance that Matthew would forgive her for using him was insulting. If Robyn had just kept her mouth shut in the first place, maybe Matthew would at least acknowledge her existence. Instead, he'd come back into the room at the police station with Reda and had spoken to Cal and Robyn as if she weren't even there. And that hurt even more than she cared to admit. Maybe if he gave her a chance to explain herself and why she'd brought him in… Maybe if he heard it from her lips, it wouldn't have sounded as bad as it had coming from Robyn's.

Still, she chastised herself for the choice she'd made and the reason she had made it. Sure, she knew that Matthew had always been fascinated by the Emerald Tablets and that it would make him ideal for bringing on board for their search. But the decision to do so, even if cemented by his excellent reputation, hadn't been a malicious one. Yet, guilt snaked its way through her whenever she thought about it. Maybe this was why she wasn't more successful in life, in business, in relationships: She didn't know how to fight for what she wanted. She didn't have a killer instinct. She'd often thought it was a strength, but it was her greatest weakness. All she had to do was take inventory of her life to see that.

It was eight thirty at night now, and she, Matthew, Cal, and Robyn were seated in Reda's living room. There were also two men that Reda introduced only as "good colleagues." But their pressed-lipped smiles and obvious submission to Reda indicated they were more like employees than colleagues. As it was, one of them was in the kitchen making a pot of coffee and boiling the kettle while the other one was perched next to a projector.

"They are aware," Reda had told them when they'd first arrived, "as I must make all of you, that everything we are about to discuss is of the utmost confidential nature. I must also be clear that if this confidence is broken, the penalty will be severe."

That had been about fifteen minutes ago, and Alex was still considering what the minister had meant by *severe*. She was taking in the room, which showed off the minister's flair for the eclectic with mismatched furnishings that somehow managed to complement each other. There were also sculptures displayed in glass cabinets, and most were pieces that represented his passion for Egyptology. A miniature replica of Tut's sarcophagus, a statue of the Great Sphinx, and the bust of a pharaoh were a few that stood out to her.

"Sorry for the wait." The nameless man who'd been sent to get coffee and tea returned to the room holding a tray and doled out everyone's beverage of choice.

Reda snapped his fingers and the other "colleague" got up and pulled down a projection screen.

"Now before we begin," Reda said, "I must emphasize again that this matter is confidential. The details we discuss are to be taken to your graves."

That was about as severe as it could get. Alex had to wonder if any defiance would warrant an express trip. At this point, nothing Reda did would surprise her.

"I've disclosed some of this information to Matthew down at the station, but now it's your turn." Reda stopped talking, as if purposely doing so to entice them. And despite Alex's reservations, her heartbeat still ticked up.

"The artifact—" Reda snapped his fingers and the "colleague" in charge of the projector clicked a button on the remote he was holding and a picture came up on screen "—as you can see here, is now missing. More directly, we believe it was stolen."

"And this is what you accused us of stealing?" Alex rushed out.

Reda regarded her. "That's right."

No apology, not even an attempt at reconciling the relationship they'd had.

"But you realize now that we weren't involved in its disappearance." She jutted out her chin and felt herself go cold, as she often did when angered.

"Yes, I do." Reda's lackluster response disclosed that he thought nothing of what he had put them through and would do it again.

"We go back *years*." Alex couldn't make herself stop, and she wasn't interested in drinking the coffee she had in her hand anymore. She set it on a nearby table. "You shouldn't have doubted my integrity."

"I sense you would like an apol—"

"Damn right, I do," she snapped.

Everyone was looking at her. Even Matthew had his gaze on her, but when she caught his eye, he looked away.

"Well, I do apologize," Reda began, "but this matter is one of urgency. So if I might continue…"

Alex gritted her teeth at his dismissal. She'd leave if she wasn't the equivalent of a trapped animal. There was no way she could excuse herself. She'd most certainly lose the dig, the credit. All she had uncovered with the nameless pharaoh's tomb would have been for naught. She owed it to herself to see this through to completion. Whatever *this* was.

Alex swallowed her indignation. "What is so important about this artifact?"

"*What is so important* is that it contains directions to the Library of Thoth and the Emerald Tablets."

Alex snapped her jaw shut and sank back against the couch.

"Nothing more to say?" Reda pressed her. He waited a few beats and continued. "Very well." He snapped his fingers again. The slide changed. It was a close-up of the artifact. "Enhancements were made, and as you can clearly see, there is an inscription on the side, which has been interpreted as a warning."

Matthew leaned forward, propping his elbows on his knees. "You told me it mentioned the Tablets and Thoth's Library."

"That too." Reda cleared his throat. "I also told you that I came across *insertions* as I translated the murals in both the burial tomb and secondary antechamber, and that one section of the hieroglyphics matched those on the side of the artifact."

"So this warning that is noted on the artifact is also in a mural?" Matthew asked.

"Yes," Reda spoke slowly. "It was found within a mural in the burial chamber. But as I mentioned there were *insertions*. More than one. These were abrupt changes of thought and expression. They were always marked by this depiction." He made eye contact with his "colleague" with the projector, who changed the slide. A drawing that resembled the artifact came up on screen. Reda gestured toward the man again, and the picture went back to the previous slide. "We also found that wherever there was an insertion, there were pictures depicting the Tablets and the Library." Reda pointed to three green rectangles of similar size with yellow rays coming out of them. They were within a box. Alex remembered a similar representation of the Tablets that Jasper found in the mural in the secondary antechamber. But they had been rectangles inside of a triangle, alluding to the Great Pyramid.

"Anyway, as you can appreciate," Reda went on, "we have a great mess on our hands. It's far more than a piece of Egyptian history that is out in the world." He snapped his fingers again. The slide advanced twice. Reda directed a laser pointer at the screen. "This was taken from the painting in the secondary antechamber. You'll notice the same image we just saw to indicate the Tablets and the Library appear again, as well as the graphic that looks like the artifact."

Alex found herself leaning forward, literally on the edge of her seat in anticipation.

"It goes on to tell of a book that was given to the unnamed pharaoh by the gods," Reda added.

"'The book' being the Emerald Tablets?" Robyn asked for clarification.

"Correct, my dear."

The energy in the room became heavy, and Alex decided to look at Robyn. She was scowling at Reda, apparently not caring for how he'd addressed her.

"Now, I remember seeing a dominant depiction of Thoth in the burial chamber," Matthew said. "And I know legends mention Thoth's involvement with the Tablets."

Reda nodded. "Well, the painting indicates that Thoth is the author. Now, you all likely know this, but the knowledge contained in the Tablets is unparalleled to any other wisdom existing in today's world. Some legends have pegged it as containing the *secrets of the universe*. Also, I was able to discern from the painting in the burial chamber that whoever possesses the Tablets is promised abundant wealth." He paused a moment. "The warning is to caution against the abuse of its power." He nodded toward the screen. "The depiction on this wall also says that only those who are enlightened dare to proceed." Reda's words fell heavy in the room, and it was silent except for the ticking of the clock on the wall.

After a bit, Reda continued. "The Tablets contain the secrets of the universe," he repeated with emphasis. "This means all there is to know about life and death, and everything in between. He or she who possesses the Tablets will not only be extremely wealthy but would be the most intelligent and powerful person in the world."

"There would be a lot of political leaders who would love to get their hands on them," Matthew said.

"And terrorists," Alex shot out, getting to her feet and pacing the room. "You mentioned these insertions and hinted at there being a map."

"Yes, but not a complete one," Reda said, dire resignation casting shadows over his face.

"Well, we need to figure this out. There has to be an insertion you're missing," Alex said.

"I wish there were, but I don't think so." Reda paused. "That's where the lot of you come in." His gaze landed on Matthew. "Assuming the rest of the map is on the artifact, we need to either find it or somehow beat whoever has it to the finish line."

"And how do you propose we do that when we don't know where that is? Kind of hard to hit a mark without a target." There was a gruff edge to Matthew's demeanor that hadn't been there before, and it saturated his tone. "I'm an archaeologist, not a detective."

"Ah, but you are selling yourself short." Reda shifted in his chair. "Do you not piece together clues to uncover legends? For example, when you set out after the City of Gold, I doubt you had a precise map to its whereabouts."

"Yeah, it didn't exactly work that way," Cal conceded.

Reda smiled. "I take it from your friend's reaction here that you had a lot of surprises along the way and needed to change approach, direction, think on your feet?"

Matthew nodded. "Yes, but—"

"*But* nothing, Dr. Connor. We need your mind on this."

"I say you find Jasper, Timal, and Seth," Matthew suggested.

Alex looked at him. "You're pointing the finger at them?"

"They are in the wind," Matthew responded coolly.

Alex shot him a glare, trying to ignore the sting his reaction had caused. "You think they are behind the missing artifact?"

"From what Reda told me, it would be possible given the timeline."

"He's right, my dear," Reda assured her.

Having Reda call her *my dear* made her appreciate why Robyn had scowled. It was bitter and hypocritical on the tail end of being hauled off by the police. But what Matthew had said and Reda had confirmed was starting to sink in. Jasper, Seth, and Timal could have stolen the artifact, and that thought stole her breath. She'd trusted them. She'd known Jasper for years. Bile rose into the back of her throat, and she swallowed roughly.

Matthew's gaze passed from Alex to Reda, and by doing so, he seemed to close the conversation on Jasper, Seth, and Timal's culpability. "Jasper had mentioned that the Tablets were linked to the Great Pyramid," Matthew said. "Did you find out any more in that regard?"

Reda smiled and pointed a finger at him. "See, you are sharp. There were several mentions of a hidden chamber in or around the Great Pyramid, but not in direct reference to the Tablets. They could be connected, though," Reda conceded.

"Rumor is that there are hidden chambers within the pyramid and around it," Alex said. "But I thought you were skeptical about that possibility." Maybe if she focused on making progress with what they did have, she'd stop scrutinizing her ability to read other people.

Reda's eyes darted to hers. "I've been wrong before. Besides, rumors are usually based on a snippet of truth. Of course, I shouldn't have to tell you that."

"What makes people think there are hidden chambers?" Cal asked, inserting himself into the conversation.

"Radar," Alex answered.

Cal arched his eyebrows. "Why not just get in there, then?"

"There are a lot of laws that protect the entire pyramid complex. It hasn't been easy to get the rights to investigate as thoroughly as we'd like to," Reda replied.

"It probably doesn't help when the minister of antiquities is skeptical of their existence," Cal called him out. "How are we supposed to get in there, then?"

"That's one of the things I'll take care of," Reda stated, unaffected by Cal's coolness.

"Sounds like a big thing." Cal shrugged when everyone looked at him. "What? It does."

Alex had to admit that Cal had a point, but she wasn't naive enough to believe the minister didn't hold sway. She was curious why he hadn't bothered to throw his weight around on this matter before. Then again, the payoff for doing so now was great.

"All right," Alex started, "I'd like to know where to concentrate our efforts. We can't just go digging all over the place hoping to get lucky."

"And that's where I can't help, and I'm hoping all of you can," Reda said. "I have some clues, but they will only take us so far. We need to get our hands on the artifact or figure out how to reach the Library some other way."

"Some other way," she mumbled. They were so close, yet so very, very far away.

CHAPTER

43

IT WAS THE *SOME OTHER WAY* that was drilling into Matthew's head. All he had to do was think outside the box. All in a day's work for him. Still, in this particular case, the answers weren't coming easily.

Matthew drank the rest of his coffee and set the empty cup on a coffee table atop a coaster. "Thing is, we have no idea where Jasper, Seth, or Timal are. They could be anywhere in the world."

"Not if they have the artifact," Reda interjected. "They'd want to be right here in Egypt."

Matthew didn't want to dwell on the alternative, but it was a possibility. "They could have sold it. Then we'd have no idea who we're looking for."

Alex shook her head. "There has to be another explanation for why they can't be found. Jasper is in love with ancient Egypt and has been working here for most of his career."

Matthew looked at her. Was she really naive enough to think Jasper wasn't behind this?

"What about Seth and Timal? Are you as confident about their innocence in all this?"

Alex flushed but didn't get a chance to respond before Robyn cut in. "Well, if Jasper has a passion for ancient Egypt as Alex said, he'd want to put his hands on the Tablets for himself and see the Library with his own eyes. He wouldn't have sold the artifact," Robyn added. "I'm not saying he's innocent. And he'd get more money if he had the actual merchandise in hand. That is, if he plans to sell anything."

"If we're to believe that," Matthew began, "it would indicate a couple of things. One, the artifact has the exact coordinates to the Library and Tablets. And two, he'd likely enlist some help before setting out after them."

"Let me guess—" Alex crossed her arms "—that's where Seth and Timal come in."

Matthew shrugged. She narrowed her eyes at him, but beyond the blaze of anger, he saw pain.

"Thing is, we can go around and around with this," Reda interjected, playing referee, "but it won't get us anywhere."

Alex worried her lip. "I just can't accept that Jasper would do something like this, even with the wealth it would bring him."

"Maybe it's not the wealth that tempted him," Reda said. "It could be the power."

Matthew was starting to paint a picture in his head, and it wasn't a pretty one. To steal something from the site, there would need to be a diversion, and the largest one of those was Jeff getting bitten by a snake. His breath caught.

"Just listen to me, Alex," he beseeched her.

She knotted her arms tighter.

"When Jeff was bitten, what's to say that Seth and Timal didn't drive off with the artifact when they took him to the hospital?" Matthew got to his feet but thought better of getting too close to Alex when she turned slightly away from him.

"You're suggesting that...that..." Alex ran a hand down the length of her throat.

Matthew prayed that she wouldn't make him finish, but she was just looking at him with big doe eyes. He stepped closer to her, risking rejection now, but she stayed put. "What if Jeff was killed because he refused to go along with the scam Jasper had going with Seth and Timal?"

"You realize how crazy you sound?" She backed away from him and held up her hands. "You said not long ago that you're not a detective, so why are you acting like one?"

"Fine. But the artifact went missing before we started cataloging." Matthew looked at Reda.

"He's right, my dear. It was in pictures from when you first discovered the tomb, but it was gone by the time cataloging started."

Alex's eyes glazed over, and she swallowed roughly.

"Cal, you took pictures of the main antechamber on different days. Can you easily bring those up for Alex to look at?" Matthew asked, not worried about offending the minister. He had provided a rather large time frame for the artifact to disappear: from initial discovery until cataloging began. Matthew was curious if they could narrow that down.

"Yeah, it probably wouldn't take much. I keep a copy of the pictures, of course, and organize them by day, time, and location." Cal got to his feet and went toward the front entry, where their luggage was sitting. He came back a few seconds later, his laptop under an arm, and sat back down on the couch. He fired up his computer and was tapping on keys in no time, but it seemed much longer because Alex was staring at him.

"All right," Cal began. Alex moved behind Cal and looked at his screen over his shoulder. "This picture was taken when we first showed up. And the artifact is there." Cal worked his fingers over his keyboard. "And this…" Cal fell silent and glanced back at Matthew, then at Alex. "I'm sorry, Alex. But it isn't showing in the pictures I took the morning Jeff died."

"That means that Jasper, Seth, and Timal are involved with its disappearance," Matthew clarified.

Alex's chin started to quiver and her body began to tremble. He hurried to her side but then hesitated, debating whether he should hug her and offer comfort or let it be. She put her arms around him before he could decide. He held her close until she pulled back. She palmed her cheeks.

"I can't believe I'm even entertaining the possibility that…" She shook her head. "That Jasper and the others…that they killed Jeff." Her eyes were full of tears, but they sparked when they met Matthew's. "Do you think he was even bitten by a snake?"

He'd already been responsible for the brunt of bad news. He wasn't about to suggest that the others could have provoked the snake to strike or that it had been something else entirely that had killed Jeff. "There's a way to find that out for sure, too, and that's by contacting the hospital."

"Let me take care of that for you, my dear," Reda offered. "You have enough on your plate as it is."

Alex nodded and sniffled. Matthew ran a hand over her hair. She leaned against his side, and he held her. In this moment, all was forgiven. So she'd used him. She'd probably had a good reason. He was losing his mind over this woman. Being used was being used no matter the excuse. But he hadn't really given her the chance to explain herself, and if anyone should know about the principle of standing on others' backs to get ahead in business, it should be him. He'd grown up watching his father's career in politics, after all.

"Now, I have more to share with everyone." Reda snapped his fingers, and the image on the screen changed.

"This is another insertion." Reda pointed the laser dot at the image of the artifact as drawn on one of the paintings, not that he needed to, as they all knew what to look for now. "In fact, I have four to share. The first one, as I'd mentioned, is a warning. The rest are more or less directions. Now, it's unclear what order they go in, but they provide a seemingly step-by-step guide on how to reach the Library and the Tablets. That is, once one knows where to start looking. This one here is a depiction that indicates there are seventeen steps that lead to the library of great knowledge. Next picture."

Another image came up, the inscription different from the one on the last slide.

Reda was staring at the screen. "Dig and you shall find."

"That one sounds like a Bible verse," Robyn said. "But it's *seek* and you shall find."

Reda looked at her. "I'm not sure of the correlation or if there is one, but this inscription also denotes labyrinths and tunnels within the Great Pyramid."

Cal winced. "I don't know about the rest of you, but I'm not in a real hurry to go back into a tunnel."

"We might not have much of a choice," Matthew told him.

"I know," Cal said. "But that doesn't mean I have to like it."

"You just need to remember why we're doing this, Cal. Besides the threat of prison." Alex's voice turned hoarse. She was obviously bitter. "We owe it to Jeff to make this right," she added softly.

Cal nodded.

"Too bad it doesn't say where within these tunnels," Robyn said.

"Again," Reda started, "if we knew that, we wouldn't be sitting around here." He snapped his fingers, and the slide changed again. "This says to proceed one hundred and fifty cubits. A cubit is seventeen-point-six inches on the short end and twenty point six on the long, so that's—" Reda's face scrunched up "—between two hundred twenty feet and two hundred fifty-seven and a half feet." Reda met Matthew's eyes and then bobbed his head. "Yes, that math is right," he confirmed his own work. "Next slide." Reda put his attention back on the screen. "This one says to go right." He sat back and clasped his hands in his lap. "As I mentioned, we don't know the order of these directions or where to start our search."

The room fell silent. Matthew looked around at everyone. Robyn was chewing on her bottom lip, looking at him. Cal was staring blankly at him. Alex was running a hand through her hair, visibly frustrated, her gaze on him, too. Even Reda was watching him.

And that was the problem with being good at something: people expected you to present solutions.

Reda seemed quite certain no more clues remained in the tomb. There was something Matthew was missing, though, something that danced around the edge of his mind. It was something that Reda had reminded him of at the police station, something that he'd said—

"The key to enlightenment lies with the pharaoh," he rushed out.

No one said anything.

"What if that was meant literally?" Matthew shot out, and he stepped toward the front door. "We could have missed something in the sarcophagus."

Alex hooked Matthew's arm and drew him back. "We already looked in the sarcophagus."

"We could have missed something." And they did—he could feel it.

Eventually, Alex nodded. "What are we waiting for? Let's get to the museum."

"I'd say let's sleep on it, but the fate of the world rests on our shoulders," Cal chimed in.

Matthew looked back at his friend, and Cal was smiling, but it was broken by a yawn.

Reda slapped Cal's shoulder in a friendly gesture. "That it does."

Maybe they would actually find the Tablets and save the world. Then again, maybe he shouldn't get too carried away just yet.

CHAPTER
44

ROBYN HAD NEGOTIATED WITH THE Egyptian Museum several times throughout her career, but this was her first time setting foot inside the building. She had to admit that she'd never imagined her reason for doing so would be to look inside the coffin of a mummy she'd had a hand in discovering. But now wasn't a good time to allow herself to get caught up in this surreal moment. She was essentially here under threat of prison time. But she needed to focus on her personal motivation, and that was to save the world as she knew it. The last thing the world needed was a miscreant wielding otherworldly power.

They were let inside the museum by a contact Reda had in the forensic analysis department. It had only taken one phone call from the minister and the doors were opened.

Reda's contact was a man in his late forties with a Roman nose and alert eyes. He had either a high forehead or a receding hairline—however one wished to see it. What hair did remain was silver.

"This is Tony," Reda offered as an introduction. "We'll leave out the last name. It's a mouthful."

Tony smiled politely and held out his hand to Alex first, then Matthew, Robyn, and lastly, Cal.

Reda went on. "Tony is a trusted member of my inner circle. He's aware of what's at stake here and has been sworn to secrecy."

"I hope that you find what you're looking for tonight." Tony's face became grim. "I do not want to imagine any of this falling into the wrong hands."

Robyn appreciated the reason for the cryptic manner in which Tony was talking to them. Reda had explained on the drive over that the museum was under video surveillance, and in some areas, that included audio, as well. She assumed Reda must have a contact in security, too. Otherwise all this would be too risky. She'd wager that the lab they were standing in now had both eyes and ears on them.

"We'd like to see what we've come for," Reda said.

"Of course. This way." Tony led them through the lab to another room. The door required a code and the swipe of Tony's ID card to open.

Cool air rushed out and kissed Robyn's skin. She walked in after Reda and Matthew, and there was the sarcophagus. It was breathtaking. It had been cleaned, and the overhead lights sparkled off the smooth gold. There was, however, something unsettling about seeing it here, out of its element, rather than where it had been placed thousands of years ago. It somehow felt as if they'd been responsible for trespassing and theft. Of course, this is what she did with Matthew and Cal: they found artifacts and relics, and brought them to the light of day for the world to enjoy. But somehow it seemed different when that "artifact" contained a once living, breathing person.

"Any luck on confirming his identification?" Reda asked Tony. "Or his heritage?"

Tony shook his head. "No to both. We haven't gotten there yet, but given the excellent shape the mummy is in, I don't anticipate any problems extracting useable DNA."

Another thing out of its element with this scenario was the science. There was no way that the ancient Egyptians ever would have imagined this type of testing would exist in the future.

"Is it…" Cal's mouth twisted in disgust. "Is it…still in there?"

"Yes, of course," Tony answered, furrowing his brow as if to ask where else he would expect it to be.

Cal stepped back and stood in the doorway.

"We're going to need to take a close look inside the coffin," Reda told Tony. "And we might need your help to take the mummy out."

"Oh no. This is where I leave." Cal spun on his heel and went out the door and back into the main part of the lab.

"Please don't touch anything out there," Tony called to Cal.

Cal put his arm out into the doorway and gave a thumbs-up. Robyn smiled. Crazy, loveable, Cal. Obviously, he was still a little squeamish about the body and latching on to his belief in a mummy's curse.

Matthew took position next to the coffin and looked over everyone. "Cal," he cried out, "we'll need you back in here."

"No way, not again," Cal shot back.

"Come on."

"Fine." Cal came back into the room and got into position around the sarcophagus, as did the rest of them.

"All right, we've got this," Matthew offered encouragement. "On the count of three." Matthew did the countdown, and they all lifted.

Once the lid was on the floor, Robyn looked inside at the mummy, taking in the beautiful golden mask and the golden fingertips that still adorned his hands. Bathed in full light, and here in the museum, it was so stunning that tears came to her eyes. This find alone was incredible, yet they were there with the intention of trumping it. That was hard to imagine.

The mummy was in pristine condition. Maybe if she could arrange for it to be showcased at the ROM, it would go a long way toward making amends with her boss. He wasn't too pleased when she'd called to say she was going to be delayed returning to Toronto. He'd responded with a curt, *Do what you must.* He hadn't even asked when she'd be back. She'd take that as his leniency having reached its end. She winced at the thought and put her mind back on the mummy and the interior of the coffin.

"There are no markings," Robyn observed. Just as there weren't any on the exterior. Both of which were unusual.

"We have to remove him," Matthew said.

Tony looked at Reda, and it was clear from his energy and panicked eyes he had hoped it wasn't going to come to that.

"We do as he says," Reda confirmed.

Tony simpered. "Minister, please, there's a proper way of handling—"

"You'll help us, and we'll be careful." Reda left no room for negotiation.

Alex winced and looked at Robyn. "This makes me nervous."

Robyn nodded. That made the three of them, pulling Tony into that fold. But she had a feeling that Matthew was on to something. Even the way his eyes had taken on a steely intent, his entire body was tense and poised, and all his attention was directed on the mummy and the coffin.

"Very well." Tony tapped a nervous hand on his leg. "We're going to need everyone's help, though." He looked straight at Cal.

"No. No way." Cal held up his hands and stepped back.

Robyn was fighting not to laugh at his facial expression—the way his lips curled in disgust and his eyes got large. Tag onto that the tension in the room, and she feared she might be on the losing end of her battle against the giggles. This didn't happen to her all the time, thank God, but sometimes awkward and stressful situations brought it on. Not a characteristic she much cared for, and it had gotten her into trouble more times than she could count.

"Cal, it won't be that bad," Matthew said.

"Humph."

"Don't be like that." There was no play to Matthew's voice. Rather, there was a little irritation.

"Fine," Cal sulked. "But if I end up haunted by this thing, I'm blaming you."

This thing? *Leave it to Cal.*

"I'll take my chances." Matthew's dry response only confirmed what Robyn had already picked up on: he was focused.

A few moments later, the mummy was lying on a steel gurney.

Alex was grinning and pointing at the bottom of the coffin. "There's a cartouche!"

Robyn hurried over to take a closer look, and sure enough, there it was. "The mummy covered it."

"Let me see." Reda nudged his way between Matthew and Cal. He pulled out his glasses and bent over the edge of the coffin. He straightened up a few seconds later, smiling. "We have our identity."

"But his name, it was…t-t-taken from him," Robyn stuttered. "It says his name?"

Reda looked at her and nodded. Her insides were tingling from anticipation.

"What does it say?" she rushed out, unable to wait any longer.

"Baufra." Reda took his glasses off but held on to them by one arm.

Robyn covered her mouth, then dropped her hands. "His existence has never been verified… Well, not before now. Not contemporarily, not archaeologically."

"So we're looking at a ghost here," Cal inserted.

She looked over at him, and he was smiling. His comment, obviously meant to be funny, just intensified her joy. With Baufra's discovery, they'd had a part in rewriting history. Robyn let out a holler and hugged the person closest to her, who just happened to be Alex. Alex hugged her back, clearly letting their past go for the moment. And no wonder. Her name would go down in—

Robyn backed out of the embrace and ran her hands down her shirt to straighten it out. She'd been thinking that Alex's name would go down in *history*, something that was obviously more important to her than people. Maybe Robyn was being a little harsh, but she had her loyalties and her values, and she'd be nothing without them. She knew she had told Alex that Matthew was a forgiving person, but she had a hard time understanding how he could so easily dismiss Alex using him.

"All right. I hate to break up the party, but we're no closer to finding what we're after. Anyone have any suggestions?" The arch of Matthew's brow displayed his frustration.

Nothing was coming to Robyn's mind, but she split her gaze between looking at the mummy and the people in the room.

Matthew raked a hand through his hair. "I don't get it."

"Okay…" Robyn paced a few steps. "The key to enlightenment lies with the pharaoh… That's what led us to here."

"Thanks for the recap," Cal teased.

She narrowed her eyes at him while secretly loving how her friend kept inserting humor into their tense predicament. "We have his name now, a name that was supposedly taken away from him." She paused there, wondering if there was something significant about that. "Why remove his name everywhere else but put it inside the coffin?"

Matthew hitched his shoulders. "It's a good question, but—"

"I know. Does it factor into what we're after?" Robyn finished, surmising what Matthew was going to say.

He nodded.

"That I don't know. We did note how much stuff he was buried with for someone who'd had his name stripped. And he had been entrusted with a great secret." She purposely held back saying the Library and Tablets specifically due to the surveillance. Her gaze settled on the mummy and his burial mask. "We should take a closer look," she said, pointing at the mask. "Maybe there's something written within the design."

Now Matthew's eyes lit up.

Reda was watching her, a smile on his lips. "Good thinking, my dear."

How she wished he'd stopped calling her that. While she hadn't minded the term of endearment before, since he'd accused them of stealing the artifact, it irked her to no end.

Matthew perched over the mummy's mask but shuffled to the side to make room for Reda.

The minister put his glasses back on and leaned in again. It would seem he needed to update his prescription.

"Do you see anything that can help us?" Matthew asked.

Reda straightened up and shook his head. "Nothing."

"What about his golden fingertips? Anything stand out on them?" Matthew's voice rang of desperation.

Reda looked briefly at them. "I'm afraid not."

The room went quiet again, and Robyn was sure the rest of them were as caught up in their thoughts as she was. She wondered if theirs were as dark as hers, though. All she kept imagining were the Tablets in the wrong hands, and the fate of the world within that person's control.

"I guess we should put him back." Matthew sounded more than discouraged. He sounded like a part of him had been broken.

Robyn looked at him. He'd been fascinated with the Tablets a good portion of his adult life, and now he'd come so close only to have any chance of realizing his dream blow up in his face—again.

Robyn and Alex stepped back as the men already had their hands on the mummy to return him to the coffin. They almost had it back inside when something hit the floor. It had made a tinking noise against the tile.

Her heart lurched, and she widened her eyes at Matthew.

"Everyone stop moving!" he said. While he didn't say anything else, Robyn received his message nonetheless.

She scanned the floor, her eyes picking up nothing. She hunched down, looking beneath the wheeled crate that the sarcophagus was on top of. And she saw it. She wanted to say that she found what had dropped in answer to Matthew's unspoken question. But for the same reason he didn't ask out loud, she didn't comment out loud. While Reda might have the surveillance angle covered, she certainly didn't need to advertise to whomever was listening in that something had fallen out of the mummy's wrappings.

Robyn shook her head and started mumbling. "Sorry, about that…" She reached her hand under the crate and picked up… *A coin?* It was about two inches in diameter, and her fingertips ran over an engraving on both sides. She couldn't examine it here without tipping off security, though. But it very well could be "the key" the hieroglyphics had referred to. She palmed the item and stood up, making sure to keep eye contact with Matthew as she did so. "I just dropped my keys. Sorry."

Matthew blew out a deep breath, but there was a flicker in his eyes that told her he'd received her message. "Don't let that happen again. You scared the crap out of me."

The others seemed to catch the underlying communication, too, and the men got the mummy positioned back inside the coffin.

"Well, thank you for your help, Tony." Reda shook the man's hand.

"Anytime, Minister." Tony smiled cordially, and it was evident their secret was safe with him.

Robyn stepped toward the door, the rest of them on her heels. Reda stopped, though, and said, "Please let me know if the DNA confirms our man's identity."

"I will, Minister."

Robyn wanted to run out of the museum but managed to pace herself. She led the way toward the two black SUVs they'd driven here. Reda's "colleagues" were each waiting behind a wheel.

Robyn positioned herself between the two vehicles and away from the museum parking lot cameras. She opened her hand. There was some light from the posts but not enough that she could make out any details.

Reda came in on her left, and Matthew on her right. He pulled out his new phone and turned on the flashlight function. He shone it on the object she held.

She ran the pad of her thumb over the surface. It was a gold coin. And as she'd suspected, there were engravings on both sides.

Reda had his glasses out again and was leaning in to see. "Do you mind, my dear?"

She reluctantly handed it to him, but he would be the only one of them who could interpret its message. Still, she felt an attachment to it.

"Ah." Reda was grinning broadly, the lines around his mouth cutting into his cheeks. "This is it."

Robyn caught Alex's eye.

"It tells us where to dig?" Alex ventured.

"Yes, I think it tells us precisely where to dig." Reda let out a wallop.

Robyn faced Matthew. "You did it," she said to him.

"*We* did it," he countered.

He put an arm around her, pulled her to him, and pecked a kiss on her cheek, but he quickly released her. He patted Cal on the back and ended up in Alex's arms.

Robyn touched her cheek as she watched them. Alex seemed to make Matthew happy. Maybe she wasn't quite the devil Robyn had made her out to be. Maybe she was the one who was like a monster—the green-eyed kind.

CHAPTER
45

THEY WERE BACK AT REDA'S house where they'd be spending the night. Cal was tucked away in one of the five guest bedrooms, pacing the room like an expectant father. Really, it was a miracle he had any energy at all. It had to be the sugar from the donuts they'd picked up on the way to Reda's.

The plan was to get some sleep and head out first thing in the morning. Apparently, the urgency of their mission had been disregarded in favor of getting some rest. Reda had put people in place to watch the area where they were planning to dig. Reda also assured them that he'd take care of getting proper permits. It made Cal wonder just how much pull the minister had.

Cal tapped his phone against his thigh. He couldn't bring himself to the look at it, though. Hours ago, he'd taken the coward's way out and texted Sophie about the delay in returning home, then silenced his phone. She had probably replied with a snippy text by now—probably more than one. And he didn't think he could handle an argument right now. While it was going on midnight in Egypt, it was the dinner hour back in Toronto. And that would mean Sophie would be awake. Maybe *too* awake.

He dropped onto the end of the bed, cradling his phone in his hands, still hesitant to look at it. He knew he'd have to defend himself again. As it was, they'd only talked a couple of times since he'd arrived in Egypt, and both calls had been short. It was no secret that Sophie didn't care for his "adventures" and cared even less about discussing them. And that cut deep. Here he was having an adventure of a lifetime, and she couldn't even feign interest or happiness for his sake. He'd held back the part about him and the others being trapped in a tomb. He could only imagine how she'd prattle on about that, all the I-told-you-so's. She'd go on about how dangerous his expeditions were and how he shouldn't be doing them. He didn't want to hear it. The truth was he'd never give them up. And now it seemed they were on the verge of actually finding the Emerald Tablets and the Library of Thoth. There was no way he could turn his back now, even if Reda gave him an option. It all excited Cal too much, and that excitement was stronger than his fear.

Even though he figured he'd never be permitted to capture the Tablets through his lens, he was fine with that. Still, he'd caught himself fantasizing about capitalizing on their discovery a few times, both financially and professionally. *If only.* Not that he'd ever do that. Too much was at stake if their discovery got out. They had to keep the Tablets safe and out of the wrong hands. But who was qualified to determine whose hands were the right ones? The thought hadn't occurred to him until now.

He flipped his phone over and steeled himself before glancing at the screen. Only one text message.

Maybe Sophie was too mad to talk to him…

He unlocked his phone and confirmed the message was from her. He winced at the simplicity of her response. *Fine.*

Oh God. She was more pissed off at him than he'd expected. He hadn't even gotten a *let me know* or *keep me updated.* Not even an *I love you.*

He gulped. The situation between them was worse than he'd thought it was when he'd left. And really, if they couldn't talk openly, it would only widen the chasm between them.

He sat there taking some deep breaths. He loved the adrenaline rush and the lack of predictability that came with quests. In contrast, his life with Sophie was quite predictable. But he liked that, too. She'd been there for him almost six years now. Whenever he'd needed her, no matter what. The only thing they never saw eye to eye on were the adventures. And if that hadn't changed after all this time, it was unlikely it ever would. The thing was, it had become pretty much a taboo subject, and he felt guilty even bringing it up.

Pain knotted in his chest. Maybe she had her reasons for distancing herself from the adventures. After all, her kidnapping, near rape, and brush with death were the result of one of them. Still, was the space between them just going to continue to grow? What if they never agreed on the matter? He couldn't let her change him or control what he did with his life. But he loved her, and relationships—at least the ones that lasted—required some compromise. That was the thing, though—*some* compromise. Not complete self-sacrifice.

He picked her number from his Favorites and listened to the ringtone. Just when he thought he was going to be shuffled to voice mail, she answered. But she said nothing.

"It's Cal."

"I saw that before I answered."

Oh, she was as cold as ice. There was zero warmth to her voice. He'd talked to strangers who were more excited to hear his voice.

He cleared his throat. "I'm sorry I didn't have a chance to update you…on the delay. Over the phone."

"I figured you would when you could."

Again, she showed no interest or concern. She wasn't being loud or harsh, but it was the undercurrent of cold indifference that was killing him.

The line remained silent, as if telling him he was to fill the void. But it wasn't as if he had a timeline for his return, and Reda's promise of severe punishment for breaking confidentiality wasn't far from his mind.

"I don't know when I'll be home." He pinched his eyes shut after he said this and waited for the yelling to start, for the barrage of questions. Neither came.

"Not sure why you called, then," she said.

Tears stung his eyes as anger raised the hairs on the back of his neck. "I just thought you might like to know where I was."

"I know where you are. Or at least I think I do."

He flinched as if hit, and his hands were shaking. "What do you mean by that?"

"Nothing."

"No, what do you mean by that?" If she thought he was going to let this go, she was mistaken.

"I meant *nothing*," she ground out.

"Fine," he spat.

"No, you don't get to be like that with me, Cal." Anger permeated her words now. "You take off to Egypt, put your life on the line, our future at risk…" She paused. "I didn't think you'd actually go."

"And why wouldn't I?" The question hurled from him without restraint or thought.

"Because I thought you loved me, Cal. I thought we meant something."

His chest was burning as agony filled him. His hand was clenched around the phone while the other one seemed to lay limp. The threat of emotion taking over him right now was very real. It was propelling up the back his throat and touching the hinges of his jaw. He was one blow from curling over in defeat or one blow away from…

He couldn't believe the thought had even come to mind. He loved her. She'd been his world for so long now. He'd wanted her to be his future. But all that came shattering down, raining over him like shards of glass shredding his spirit. "Are you ever going to support me going on these expeditions?" The question ripped from his throat.

"You know how I feel about them." Her tone left no room for an apology and didn't hint at any willingness to compromise.

He closed his eyes, pulling strength from somewhere deep inside, hoping to be brave enough to do this. He had the right to be true to himself without feeling guilty about it. "I think… I think." He cleared his throat. "I think we should…take a break."

Silence.

His heartbeat pulsed in his ears, and if he listened hard enough, he swore he could hear his heart literally breaking.

She sniffled. "Well, I guess we've had a good run."

"Don't you pull out that crap with me. Not now." She could have said pretty much anything else and it wouldn't have ticked him off like that had. It was a favorite line of hers that she'd pull from her arsenal whenever they argued. Really, it was a manipulative tactic. He softened his voice, reining in his temper. "You really think this is easy for me?"

The line went dead. She'd hung up.

He sat there holding the phone, wishing that he'd told her he loved her. Because he did, and he probably always would. A part of him wanted to call her back, beg for forgiveness, tell her that he'd overreacted, but he couldn't bring himself to move. Sure, she understandably had an issue with his going on expeditions, but she claimed to love him. He should be allowed to talk about his adventures; he couldn't go the rest of his life censoring what he said. His soul was whispering that he'd made the right call and that he had the right to love himself, too, and do what made him happy. He could only hope that this ache is his chest would go away. But he had a feeling that would take awhile.

CHAPTER
46

REDA HAD RUN THEM THROUGH his interpretation of the coin before they headed out to the Giza pyramid complex. Now, Matthew, his friends, and Reda were standing at the base of the Great Pyramid, one of the Seven Wonders of the World. Matthew had been here before as a tourist, but the awe of that trip couldn't rival the thrill that came with today's purpose.

It was six o'clock in the morning, hours before the site would open to the public. And as Reda had promised, he had the connections to secure them access.

Matthew, Cal, Robyn, Alex, Reda, and his two men were standing at the back of the pyramid, facing south toward the boat pits and, farther out, a modern-day road. The Great Sphinx was ahead and to the east. To the southwest was the Pyramid of Khafre, and beyond that, the Pyramid of Menkaure.

"It said two hundred twenty-five cubits due south from the middle of the structure," Matthew reiterated, certain he remembered what Reda had told them about the coin's inscription.

Reda nodded. "Approximately three hundred thirty-eight feet."

Matthew looked in front of them. He'd guess it would take them past the road. "Just refresh my memory of what's on the other side of the road," he said to Reda.

"We have the Mortuary Temple of Khafre and Khufu's causeway."

Matthew nodded. He knew there were many structures and

landmarks within the pyramid complex but couldn't recall the positioning of everything.

He took out his phone, using an app to track distance, and took his first step. The others fell in line with him. As he'd guessed, it took them past the road. They reached three hundred thirty-eight feet before they hit the causeway. "This is where we dig."

He looked at Alex and stepped back for her to get into position with the ground-penetrating radar machine. She took it out of a cart that Reda had one of his men drag behind them. In addition to the machine, it contained their bags, various tools, and a tent for shelter. She connected the readout module to the radar machine and turned it on. Matthew hovered over her.

She stopped moving and glanced over a shoulder. She was smiling at him, but said, "A little space might be nice."

He held up his hands and backed up. If they were alone, he'd call her out on that. Last night she hadn't wanted any space between them.

"All right, it's reading something..." Alex focused on the screen. "It's reading a depth of twenty-five feet." She walked a bit farther. "And there's definitely something down there. It could be a tunnel."

"Let's get digging, then." Reda handed Cal a shovel.

Cal didn't reach for it. "Who's going to take pictures?"

"Come on, help an old man out," Reda pressed.

Cal took the shovel, albeit reluctantly, and turned to Alex. "Where are Andres and Danny anyhow?"

"They're keeping watch over the tomb and base camp," Alex replied.

Matthew was watching his friend, unsure what was going through his mind. He wasn't exactly being himself today. He seemed fine one moment—even happy—and the next he was scowling. Come to think of it, Matthew hadn't seen Cal lift his camera to his face once since they'd arrived at the pyramid complex. Matthew knew that Cal had planned on calling Sophie last night, and this morning, when Matthew had asked how it went, Cal had simply said it went fine. He hadn't exactly been forthcoming, now that Matthew was giving it some thought. And that likely meant the conversation hadn't gone well.

Matthew took a shovel from the cart, and Alex exchanged the machine for one, too. Robyn was ahead of them and already heaving sand over her shoulder. Same with Reda's two men, who were excavating like eager hounds on the scent of a groundhog. Reda stood back, watching.

After a while, Reda snapped his fingers, and the projector man from last night sauntered off a short distance with Reda and pitched the tent. Everyone else spread out a bit and stayed focused on digging.

Matthew moved in next to Cal and leaned toward him. "Everything all right with you?"

"Yeah, sure." Cal heaved a shovel full of sand over his shoulder.

"So the call with—"

"I told you it went fine." Cal put his back into the next pitch of his shovel.

So you guys are good? Maybe Matthew was pushing harder than he should, but he and Cal went way back.

Cal emptied his shovel a few more times and then looked over at him. "Are you going to help us or just stand around?" There was a hint of jest in his voice, but his gaze squashed the attempt.

That answered Matthew's question. Something had happened during their phone call last night. But he'd have to wait to find out exactly what.

Matthew got to work, and it wasn't long before he was wiping his brow with the back of his hand. The sun was out and already powerful. Factor in the manual labor, and it made him one sweaty mess.

Shadows suddenly moved over him, and he turned to see the source. Five armed men were standing there watching him and his friends.

Matthew glanced over at Reda, who was seated under the tent. Reda just smiled and waved. The armed men were obviously here on his orders. And the added security probably meant the complex was open to the public now or soon would be.

No wonder it was getting so hot. It would be nearing nine in the morning.

They carried on, though, and spent hours digging. Matthew's shirt was soaked through when they took a break for lunch. At least Reda's two "colleagues" had gone back to helping them dig, and as a team, they were all making real headway.

Once the tourists arrived, they were curious, walking by as close as the armed men would let them get. They wore their baseball caps and Ray-Bans, and gulped from bottles of water.

By the time the tourists had cleared out, Matthew and the others had dug down about twenty-one feet. Four more to go, and, thankfully, the sun was starting to sink in the sky and a breeze was coming with refreshing impact.

At six o'clock, they took a short break for dinner, which was just some deli sandwiches Reda had someone bring in. Matthew sat down, and it felt so damn good. Getting his body to move again was going to take effort. He took a bite of his sandwich and followed it with a large swig of water.

He looked around at everyone who had been digging. They looked about as wrecked as he felt.

"We're not going to make it," Cal lamented, pulling from Matthew's mind, and lolled his head forward as if he was going to hit the table.

Robyn was the first to laugh at his dramatics, and the rest followed suit.

"Only a couple more feet," Matthew said, smiling, as he found the gumption to motivate the others.

"Four, actually, but who's counting?" Robyn smirked.

He smiled at her and let the expression carry for Alex and Cal. "What do you say we get it behind us so we can get to the real adventure?"

"Sounds good to me." Alex was the first up and out of the tent, and Matthew followed.

The opening they'd dug out was wide enough for six people to work next to one another. He got back to digging, staying focused on their goal.

Day turned to night, and portable lights were brought out. He dug his shovel into the earth, prepared to pull out more sand, but it hit a hard surface. "We're there!"

Reda's "colleagues" got in there and cleared out the rest of it. They came to discover that Matthew had been standing on top of the tunnel and his shovel had struck stone. Two feet to the right of that was a sealed entrance.

Reda snapped his fingers, finally standing up from his perch. "Go get it," he said, sending the projector man off and running.

He returned with a ratcheting system they'd brought just in case they ran into this. It would offset the weight of the stone seal and allow them to move it out of the way. After it was rigged up, and with persistence and determination, the stone started to move. Then it was lifted out of the way.

Behind it was darkness.

Cal groaned. "Here we go, again. Into the belly of the beast."

Matthew laughed at Cal's reference to the movie *Lara Croft: Tomb Raider*.

The four of them grabbed the oversized backpacks and miner hats they'd brought along.

Cal stepped back and gestured to Matthew. "By all means, you go first."

Matthew quirked an eyebrow. "You sure that you want to be the last one in?"

"Why? What's wrong with bringing up the rear?" Cal's eyes widened in panic.

Matthew laughed and pushed his friend gently toward the opening.

"And out the demon's ass," Cal said, ducking inside the tunnel. He was nothing if not dramatic—and a movie lover.

Matthew looked up at Reda, who was standing back from the entrance with his two right-hand men. "You're not coming down?"

"Not this trip," Reda began. "But please make sure that your friend takes a lot of pictures."

Matthew smiled at him, adjusted his hat, flicked his headlamp on, and stepped inside the tunnel. It was about five feet wide by five feet tall, just like the one that had collapsed out at the dig site that first day. His breath caught, the correlation between the two tunnels playing with his mind. Still, his stomach fluttered with excitement and anticipation at breaching the unknown. The fact that the tunnel had been sealed thousands of years ago didn't help his nerves. Nor the fact that the mission they were embarking on now was solely to save the world.

No pressure.

"We need to go at least two hundred twenty feet down the tunnel," Matthew said, pulling from one of the insertions in the tomb's murals. There was no sign of the seventeen steps, so it seemed that landmark would come later.

Alex brushed past him and Cal. After a bit, she stopped walking and pointed to the right. "There's a staircase."

"Seventeen stairs," Matthew whispered, awe overtaking him.

"The tunnel keeps going straight ahead of us, too, Matt," Alex added.

"It probably snakes into the Great Pyramid." An assumption, but

Matthew would wager it was a likely one. It would give a literal meaning to the Tablets being linked to the Great Pyramid.

"If that's the case, it's a miracle this tunnel hasn't been discovered from the other end," Robyn interjected.

"It could be one of the hidden passages that archaeologists are aware of but haven't yet gotten to," Matthew said.

"But why go to all the trouble of putting the location of the Library and Tablets on some coin and burying it with other clues miles from here if someone could just randomly come across it otherwise?" Cal raised his brows to emphasize his point. And he had made a good one.

The key to enlightenment lies with the pharaoh.

They'd found the coin with directions on where to dig, but the missing artifact had mentioned the Library and the Tablets. And it seemed Jasper, Seth, and Timal had seen fit to steal it. There must be a use for it they had yet to figure out.

"We just might need the stolen artifact in our hands," Matthew said.

"Well, I sure hope you're wrong about that," Robyn began, but she didn't need to finish. If he was right, they were screwed, because they obviously didn't have it.

Matthew took the lead down the stairs. The steps were about three feet wide and half a foot high. He counted them as he walked and reached the bottom after the seventeenth stair.

He swept his flashlight ahead of him. The beam of light picked up shelves full of scrolls. "We're here!"

CHAPTER
47

MATTHEW STEPPED INTO THE ROOM and found he was able to stand at full height with inches of clearance above his head. He pulled off his bag and took a flare from one of its pockets and turned it on. Light burst forth from it, causing him to squint. But once his eyes adjusted to the light, he was left speechless by the splendor that was before him. He let his bag drop to the floor.

Alex stepped into the room and spun around slowly. "This is…"

Robyn's mouth was agape, and Cal's camera was to his face, the flashes of his photography serving as mini strobe lights in the room. There was a lot to capture.

Matthew looked around, taking quick stock of the space. There were two sections of shelving made from stone bricks. Each had three rows and were stacked with scrolls.

Between what could best be described as bookcases was an area the size of a doorway, which was set back in the wall about six inches. The ceiling was arched in that section, as well. Matthew touched the stone in the inset section. The surface was smooth, and it made him think of the door they'd found in the hidden room in Baufra's tomb. But there wasn't enough of a crack around the frame to pry it open with a shovel. Still, he had a gut feeling that something was behind it.

"I think this is a door." Matthew pressed his fingers against the stone and pushed. No give whatsoever. It seemed too solid to break through. "There's got to be a way to open this, and it's probably somewhere in this room. A hidden switch or something. Spread out and look for it."

"I'll go tell Reda." This came from the projector man, and he ambled out of the room. Matthew hadn't known he'd even tagged along.

"Where are we supposed to look, Matt?" Robyn asked. "There are scrolls everywhere. Nothing is exposed on the walls that I can see."

Really, there was only one thing they could try. "Very, very carefully pull all the scrolls off the shelves."

The others set down their bags beside Matthew's and got to work. Matthew took the right section with Cal, and the women worked on the left.

They removed the scrolls one by one, vigilant not to damage any of them. Surprisingly, they remained intact and rather sturdy for having been down here for thousands of years. They were piling them neatly in a corner of the room.

Matthew was pulling out a scroll from the top of a stack when he caught a glimpse of something on the wall behind it. He continued to clear the rest of the scrolls from the area and set them on the floor. Afterward, he moved in on the space they had occupied, wanting to take a closer look.

"Matthew!" Alex cried out. "I found something!"

Matthew took another few seconds to study his find. There was a slightly curved, horizontal slot in the middle with four indentations surrounding it in the shape of a square. The one in the middle was larger than the others and rounded inward. Imagining a box around them, he'd say it was about fifteen square inches. It made him think it might be a type of switch plate.

"I found something, too. Does it look like this?" Matthew stood up and stepped back, pointing to what he'd discovered.

Alex indicated where she'd come from.

He hurried over to where Robyn and Cal were still huddled around Alex's find. It was identical to what he'd found behind the scrolls on his side of the shelving.

This time he dipped his fingers into the indentations. The pattern was familiar to him, as if he should know what it belonged to. And just as he thought that, he said out loud, "They separated the lock from the key."

"Aren't most keys and locks separated?" Cal raised his brows.

Matthew smirked and shook his head. "Stop thinking so literally. I just meant there was a lot of distance put between them on purpose." He got up and headed to Alex. "Look." He gestured to the switch plate he'd found. "Remember the pictures of the artifact? It came to a point like a pyramid at the top but had a disc—" he pressed a finger to the larger curved slot in the middle "—and the corners of the artifact had taller points in each corner. Imagine holding the artifact on its side… The top of the artifact is the key."

"I knew you'd prove invaluable."

The man's voice came from behind Matthew. He and Alex hurried to pile the scrolls back on the shelf to conceal the switch plate he'd found. And just in time, as Jasper entered the room. He didn't seem to have noticed.

"How did you get in here?" Matthew growled.

"What's happened to Reda?" Alex demanded as she stepped toward Jasper, stopping inches from his face. "Did you kill him and the other men the way you did Jeff?"

Matthew took a deep breath. It seemed like a good time to slow down and think. He hadn't heard any gunfire, and surely, if there had been, it would have echoed down the tunnel. Then it hit him: Reda was in on it.

Matthew came up beside Alex. "No, he didn't kill him," he said. "Reda's part of this little scheme."

Reda stepped into the room, clapping slowly. "Very well done, Doctor."

Matthew glared at him.

Reda turned to Alex. "Though your concern for my welfare is very touching, my dear."

Alex spat in the minister's face.

Reda wiped it off with his hand. "How very charming." He curled his lips in disgust.

Matthew's body tensed, each muscle poised to strike. "How long have you been working together?"

"Since near the beginning of this debacle, I'm afraid," Reda replied.

Alex shook her head, her face reddening and teeth grinding—a clear mix of anger, hurt, and confusion. "I don't understand."

"Jasper was wise to recognize an opportunity and seize it." The minister grabbed a fistful of air and pulled it back to himself. "He knew that I'd notice the missing artifact—or he couldn't be sure that I wouldn't." Reda turned to Cal. "He knows I like my pictures."

"So he approached you and made a deal?" Matthew rushed out, not wanting to delay this agony and in a hurry to piece everything together.

The minister nodded. "That he did."

"I don't understand. Why involve us?" Matthew stepped in front of his team.

"You got us here," Reda said matter-of-factly.

The thoughts were spinning in his mind, but he couldn't catch and connect them. "But you have the artifact, and you know how to read hieroglyphics."

"Yes, but in the end, it was you who found the last—or should I say, *first* clue." Reda's gaze settled on Matthew. "You were smart enough to take us back to the sarcophagus. So easy to see in hindsight."

Anger blossomed in Matthew's chest. They'd been pawns from the moment Reda and his allies had reached a dead end with the artifact. Yanking them into the police station had been a ruse to force their cooperation.

"I see it's all starting to become clearer to you, Doctor." Reda took a few steps. "I needed all of you motivated to find the Library."

"Or more precisely, to lead you to the Emerald Tablets." Matthew clenched his jaw, feeling more used now than he had when he'd learned Alex had only invited him to the dig because of his reputation.

"Yes." Another grin from Reda, and this one sent chills lacing down Matthew's spine. "Without your talent for uncovering legends, we may never have found the coin or even thought to revisit the sarcophagus. I knew that by coming after you at the airport, arresting you, and dragging you into the police station, I would get your attention," he said, confirming Matthew's theory. "And then when I believed your innocence—of course, I knew you were innocent all along—you became fired up to help."

"The threat of prison also came up," Cal snapped.

Alex lunged forward, but Matthew held her back.

Reda went on as if Alex hadn't reacted and Cal had said nothing. "Oh, yes, and I ratcheted up your interest in helping me by providing you with some personal motivation."

Three more silhouettes were cast on to the wall in front of Matthew.

"Dead man walking," Cal said coolly.

Matthew turned to see who had entered.

"Jeff!" Alex snarled. She lunged again, this time for Jeff, but Matthew didn't bother trying to hold her back. She slapped Jeff across the face. "You faked your own death? You put me through—" She put her hand to her chest, and Matthew hurried over to her and put an arm around her. "Your wife, your daughters—they think you're dead. Why would you do that to the people you love?"

Jeff was staring straight at Alex as if the words she was saying flew right over him.

Alex let out a few deep breaths. "How did you know I wouldn't want to see your body before it was shipped back to the States?"

"You don't like dead bodies unless they're mummified—" Jeff gestured to Matthew "—and I knew you'd be all right."

"You son of a bitch!" Alex dove toward Jeff again, but he pulled a gun on her.

Jasper and Reda's two right-hand men—who were the other two men who had accompanied Jeff—pulled guns, as well.

"What? Now you're going to shoot us?" Alex was bordering on hysteria, and Matthew stepped in front of her.

Two more figures entered the room.

"How rich," Matthew scoffed when he saw Seth and Timal. Seth was holding the artifact.

"This is getting to be a regular ole party down in here, and not a fun one," Cal added blandly.

"All of you were in on this?" Alex was shaking her head. "I can't believe it."

Matthew's mind wandered back to the police presence and how Reda had just been able to walk them out of the station. "That sergeant's in your pocket, too, isn't he?"

"Did someone mention me?" Youssef stepped into the room.

"If any more people come in here, we'll run out of space and oxygen," Cal said.

Matthew shot him a glare. He understood that his friend didn't handle pressure well, but he had to shut up.

"But…" Alex voice trembled. "But why do this? You're the minister of antiquities, a respected man…"

"I'm about to retire, and I want to be remembered for something great." Reda peacocked his stance. "Also, the wealth and the power are great advantages. Can you imagine what it will be like being the only man in the world with the Tablets?"

"You are disloyal and a thief. You disgust me," Alex fired back. She looked around at the men in the room. "Did you hear what he said? He said, 'What it would be like to be the *only* man.' None of you fools are included in his grand aspirations."

"Now, now," Reda cooed. "They know their place. Unlike you." He snapped his fingers, and the men spread out and started moving across the room.

Matthew curled his fist and raised his arm, but one of Reda's "colleagues" grabbed his wrist, pulled it behind his back, and pinned him to the wall faster than Matthew could react. He bucked against the man holding him to no avail.

He looked at his friends. They were all being secured, too.

Matthew was seeing red. "You're not going to get away with this."

"Oh, but I already have. And all of you, well, you've served your purpose."

"You're going to kill us?" Cal practically squeaked out.

"Of course," Reda said with a smirk, "but you can't say I'm not a gentleman. I'll let you hang around long enough to watch me retrieve and walk off with the Tablets. I don't even care about the rest of this." He gestured around the room to indicate the scrolls. "Consider it a consolation prize. One that you'll be able to enjoy while you rot down here." He snapped his fingers, and Jasper took the artifact from Seth.

"Now, where does this go?" Jasper asked Matthew. He obviously hadn't seen where the switch plates were.

The man who had been holding Matthew let him go. Matthew jutted out his chin. If they were going to kill him anyway, why would they think he'd tell them?

"Tell me," Jasper barked. He nodded at the man who was holding Robyn, and the man pressed his gun to her temple. "Do you really want to watch her die right here, right now?"

Matthew's eyes widened, and he took a deep breath. The panic was churning in his belly, but he had to keep it together. He made eye contact with Robyn, the terror in her eyes breaking his heart. "Over there," he said and pointed to the switch plate that Alex had found.

Jasper gave the gunman a curt nod, and the man removed the gun from Robyn's temple. "That's what I thought," Jasper said drily.

CHAPTER
48

IT DIDN'T SEEM LIKE THERE was any other option but to sit back and see what happened. They were outnumbered and outgunned. But Matthew wasn't a sit-back-and-see type of person. At the same time, he had to be careful not to start a bloodbath. He couldn't let his friends die.

Cal and Robyn weren't armed, but he and Alex were. She'd given him a handgun when they had been grabbing supplies for the dig. Matthew was thankful that Reda hadn't been around to see that. He was also thankful the weapons were concealed by their clothing. They might have the element of surprise working in their favor.

The guy who had manhandled Matthew now stood across the room glowering at him. Matthew had no doubt he would be all too happy to pull the trigger if given even minimal provocation.

Matthew turned to look at Jasper who was at the switch plate, the top of the artifact already inserted into it. He gave it a push, and the hidden door started to move, stone scraping against stone. As it opened, cool air rushed into the room, sweeping over Matthew's skin and giving him goose bumps.

Reda slipped inside the moment he could fit his body through. A few seconds later, he was laughing.

Matthew's breath caught at seeing him holding a tablet that was about one foot wide, two feet tall, and one inch deep. It resembled depictions of the Tablets in textbooks. Writing was engraved across its face, and the emerald was the deepest green Matthew had ever seen. It was absolutely beautiful. And it was real. Believing had gotten him to this point. He was robbed of totally reveling in this accomplishment, though. Armed men and evil intent surrounded them, and they were here for the Tablets. He couldn't allow any of them to leave with them.

"We did it, gentlemen!" Reda declared in triumph.

Bile rose into the back of Matthew's throat, and he swallowed roughly.

Reda's "colleagues" carted out two more Emerald Tablets.

"This is all of them," the projector man said.

Matthew looked at his friends, who appeared as nauseated and defeated as he felt. Robyn lowered her eyes and took a deep breath.

Matthew turned back to Reda and his men. All of them seemed enraptured by the Tablets.

Under different circumstances, he would be, too. After all, they held the secrets of the universe, the ability to traverse Heaven and Earth, and abundant wealth. It read like a fable, but he had latched on to it with the innocence of a child, even though he'd been a grown man when he'd first heard about them. And now they were only a few feet away from him. And what he had feared had become a reality: the fate of the world was in the hands of one evil man.

Reda came over to Matthew. "See what you have helped me to accomplish?"

"I didn't do any of this for you." It took all Matthew's willpower not to knock out the old man or to draw his gun and squeeze the trigger. But then again, maybe this was the time to make a move. Reda's men were distracted. They had even holstered their weapons to admire the Tablets. And Reda was close enough to grab…

He'd be taking a risk, not knowing how devoted these men were to Reda, though. But there wasn't really another option right now.

Matthew slowly pulled his handgun from the holster at his lower back and grabbed the minister.

Reda gasped loudly. His men looked up from the Tablets.

"Step away from the Tablets and put your hands up," Matthew directed.

"What do you think you're doing?" Reda wriggled, trying to break free of Matthew's hold.

Matthew tightened his grip and put the gun in his face. "I said *step away*!" he roared.

The men seemed to hesitate, but a few seconds later, they complied with Matthew's command.

Matthew now had a clear shot at the Tablets on the floor. It was as if they were sitting there taunting him. The power they held would destroy the world. If it wasn't Reda, it would be another person set on their own agenda—a world power, a terrorist group. Bloodshed and chaos would govern humankind. There was no safe place for the Tablets to be. He raised his gun and pulled the trigger, firing off rounds at each Tablet until all that remained were tiny fragments of emerald.

"What have you done?" Reda yelled.

Smoke was still coming from Matthew's gun, and he already had it pointed at the minister again.

"What I had to do," Matthew said through clenched teeth.

"Shoot all of them!" Reda barked to his men.

"If any of you pull your weapons, I will shoot him," Matthew yelled, ice lacing through his veins. The men remained still, all looking at him.

Matthew didn't know what the next step was, though, as he hadn't thought this through that far. He'd been rash and impulsive, and he just hoped it wouldn't bite him—or his friends—in the ass. His gaze went to the room where the Tablets had come from, his mind on the second switch plate they'd found. Did it do the same thing as the one the artifact was in or something else? He shook away the thoughts. It probably didn't matter right now. He had to get him and his friends out of here. And he finally figured out just how he'd do that.

"Put your guns on the floor," he ordered. He paused a beat, riding the waves of adrenaline that were making him feel lightheaded. "And don't even think about making a move, or I'll kill him." Matthew pushed the muzzle of the gun harder into Reda's cheek.

"Ouch!" Reda jumped, and Matthew pulled the gun back enough to see the red burn mark on his cheek. Matthew put the gun back to the man's cheek, humanely keeping a little space between the muzzle and Reda's flesh. Still close enough that he'd likely feel a radiant heat.

"Do as he…" Reda's words came out mumbled.

His men relinquished their guns.

"Now, move into that room," Matthew instructed.

They stared back at him, all of them hesitating.

"Don't make me—" Matthew thrust the weapon against the minister's cheek.

"Shit!" Reda cried out.

The sergeant held up his hands and was the first to obey. The rest filed into the room behind him. The group of them barely fit in the room all at once.

"Alex," Matthew said, "close the door. Robyn, Cal, grab a weapon, and if one of them so much as twitches, shoot them."

Robyn and Cal hurried to do as Matthew said and got into position.

Jasper was practically foaming at the mouth. "You can't just lock us up down here."

"Watch me." Matthew tilted his head toward Alex.

She removed the artifact and set it on a shelf. The door started to slide closed.

Timal rushed for the door. "Please, don't—"

In a split second, Alex had her gun in his face, and he backed up. The door sealed shut in front of him, enclosing Reda's men inside.

The minister's entire face was a bright red. "Are you out of your fucking mind?"

Matthew was tempted to backhand him with the butt of the gun, but he still had a use for the man.

His men's protests continued, muffled from behind the door, but Matthew wasn't listening. His gaze went to the floor and the shattered Tablets. His heart sank at the sight, but he knew he'd done what needed to be done.

Alex came over to him and touched his upper arm. "I can't believe they're gone forever," she said, as if sensing what he was going through.

Matthew looked at her. "Some things just aren't meant to be found."

She nodded and let out a deep breath.

"So what now?" Cal wiped his head. "We can't exactly waltz on out of here. Who knows how many other men Reda has guarding the exit."

"That's why we're using him as our ticket out of here." Matthew nudged Reda.

Reda cackled. "You're all going to die."

Oh please, let me knock him out before this is all over...

"Move." Matthew kicked the back of the minister's legs to get him going, because a gun to the head clearly wasn't motivation enough.

They made their way out of the room, up the stairs, and down the tunnel. When they reached the exit, they found themselves facing the barrel end of two assault rifles.

"Don't shoot, you idiots," Reda barked. "He's got a gun to my head."

They stepped out into the night air, and Matthew counted five men, including the two immediately in front of them. They were the same men who had watched over their digging. The other three seemed to see what was going on and crowded in toward the tunnel.

"Stop or I'll shoot him," Matthew threatened. They stopped in their tracks.

"I'm going to need you to set down your weapons and put your hands in the air," Matthew said.

Alex came up on his left, Robyn on his right, and Cal on her right. They all had guns aimed at the men. The seconds ticked off, and it felt like an eternity, but Reda's cohorts finally lowered their weapons and put up their hands.

"I'll need a sat phone," Matthew said to Reda. "Where can I—"

"In the tent," the minister hissed.

"Alex, go get it. Call the US and Canadian embassies."

"Both?" she fired back.

"Let's just say after everything that's happened, I prefer to cover my bases." Matthew smiled at her and Cal and Robyn, who had gathered the men's weapons.

What do you know? We actually pulled this off.

CHAPTER
49

THE LIBRARY AND THE TUNNEL system would be swarming with authorities soon. Matthew had counted off twenty military officers as they headed down there. He'd already told the men in charge about the artifact and how to open the door to the secondary room to free Reda's accomplices.

Before they'd arrived, Matthew had sent Alex and Robyn down to collect the shards from the Tablets and put them into their bags. It was one thing that the scrolls were out for the world to see, but it would be best if the Tablets remained a myth. And while it was possible the scrolls contained arcane knowledge, he couldn't justify destroying everything. As far as the military was concerned, Matthew and his friends had captured conspirators against Egypt while searching for the Emerald Tablets and the Lost Library of Thoth. Given that the artifact was there for the military to see and its inscriptions could be deciphered, Matthew was forthcoming about the Tablets but said they hadn't found them.

Now Matthew and his friends were standing outside the tunnel entrance, watching as Jasper, Jeff, Seth, Timal, Reda's two right-hand men, and the police sergeant were carted out in cuffs.

The officer who had already cuffed Reda walked him past Matthew and his friends.

"Good luck getting a new person to fund your dig, sweetheart," Reda said to Alex.

"Y-you?" Alex stammered.

"And you—" Reda's nostrils flared when he looked at Matthew "—you've ruined everything!"

Matthew waved at him and grinned wildly. "Have a nice life, *Former Minister.*"

Reda scrunched up his face and hurled spittle in Matthew's direction, but it didn't come close to hitting him. It did, however, land on the side of the officer's face.

Cal winced. "Oh, that's not good."

The officer punched Reda in the face. Matthew withheld the laugh he really wanted to bark out. He may not have gotten his hit in, but that had been satisfying as hell to watch.

Another officer came out of the tunnel and announced, "It's clear down there," to the commanding officer.

"Good job. Now get them all out of my face," the commanding officer said, walking toward Matthew.

"We'd like to ask a favor, if we could," Matthew said.

Cal bumped his elbow. "We do?"

Matthew turned to Cal. "Uh-huh." He looked back to the officer. "We'd like the honor of going inside one last time."

The officer seemed to consider Matthew's request a little too long for comfort. He smiled at all of them. "Take your time," he finally said, tossing in a smile.

"If we could have our privacy while we're down there," Matthew said, hoping he wasn't pressing his luck, "that would be very much appreciated. We've been through a lot and—"

"And you made quite the discovery, which will be carted off to museums. Go—" he smiled "—enjoy your find and take all the time you need."

"Thank you." Matthew hesitated. "Speaking of the discovery…"

"Nothing has been touched," the officer told him. "Well, except what was necessary to open the door." He walked off.

Matthew turned to his friends. "We need to grab our backpacks and miner hats."

"I'm not sure I really need to go back—" Robyn's protest died on her lips. She must have read Matthew's eyes and seen that he had something specific in mind.

"A little while won't hurt," Robyn consented.

They loaded up with their bags and hats, which they'd set aside during the hours that passed from calling the embassies until now. "Cal, you lead the way," Matthew said.

Matthew let everyone else go ahead of him, though he couldn't wait to reach the Library.

Robyn turned to him. "You're thinking about that second switch plate, aren't you?"

Matthew just smiled and shrugged playfully.

When they reached the room, the artifact was exactly where the officer would have left it to open the main door—in the switch plate on the left. Matthew picked up the artifact and headed straight for the shelving on the right. He set the object down just long enough to expose the second switch plate.

"What do you think it will do?" Alex asked, speaking over his shoulder.

"Guess we'll find out." Matthew pushed the artifact into the switch plate. The sound of stone scraping against stone filled the room again.

"There's another door," Robyn exclaimed. "It sounds like it's inside the room where the Tablets were."

Alex turned to Matthew. "How did you know the one I found would open the door to the first room?"

Matthew shook his head. "I didn't."

"Okay, so what do you propose?" Robyn put her hands on her hips, and her eyes lit up. "We have to open the main door, then someone has to go inside and stay there while it closes behind them so we can open the other door," she said, answering her own question.

"And then go into the next room that opens up," Matthew finished. His gaze went to Cal.

Cal held up his hands. "Why are you looking at me?"

"You're not going to send the women in there, are you?" Matthew glanced at the women, certain he'd set the stage for a protest.

"Hey, one of us could do it," Robyn rushed out, seemingly offended, and she gestured between herself and Alex.

"I wouldn't want you to break a nail," Cal teased, stepping toward the room.

"Ooh." Robyn pushed him, and he lurched forward and caught his balance on the wall.

Cal looked over his shoulder and glared at her. "Watch it."

"You deserved that," Alex said in Robyn's defense, a smile playing on the corners of her mouth.

"I'm just fooling around. Geez." Cal clawed at the air but shrank back when Alex waved a fist.

Matthew was laughing, as were Robyn and Alex.

Cal indicated the closed door. "Just get on with it."

Alex removed the artifact from the secondary switch plate and put it into the first one. The door opened. "Get in there, sugar pie."

Cal squinted at her. "Grr."

"Just call out when you're ready for us to open the main door back up. We'll wait for your signal," Matthew clarified.

Cal gave a thumbs-up, and Alex removed the artifact. She waited for the door to completely close before inserting the artifact into the second switch plate.

"Cal?" Matthew called out.

There was no response, but it was far too soon to panic that something bad had happened. Besides, Cal was a screamer...

A minute passed, and Alex asked, "Do you think we should open the main door again?"

Matthew shook his head, holding firm. "He'll let us know."

A few more minutes passed.

"Let me outta here," Cal shouted.

Matthew smiled at the ladies, and Alex opened the main door. Cal was standing there with the cheesiest grin Matthew had ever seen. And at his feet were three Emerald Tablets.

Alex was looking from Matthew to the Tablets. "How did you know there was a second set?"

"I didn't. But something so important would warrant a backup, don't you think?" Matthew reasoned. "Or maybe the others were decoys, even. It's also possible all six were different." He winced at the thought, but really, he'd had no choice but to destroy the first three.

"But you seemed so sure of something when you shattered the other Tablets," Alex said.

"I was sure I didn't want them to end up in Reda's hands—or anyone else's for that matter. They were meant to remain hidden until humankind was ready for them. And that time certainly isn't now. Honestly, I don't think that time will ever come."

"But you found them, Matthew. Twice, technically," Alex said softly. "Now what are we going to do with them?"

His mind was on the room within a room and how they'd found that small one in the tomb, too. In Baufra's tomb, the room had been empty. Were the Tablets moved here or—he swallowed roughly—were there more Tablets out there to be found?

"Matt?" Alex prompted, yanking him from his musings.

"I haven't thought it all through yet, but we definitely need to get them out of here." He pointed toward their bags, which were still on the floor. "I figure if we put one in each of them, they won't be too heavy to carry."

He realized then that he hadn't even touched them. He paused and went over to the Tablets. He ran his hands over the smooth green gemstone. All these years of fantasizing about their existence… And he'd found them all right. Now what was he going to do with them?

CHAPTER

50

The moist, salty air was invigorating after the month he'd spent in the desert. Matthew was at the stern of a chartered yacht, leaning against a side railing with the bags containing the Tablets at his feet. He inhaled deeply and closed his eyes.

His right arm was wrapped around Alex, Robyn stood to his left, and Cal was on her other side. The only other people on the ship were the captain they'd hired and a deckhand. They were nonnegotiable with the charter company, but Matthew had insisted that they sign confidentiality agreements. But the plan was to do what they'd come to do as discreetly as possible.

"Sir?" Matthew turned and saw that it was the deckhand who had addressed him. "You asked to be notified once we were over the Calypso Deep. We're here now."

Matthew looked out at the water. To think that the bottom was estimated to be 17,280 feet down and they were just floating over it, was somewhat humbling. "Thank you."

The deckhand gave a little dip of his head, folded his hands in front of him, and stayed put to see if Matthew had further instructions.

"We'll need complete privacy for the next fifteen minutes, please," Matthew said.

"Absolutely, sir. Will that be all?"

"When I say complete privacy, I would prefer that you and the captain spend that time at the front of the ship," Matthew clarified.

"No eyes on you." The deckhand nodded. "I understand."

"Exactly. Thank you."

"Very well. I will tell the captain. Will that be all, sir?"

"Actually—" Matthew glanced at his friends "—after the fifteen minutes, please bring out what we talked about earlier."

"Will do." With another nod, the deckhand left.

Matthew looked over the side of the boat. The Tablets would be buried forever in these depths. They would be safe. Humankind would be safe.

Alex nuzzled up against him again. "Are you sure you want to do this?"

He wrapped an arm around her. "It's not a matter of *want*. It's the right thing to do."

He didn't need to share that he had been having some reservations about pitching the Tablets into the sea. They were thousands of years old and priceless. And their continued existence would prove that he wasn't crazy for believing in the Tablets. But they contained vast, otherworldly knowledge that could destroy the world. By getting rid of the "evidence," he and his family—and the world—would certainly be safer. Still, it was a bittersweet position to be in. He'd longed to find them for years, and now, only a brief few would even know they'd existed.

Alex gave him a relaxed smile and leaned her head on his shoulder.

"All right, let's do this." Cal clapped his hands like an excited child.

Apparently, he doesn't have any reservations.

Regardless, it had to be done. Matthew reached into the bag closest to him, his stomach a knotted mess. He didn't typically uncover legends only to bury them again. He let out a deep breath as he slipped the first Tablet out. As much as part of him didn't want to toss them overboard, he didn't want to put that onus on anyone else.

He lifted the Tablet, mentally estimating its weight at about twenty-five pounds. He made sure to keep it in front of his body to protect it from any prying eyes—just in case. Then he looked at his friends one more time for the strength to do this.

Alex and Cal were watching him. Her eyes were encouraging and compassionate, as if she understood his secret turmoil, while Cal was grinning and gesturing to the water. Matthew glanced at Robyn. She pressed her lips together and nodded. He took that as silent reassurance that he was doing the right thing.

He turned back to the water and tossed the first Tablet overboard. As it left his hands, it was as if a heavy emotional weight had also been lifted from his chest. It only confirmed that he was doing the right thing.

He did the same with the other two Tablets and the shards from the Tablets he'd destroyed. They still didn't know if they were duplicates, decoys, or additional Tablets, but it wasn't worth the risk of investigating further. None of them had the expertise to decipher them, and bringing in outside help was certainly not an option. When every piece was overboard, they stood silently for a few moments.

"I couldn't have done any of this without you," Alex said, eventually breaking the quiet and leaning in to kiss Matthew's cheek. She pulled back. "By that, I mean *all* of you."

Cal groaned. "Uh-huh." But he was grinning, obviously just giving Alex a hard time.

"I mean it," she insisted. "Cal, you took amazing pictures, but if you didn't stay up with the radio that night, we might still be down in that tomb. And Robyn, your knowledge of Egyptian history was invaluable. Your help with cataloging was greatly appreciated."

"Thank you," Robyn replied.

"You're very welcome. And you, Matt—"

"Oh no. It's about to get mushy in here, I can feel it." Cal shook his head and laughed.

Alex raised a fist to Cal. "You're going to *feel* this." Her feigned seriousness crumbled quickly, and she chuckled. She looked at Matthew. "You've been a friend to me through this entire journey—when we thought Jeff had died and even before that. And if it wasn't for you, we never would have found the Tablets. You thought of the mummy's coffin. You were insistent that something was there. And you were right." Her tone turned somber. "Robyn and Cal, would you mind if—"

Robyn held up a hand. "We'll give you some time alone."

She and Cal went to the other side of the boat, far enough that they would be out of earshot.

Matthew faced Alex. "What is it?"

"I just wanted to apologize for…" Her gaze drifted away from him briefly. "For using you. God, that sounds so horrible out loud."

"Did you intend to hurt me by doing so?" he asked.

"No," she was quick to reply. "Not at all. Gosh, you're a great guy. I just thought…"

"That my reputation would help build yours," he finished for her.

Her cheeks flushed, and she tucked a strand of hair behind an ear. "Yeah."

"I would have come, even if you had been upfront about it."

"Even now?" Her eyes flicked to the water, no doubt alluding to the Tablets.

"Even now." He paused. "We found them. And we've confirmed Baufra's existence and that he was a pharaoh, in addition to finding his tomb. The history books will need to be rewritten. It's incredible." He smiled at her. "Congratulations *to you* on leading this expedition."

"You're so amazing." She threw her arms around him and pecked countless kisses on his cheeks. "Thank you, thank you, thank you."

He couldn't help but laugh.

A few minutes later, they were still facing each other but had fallen quiet.

"What are you going to do now?" he asked. "Reda was funding the dig?"

"I'll be appealing to the Egyptian government to let me continue the work I started. There's a lot still to be done there."

"There definitely is." His gaze drifted out to the water.

"Matt?"

He looked back at Alex. "Yeah?"

"Don't take this the wrong way, but I hope you get on your plane this time." She smirked.

"That makes two of us." He touched her cheek and tenderly kissed her. He pulled back. "It's been quite the adventure, hasn't it?"

Her eyes were glistening with tears. "Oh yeah. Especially since you arrived."

He drew her to him, swept her hair back, and kissed her forehead. "You stay safe out here."

She gave him a lopsided smile, but she sniffled. "You know, it was a much safer place before you got here. Really, it was only after you arrived that all hell broke loose."

He held up his hands. "You're blaming me for the tunnel collapsing?" He was teasing her, just as she was teasing him. He felt his breath hitch and a small splinter in his chest. "I'll never forget you."

"Me neither." She kissed him softly on the lips. "I hope you'll come back and visit."

"I just might do that," he said vaguely. He had to play it a little nonchalant; he had to protect his heart somehow.

"Sir?" The deckhand had returned and was holding a tray of four full champagne flutes.

"Ooh, champagne." Robyn came over, Cal trailing behind her.

Each of them took a glass, and the deckhand excused himself.

Matthew lifted his glass. "To saving the world."

The toast rang back to his ears from each of his friends, and they clicked glasses.

The champagne was dry and delicious, and today—what they had done—was certainly worth celebrating. Alex's and Robyn's smiles touched their eyes, but Cal's were flat, even as his lips curved upward.

Something was definitely wrong. "Can you ladies excuse us?" Matthew asked, getting Cal to look at him.

"For a little while." Alex winked at Matthew.

"We'll be fine." Robyn chortled and clinked her glass against Alex's again.

Matthew was happy to see they were getting along. They had so much in common.

On second thought, maybe they had *too much* in common…

Cal was standing at the railing on the other side of the ship. Matthew joined him. He didn't say anything, just stood there, gazing at the water, sipping his drink.

"Sophie and I…" Cal cleared his throat. "We broke up."

Matthew looked over at his friend, his heart aching for him. "I'm sorry, Cal."

"She just couldn't accept that I love going on these treasure-hunting expeditions with you. Or *adventures* as she calls them."

"I don't know what to say." And the truth was, Matthew didn't.

"Well, there's really nothing to say." Cal's eyes were riddled with pain. "She can't accept that part of my life, and I'm not ready to give it up."

Matthew was watching his friend, wishing there was something he could say or do to ease his pain. "Maybe once you get home, talk things out..." Matthew's voice trailed off.

"Well, I guess we'll find out soon enough." Cal downed the rest of his champagne. "I love her with all my heart, Matt."

"I know you do."

"But I need her to support me. I don't want to feel guilty every time I leave on an adventure with you. It's not fair to force me to give them up." Cal peered down into his glass, his eyes full of tears.

Matthew put a hand on his friend's shoulder.

"Why do you guys look so serious?" Alex called from the other side of the ship, doing so in a voice that mimicked a line from *The Dark Knight*.

Matthew winced, but Cal laughed.

All right, maybe his friend would be fine.

"I'm just really ready to be back home." Cal scratched furiously behind one of his ears.

Matthew quirked his eyebrows.

"Sand," Cal explained. "It doesn't matter how many times I shower."

"Let me guess," Matthew said, "it gets everywhere."

Cal pointed a finger at him. "You got it, my friend."

"You guys are crazy," Robyn shouted.

"If we're crazy, you're crazy," Cal shot back in a singsong voice.

The women were laughing and heading toward him and Cal.

"I hope you're not having regrets about what we've done," Alex said to Matthew.

He held up his glass. "Let's put it this way... No one's going to find them."

"Yeah, I think we can be pretty certain of that." Robyn smiled, but Matthew watched her gaze drift to Cal and turn serious. "Are you all right?"

"I'm fine," Cal mumbled.

Matthew shook his head. The word *fine* must be such a trigger word for shrinks.

Robyn's eyes flicked to Matthew, who then looked at Cal.

"I was just telling Matthew that Sophie and I are over," Cal said.

Robyn's mouth gaped open, and she didn't say anything for a few seconds. "I'm sorry, Cal. What happened?"

"I was just telling Matt."

Matthew noticed Alex's cheeks turn bright red, but he shook his head softly to let her know not to worry about her earlier joke. There was no way she could have known they actually were having a serious conversation.

"Well, we can talk about it later," Robyn said, "or not at all, if that's what you want."

"Maybe we'll be able to patch things up." Cal sounded hopeful but not as if he bought into it quite yet. "It's just that I love exploring the world with you guys and going on our adventures. But it's too much for her. Neither of us should have to change who we are to be together."

Robyn licked her lips. "Everyone deserves to do whatever it is that makes them happy." The corners of her mouth twitched, and then she smiled. "Unless, of course, that's destroying the world as we know it." She winked at Cal.

"Yeah, that's a big *unless*." He smiled back at her and then at Matthew.

In that moment, Matthew was certain his friend would, in fact, be fine, no matter what ended up happening with Sophie. He locked eyes with Alex, thankful to have gotten to know her better over these past few weeks. But when he looked at Robyn and Cal, his two closest friends in the world, he was overwhelmed with gratitude for having them in his life. He couldn't imagine not having them with him on future "adventures."

He lifted his empty glass. "I think we need more champagne."

Catch the next book in the Matthew Connor Adventure Series!

Sign up below
to be notified when new Matthew Connor titles are available for pre-order:

CarolynArnold.net/MCUpdates

By joining this newsletter, you will also receive exclusive first looks at the following:

Updates pertaining to upcoming releases in the series, such as cover reveals, book descriptions, and firm release dates

Sneak peeks of teasers and special content

Receive insights giving you an inside look at Carolyn's research and creative process

Read on for an exciting preview of
Carolyn Arnold's police thriller
featuring Madison Knight

POWER STRUGGLE

CHAPTER
1

DEATH WAS NOT DISCRIMINATORY, but murder was certainly selective. At least that's what Major Crimes detective Madison Knight had learned in her twelve years with the Stiles PD.

She looked down at the male victim. He was single, fifty-nine, and lying on the king-size mattress in his master bedroom. Silver sheets were covering him to his hips, leaving his upper body bare and exposing multiple stab wounds to his chest and abdomen. Blood was everywhere, staining the bedding and spattered on the walls and ceiling.

Normally, being immersed in such a messy murder scene would make Madison's stomach churn. She'd most certainly feel a burning drive to get justice for the victim. But this time, she was devoid of emotion, flatlined like the man on the bed. If anything, there was lingering bitterness and underlying anger. Because she knew the victim. Jimmy Bates. The man who had killed her grandfather.

Because of Bates, her mother had lost her father as a teenager and her grandmother had to bury the love of her life before Madison was even born. And all this because Bates's father had been the numbers man for the branch of the Russian Mafia that operated out of Stiles, and Madison's grandfather, a police sergeant, had put him away.

Madison pinched her eyes shut briefly. A darker part of her was finding some sort of redemption in the fact that Bates had exited the world not of his own volition. Just as he had snuffed out her grandfather's life, someone had taken Bates's. A working out of Karma as it were…

"Are you all right?" asked her partner of seven years, Terry Grant. He had a light complexion and never had a blond hair out of place, always ran before breakfast, was a loving husband and father to a baby girl named Danielle. He was three years younger than Madison's thirty-six.

She turned to see that he hadn't come into the room alone. Higgins, the first officer on scene and her former training officer, stood next to him. Both men had given her time to be alone with the scene and Bates after learning the vic's identity.

"I'm fine." Her response had come out way too quickly to be believable.

She looked back at the body. Both his arms were over his head and tied to the barred, wooden headboard with zip ties. She let her gaze trail down to his ankles, to see if those were also restrained, but they were still covered. She'd have to wait until the scene was processed to find out.

Given the number of stab wounds he had, though, it was likely that both his arms and legs had been bound, which indicated that the killer knew where to strike to delay death and invoke torture. While the former indicated a professional, the latter suggested the killer may have been after something.

Madison scanned the room. A television was mounted on the wall at the end of the bed, and it was on at a low volume and tuned into a popular crime drama.

Odd how reality can mimic fiction.

"Winston should have sent someone else." Higgins sounded apologetic for the Major Crimes sergeant's decision to include her in the case.

She met his gaze and dismissed his comment with a wave. "He probably didn't even know the ID on the vic when he made the call." She returned her gaze to Bates, analyzing whether he'd paid and suffered enough for his wrongdoings. In life, he'd served a full twenty-five-year sentence, but when he'd gotten released nineteen years ago, it hardly seemed like enough punishment. Was his murder finally enough to satisfy her personal scales of justice?

As her mind relaxed, and she took in the scene, she sensed a familiarity about it. The numerous stab wounds, the bound wrists...

The woman was laid out on the couch, her arms open wide, one resting

against the back of the sofa, the other raised in the air, its wrist twisted
back at an unnatural angle. Her torso was stained red with blood, which
extended to the sofa and the floor. It was as if a can of red paint had been
dumped on top of her.

"It looks like she was stabbed dozens of times. The killer must be a professional, too."

At the time, bile had risen in Madison's throat. The odor, the sight—
it had been all-encompassing.

The woman's name had been Lillian Norton, and the man who'd killed
her had been a Russian Mafia hit man by the name of Constantine
Romanov—the same hit man who had almost succeeded in raping
and killing Madison ten months prior. Lillian's longtime boyfriend
had worked as an attorney for the mob, and she'd been tortured for
information.

With Bates's father's involvement with the Russian mob, as well, it
didn't seem like it could be a coincidence that Bates's murder resembled
Lillian's. And all the stab wounds, the bondage, the time it would have
taken, and the seeming lack of concern over getting caught fit with
Constantine's personality. But if Madison was going to entertain the
idea that Bates was killed by the hit man, that meant—

God, no, please don't tell me he's back.

Madison put a hand to her stomach as her eyes filled with tears. She
blinked them away, willing herself to compartmentalize her thoughts.
Constantine had escaped police custody and fled the country. Intel
indicated that he'd returned to Russia, and he'd be flagged the moment
he landed on American soil. Of course, criminals found ways to work
around things like that.

She took a deep, steadying breath.

It had to be paranoia that had her dragging the Russian hit man into
Bates's murder. After all, the recent loss of her friend and fellow officer,
Barry Weir, had the flashbacks surging again periodically. Before his
death, they had been starting to ease. Plus, a connection between Bates
and the Mafia hadn't even been established.

It was definitely best to keep her suspicion of Mafia involvement to
herself for now. "I'd say we're probably looking for a professional," was
all she said.

Terry nodded. "Given all the blood, I'd say the vic was alive for most of these stab wounds. That means the killer knew where to strike."

"I agree." Usually the person to find a body was the first under suspicion, and Madison's mind went to the woman she'd seen talking to an officer when they showed up. She was in her twenties and beautiful with long, honey-colored hair. She could have been any number of things to the deceased—a daughter, a lover, a wife, or in this neighborhood, a housekeeper. While she didn't strike Madison as a killer, first impressions could be wrong. Madison turned to Higgins. "Who's the woman who found him? The one talking with Officer Tendum earlier?"

"That's right," Higgins said. "Name's Yasmine Stone. She worked with Bates, as well."

"As well as what?" Madison asked.

Higgins shrugged. "She claims they were sleeping together."

"*Claims?* You don't believe her?" Terry asked.

Higgins's gaze hardened. "I don't take anything at face value."

Terry pointed at Higgins, then said to Madison, "Now I see where you got your skepticism."

"She *claims* she found him just a couple hours ago." Higgins slid his glance to Terry, as if to punctuate his word choice. Maybe Terry was right and she had inherited her doubt of people from her former training officer. But in their line of work, it was better to be wary than gullible.

"She made the call to us at seven," Higgins added.

Terry nodded. "And you said she worked with Bates?"

"That's right. Berger & Stein. It's an accounting firm downtown."

Madison recalled their logo on the top of a high-rise. "Huge company."

"That it is," Higgins replied. "Bates was sort of a bigwig accountant there, according to Yasmine," Higgins began. "She reported to him."

"That could explain how he afforded all this." She was referring to Bates living in Deer Glen, a prestigious gated community, and doing so alone in a two-story house that was large enough for a family of six. Not to mention the grand entry with the curved staircase, marble flooring, high ceilings on the main level that were easily twenty feet, and the chandelier in the foyer that had probably cost thousands of dollars. But Madison couldn't help but wonder if that was the only explanation for his wealth. Was an ex-con that lucky, or was it a matter of a son being like his father? Had Bates taken after his father by cooking the books for the Russians after he got out of prison? By extension, was the accounting firm connected with the mob?

"How long has Bates been working at Berger & Stein?" she asked.

Higgins shook his head. "Don't know. I hadn't gotten that far with her. It's possible that Tendum knows by now."

Madison nodded and made a mental note to find out.

"His old man was an accountant of sorts, too," Terry said.

She met his gaze, and her partner seemed to be prying into her mind through her eyes. Was he thinking the Russians might be involved with Bates's murder? She wasn't convinced yet based on the evidence, and she couldn't allow her past to interfere with her judgment. While she might not care that Bates was murdered, she still had a job to do, and she'd make sure his killer was caught.

"That he was," she said impassively.

"It probably wouldn't hurt to see if Bates had any connections to the Mafia," Terry suggested. "It's not often we see violent murders like this in Stiles." He raised a brow at Madison.

Was he baiting her? She glared at him. She couldn't let herself give into her paranoia; she had to remain objective. "We had that case two Christmases ago—the woman who had her throat slashed in her kitchen."

Terry didn't say anything. He just held eye contact with her. Was he going to bring up Lillian Norton? No, Madison wasn't going to give him the chance.

"We'll look at it from the Mafia angle, of course, but we need to dig into Bates's life," she said, "see who would have had motive to kill him. And we should start by talking with Yasmine."

Higgins touched her shoulder. She flinched, and he pulled his hand back. His brow creased, and his lips pressed downward in a concerned frown. "If you're not comfortable with this case, I'm sure Sergeant Winston would understand."

"He's right, Maddy," Terry chimed in. "As you said, he probably didn't even know the victim's identity when he assigned you. If he did—"

She jutted out her chin defiantly. "I'm staying on the case."

The last few months had mostly passed without an altercation between her and Sergeant Winston. They were working better together than they ever had. After Barry's death, they had moved past their differences and navigated his murder investigation as a team. Even in the cases following that, things had proceeded more smoothly than before. For her to go to him now and request to be pulled from a case would be tantamount to admitting defeat. And all she needed was to resurrect his outdated mentality that law enforcement should be a boys' club. And she knew the request would somehow become about that.

"I'll be fine," she started. "What happened with Bates and my grandfather was a long time ago. I never even knew him." But she had seen pictures and was told that she got her light complexion and blond hair from him. He'd only been blond until he was six, but the rest of her family were brunettes with brown eyes. She'd inherited her dark eyes from them.

Terry tilted his head. "Are you sure? This one *is* personal."

"I'm *fine.*" She turned her back to Terry then, not wanting him to see the lie in her eyes. But now she was facing the bloody side of the room, and the situation was starting to sink into her awareness. Even still, she couldn't rouse empathy for Bates.

"Just so you two know, Crime Scene should be here any minute now, and I've made the call to Richards, too," Higgins said.

Cole Richards was the medical examiner, and the sooner he arrived, the sooner they could get some real information.

"Thanks, Chief," Madison said, using her affectionate nickname for him. She smiled at Higgins, plastering on a strong front. Inside, however, her heart was racing and her mind was whirling with thoughts, the foremost of which was that, if Constantine was back in Stiles, it was likely only a matter of time before he'd be coming after her to settle an old score.

CHAPTER
2

MADISON WAS ABOUT TO STEP out the front door of Bates's house when she noticed the security system keypad mounted on the wall. She pointed it out to Terry, who was a couple of steps behind her. "We'll have to get access to his records with the service provider."

"And that may only help us if Bates actually used it," Terry countered with a shrug. "You'd be surprised how many people have security systems but fail to arm them, especially when they're at home."

"Not much point to having one, then." Madison stepped outside, the cold December air forcing her to do up her coat. The medical examiner's vehicle was at the curb, and Cole Richards and his assistant, Milo, were headed toward them.

Richards smiled, showcasing bright-white teeth that stood out in contrast to his dark skin. "Detectives."

Madison smiled in return. Maybe if she just worked to stuff all her thoughts of Constantine deep inside, then no one else would see how truly shaken she was that he could be back in Stiles. Besides, something about Richards always set her at ease, and she respected his work ethic and values. At one point, she might even have had a bit of a crush on him. Of course, the fact that he was married nixed any possibility of a relationship there. "You beat Crime Scene."

"I know. That rarely happens," Richards conceded. "And I don't like it when it does because it holds me up."

Usually investigators made their way around a crime scene, collecting evidence and snapping photos of the deceased and the immediate area around the body, before the ME could get started.

The sound of a vehicle had them turning toward the road where the forensics van was parking.

"Speaking of…" Richards made a move to go inside with Milo, and Madison and Terry stepped back to let them pass.

Cynthia Baxter, the head of the crime lab and Madison's best friend, was a bit ahead of Mark Andrews, who was one of three employees that Cynthia oversaw. Each of them had a specialized skill set. Cynthia was great with technology, documents, prints, and other patterned evidence; Mark excelled with trace evidence; and the other two employees were trained in firearms, ballistics, and forensic serology.

Cynthia's dark hair was swaying in a ponytail, and the pendulum kept going when she stopped in front of Madison and Terry. "He's not going to let us live this down, is he?" She pointed toward the front door, implying Richards and the fact that they'd arrived after he had. Normally her shoulder-length brown hair was down, not that it mattered how she styled her locks. There was something about her—even Cynthia didn't know exactly what—that made men fawn over her. She had played that to her advantage for years until Lou Stanford, another major crime detective, put a ring on her finger. Of course, they still had to officially tie the knot, but the commitment was made.

Madison shook her head. "I don't think so. He doesn't much care for it when it happens."

"That I know." Cynthia moved to the side and turned to Mark. "You go on ahead of me. I'll be in shortly."

Mark acknowledged Madison and Terry with a head bob as he walked inside, but his ponytail didn't sway as much as Cynthia's. He kept his tied low at the back of his neck. In fact, Madison had never seen his hair down.

Madison turned back to face her friend, who locked eyes with her, something Madison would have preferred to avoid because Cynthia had the ability to read minds…or so it seemed. Maybe if Madison pressed on with the case specifics, Cynthia would be distracted enough to drop her focus from Madison. The last thing she wanted was for her friend to see her true feelings, to know that she wouldn't be solving this murder fueled by her regular drive to find justice but rather to quell her suspicions about Constantine's return.

"The victim has a security system," Madison blurted out. "That might provide us with some leads."

"Victim? So either the victim hasn't been ID'd yet or you knew them. Which is it?" Cynthia was scanning her eyes, and Madison knew she'd messed up. Madison always preferred to use names over *victim*.

Madison wet her lips, glanced at her partner, and then turned back to Cynthia. "The latter."

Cynthia's gaze became more penetrating. "Did you know them well? Are you okay?"

When Madison didn't respond, Cynthia eyeballed Terry. "She should probably pull herself off this case," he said.

"Hey, I'm right here," Madison spoke up. There wasn't anything more irritating than being talked about when one was present. "And this victim's identity isn't going to stop me from working this case. No one is."

Cynthia raised an eyebrow. "All right, now I'm curious. Who is it?"

"It's Jimmy Bates." Madison said it in the most detached tone she could muster.

"Jimmy Bates?" Cynthia's voice raised a few octaves. "Isn't that the man who—"

"Killed my grandfather?" Madison finished. "Yes."

"What happened?"

Madison hitched her shoulders. "You'll see for yourself soon enough."

"He was stabbed multiple times," Terry offered.

Cynthia didn't break her eye contact with Madison. Maybe it was best to just come out with her notion that Constantine might be behind Bates's death, but even her close friend might think she was crazy given how little they had at this point. No, she needed some more evidence first. At least a direct connection between Bates and the Mafia.

"Stabbed multiple times?" Cynthia paused. "We don't see that too often. The last case I remember was that woman... What was her—" Her eyes widened. "Constantine killed her."

That didn't take long...

"Her name was Lillian Norton," Madison replied calmly, proud of her reserve considering the jumbled mess she was inside.

"You don't think...?" Cynthia let her implication go unspoken, but her face paled.

"It's too soon to tell who's behind Bates's murder." Madison sounded steadier in that conclusion than she was in her gut.

"Huh… That doesn't sound like the Maddy I know." Cynthia angled her head. "Lillian's name just popped right into your head when I brought up the stabbed woman? I doubt that. You'd already noted the similarities between the two murders, didn't you?"

Terry turned to face Madison now that she'd been called out. Maybe she should just admit to that much. "I did."

Terry's brow furrowed. "Why didn't you say anything about Lillian upstairs?"

"Why didn't you?" she fired back, and Terry shook his head. "Listen," she said firmly, "we have to look at this murder from all angles, and I'm not going to get stuck on one guess. Now, if you'll excuse us, Cynthia, we need to question the vic's girlfriend and coworker." Madison stepped down the walk toward the driveway, her mind spinning and emotions cresting.

"If you think he's back," Cynthia called out, "you should get protection, just to be safe."

Madison spun to face her friend. "I'll be fine." And there was that word again. She'd been saying *fine* a lot today. When she'd first started seeing a shrink—under mandated orders after her ordeal with Constantine—her doctor had pointed out that she used the adjective often, and that it was a means of deflecting how she truly felt.

"You'll be fine? What if you're not?" Cynthia's shoulders sagged, and her face drained of color. "You need to at least remove yourself from this case. If Constantine's back…"

Madison's body stiffened. Hearing her friend say his name again and seeing her so visibly upset shook Madison to her core, weakening her resolve to just deal with this investigation one step at a time. Her mind was telling her to let go of the idea that Constantine killed Bates, but her heart wasn't buying it. Bates's murder, and what it represented from her perspective, was truly a nightmare she wished she could wake up from, but she wasn't going to cower in a corner. She wouldn't let him win.

"If he's back and he's going to come for me, he'll do it whether I'm working this case or not. Now," she said, "we really do have work to do."

Cynthia waited a few beats. "Just be careful."

"I will. I promise." Madison walked away, and while Cynthia didn't say anything else, Madison could feel her friend's eyes on her back.

"She's right, you know." Terry stepped in line with Madison.

She couldn't bring herself to glance over at her partner. Her body was quaking, a mixture of fear and anger. The latter won out. She met his gaze now. "What? That I should go into hiding? No. He doesn't control how I live my life."

Terry shook his head. "Not hiding, no. But if you really think he's back, you should take precautions."

Madison let out a deep breath. "How about we prove he's back in town and go from there?" she suggested coolly, keeping her strides wide and determined.

She headed toward Tendum, who was in the car with Yasmine Stone, presumably taking her statement. Madison made eye contact with him and gestured to him with a curled finger. Tendum nodded in receipt of her unspoken message to come out and update them, and joined Madison and Terry by the trunk of the car.

"What can I help you with, detectives?" The twentysomething officer's eyes were alert, and his cheeks were flushed with the cold air.

Madison rubbed her hands. "How are you making out with her statement?"

"Almost finished." Tendum's gaze went to the car, and Madison sensed he was eager to get back to Yasmine. "Is there something you need to tell me?"

"We'll be taking her downtown shortly." Madison stepped farther away from the vehicle, and the men followed her. She didn't want Yasmine to overhear them. "I just want to make sure you ask a few specific things so we can see if she replies the same way when we ask the same questions later."

"Understandable," Tendum said. "Shoot."

Shoot? Sometimes the officer's age really didn't do him any favors.

"But first, I want to start with your impressions," Madison said. "How does she seem? Shaken? Distant? Angry? Shocked?"

"I'd say she's scared and shaken."

Madison hadn't expected that. "Have you asked her why she's scared?"

"She said finding him 'like that' was unsettling and that it's scary how we can be here one minute and gone the next."

"So she's analyzing her own mortality. Quite a natural reaction," Terry chimed in.

"I'd say there's more to it," Tendum ventured. "She's shaking and biting her bottom lip quite often and fidgeting with her hands."

Those traits could indicate shock, nervousness, or guilt. After all, she had the attention of Stiles PD and not in a good way. The person to find a dead body always fell under suspicion.

"Did you push her further on why she's so scared and unsettled? Try to break her?" Madison asked.

Tendum nodded. "I did, but I didn't really get anywhere."

Hopefully Madison would be able to apply enough pressure to squeeze something more out of the woman once they got her downtown. "When did she last see him alive?"

"She said she came over last night for a booty call at about eleven and left before midnight."

"And then she came back early this morning? Why didn't she just spend the night? Did you ask her that?" Madison snapped at Tendum without meaning to. She had to be on edge about the prospect of Constantine being in town.

Tendum fumbled with his notepad and thumbed through it. A moment later, he looked up, eyes blank. "I didn't think to..." Tendum seemed embarrassed as he scribbled something down.

"Maybe the guy just preferred to sleep alone," Terry interjected.

Madison glanced at her partner, defender of the newbies. She pointed to Tendum's book. "Make sure you ask her."

Tendum tapped the end of his pen to the page. "I will, Detective. I've written it down."

"And the house has a security system," Madison added. "Did you ask her anything about that? Whether it was armed when she showed up today? If she has a code and a key for the door?"

Tendum was just staring at her.

"You did see the system, right?" she pressed.

"I...did," Tendum admitted. "But I didn't think to ask her either of those questions."

"Well, add that to your little list, then," she responded.

Tendum winced and scribbled in his notebook again.

Madison took a few staggered breaths to bring her rising impatience under control, and then asked, "And was he all right when she left him last night?"

"Yeah, he was fine."

"So you asked?"

The young officer flushed. "Yes."

"What about how long she's been seeing Bates?" Madison asked, keeping the questions coming.

"For a few months now," Tendum responded without consulting his book. "She couldn't remember exactly when but figured they started seeing each other around October or thereabouts. Before you ask, she's worked with Bates for a year." He squared his shoulders as he regained his confidence.

Good work, Newbie, but it will take more to impress me...

"Have you run her background?" Terry asked before Madison could comment aloud.

"Yeah, of course. Nothing of interest there, though. Like, no criminal record anyway."

Like? Tendum's youth sprouted through the cracks.

"Is there anything else or should I finish up?" Tendum asked.

"Finish up. Ask her those questions—" she pointed to his notebook "—have her sign off on what she's told you, and then we'll take her downtown."

Tendum nodded and headed back to the cruiser.

A few minutes later, the car doors opened and both Tendum and Yasmine got out. Tendum gestured for her to stay next to the car, but he headed over to Madison and Terry. Yasmine pressed a cheek to her shoulder as she waited.

"I asked about the security system," he said when he approached Madison. "She says she has a code and a key."

"And why did she leave at midnight only to return this morning?" Madison asked.

Tendum glanced at Terry but directed his response at Madison. "It was as Detective Grant said: he likes to sleep alone."

"All right. Tell her to come over," she directed.

Tendum gestured for Yasmine to join them. When she did, he made the introductions. "These are detectives Madison Knight and Terry Grant."

Yasmine tucked a stray hair behind an ear but didn't say anything. Her eyes were wet with unshed tears, and her complexion was blotchy.

"We'd like to take you downtown, ask a few more questions," Madison said gently but without room for negotiation.

Yasmine gave Tendum an uncertain glance before following Madison. "I'm not sure why I have to speak with you now."

"It's standard procedure," Madison assured her.

"But I didn't do anything." Yasmine stopped walking, her words full of panic as she rubbed her arms.

Madison turned toward the girl. "As I said, it's standard. It shouldn't take too long. We just have a few questions."

A tear fell down Yasmine's cheek, and she wiped it away before continuing to follow Madison.

Also available from
International Bestselling Author
Carolyn Arnold

POWER STRUGGLE

Book 8 in the Detective Madison Knight series

One hit man who's back for revenge.
One detective who's not going down without a fight.

It's been ten months since Detective Madison Knight almost died at the hands of Russian Mafia hit man Constantine Romanov. She hasn't seen hide nor hair of him since he escaped police custody and fled to Russia soon after his arrest, except now her latest murder investigation gives her reason to believe he's back in town. Seeing as the victim is the man who killed her grandfather, her perspective may be a little skewed, but with the MO smacking of Constantine and the victim's connections to the mob, she finds it hard to be objective. Still, she's doing her best to consider all the evidence.

When she receives a threatening letter from Constantine, however, her suspicions are confirmed. And he's made it abundantly clear that not only does he plan to finish what he started but he has her family and loved ones in the crosshairs, too. Madison vows to do whatever it takes to save them, but as the hours race by, the body count rises. And the stakes only get higher when Madison's sister, Chelsea, goes missing.

Now, Madison's only play is to take Chelsea's disappearance for what it really means: Constantine is calling Madison out for one final showdown. And they won't both survive…

Available from popular book retailers or
at CarolynArnold.net

CAROLYN ARNOLD is an international bestselling and award-winning author, as well as a speaker, teacher, and inspirational mentor. She has four continuing fiction series—Detective Madison Knight, Brandon Fisher FBI, McKinley Mysteries, and Matthew Connor Adventures—and has written nearly thirty books. Her genre diversity offers her readers everything from cozy to hard-boiled mysteries, and thrillers to action adventures.

Both her female detective and FBI profiler series have been praised by those in law enforcement as being accurate and entertaining, leading her to adopt the trademark: POLICE PROCEDURALS RESPECTED BY LAW ENFORCEMENT™.

Carolyn was born in a small town and enjoys spending time outdoors, but she also loves the lights of a big city. Grounded by her roots and lifted by her dreams, her overactive imagination insists that she tell her stories. Her intention is to touch the hearts of millions with her books, to entertain, inspire, and empower.

She currently lives London Ontario with her husband and beagle and is a member of Crime Writers of Canada and Sisters in Crime.

CONNECT ONLINE
Carolynarnold.net
Facebook.com/AuthorCarolynArnold
Twitter.com/Carolyn_Arnold

And don't forget to sign up for her newsletter for up-to-date information on release and special offers at CarolynArnold.net/Newsletters.

Lightning Source UK Ltd.
Milton Keynes UK
UKHW01n1828251018
331215UK00003B/64/P